GEORGIA BRIDES

GEORGIA BRIDES

THREE-IN-ONE COLLECTION

PAIGE WINSHIP DOOLY

BARBOUR
PUBLISHING

The Lightkeeper's Daughter © 2010 by Paige Winship Dooly
The Displaced Belle © 2010 by Paige Winship Dooly
The Reluctant Outlaw © 2010 by Paige Winship Dooly

ISBN 978-1-61626-468-0

All rights reserved. No part of this publication may be reproduced or transmitted in any form or by any means without written permission of the publisher.

All scripture quotations are taken from the King James Version of the Bible.

This book is a work of fiction. Names, characters, places, and incidents are either products of the author's imagination or used fictitiously. Any similarity to actual people, organizations, and/or events is purely coincidental.

Cover design: Kirk DouPonce, DogEared Design

Published by Barbour Publishing, Inc., P.O. Box 719, Uhrichsville, Ohio 44683, www.barbourbooks.com

Our mission is to publish and distribute inspirational products offering exceptional value and biblical encouragement to the masses.

Member of the
Evangelical Christian
Publishers Association

Printed in the United States of America.

Dear Readers,

Thank you so much for taking this journey through Georgia with me! I really enjoyed writing about the various areas of this wonderful Southern state and I hope you enjoy it, too.

As a Southerner, I'm partial to the South, and Georgia doesn't disappoint. It's a beautiful place that is full of history. The area provides ideas for a multitude of stories with the mountains, coastal areas, and everything that's in between. Savannah, so rich in culture and beautiful architecture, is an area I'd love to use as a story setting in the future, but for this group, I decided to use a quieter island with one of the few remaining lighthouses as the setting for book one.

I love to put my spunky historical heroines in the path of head-strong alpha males. The combination guarantees sparks will fly between the hero and his lady. *The Lightkeeper's Daughter* tells the story of a disillusioned preacher returning home to find peace. Instead, he finds that his former fiancée's father is missing and she's determined to find him, despite tropical storms and villains that lay in wait, and the fact that she's just regaining her vision after an accident that took her mother's life.

The Displaced Belle takes place north of Atlanta. The heroine must return home to the family plantation after being sent away by a hateful step-father. She has to get her siblings out of the family home. The hero is an unhappy gambler who just wants to be left alone, but ends up with a gaggle of people he has to care for. In the end he can't resist the damsel in distress and helps her with the plan to rescue her sisters and brothers.

I had fun with *The Reluctant Outlaw*. It seems most outlaws are male, so I put a spin on this one and made the heroine an outlaw with a conscience. Her brothers aren't any too happy with her to start with but are especially annoyed when she shows up with a preacher, who is a part-time sheriff in hand. I think her struggles to do the right thing reflect the heart of most of us who want to follow the right path in life.

I'm glad you picked up this book to read. I hope you enjoy it and find your faith stronger after cheering on the characters.

Enjoy!
Paige Dooly

THE LIGHTKEEPER'S
DAUGHTER

Dedication

Thanks Mom and Dad for your love and support through the years and for your encouragement when it came to my writing. I love you both!

Chapter 1

Little Cumberland Island, Georgia, 1867

I know Papa's coming back, Samson. Don't try to tell me otherwise."

Hollan climbed to the top of the largest sand dune with Samson following close at her side. As they neared the peak, he nudged past her and plopped onto the sand. She sank down beside him. Her stamina wasn't keeping up with the rapid improvements in her vision. They'd searched for her father as far as she dared. With her eyesight coming and going, she was afraid to go too far. "We just need to find him, that's all."

Samson released a small whine.

"With Mama it was different. I knew she was gone. My heart knew. But this time, with Papa—" She stopped a moment and gave her next words some thought, then shrugged. "I don't know. With him, it's different. He's out there somewhere. I'm sure of it. We just need to figure out where. It's only been a day."

Samson lifted his furry head and raised an eyebrow.

"You think I'm crazy, don't you, boy?" She reached over and ruffled his tawny fur before settling on her back beside him.

The cloudless blue sky overhead stretched in all directions. The gentle breeze blew in off the water, carrying with it the salty scent of the ocean. Hollan inhaled deeply.

Her vision had steadily improved during the past few months, going from nothing but blurred shapes, as it had been for most of the past three years, to dim but specific outlines of objects and people. She hadn't told her father about the improvements, not wanting to get his hopes up if the experience was fleeting, but every day brought her more clarity.

Until now. . . . This moment brought her colors and clarity and. . .

"Samson!" She shot to an upright position and looked around.

Samson raised his head and barked, alert for pending danger. When he didn't see any, he looked at her in confusion.

"I *saw* your eyebrow quirk! I can see you staring at me like I've finally lost my mind. I can see the sky and the water and—oh Samson! I can see it all!"

The ocean-side view spread before them. Hollan could see every detail clearly: the sea oats, the waterline, the birds, a faraway boat on the horizon.

"Samson, I can see the water." Hollan held her breath, afraid that if she moved wrong or breathed too deeply the vivid scene in front of her would melt away. "Not only can I hear the waves, I can see them."

The sun played across the water, causing it to sparkle. A fin cut through the surface, though from this distance Hollan couldn't tell if it belonged to a dolphin or a shark. The movement—straight up, then forward for a few feet, then straight down—more closely resembled that of a shark. Dolphins tended to move in arched patterns, rolling up over the surface and back down, and they usually appeared and disappeared over and over until they moved out of view. She longed to see a dolphin. It had been too long.

Samson didn't respond other than to stare. She leaned down and peered into his dark brown eyes. She hadn't looked into a set of eyes in more than three years, and Samson's doggy eyes were just beautiful. It was a perfect moment. Samson reacted to the direct contact by wagging his tail.

"I know, Sam. This is a gift. It's precious."

Her vision blurred, and she panicked, wiping quickly at her eyes. She stared down at her hands. Tears. She could see the crystal clear liquid on her fingers. Her vision wasn't receding. The tears caused the blur.

"If only I could see Papa, Sam." She looked into her dog's eyes again. "He'll come home soon, right?"

Samson laid his head on his paws and stared out over the water.

Dark storm clouds appeared on the horizon.

"The next storm is already on its way, boy. I guess we aren't going to get a break in the weather for as long as I'd hoped."

Hollan wanted to savor the view, but she knew with her vision coming and going she needed to do some chores while she was still able.

⬧⬧

"Maybe he's not coming back." Hollan whispered aloud the words her heart had wondered about for the past three days. Words she hadn't wanted to voice because stating them might make them real. Each passing day caused her more concern. Her father had never left her, not even for a day, and there was no way he'd leave her now unless he had no choice. Had she lost him to the most recent violent storm? She'd lost her mother during a similar squall three years earlier. She pushed back her panic and forced herself to take a few deep breaths. Perhaps he'd only been hurt. But deep down she knew even if he'd been hurt, he would have found a way to get back to her. Just as he always had in the past.

She squeezed her eyes shut against the thought, warding off the image of her injured father needing her when she was unable to find him. The reality that she'd kept pressed against the back of her mind insisted on forcing its way forward. If her father had been injured enough not to make it back, surely he wouldn't be alive three days later. Their part of the island wasn't that big.

Hollan faced the ocean and listened to the harsh waves as they crashed against the sandy shore—the sound the last remnant of the most recent destructive storm. The beach would be scattered with debris—driftwood, seaweed, and other odds and ends that always washed ashore with the waves.

But she wouldn't know at the moment. Her vision had returned to its blurred state. She didn't worry about it too much. It had reappeared with vivid crispness several times during the past couple of days. The clarity stayed longer and came with more frequency each time. She prayed her vision would return in full at some point, but she'd adapted to not seeing, too.

She hadn't spent much time with God lately. The realization caused a catch in her heart. Her prayers at the moment were rote, but she told herself she'd do better in the future. She'd spent most of her time during the past three years just existing. Her uncle had to be very disappointed. He'd told her as much, but in her newly blind state, she hadn't really cared. And ever since, she'd drifted away from everyone except her father. And now he'd somehow drifted away from her. Maybe God was trying to get her attention.

The briny scent of the sea and the taste of salt on her lips reassured her that not everything had changed. But without her father, Hollan's small world would never be the same. Two facts prevailed and tried to drag her down into depression. Her vision had faded, and her father hadn't returned. She fought hard to keep her positive outlook, but it all felt so confusing.

While the familiar scents and sounds reassured, a tremor started at her leg and steadily worked its way through her stiff body. She wasn't cold. The warmth of the early autumn sun beat down on her shoulders. She wrapped her arms tightly around her torso, as if the action could stop the shaking. She was afraid that if she let go, she'd fall into a million pieces.

A bark in the distance announced Samson's arrival. Hollan whistled for him, and he barked a response. A few moments later, he brushed up against her. His panting gave away the exertion of his latest hunt.

"Still no sign of Papa, Sam?"

The dog only whined and leaned against her thigh. If Samson had found his master, he'd have let Hollan know.

"I didn't think so, boy, but we'll be fine. I still feel confident that Papa's out there somewhere." She reached down to rub his head. And they *would* be okay. Just as soon as she figured out a way to take over her father's job as lightkeeper, her life would steady and move forward again.

Hollan had no idea how long she stood there, staring sightlessly at the water, but when dark clouds covered the warmth of the sun, and dampness from the brisk ocean breeze permeated the light cotton of her long dress, the tremors turned to shivers of cold, and she urged Samson to move back toward their home.

My home, she corrected herself, her steps slow and careful. Now that she was alone—and until her father returned—she was in desperate need of a plan. She passed through the shadow of the lighthouse and raised a hand to caress the cool stone of its base. The lighthouse had remained dark through the majority of the war. They'd only recently resumed operations. She'd need to go up there soon and ready things for the night's work. Whenever her vision cleared, she hurried around and did everything necessary for the next few hours. She'd spent enough time in the lighthouse to do the basic chores even with her limited sight. When her vision dimmed, she was forced to let the lighthouse sit in darkness, too.

But first she needed to prepare a missive for her uncle. She continued toward the cottage, counting backward through the past few days. The supply boat—if it had fared well through the storm—would arrive later that afternoon. When the young captain, Fletcher, found her alone, he'd surely insist on bringing her back to the mainland. She'd argue with him, and he'd agree to search the island for her father, but after, even if she talked him out of forcing her away, she'd only have a day's worth of time to plan before her uncle descended.

The abrupt pain of her bare foot stubbing against the lowest stone step of the cottage pulled her from her musings. She reached forward to catch her balance against the wooden door, barely preventing a headfirst tumble into the garden to her left. The pain was intense, and she clenched her teeth, blowing a few panting breaths through tight lips to ward off the ache before tentatively putting weight on the aching appendage. She'd likely bruised some toes, but they'd soon be fine as long as she was careful. Though her vision was steadily improving, she needed to pay more attention to her surroundings.

A wry smile formed on her lips as she clung to the solidity of the door and hobbled up the final two steps. Hadn't her father said the same thing to her many times before? The thought brought him closer. Perhaps he wasn't so very far away. His words and teachings, especially the ones about Jesus and His unfailing presence lived on inside her. The thought brought her a moment of peace, but the reality of the reason for the thought again caused tears to threaten. She'd never before been alone. Though she was strong and resilient, she needed to have someone close by. Her father had taught her that with Jesus as her Savior, she'd never be truly alone. But while that was all good and well during his suppertime teachings, it didn't really seem to help right now when she lived alone in darkness and needed to find her way.

She shook away the panicked thoughts and chastised herself. More importantly, she needed to write her note before giving in to the cloying and ever-present grief and concern about her missing father.

The wind blew harder, and Hollan hurried to open the door, suddenly anxious to be safely tucked inside the dimly lit interior of the cottage. Samson nudged in front of her and trotted to his usual position near the dying embers of the fireplace. Hollan closed and secured the door then felt her way across the room until she bumped into the small dining table nestled against the far wall. She reached forward and located the lamp with one hand while the fingers of her other hand searched along the rough wood of the table for the nearby matches. The familiar routine soothed her.

Light flared, and she tested her eyes. Though she could see a dim outline of most items in the room, she couldn't see anything clearly.

She moved a few feet across the floor to the hearth and nudged Samson out of the way before leaning down—mindful of her dress hem—to carefully stoke the fire. Years of practice made the chore easy, and she took a few moments to bask in the warmth of the crackling wood. When the flames had dried her dress and heated her skin, she sighed and moved to sit at her small writing table, ready to carefully formulate the brief note for her uncle. The change from the light of the fire to the dimmer light of her writing table didn't help her mission. But in all reality, it didn't matter. Even without the contrast of moving from the bright fire to the blank paper, she could just barely see well enough to discern the letters as she formed them on the blank page. Though not an easy task, she did her best to make the note brief and her correspondence legible.

She considered walking down to the dock to meet Fletcher but decided it was best to wait for him to come to her while she rested her throbbing toes. If she were to stumble or get hurt on the path, it would only fuel Fletcher's potential determination to take her back with him. Instead, she'd sit tight and pray, with the hope that God would answer her prayer by providing her with a way to remain on the island.

Chapter 2

Jacob topped a slight rise and reined in his horse, scowling as he took in the view spread before him. He'd come home. He ignored the anxiety that invaded his thoughts as he contemplated the hostile reception he might receive and instead focused on the beauty of his surroundings. He'd missed the ocean. And if he had to admit it to himself, deep down he was glad to be back.

He had a lot of wrongs to right, and after one quick stop, he'd start the process with Hollan.

The dirt path he'd traveled led directly to the thin strip of water that separated the mainland from Little Cumberland Island. A larger dirt road bisected the path, leading to the tiny village where he'd grown up. Small fishing vessels bobbed on the dark blue water, each one filled with occupants in various stages of securing their catch. The fishermen pulled nets laden with their bounty from the salty water, while others prepared to toss their nets back in from a better vantage point. A few scattered figures walked along the shore, enjoying the brilliant day, some feeding the seagulls and others looking for seashells. Out on the island, the lighthouse stood tall on the distant horizon, keeping watch over the mouth of the Satilla River and the coast.

Jacob figured he should feel some sort of reluctance at the thought of returning home to the seaside town as a prodigal of sorts, but instead relief loosened the tightness from his shoulders now that he'd arrived at his destination. His burden felt much lighter.

Three years earlier, he'd left his hometown behind. By day he'd lived life as a traveling preacher. At night he'd scoured the surrounding towns, looking for his outlaw father and brothers. In both endeavors, he'd been full of expectations and enthusiasm. Yet life on the road had left him surprisingly empty and alone. He'd thought doing the Lord's work would bring him contentment no matter where he was and that by bringing his family to justice he would in some way undo the evils they'd committed. But instead the process had drained him.

He had one more brother to track, but for longer than he wanted to admit, the tug to return home had consumed him. When his brother's trail turned and led toward home, Jacob felt the first flicker of hope in a long time. He knew God had a plan for his return. And now that Jacob had returned, for the first time in a long time he felt reassuring peace flow through him. He felt confident that he'd soon locate David and that justice would prevail.

Jacob turned the horse and urged him toward the village. First order of business was to find his good friend and adviser, Edward Poe. He'd start at the tiny parsonage. Jacob held his head high as he rode, not missing the glances that followed his progress as he passed, nor did he miss the way the townspeople bent their heads close together to whisper as he moved by.

The double doors at the front of the small whitewashed church were propped wide open, and they welcomed Jacob inside. He swung down from his horse with a smile, secured him to one of the hitching posts that stood sentry under the shady magnolias flanking both sides of the front steps, and pulled his hat from his head. As he walked he slapped the dusty brim against his equally dusty pants in a vain effort to shake off the remnants of the trail. With a sense of anticipation, he moved forward and entered the cool interior of the worn clapboard building.

Edward sat at a small table in an alcove just inside the front of the church. He had one elbow propped against the surface, his hand resting against his forehead while his other hand clutched an open note. The parson's eyes were closed and his white-topped head bowed in apparent prayer over the missive.

Jacob remained silent until Edward lifted his head, finally aware of his presence.

"Jacob Swan!" Hurrying to his feet, Edward came forward and pulled Jacob into a warm embrace. "You've come home. After all this time and those few notes insinuating your intent, you finally followed through!"

"I did indeed." Jacob smiled at his mentor. "I couldn't find peace on the trail and decided I'd best come back before the good Lord found a more blunt way to send me home to my roots."

Jacob stood with arms crossed and feet squared and grinned at his favorite teacher.

Edward studied him. "You had some concerns about your return. Have those worries lessened?"

Jacob shook his head. He tried to fight off the urge to pace but finally gave in and moved a few steps away and back in the small space behind the pews. Edward followed his movements with knowing eyes.

"You're nervous about your reception."

Jacob glanced out the church doors, watching as a couple of people moved past the entrance. "I am. It's the only thing that's held me back from coming sooner. My family. . ."

"Your family made their choices, Jacob. Those choices weren't yours, and the people around here all know it."

"I'm not sure my neighbors will see it that way. The townspeople are already talking."

"Well, that's their problem to live with until they see the truth. And you know how they love to talk. In the meantime, all that matters is that you've come home. I know several people who will rejoice at that news, Ettie being one of them."

Jacob smiled at Edward's mention of his wife. "I look forward to seeing her. Before I do any visiting, though, I need to finish some details of my return. I'll need a place to live. I need to locate work—and even though you think my father's and brothers' actions won't be held against me, I suspect I'll have a hard time securing a job."

"Tell me something." Edward frowned as he mulled over Jacob's words. "With all your concerns, why did you come back?"

"The Lord called me here. I stayed away until I couldn't refuse, if that makes any sense. The past year has been hard. Each time I tried to ignore the quiet voice urging me to return, things became harder on the circuit. I'm tired, and I need a change. More than anything, I want to right my brothers' wrongs. I want to make up for my father's poor choices."

"I see." Edward nodded. "That's a pretty strong order. But to put things in perspective, it's not uncommon for a traveling preacher to wear out if he doesn't take time to stoke the fire—especially if he's chasing his own demons at the same time." He sent Jacob another knowing look. "And after so many years on the road, giving to everyone you come across, you need to be refreshed. You need a break, yet you need to find a way into the hearts and lives of the locals." He glanced at the note on the table, and his features transformed with excitement. "And I think I have just the solution."

Jacob's eyes narrowed. Edward's *solutions* always came with a price. Sometimes a very high price.

"Don't look so suspicious." Edward clapped him on the back and motioned to the rear pew. "I think your timely arrival might just be an answer to my prayer. Sit."

Jacob sat. How he'd gone from confident warrior to submissive schoolboy in a few short moments he didn't know.

Edward joined him. "You're not sure what the townspeople's feelings will be now that you've returned. Correct?"

"Yeeesss." Jacob drawled the word out, knowing his agreement came with a catch.

"If you were to marry one of the town's darlings, it would go a long way in clearing the path toward your redemption, would it not?"

"Marriage?" Jacob's voice rose in volume and pitch. He jumped to his feet, ready to flee. "You just said my family's actions were not my own. Now you're using the situation against me to force me into marriage?"

"You know I wouldn't force you to do anything."

"I didn't come home to marry."

"I'm sorry. Is there someone else, another woman who holds your heart?" Edward asked in surprise. "Is this the cause of your return?"

"Another woman? Of course not! You know there is only one woman for me. The only woman I'll ever love is Hollan. And my father's and brothers' actions ended any chance for that marriage. After what they did to Hollan and her family. . ." He shook his head. "I can't believe you asked if there was anyone else. I'm constantly on the move. When would I have time to build a relationship with a woman? There's no one out there waiting for me. My family's legacy chases away any desire I might have to marry." He ignored Edward's motion that he be seated and paced the room again. "Marriage is the furthest thing from my mind."

"You have no intention of settling down?"

"I do want to settle down. I just prefer to settle alone."

"And there's no one—besides Hollan—who holds your heart?"

Jacob hesitated before answering. He had a feeling his words were throwing him headfirst into Edward's plans. "No. You know my father was an evil man. I watched my father's actions pull the life from my mother. I watched him break my brothers with his cruelty and then watched my brothers hurt the women in their paths. I won't do that to anyone else."

"How many times do I have to remind you? You aren't your father or your brothers."

"I understand that, but I am my father's son. My brothers treated the women in their lives in the same exact manner as my father treated my mother. Or should I say, *mistreated*."

"You didn't agree with your family's lack of morals back then. Why do you think you'd be like them now?"

"I won't marry, Edward. I won't take on a carefree bride, just to make her into a miserable wife."

Edward's face fell. "I see."

Jacob stopped in his tracks, suspicious at his mentor's abrupt change of heart. It wasn't like him to give up so easily. Whatever Edward needed must be very important to him. And Jacob owed the man. . .owed him a lot. When all the other people in town turned their backs on him, Edward had given Jacob a home. More importantly, from the time he was a boy, Edward had taught Jacob about his faith. He'd shaped Jacob's whole future from that of an outlaw to one as God's chosen. He and Ettie had encouraged him during the years he fought in the war. There wasn't much Jacob could deny the older man. But marriage?

Jacob battled his inner thoughts and lost.

"What—or who—do you have in mind?" He folded his arms and spat the words out, hardly the picture of amiability, but marriage was a big request.

Edward walked over to the table and picked up the note. "I received this shortly before you arrived. I've been praying ever since."

Jacob pulled the paper from his mentor's hand and read the words carefully. His heart tightened with each word of the missive. "Hollan."

"Yes, Jacob. And she's all alone. Well, not exactly alone at the moment. I've sent Sylvia over to stay until I could find a better solution."

"Sylvia?"

"Hollan's mother's best friend. She's a widow. The night of your family's rampage, Hollan's mother passed away. Hollan was injured. Sylvia went over to care for Hollan and her father until Hollan could manage alone."

"I remember Sylvia." Jacob winced. "I'm glad she was there for Hollan. I never wanted her hurt."

Edward paused. "You still love Hollan."

"I will always love her, but that night when my family left town, things between us changed." He held out the note for Edward. Edward ignored it, letting the note burn a path through Jacob's fingers. *Hollan had touched this paper.* "Ettie would want to bring her home to the parsonage, wouldn't she?"

Edward nodded. "Of course. And Ettie would be ecstatic at the chance to fuss over Hollan. But do you really think Hollan would be happy with that arrangement? You know my niece. She loves her life on the island. Bringing her here would be the worst thing we could do."

Jacob felt the weight of responsibility press down on him.

"Surely there's another solution. If Sylvia is with her, I could go over and stay at the lighthouse. I could do the necessary work—I often helped Gunter with the lighthouse—while Hollan could remain in her home." His thoughts made so much sense that the burden lifted. Edward would have to see the perfection in his plan.

"Sylvia can't stay. She's only there for a few days. After that she'll return to the mainland. If I can't find another solution, Hollan will have to return with her. That'll break her heart. And she's already been through so much."

Guilt ricocheted through Jacob's heart. She'd been through so much because of him. If Jacob kept his gaze toward the door, he'd be able to walk away from the situation. His conscience and sense of obligation would likely send him right back in, but he'd have had a chance. Instead he looked into Edward's eyes, and the pleading there settled his fate. He couldn't tell him no. Not after everything Edward had done for him.

"I can't just go out there and man the lighthouse and watch over her from afar?"

"You know people would talk. It would add fuel to the fire regarding your relationship and would tarnish Hollan's reputation. Make things right, Jacob. Go out there and finish what you started."

"Marriage, huh?"

Edward nodded. "It would be the only way, for propriety's sake. And if you truly have no desire to marry for love, a marriage of convenience wouldn't be such a bad thing, would it?"

Jacob shrugged. "The only way I'd ever marry would be for love, but Hollan will never have me. You know how things ended. What my brother did—"

Edward cut him off. "Think about the good that will come of this. With or without this marriage, I'm sure in time you'll find your neighbors' acceptance. Without being married at that time, with your charm and handsome demeanor, the womenfolk will line the eligible ladies up at your door, trying to get you settled. If you marry Hollan, the process of acceptance will move more quickly, without all the matchmaking that will surely come your way."

Jacob shuddered.

Edward took the action as encouragement to continue. "You'll soon be able to relax on the island. You know Hollan is independent and undemanding. The situation will be perfect for both of you."

"Speaking of Hollan, how do you expect her to react when you arrive on the island with her new husband?"

Edward grinned. "She'll be so happy to be able to stay on her beloved island, she'll welcome the idea with open arms. She once loved you, Jacob. She'll soon learn to love you again. I'll explain things to her as soon as we arrive. She'll embrace the idea."

Jacob raised his hands in surrender. "I guess you'd best prepare to board my horse."

Chapter 3

W e're doing *what*?" Hollan's words ended in a shriek. "I—you—what? No. No! I won't do this. You want me to marry a complete *stranger*?"

"Jacob's hardly a stranger, Hollan. You two were engaged. You've known him since you were young."

"Oh yes. I remember. Right before he ran off with his outlaw family after they pillaged the town. The night my mother. . ." Hollan let her voice drift away as she stomped away from her uncle and headed for her place of refuge—the sand dune overlooking the ocean—wanting to leave everyone behind. Her astute hearing told her that her uncle ignored the fact that she'd purposely left him in her dust and continued to follow along.

"He didn't run off with them. He went after them to bring them to justice."

Hollan spun to face him. "How can you want this for me? How will this *fix* my present situation? Our love disappeared along with him the night he left. An arrangement like this will only bring more problems." She figured her horrified words could be heard all the way to the mainland, but she didn't care. What was her uncle thinking? "There must be another way."

Her uncle raised his gentle voice so he could be heard above the wind that blew in off the water. "I'm open to suggestions, Hollan. You need to be reasonable. You know you can't stay out here alone. Do you have a better plan?"

Hollan would find one. She had to. Anything was better than an arranged marriage to someone she no longer knew. The man she'd known no longer existed, if he ever had. She hadn't seen Jacob in years. The night he left, Hollan had lost her mother, her vision, and Jacob's love. It was a night she never wanted to think about again.

The man had outlaw roots, plain and simple, and in the end, when it mattered the most, those outlaw tendencies seemed to come to the forefront. Why else would he run off with his outlaw family and leave her to pick up the pieces? It didn't matter how long or how well Uncle Edward had known the man. Hollan didn't want any part of this.

Soon after Jacob had left—after she'd recovered from her accident—she'd made the decision to never marry. With her visual difficulties, she'd feel like a burden in the eyes of whoever ended up with her. She'd lose her independence. Her mother had unraveled on that horrible night, and she could only imagine why. If her mother had been happy, why would she have jumped from the lighthouse?

For her uncle to be desperate enough to marry her off to an outlaw, she was in a worse situation than she'd ever imagined. Marriage in any situation wasn't a good idea, but this was oh-so-much worse.

"How can you not see that this isn't an option for me?" Her mother's desperate attempt to escape from their life closed the door on that idea for Hollan years ago.

"Your mother wasn't of sound mind, Hollan. The accident wasn't what you think. Your parents had a wonderful marriage."

"What changed that? If something could go so horribly wrong in their marriage, how am I to know the same thing won't happen to me?" A balmy wind blew around her. She breathed in the comforting scent. "And I already come along with enough of my own challenges—challenges that would cause undue burden even in the strongest of marriages. Even in a marriage filled with love, which this one won't have."

"The two of you loved each other before. I know you can find your way back to each other and love again. As for your mother's accident, we do need to discuss it further, but now isn't the time. Just know her decision that night had nothing to do with her love for you or your father." Her uncle's speech ended, and he stood silently beside her.

Her father and Sylvia both wrote Hollan's mother's demise off to an unstable mind, but she couldn't understand that. Why hadn't her father been able to fix whatever was wrong? Why hadn't the need to be around for Hollan been enough to keep her mother's mind intact? What could be so awful that her mother thought the answer lay in plummeting from the deck that ran around the lighthouse? In any case, her family history didn't bode well for marriage, especially when marriage to her came with the additional challenge of dealing with a sightless wife.

Well, she amended, her heart jumping with a momentary lilt—*a* partially *sightless wife*. Her vision still improved daily, returning in bits and pieces. Even now she could see the outline of Sylvia's slightly curved figure to her left and her uncle's more barrel-shaped chest to her right. A bit of a distance away, the bright midmorning sun highlighted the tall figure of her husband-to-be.

Hollan turned toward her caretaker. "Sylvia, you'll stay on to help me, won't you? I'll make sure you're well paid for your time. And Fletcher can take over the lighthouse. You know you're both welcome here."

Fletcher was a good man and a hard worker. After dropping off her uncle and Jacob, he left with the supply boat to fulfill his normal workday, even after the long night of tending to the lighthouse.

Sylvia moved forward to place a reassuring hand against Hollan's cheek. "You know I can't stay, dear. We've had this talk. I'm needed in town, and Fletcher's work doesn't allow him to be out here on the island. He can't continue to work the lighthouse *and* run the boat. You'll be fine with your uncle's arrangement. You know he wouldn't do anything to hurt you."

"But Sylvia, I—"

Her caretaker dropped her voice to a whisper and leaned close as if Hollan hadn't spoken. "And we all know how much that man over there once loved you. You'll find your way back to him again." She planted a soft kiss on Hollan's cheek and moved back toward the house.

"But—Sylvia! Wait."

"I can't, darling. I need to pack up and be ready to go when Fletcher returns."

"Argh!" Hollan stomped her foot.

The action was rewarded with a deep chuckle from up the hill. *Jacob. The heartbreaking outlaw.* She ignored him and spun back around to her uncle.

"An outlaw, Uncle Edward? Is that really what my future has come to? Am I such a burden that only he will take me?"

"I don't consider you to be a burden at all. As a matter of fact, your aunt Ettie and I would like nothing more than to have you pack up and return to the mainland to stay with us. We can forget this conversation ever happened, and you can start anew in our home. You do have a choice."

Hollan turned away so he'd not see her face crumple at the dismal choices set before her. She loved her uncle and aunt, but she loved her island, too. "Marriage to an outlaw or I leave the only home I've ever known to start over again in town. And what a choice it is."

"Don't sound so despondent, dear one. You know I'd never do anything to hurt you. And Jacob isn't an outlaw."

"The history of the Swan family made it all the way out here, Uncle. I know what his family did."

"Their history isn't Jacob's. You knew him as a boy and as a young man. He's a good person. That hasn't changed. He wasn't with his brothers or father when they pillaged and set fire that night. Their actions have caused him enough pain, and I won't have you joining in with the townsfolk and judging him unfairly. Jacob is a wonderful man of God. He wants nothing more than to live in peace, free from the demons that pursue him. He only seeks quiet and relaxation. The marriage will be in name only, for propriety's sake. You both seem determined in your quest to avoid marriage. Perhaps this arrangement will protect you from the very institution you both abhor."

Hollan couldn't help but laugh. "Marriage will protect us from marriage? That makes no sense."

"Nothing much makes sense lately, Hollan." Her uncle sighed. "But if you're both sure you don't want to seek out love and settle down with someone else— someone else you care deeply for—then this arrangement is for the best. You'll have the protection you require and, in exchange, someone to run the lighthouse."

"And what will Jacob get?"

"The quiet life on the island will agree with Jacob and will salve the scars of his past. I have no doubt he'll like it here. The two of you loved each other before. I know you'll take care of each other, even if your love is gone. You'll see the good in him. And in time the townspeople will see it, too."

Hollan started to ask what scars he carried but figured with his family history it was obvious. When Jacob went to serve in the war, his brothers and father had evaded any type of service. They'd been suspected of pillaging and raiding local towns instead.

"If you don't want to agree to this arrangement, you'll need to head up to the house and pack your things. We'll leave late afternoon when Fletcher returns for his mother."

"I marry Jacob, or I leave the island." The whispered words blew away on the breeze. "I can't leave my island. It's all Samson and I have left. It's our home."

"Then you agree to the marriage?"

She thought hard, but no better solution came to her. "Yes, Uncle Edward. Prepare the way for my wedding. I guess I'll marry the outlaw."

"You'll marry a gentleman. I'll have you see it no other way."

"Perhaps you should reintroduce me to my groom." She folded her arms at her chest and refused to turn around to see if Jacob stood nearby. "Is he still standing on the hill listening?"

Her uncle chuckled. "No, he fled after your foot stomp. He's down the beach a bit with Samson."

"With Samson? The traitor."

They fell into step together and headed in that direction. The sound of the surf rose in volume as they neared the shore. Hollan's bare feet sank into the soft sand, and an impetuous thought made her smile. What would her new husband think of her perpetually shoeless state? Perhaps he'd never know. But with the loss of her sight, she needed to use each and every sense she could. She loved to feel the textures of the ground around her. And she found the sensation of sand beneath her toes to be her favorite sensation of all. She wouldn't have that pleasure in town. She'd made the right decision, even if it was scary and hard.

She stopped momentarily to breathe in the always-present, reassuring scent of her surroundings. Marriage couldn't be worse than losing the island. She'd come through this and be just fine on the other side. She was not her mother.

Her uncle's voice broke into her musings. "Samson seems content. He's retrieving sticks thrown into the water by Jacob. Maybe the animal sees the merit of the situation better than you do."

"Samson doesn't make up with anyone, Uncle Edward. You know that. All the changes of late must be muddling his little doggy brain."

"That dog has more brain than most men I know, your fiancé not included."

"My fiancé." She groaned.

"Your fiancé only for a short while." Her uncle's voice held a hint of laughter. "Before you have a chance to get used to the idea, your fiancé will be your spouse."

"Maybe I could have a bit more time to get used to the fiancé angle before we jump into marriage?" she asked hopefully.

"Take all the time you need. After reintroductions, you'll have the better part of the next hour to get used to the spouse part of the idea. You'll get through this just fine."

Hollan stopped, and Samson ran to her side. She ran a clammy hand self-consciously through her wind-tossed hair. The hot sun beat down on her back. What must her husband-to-be think of her? Did he, too, see the ceremony as "something to get through"? Would he someday mourn his loss of choice in handpicking a bride in the future? He'd already turned his back on her once. Would he spend the rest of his life regretting her?

She squared her shoulders and moved forward. She wouldn't be pathetic. Her fiancé would meet the independent woman who was his future wife.

Chapter 4

Jacob, Hollan thought it best that you meet again before you marry."

The introduction felt odd, but as Edward led the beautiful but reluctant woman closer, Jacob realized she might as well be a stranger to him. Hollan had matured and grown even more beautiful, something he hadn't thought possible three short years earlier. She wore her auburn hair pulled up, but stray wisps blew around her face. She reached up to hold them tentatively away from her delicate features. He saw only a glimpse of her warm brown eyes before she looked away.

Jacob wondered if she felt as awkward in the situation as he did. Outwardly she seemed completely calm, but judging by her earlier response, she, too, felt the tension. And how could she not? Her life had taken on a myriad of changes in a very short time.

"Hollan." Jacob stepped forward. "The years have been good to you. I'm pleased to see you again." He winced. Perhaps those weren't the best choice of words to say to someone who'd lost almost everything they valued.

She reached a dainty hand his way, and he took it briefly in his own. She looked toward him, though her eyes didn't meet his. A slight smile tilted up the corners of her mouth as her chin dipped in a nod of acknowledgment. "I'm pleased to meet you again, too." The forced smile stayed in place as she bit out each word.

Jacob held back the laugh that threatened at her forced words. He wouldn't do anything to jeopardize their future together, but she was anything *but* pleased. Her choices had been reduced to a life in town away from everything she knew and loved or a life married to—as far as she was concerned—a complete and total stranger who had already wreaked havoc in her life once before. That their marriage came with her uncle's blessing didn't really matter at this point—he was a stranger to her all the same.

An unexpectedly protective urge slammed through him as he held her soft hand in his, even as he felt the strength in her own response. She squeezed his hand once and released him.

"I'll leave you two to get acquainted. I have several things to attend to before we do the ceremony."

Jacob didn't miss the momentary panic that moved across Hollan's face. She wasn't as calm as she tried to let on. He'd do his best to put her at ease, but in reality he was just as nervous and shaken up.

They stood quietly for a few moments as her uncle made his retreat. Jacob loved the man, owed him his life, and would do everything in his power to make things easier for his former fiancée.

"Shall we walk?"

"Walk?" Hollan stuttered over the word, glancing up the coast.

"You know, one foot in front of the other as we move along the shore?" He figured the distraction of movement would be better than awkwardly standing there. "We should at least try to get acquainted as your uncle suggested. It's been a long time. We have a lot to discuss."

"I suppose."

"If I may?" He reached for her hand and placed it against his bent arm. She stiffened, and he thought she might pull away, but then she relaxed and accepted his assistance. He felt the heat from her fingers through the rolled-up sleeves of his thin cotton shirt. The sensation was pleasantly familiar. He'd missed her touch. He suddenly realized this wouldn't be nearly as easy as he'd imagined. The heart of stone he'd envisioned at his core was suddenly turning to mush.

They began to walk, and he took care not to let the waves break against her long dark skirt. A few times he led her higher up the beach to avoid an especially aggressive wave.

"What did you want to talk about?"

"Guidelines." Which, based on his response to her touch, they now needed worse than ever.

Her brows drew together. Her hand tightened against his arm, and her steps faltered. "Guidelines? Such as?"

"I know you aren't exactly excited about this arrangement."

He hesitated when she laughed.

"That's an understatement." Remorse immediately replaced the smile. "I'm sorry. It can't be much easier for you. You're making a great sacrifice and doing me a huge favor by allowing me to remain here, for reasons I can't even imagine."

The way his emotions were tossing about—much like the faraway ship moved across the storm-tossed sea—it didn't make marriage to her feel like such a sacrifice. He cleared his throat. "I'll be fine. But I want you to have peace with the situation, at least as much peace as possible. I want to do what I can to make the adjustment easier for us both."

She stopped. "Why are you doing this? What's in it for you? I want to hear your reasons from you."

"I think that answer is obvious. I know your uncle went over it with you. But to reiterate, we each have something the other needs."

"And what would that be?"

He reached for her wrist as she pulled away. Her rapid pulse beat against his fingers. He prayed for the words that would help soothe her fears as he again tucked her hand firmly in place. They continued walking at a leisurely pace.

"You aren't the only one who's had a rough time of it. You know I owe your uncle a great deal. I owe you, too. The night I left town, after what my family did, I couldn't face you. I needed to get away." He didn't really want to hear the specific details of what his brothers had done, but he left her the opportunity to discuss that night if she needed to. Otherwise, the details would come out in time.

"And yet you've returned."

"Yes." He was surprised she didn't lash out or want to discuss the details. But perhaps she'd never want to discuss it. He glanced down at the sand as they walked, and a delicate shell caught his attention. He bent to pick it up. Most of the shells on the beach had been broken into jagged pieces by the strong tides before they ever finished their tumble to shore. He started to throw his find into the ocean, but instead he carried it as they walked along, turning the smooth object over and over with his fingers. This shell, which looked so delicate, had to be strong to have made it through the rough waters in one piece. It reminded him of the woman who walked beside him. "The trails didn't hold the answers I'd hoped for."

"And you expect to find the answers out here?"

"The answers will come in time. Here I'll find quiet and relaxation. At least that's what Edward tells me." He grinned her way, even though she wouldn't notice. The smile carried on his words. "I suppose that remains to be seen."

Judging by the effect the gently breaking waves about a dozen feet out were having on him, Uncle Edward was correct. He felt a peace here he hadn't felt on the mainland. Or maybe it was the gentle nature of the woman walking beside him that charmed his heart. He hoped the feeling was mutual.

"I won't get in your way."

Not quite the response he'd envisioned and hoped for.

"I don't want you to avoid me. I don't want to force any changes on you."

"What *do* you want from me?"

"Pardon?"

"What are your expectations?"

"I have no expectations. I haven't had time to think of any."

"I guess that's true. Where do you plan to sleep?"

Again she had him grinning. "You don't tiptoe around your thoughts, do you?" He hadn't smiled this much in years.

"I try not to. You know my father. He taught me that if a question is good enough to think about, it's worthy of putting into words."

His father's teachings had been far different. "I always liked your father. But to answer your question"—he turned back and glanced at the lighthouse—"your uncle said there's a room at the base of the lighthouse that would serve well as my living quarters."

Her features relaxed as she released a soft sigh. He hadn't noticed she'd been holding her breath while waiting for his answer.

"Indeed. He's right. That will work out nicely. The room is already set up with a bed. My father would often stay out there during difficult weather. Except for the night he disappeared." Her voice tapered off. A scowl marred her features.

"Fletcher said he searched the island."

"He did. But I don't feel as if my father is gone." Her grip tightened against his arm. "When my mother—died, after I came to, I knew instantly that she was no longer with us."

"I'll continue to look for him. If he's here, we'll find him."

"Thank you." For the first time her smile appeared to be genuine. "Fletcher and Sylvia seem to think it's shock talking when I say that. My uncle surely thinks the same." She shrugged.

They turned and headed back toward the cottage, the silence around them broken only by the cries of the seagulls.

She abruptly appeared to shake off the melancholy mood along with whatever thoughts were on her mind by quickly changing the subject. "I'll make your meals of course."

"That would be nice."

A most charming blush colored her cheeks. "You can eat in your room or up in the lighthouse if you'd prefer, but I won't mind if you'd like to join me at mealtime, either. I'd appreciate the company." She dropped her hand from his arm and hugged her arms around her torso.

Though in all likelihood she was only trying to be charitable in order to please her uncle, and judging from her actions hoped he'd say no, he couldn't stop the words that instantly popped out in response to her invitation. "I'd like that."

"You would?" Surprised, she stumbled and would have fallen had he not grabbed her by the arm. "Well, then. . .ouch!"

He'd been so mesmerized by Hollan and her enticing personality that he hadn't paid enough attention to all the broken shells and the uneven shoreline on this part of the beach. He should have been more diligent. Edward was counting on him to keep Hollan safe.

"What happened?"

"I'm fine." She waved him away, a look of desperation on her face as she tilted her head and listened to the sounds.

Jacob could only hear the surf breaking at their feet along with the calls of seagulls from up ahead.

"We're almost back to the cottage. Sylvia has been feeding the gulls about this time every day, and I can hear them begging up near the lighthouse." She took a cautious step, gasped, and closed her eyes in pain.

"You're hurt. Let me have a look."

"No."

"You're soon to be my wife. I don't think it will hurt for me to take a look. One of the shells must have cut through your boot."

"I'm not wearing any boots." She sighed. Frustrated, she scrunched her fingers in her hair. More loosened tendrils of auburn hair blew around her face. "I like to feel the sand under my feet."

She started when he laughed out loud.

"You find the notion funny?"

"I find you to be quite funny." He scooped her up in his arms and carried her away from the shells.

"I beg your pardon! Jacob, put me down!"

He had no intention of putting her down. She felt too good in his arms. "I will as soon as we get past these broken shells." He settled her on a large piece of driftwood before dropping to his knees in the sand. "Let me see the damage."

With a sigh she allowed him to look at her foot.

"There's still a fragment embedded in your skin. You're bleeding. No wonder it hurt to walk." He gently tugged the shell loose, but Hollan still gasped and patted at his arm.

"Ah, that hurt!"

"Sorry. The fragment is out now, but you can't walk on your foot. You'll fill the cut with sand. Stay put for a moment." He pulled a handkerchief from his pocket and walked down to dip it in the water.

Hollan stood, apparently planning to follow him.

Some things never changed.

"Must you always be so stubborn?" he called. She'd been an opinionated handful since the first day he'd met her. "I said to stay put. The last thing you need is an infection, and these shells can give you a pretty nasty one if you aren't careful."

He hurried to where she'd settled back down on the log.

"And you're as boorish as ever." She crossed her arms as she huffed out the words.

He brushed at the wound, but the sand wouldn't come free. "I'm going to have to carry you back down to the water. You'll need to hold your skirt up while I dip your foot in the ocean."

"You'll do no such thing. If you'll lend me your handkerchief, I can make a bandage. When we get back to the cottage, I'll make a poultice out of herbs."

"I'm sure you will, and that'll be fine, just as soon as we get all the sand out." He didn't give her a chance to argue as he lifted her up in his arms.

"Put me down," she hissed.

He walked to the water's edge. "Ready?"

"No."

Ignoring her, he dipped her foot into the ocean, soaking her skirt hem with seawater in the process. "There. That ought to do it."

"My skirt is drenched."

"I said you'd need to hold it up."

She glared his way. "And I *said* I wasn't ready."

"Would you have ever been ready?"

"No."

"Exactly."

She balanced on one foot until an overzealous wave knocked her backward. Jacob steadied her.

Her breath came in small huffy bursts. She was angry.

"Now see?" She poked him in the chest with her index finger. "This is exactly the behavior I worried would come along with our marriage."

"If you're referring to the fact that I just cleaned your wound and saved you from a tumble in the water, your worries are for naught. Speaking of our marriage, you might have all the time in the world to stand here and argue, but I have a wedding to attend."

"Unfortunately, so do I, and I'm going to arrive looking like a drowned rat."

"I recall asking if you were ready."

"And I *recall* saying no." She started to hobble up the shore.

"Stubborn woman! You're going to get the wound full of sand again."

"I'll—"

He didn't give her a chance to finish. Instead he flung her over his shoulder like a sack of potatoes. She shrieked and pummeled him on the back as he stalked up the path with long strides.

He might as well face her uncle head-on. At the rate they were going, the wedding was likely off anyway. Jacob didn't like the thought. He still had feelings for the feisty woman in his arms. But less than an hour earlier, Edward had entrusted into Jacob's care a healthy, pristine niece. Jacob now returned her injured, wet, and angry. The whole ordeal was anything but peaceful and relaxing. In all honesty, dealing with the townspeople couldn't possibly be any more frustrating than this.

Jacob didn't relish the thought of facing her uncle with his obvious failure, but the sooner they got the ordeal over with, the sooner they could put this mistake behind them.

Chapter 5

Uncle Edward's booming laugh welcomed them back to the cottage. Hollan didn't need to see his face—a feat that would be impossible even if she could see, thanks to her present dangling-upside-down-over-Jacob's-shoulder position—to know that the laughter was at her expense.

"I'm thrilled that you find my situation so immensely amusing, but perhaps you could stop laughing long enough to make him put me down." Her indignation was wasted on the man. She couldn't be heard over the laughter with her face and voice muffled against the back of Jacob's shirt. She tried to ignore the strength of his muscles, but it was hard to do while feeling the solid resistance as she again pummeled her fists against his back.

Jacob apparently heard. Or maybe the hard pinch to his side alerted him to her fury. He dumped her unceremoniously on her feet, only mindful at the last moment of her injury. "Thought I was going to drop you on your sore foot, didn't you?"

His voice was low, for her ears only, and she shivered at the intimacy. His closeness unnerved her. She limped a few steps away.

"You're hurt!" Immediately contrite, her uncle appeared at her side.

"Of course I'm hurt. Do you think I'd let him carry me up the dunes in that humiliating manner for the fun of it?" She sent another ferocious glare in Jacob's general direction. She didn't miss his chuckle.

"She hardly *let* me do anything. I had to take matters into my own hands. And it's only a surface wound, Edward, nothing to be alarmed about. Hollan will be fine."

"*Only* a surface wound? At the beach you acted as if I'd bleed to death without your immediate intervention."

"No, I only said the wound would fill with sand and increase the risk of infection, which reminds me, you do need to let Sylvia apply that herbal poultice."

"Help her over to this chair, Jacob, and we'll get her taken care of." Edward summoned Sylvia, and after a quick peek at the wound, she hurried off for the supplies. "Fletcher arrived at the dock just before you two made your appearance. He should be here shortly. As soon as he is, we'll get this wedding started."

Hollan sputtered. "You mean you're still planning the wedding, even after all this?"

"Indeed. Why wouldn't I? Jacob just proved he could deal with you quite nicely."

"Deal with me? You consider slinging me over his shoulder against my wishes *dealing with me nicely*?"

"Compared to the alternative, yes. The gash isn't life threatening, but walking on it wouldn't have been wise at all. Jacob made the best decision for you, based on the options."

Hollan snorted and shifted in her chair, turning her back on both of them.

"Dear, have you changed your mind?" She heard concern buried beneath the humor as her uncle placed a hand on her shoulder. "If so, you can pack a small bag and leave on the boat with us. We can collect the rest of your things later. Jacob can stay and tend to the light."

Hollan considered his offer. The emotions she felt when Jacob stood nearby concerned her more than any of his actions. She knew he had only her best interests at heart. But she hadn't expected the old feelings to come rushing back in such a vivid way. A part of her she'd thought long dead had come back alive in his presence. The realization scared and unnerved her.

"No, I'll be fine." And she would be. She wasn't leaving her island. Samson plopped down beside her with a contented sigh, breaking the awkward moment. "Samson seems happy enough to hear he still has a home."

"He could have stayed out here with me." Jacob stood nearby, listening.

Hollan wished she could see Jacob's expression. Was he disappointed she hadn't taken her uncle up on his offer? Would he have preferred to stay at the lighthouse alone? She thought about it a moment and decided she didn't care. She hadn't made him come out to get hitched, and if he had his doubts, they were his problem to deal with.

"Aunt Ettie's going to be upset about missing the ceremony." She addressed the statement to her uncle.

"I asked if she wanted to come, but she was so sure you'd turn us down flat, I couldn't get her in the boat."

"She still hates it out here. She's never cared for the island."

"She loved your mother like a sister. And though she wanted to be here with you, she can't deal with coming to the island just yet. I think she fully expected you to return to the house with me."

"I understand. Tell her I'll be in to see her soon."

"She'll want to have you both over for dinner."

"We'd like that." Jacob spoke for them both. "Ettie is a wonderful cook."

Hollan wondered about the fact that it didn't bother her that he spoke of them as a couple. Instead, it felt natural. Comforting.

Sylvia arrived and busied herself with tending to the cut. Fletcher arrived at the cottage, and the men exited and walked over to the dunes. A short time later Sylvia had Hollan bandaged up and ready for the ceremony. She helped Hollan into her prettiest blue dress—a color Hollan belatedly remembered was Jacob's favorite. She blushed, wondering if he'd think she'd chosen it especially for him.

"You look beautiful, Hollan. Your mother would be proud."

Hollan hugged the older woman, not sure she agreed. Her mother would have wanted Hollan to marry for love. They'd talked about it many times before, back in the carefree days when she was happily engaged to Jacob. Though the man remained the same, the circumstances had changed.

When Hollan didn't answer, Sylvia cupped her cheeks. "Your mother would understand."

Hollan nodded her agreement. "I'd like to think so."

"Jacob is a good man. If you give him a chance, he'll make you very happy. I think God has something beautiful planned in all of this."

Though Hollan wasn't so sure about that, she hoped her friend was right.

They decided to say their vows on a dune overlooking the ocean. The whole situation felt surreal. The wedding, although very similar to the one in her dreams—the wedding she'd wanted the first time before Jacob left—seemed a farce. The man standing beside her was nothing more than a stranger, and only a handful of loved ones stood alongside to witness the event.

Other than those few *minor* details, she thought wryly, the afternoon couldn't have been more perfect for their ceremony. Hollan loved being serenaded by the seagulls that flew over their heads. The ever-present sound of the waves crashing onshore brought a familiar comforting reassurance. She knew the sounds inland would be similar—the small village was a coastal town after all—but she wouldn't hear the roar of the surf from the Atlantic Ocean. She wouldn't be able to tell weather conditions solely by the force of the waves hitting shore. She'd not be able to wade along the tide line, nor would she be able to wander freely as she did now.

She had Jacob to thank for that. His presence allowed her to remain where she wanted to be. She turned her attention to the man at her side. She wished she could see him more clearly. As it was, the sun silhouetted his broad shoulders, and she could tell he wasn't the skinny boy who'd left her behind. She wondered how the planes of his face had changed with the years. She felt sure her vision would clear again. She'd see him soon enough. And even if she didn't, she had the details of the past tucked away in her memory. His sea green eyes wouldn't have changed, but his hair apparently had. Judging by the way the strands blew around in the wind, he'd let it grow longer than before, but she imagined the strands were the same sun-kissed color they used to be. He never had been one to stay indoors any more than necessary.

Her uncle's voice intruded on her musings. "I think we're ready. We need to finish up and be on our way." The usually wordy man surprised her as he made quick work of the ceremony.

"Jacob, you may now kiss your bride."

Before Hollan could work up a full panic, Jacob leaned forward and gently touched his lips to hers in the most gentle of kisses. Against her will, her heart began to soar.

❧

The first few days of their marriage were awkward to say the least. Jacob could see the strain as Hollan tried to work into a steady routine of normalcy. They started each day with breakfast. Hollan worked hard to have the meal on the table before he arrived at the cottage door.

"You aren't normally an early riser, are you?" Jacob asked during their meal on their fourth morning together.

"Why do you ask?" she questioned, hiding a yawn behind her hand.

He laughed. "You're about to fall asleep in your eggs. At first I figured you weren't sleeping well due to our new role as—neighbors."

"We aren't simple neighbors, and you know it." She swiped his half-eaten plate of food from in front of him and made her way to the counter. "We're in a completely unique situation, and I do find myself losing sleep trying to make sense of it all." She snatched up a rag and returned to the table, wiping hard at the crumbs.

"You trying to wipe clean through the wood?" He stayed her hand with his.

Her breathing hitched, and she quickly pulled away. "Don't you have a light-house to tend to?"

"Again the lack of subtlety." He enjoyed putting a blush on her cheeks. He stood and pushed in his chair. "But yes, I do need to wipe down the lens."

"Don't forget to trim the wicks. And refuel the lanterns."

"Did all that before coming in for breakfast. Some of us get up early."

"Or never go to bed at all," she muttered.

"I sleep. I just don't need a lot of it. I sneak in a few hours before dusk and in between work."

Hollan rolled her eyes.

"Let me know if you need me." He wondered if she'd ever truly need him. If she'd ever care about him the way she used to.

He closed the cottage door behind him and walked over to the lighthouse. He climbed the multitude of narrow stairs that led to the top level. The day was clear, and he could see a good ways out. As had become his habit, he went around the entire walkway, looking for any sign of Hollan's father. If the man hadn't washed out to sea, he didn't know what had happened to him. For Hollan's sake, he hoped they'd someday find out. Hollan told him the lighthouse inspector was due for a visit within the month, and if her father hadn't returned, they stood to lose the contract. In the meantime, he'd do everything he could to keep the light in good working order.

Jacob slipped into Hollan's father's cleaning coat. The lens had to be immaculate at all times in order to work properly. He first wiped away all loose particles of debris with a feather duster. He then used a fine cloth to carefully remove any smudges left by the oil. The prisms were delicate and easily scratched, so he always made sure to touch them with caution.

He spent longer than he'd intended on the job, and the sun tipped slightly toward the west before he headed to the cottage for the midday meal. Hollan waited in a chair out front, staring toward the horizon, her forehead creased with concern.

"Is something wrong?"

"It's getting ready to storm." She motioned toward a cloth-covered plate that sat on a small table tucked between the two chairs. Samson lifted his tawny head and wagged his tail in acknowledgment before lowering his chin back down to rest upon his front paws, his favorite napping position.

Jacob surveyed the horizon. He saw some dark clouds, but he knew Hollan and her father recognized the signs of a serious storm much better than he. "Will it be a bad one?"

"I'm not sure." She'd balled her handkerchief into a small mass. "I just know the weather's turned. The seagulls have taken refuge."

He hadn't noticed, but now that she mentioned it, the ever-present birds weren't anywhere around.

"Tell me what I need to do." He didn't bother with his plate.

She smiled, but the lines around her mouth betrayed her tension. "First of all, eat. If it's a big storm, you'll be busy later."

"Then talk to me while I eat." He lifted his plate onto his lap and took a bite of crab cake. It was delicately seasoned and cooked to perfection. She'd garnished the plate with a side of tomato that he'd picked fresh from her garden earlier in the day. "This crab cake is wonderful. The tomato looks good, too."

"Thank you," she said absently. Not one to be easily distracted when she had her mind set on something, she continued to stare toward the horizon. "Do you see any clouds?"

He glanced at the ocean as he took a sip of water. "There's a darkening of the sky way out, but otherwise it's blue."

"The storms move in quickly. We'll need to batten down everything we can. The chairs and table need to go in the storage building, along with anything loose. I'm sure the process is the same as the one you'd go through in town."

"You're thinking this will be a large storm?"

"According to the birds, yes. But we won't know how large till it hits."

For the first time, he saw a chink in her armor. She'd been great about their whole situation, but her nervousness over the storm's approach was palpable. He reached over and clasped her hand with his. "God is sufficient for all our needs, Hollan. Always remember that. We'll be fine."

She didn't look convinced. "I've lost both my mother and my father in storms. They'll never be my favorite thing."

"That's understandable."

The wind picked up. The cloth that had covered his plate blew off the table, and Jacob jumped up to chase it. He glanced back at the horizon and saw the churning clouds moving closer at a quick pace.

"It's coming," Hollan stated.

"Yes." He gathered the plate and his mug and carried them into the house. He returned for Hollan. "Come. You'll be more comfortable inside."

Hollan shook her head. "I'll help with the preparations. Do you need to do anything with the light? It'll be needed more than ever during the storm."

"I have everything ready."

They worked around the yard, stowing any loose gardening gear in the storage building. The sky darkened. Clouds passed over the cottage and covered the sun. Hollan shivered.

"I need to light the lanterns. Let me see you into the house."

"I'd like to wait out here if you don't mind. I'll move in before things get rough."

"As you wish. But I'd feel better if you waited inside."

"Will you wait out the storm in the lighthouse? Or would you"—she hesitated—"consider waiting it out with me?"

"I'll be back as soon as my duties are taken care of."

Relief flowed across her pretty features. "Thank you." She waved him away.

He hurried through the motions of lighting the wicks that he'd already trimmed to the perfect length. He'd need to return in about four hours to trim them again, but as he looked around everything else was in order. The rain had begun a few minutes earlier, but now it came down in earnest. His cozy room waiting below beckoned him—he'd be drenched before he ever reached Hollan—but he'd given her his word. He didn't want her sitting through the storm alone, frightened.

He'd just exited the door at the base of the lighthouse, when a gust of wind slammed it shut behind him. The wind pushed him along as he moved toward the cottage. Hollan waited in the doorway, anxiety written across her face.

"I'm here, Hollan. I'm coming. Stay put."

Samson heard Jacob and shoved his way through the narrow opening, knocking Hollan off balance.

"Samson, no!" Hollan lunged for the escaping dog. She struggled to retain her balance against the force of the storm, but the wind caught her skirts and twirled them in a tangle around her legs. Before Jacob could get to her, she fell, tumbling down the steps with a scream. Her head hit the stone walkway, and she lay unmoving in a crumpled heap.

Chapter 6

Samson turned at once, hurrying back to his mistress. Jacob pushed him aside and scooped Hollan up in his arms.

"C'mon, Samson, let's get her inside." Rain blew through the open doorway as Jacob entered. He hurried to deposit Hollan on the quilt-covered bed. He forced the door shut before turning to stoke the fire. Though the fire burned warm, the light wasn't bright enough for him to check Hollan for injuries.

He lit a lamp and placed it on a small table near the bed. Samson, panting, stood with his front paws on the edge of the bed. He whined and licked Hollan's hand.

"She'll be fine." Jacob hoped his words were the truth.

The dog looked unconvinced.

"Hollan, can you hear me?" Jacob caressed Hollan's cheek with the back of his hand.

She remained still, her skin pale against the bright pastels of the quilt. He'd give anything to see her brown eyes open to peer into his. A trickle of blood ran down the side of her cheek. With careful fingers, Jacob tenderly sifted through her hair until he found the wound. It didn't appear to be deep at first glance, but with the amount of blood loss, it needed his attention.

First, though, he had to get her out of her wet shoes and dress. "Samson, help me out here. Hollan will tan my hide if she thinks I took any liberties with her."

Samson turned tail and headed for the fire, though he did thump his tail three times in sympathy before curling up into a cozy ball. Or at least Jacob imagined the thumps were a show of sympathy.

"She's my wife, buddy. It's fine, really."

Then why, he asked himself, *am I talking to the dog like he can understand or even cares about my justification of what I'm about to do?*

"She'll get pneumonia if she continues to lie here in a wet dress."

Samson snorted, and Jacob figured it was the dog's way of laughing at his dilemma. Or maybe the sound was just a contented sigh because as a dog Samson didn't have to worry about such things. Or maybe it was just a random dog sound that had nothing at all to do with the crazy individual who was talking to him, trying to figure out the inner workings of a dog's brain when he really needed to be caring for the woman who lay helpless in front of him.

Jacob decided to ignore the irritating thoughts that were pummeling through his head, and with purpose he unhooked Hollan's boots and slipped them off her slender feet. Though he knew she hated it, she'd taken to wearing the boots ever since she cut her foot on the shell. He doubted the habit would continue after she healed.

Next his clumsy fingers unfastened enough tiny buttons down the front of her dress to rival the amount of stairs in the lighthouse before he was finally able to pull the wet material down and over Hollan's arms. He tugged it down over her waist and away from her motionless body. He was relieved to find her underclothes dry, so he was able to leave her covered. Her petticoat and camisole did a fine job of keeping her modesty intact. He did a cursory examination for further injuries before tucking the blankets around her. He slipped the wet quilt from the bed and with a sigh of relief that the deed was done, moved the quilt and the dress nearer to the fire to dry.

Jacob dipped some warm water from the pot that hung over the flame into a small bowl. A huge gust of wind blowing against the cottage made him jump. The storm was intensifying. It sounded like this one might turn into a full-fledged hurricane. At least in her present state, Hollan wouldn't worry about their safety.

The search for rags took a bit longer, but soon he was back at Hollan's side, ready to clean her wound. He said a quick prayer of thanks that he hadn't seen any other signs of injury while he settled her in. He could only pray the head wound wasn't as bad as it looked.

"It's already stopped bleeding, Samson. That's a good sign, don't you think?"

This time Samson didn't even bother to open an eye. Jacob found it reassuring that the dog didn't seem nervous about the storm.

"I'll take that as a sign that you trust she's in good hands," Jacob muttered as he cleaned the wound. Now that the bleeding had stopped, the cut didn't appear to be deep at all.

A lump was forming under the gash. Jacob was cautious as he smoothed Hollan's auburn hair away from her face. Even now she was so beautiful. "You're going to be all right, Hollan. I'm here with you."

He couldn't do anything more for her for the time being. He slipped into some of her father's dry clothes that he had found in a trunk across the room and hung his own clothes to dry. He finally settled in a chair beside Hollan's bed and began to pray.

❧

Hollan opened her eyes and peered into the dusky gloom. The effort was rewarded by a shooting pain that forced her to close them again. She struggled to get her bearings. She remembered the storm and Samson slipping past her.

She'd reached for him and had fallen. She had no memory beyond that, except for waking in the bed minutes earlier.

I hope the injury didn't affect my returning vision. Slowly, realization flowed over her. She'd opened her eyes and had *seen* into the gloom. She'd been able to see perfectly. The few images she'd been able to take in were engraved upon her mind. The fire burned low. Samson slept near the hearth, closer than was safe, as usual. Her dress and a quilt, along with a set of men's clothes, hung on the backs of chairs near the fire to dry.

Men's clothes hung by the fire? She noticed the sound of deep breathing from a chair pulled up close beside her. She opened her eyes again, slower this time to let her eyes acclimate, and for the first time in three years she stared fully into the handsome face of the man she'd once loved. Jacob was stronger, sturdier, but still as striking as ever.

"Jacob." She whispered the word softly, but his eyes flew open as soon as she uttered it.

"Hollan." He slipped from the chair and onto his knees beside her. "How do you feel?"

She couldn't stop looking at him. "Dizzy."

"You hit your head pretty good right about here." He touched his fingers near the wound then caressed lightly down her temple. "You gave Samson and me quite a scare."

"I'm sorry." She shivered at his touch. To cover her reaction, she reached up and felt the raised bump.

"I hardly think you meant to do it." He pulled her hand away from the wound and smiled. "I cleaned the injury, but you'll want to be careful. It will be tender for a few days."

"Thank you." She peered over his shoulder. He didn't release her hand. He was too close. She felt vulnerable. "Has the storm passed?"

"Not completely, but it has calmed down some."

Her head ached. She closed her eyes and listened to the rain pattering against the roof. The aroma of simmering stew set her mouth to watering. And Jacob hovered nearby. The thought made her tremble.

"You're shivering. Let me stoke the fire."

It wasn't the cold that caused her tremor. She felt plenty warm in the cocoon of blankets he'd apparently tucked around her. It was his gentle touch that made her shiver, that stoked a whole other fire and set forth a new longing within her, a longing for things to be as they had been before. Back when he wanted to marry her out of love, not obligation. Before he left town, before she'd lost her sight, and before she'd lost her parents.

She studied him as he moved about the hearth, stepping carefully over the sleeping dog. His hair was indeed longer. He'd pulled it away from his face, which accentuated his high cheekbones. He smiled as he worked, his features relaxed with relief. When he leaned in from the far side, the fire flared, and she could see the green of the eyes she'd missed looking into for so long.

A sudden panic ran through her. Her vision felt different this time. It felt permanent. She couldn't put her finger on the change, but she had peace that her vision would remain. What if, now that she could see again, Jacob decided she no longer needed him and he was free to move on? He could have their marriage annulled and return to his previous plans—whatever those plans might have been. Surely he had some. She wasn't ready for more changes. Not yet anyway.

"What are you thinking?"

Hollan jumped. She hadn't noticed him crossing the floor to her side.

"Tell me your thoughts. You looked scared there for a moment." He pulled his chair closer and settled beside her. "Whatever your concerns were, don't worry about a thing. I'm here, and I don't intend to leave."

So you say now. When you find out you don't have to watch out for me anymore, you might feel differently.

She so badly wanted to stare into his eyes. Instead she closed her own and feigned weariness. "If you don't mind, then, I'll rest for a little bit longer."

"Do you really want to sleep, or are you merely avoiding the truth?"

"The truth?" Did he still know her so well after all these years? Had he noticed the change in her as she savored the familiar sight of his face?

"I think I understand. You're uncomfortable with our arrangement, yet you fear being alone. I'm sure this isn't easy for you."

So he didn't know her vision had fully returned. If she kept it that way a bit longer—at least until she had her bearings about her and could come up with a new plan—it would give her more time to think things through. Her head hurt and everything felt too overwhelming. She'd be able to make better decisions in the next few days.

"I feared being alone through the storm far more than I fear your closeness." There. She'd said it. But she wasn't sure that was completely true. His presence brought about a sense of awareness and accentuated an emptiness she hadn't noticed before he'd arrived back on the island. Already his presence brought her a sense of peace that she didn't want to lose. The fear of losing him so soon rivaled the fear of the storm. "At least, for the moment I *think* that's true." She cringed. She should probably stop talking until she had more rest and could think through her words, *before* stating them, with a clear mind.

He leaned close, his lips near her ear, causing tiny bumps to rise up on her forearms. "My closeness makes you nervous?"

She ordered her eyes to remain closed, though she longed to open them and see his face. She could feel the warmth of his breath on her skin.

"Yes," she admitted through clenched teeth. The man was toying with her. She didn't feel as bad about keeping her returned vision a secret at this rate. Here she lay helpless in bed and he used the situation to his advantage. She held back her smile. Deep down she didn't really mind his teasing.

Now he raised a finger and caressed her cheek. His touch was so gentle, so considerate; the act caused tears to form in her eyes. Her emotions were all over the place.

She opened her eyes. "I have a confession to make. My vision comes and goes. For the moment my vision has returned."

His face lit up. "That's wonderful news!"

"It is, but I'm confused and overwhelmed." And that was the pure truth. Hollan hadn't felt so mixed up and inundated with changes since she'd lost her mother.

"Have you prayed about it?"

She released a small breath and stared at the beams that ran across the ceiling. "I haven't prayed about much of anything in a long, long time."

"You don't believe anymore? You've lost your faith?"

The disappointment and concern in his voice had her firing off the first answer that came to mind. "No!"

She hesitated before saying anything more and analyzed his question a bit more thoroughly. *Had* she lost her faith? At the very least, she'd buried it beneath the pile of rubble that had been her former life.

"I'm embarrassed to say I haven't given it much thought lately." Guilt pricked at her conscience. If her faith had been strong, would she have let it drift away so easily? Most people used their faith to get them through the tough times—they didn't forget about it completely. "What does that say about me?"

"It says you've been through a lot." He shifted his position. "Is God still in charge of your life?"

"I guess so. . . I mean, yes, I want Him to be. I haven't given it much thought before now."

"God understands anger. But you can't let the anger make you so bitter that you turn against Him."

"No, of course not. Yet that seems to be exactly what I've done. That night. . . I lost so much."

"I know what you lost." Jacob tightened his grip on her hand. "Do you want to tell me about it? I feel responsible."

"How could you be responsible when you weren't even here?" She hadn't meant the words to sound so venomous. It might help to talk about it, to share with Jacob what happened that night. "Mama and I were talking about the wedding when we heard a noise outside. Mama went to check. A storm lurked over the water, and the wind had started up. I stayed inside and continued to work on our dinner, and the next thing I knew, Papa came in through the door. He said he'd sent Mama inside."

She untwisted and smoothed the sheets she'd wrung tight with her hands. He reached over and massaged away the tension that had gathered in her clenched hands. His touch encouraged her to continue. He deserved to know. The experiences had shaped her into the person she was today.

"Mama hadn't returned, and we both knew something wasn't right. Papa was upset and ran to check the beach while I searched the grounds around the house. Neither one of us thought to check the lighthouse, because Papa had just come from there. After looking out over the dune, I turned to go back to the house and I saw a flash of color from the ledge that circles the light. Papa couldn't hear me, so I went up without him. Mama had been crying, and she stood at the rail, much too close to the edge with the storm brewing around us."

Her breath hitched.

Jacob wiped away a tear she hadn't realized she'd shed. "Maybe now isn't the best time. You need to rest, not get more upset."

His voice was husky, full of emotion, and she wondered at the remorse she heard in his tone.

"No, I need to do this." She took a deep breath. "I went out there, and the wind buffeted around me. It almost blew me over the edge. My mother didn't even acknowledge my presence. I called to her and tried to pull her back inside, but she shoved me away. I fell against the stone wall and hit my head. When I came to, I'd lost my sight and Mama all in one fell swoop. Papa saw us up there, but before he could get to the top, Mama had jumped."

"No one knows why?"

"No, we never found out. She took her secret to the grave." Her voice had dropped to a whisper, but now she laughed, the sound harsh in the silence. "What kind of mother does that to her child—even if the child is almost grown? What type of wife abandons her husband in such a painful way? How could she have done that to herself and to us?"

"Hollan, maybe she didn't jump. If the wind was that strong, maybe she fell over accidently."

"Why was she up there?"

"I don't have the answers to those questions, Hollan. I wish I did."

Hollan understood his confusion.

"I know. I don't really expect you to. But therein lies the reason for my silence and distance from God. It wasn't a conscious choice I made, but I stopped communicating with Him." She hesitated. "I haven't forgotten my father's and uncle's teachings. I've even talked to God a bit lately. But still I've drifted away."

"Now that you've realized this, are you ready to make things right with Him?" She nodded. "I am. I want to find my way back."

"He'll calm your fears and will help you sort through all the changes you're experiencing." He chuckled. "Changes we're both going through. If we work as a team, perhaps we can make sense of it all and see what God has for us. Let me pray with you."

Jacob clasped her hand and leaned forward to rest his forehead against it. She clung to him like the lifeline he was. The strength and confidence in his warm voice as he prayed washed over her.

"Lord, we join together in prayer and thank You for keeping us safe through the storm. Help Hollan back into the fold, Lord, and use me to make the process easier. We ask that You bring Hollan clarity of mind and calm her fears in all situations. She wants You to take control of her life. Guide her in all things. . . . In Jesus' name, amen."

Hollan listened as he finished up his prayer and felt a sense of peace flow through her. She released to Him all the fears and concerns she'd carried. For the first time in a while, she felt the burdens she'd carried alone lift. She held only one small concern back for herself. She knew she was supposed to turn *everything* over to God, to let Him watch over all aspects of her life, but in this one small area she still felt she needed to keep control, at least for a little bit longer. For now, for just a little bit longer, she still felt the need to keep the permanent return of her vision a secret from Jacob.

Chapter 7

After two days in bed, Hollan couldn't wait any longer to get out and explore the island. She understood Jacob's overprotective nature after a blow to her head, but she wanted to get up. She had a lot to celebrate. Her *vision* had returned! It hadn't wavered once. She sent a covert glance at Jacob. And neither had the man she still loved. He'd returned and now stayed close to her side. But that all-important detail aside, at the moment she only wanted to see the places and things she loved through new eyes. And even better would be to see everything with Jacob by her side.

"We're going out to explore today." Hollan settled at the table, not leaving her comment up for debate. "I feel completely ready to go outside and breathe in some fresh air. If I have to stay inside another day, I'll surely go insane."

"You will, huh?" Jacob set an aromatic plate of eggs in front of her before taking his seat. "We certainly don't want that. A little fresh air won't hurt, but you'll need to take it slow."

"Yes, doc." She busied herself with eating, not wanting to waste a moment of the brilliant day that waited outside their doorstep. "Jacob, these eggs are wonderful. Where'd you learn to cook like this?"

"All over the place." He stabbed at an egg, and she took the moment to study him. His damp hair was slicked back from his forehead. "When you travel like I did, you meet up with a lot of different people. I had to work a lot of odd jobs in order to make ends meet."

"How did you end up choosing to do that? What made you decide to become a traveling preacher? I don't remember you ever talking about wanting to do such a thing."

What she really wanted to ask was why he'd left her behind. From the way he froze in place, fork halfway to his mouth while contemplating his answer, she knew she'd hit a sore spot.

"That night I left, a lot of bad things happened." He laid his fork down and reached over to toy with her hand. She had a hard time not staring into his eyes. She wanted to lose herself in them. But he couldn't know about the return of her vision. Not yet. She didn't want him to leave. She wasn't ready for that possibility. She needed more time. She needed to solidify their relationship.

"I remember."

"I know you do." He pulled his hand away and ran it through his hair, the gesture reassuringly familiar. "I couldn't face anyone after what my father and brothers did to the people of our town. So when they fled, I chased them up the trail. They scattered, and I tailed them one at a time. Each time I'd catch one, I turned him over to the law." He picked up his fork and used it to push the eggs back and forth, but he didn't eat any of them.

"That had to be hard." Hollan ached for him, for the pain he had to have felt each time he had to turn in a brother. "You found your father, too?"

"Someone else found him first. I found his body soon after."

"That's awful." What else could she say to that? Though she longed to know what had happened to her father, finding his body wasn't something she could imagine. She didn't want to contemplate it further. "And the others, what happened to them?"

"I found all but one. They'll spend a lot of time behind bars, if not worse. I didn't stick around to see what happened."

"Which one evaded you?"

"David."

He seemed to be studying her face for a reaction. She stared at his chin. His expression turned quizzical when she didn't have one.

"So you decided to let him go, and instead you returned home?"

"No, I trailed him back this way. I don't intend to stop looking until he joins our other brothers behind bars."

"So you're only here for a short while?"

"I married you, Hollan. I'm with you for life. I meant my vows when I said them."

Her heart leaped at his words. Maybe she wouldn't have to keep her secret as long as she thought. She tested him.

"But you were forced into the marriage. You might change your mind if. . ." She let her voice trail off, not sure what to say.

"If what?" His voice held a chuckle. "I made my commitment for life, Hollan."

He stood to gather their plates and moved out of her line of vision. Her *newly returned* vision. A hint of a smile broadened her lips. She savored the thought and forced herself not to track him with her eyes.

"Well, I don't know. What if you get bored? What if you catch your brother and want to travel again? I understand you wanted to return home and right the wrongs of your family, but once that's all behind you, maybe you'll want to wander again."

"Not likely." This time there was no humor after the statement. "A person can only wander for so long before life catches up with them. And in my case, it was time for me to return."

"So what about David?"

He helped her up from her chair and led the way to the door. "I'll know what to do when the time comes. God has led me to each of them in turn. I don't know why David came back. He already caused all the pain he possibly could. But for whatever reason, God has been urging me back this way for a while now, and I've ignored Him. Next thing I know, my quarry turned this way and led me home."

"Interesting." Hollan wished he'd come back because he missed her. But they were married and working on their new relationship. That had to be enough. She'd try to be patient and see what happened next.

"Enough of that. Let's go explore and see what the hurricane did to our home."

Our home. The words were so simple, yet they meant so much to her. She wasn't alone anymore.

Jacob tugged her toward the inland channel. "How about we start at the dock? I want to check the boat."

Hollan nodded her agreement.

Jacob led her down the path toward the water at a leisurely pace, walking slightly ahead. She held back just a bit, wanting to look around without him taking notice. She savored every single sight. The brilliant green of the trees stood out against the vivid blue of the sky. The seagulls circled overhead, scavenging for small crabs and fish. They neared the sandy beach, and the water lapped at the shore, tossing tiny shells and clams with the movement. The sea oats danced in the slight breeze. Hollan wanted to dance along with them. Pelicans and herons dove for their dinner in the distance. And decidedly the best view of all was that of Jacob walking just ahead of her. Her beloved Jacob. She studied his broad shoulders and the way his waist narrowed at the hips. The muscles in his arms flexed as he cleared debris from their path. The sun shone off his golden hair, which he'd again pulled back and tied at the nape of his neck. He was truly a striking man.

Jacob's grunt pulled her from her perusal. He'd stopped just ahead of her. She wanted to wrap her arms around him and press her cheek against his back, but instead she hurried to stand at his side. She glanced at the dock.

Only one thing seemed to be missing—one major thing. She put her hand to her forehead and scanned the open waters.

"The boat's gone." Jacob stated the obvious just before Hollan blurted it out. At the rate she was going, she'd surely clue him in about the return of her sight. Jacob didn't notice—he was too focused on the missing boat.

"Gone. . .where?"

Jacob reached over to clutch her hand. "I have no idea. I didn't think the storm would have done that much damage to this side of the island. It's more protected."

"Odd."

"Yes, it is." His voice held a funny tone.

"Are you thinking someone tampered with it?"

"I'm not sure. But it can't have floated off on its own."

"The supply boat won't be here for days. This means we're on our own until then."

"It looks that way." They'd reached the dock, and Jacob released her hand as he bent low to check out the dock and surrounding water. He stood back up, hands on hips, and glanced around again. "This is so strange. There's no sign of it at all."

"The storm likely blew it away. I doubt we'll ever find it."

"What now?"

"There's nothing we can do until Fletcher returns."

He clasped her hand again and led her down the shoreline path. His hand felt solid and reassuring. "Let's walk some more. Maybe it washed ashore. If so, we'll come across it. If not, I still want to see what other damage the storm did to our island."

They walked in silence, and more than once Hollan's eyes blurred with tears of happiness. A lizard skittered across the path and disappeared in the overgrown foliage to her left. A large turtle floated in the water just offshore. The water was so clear here that she could see the turtle's shadow on the sandy bottom as it moved along. A mockingbird sang from somewhere in the dense trees overhead. She'd missed these sights dearly. And because she never dared to walk very far, she'd missed a lot of the shoreline's sounds. Hollan took a deep breath, breathing in the salt-laden air. The vivid blue of the sky almost hurt her eyes, but she embraced the sensation. She'd never been happier to squint.

Jacob slowed. "Where does that path lead? I've never noticed it before."

"What path?"

Jacob tugged her inland, a small path barely visible through the dense jungle of palmettos and scrub that made most of the island impenetrable. "It leads through the undergrowth. It looks like at one time it would have been used quite often, but now it's almost completely overgrown."

"Sounds like the path to Amos's old place." Hollan was beginning to hate the farce she'd put into motion. If only she had complete surety that the return of her vision wouldn't cause a negative change in their budding friendship.

"Amos?" Jacob took the lead through the tunnel of vegetation. Hollan's skirts were snagged and tugged by the ends of the palmettos' sharp fronds. She didn't care. She'd happily sacrifice the old dress she wore for the experience and adventure of refamiliarizing herself with the interior of the island. Especially when it meant Jacob would hold her close against his side as he did now.

"He helped my grandfather when he first took over the lighthouse, before my father had the contract. He had a small shack somewhere around here."

"Let's find it."

"If it's even standing." She laughed. "It's been around for a long time, and you know how harsh the weather can be."

"It's still here."

Sure enough, it was. And it looked surprisingly solid. Of course she couldn't admit that to him.

The door screeched as he pulled it open. Hollan screamed as a bat flew out, barely skimming her head.

"Sorry about that." Jacob pulled her into a quick embrace. "It's gone now."

Hollan shuddered. She'd never liked the creatures of the night. Suddenly the area felt dark and oppressive. She couldn't imagine how much worse it would be if she couldn't see. Snakes loved to lurk on this section of the island, along with alligators and all sorts of other creatures.

"If you've seen enough, I'm ready to go back to the shore."

"No, actually, I want to look a little closer. Other than the bats—"

"Plural? I thought there was only one!" Hollan reached up and scrubbed at her hair with both hands. "They're gone, aren't they?" She spun in a circle.

"They all flew away. You're fine." She didn't comment on the chuckle she heard in his tone. He stood in the open doorway. "But it looks like someone has been here recently. The interior isn't as rough as I'd expect after all these years."

Hollan stepped closer and grabbed hold of Jacob's arm. "Someone or—something?"

"Someone. The floor is cleared, and there's a sign of fire. Let me duck inside."

"All the more reason to leave."

"I'll only be a moment."

"You do know there are snakes and gators around here? Don't leave me for long."

Hollan hugged her arms around her waist and scoured the area for signs of predators. A bubbling stream ran along the opposite side of the small clearing. Though she much preferred being outside in the open rather than being inside the tiny bat-infested cabin, her mind was quickly conjuring up quite a few alarming scenarios of possible creatures lurking at her feet.

"Um, Jacob? I'm hearing scurrying sounds in the brush. Not something I like to stand here and listen to. My imagination's racing out here."

"I'm ready." His sudden appearance at her side made her jump. "Let's get you out of here. But I'll be watching the place, and if someone is using this cabin, I'll find out."

"Sounds good to me. Meanwhile, I'll stick to waiting on one of the nice, clean, wide-open paths on the beach when you check."

Jacob laughed.

They cut across the island toward the ocean and reached the main path. Hollan breathed a sigh of relief. The sigh ended in a cough as she inhaled the sharp odor of rotting fish. Quite a few of them lay scattered at their feet. "Whoa. Lots of fish washed ashore in this area after the storm."

Jacob turned her way, eyes squinting, his forehead creased. Hollan covered quickly, waving her hand in front of her wrinkled nose.

He laughed. "It *is* a bit potent."

"It's the aroma of home. I like it."

"You are an island girl through and through, aren't you?"

"Always and forever." Hollan couldn't imagine living anywhere else. She didn't want to *think* about living anywhere else.

"Hollan, there's something we need to talk about."

Her heart plummeted. Here it came. She didn't want to hear what he had to say. "Oh listen! The waves are louder and the birds more vocal. We're nearing the ocean side, aren't we?"

"Yes." He squeezed her hand. "Hollan, don't change the subject."

Intent on savoring the newest view, she didn't answer. The Atlantic Ocean seemed to stretch out forever before her. Shells scattered at her feet, begging for her attention. She loved walking with Jacob, but she couldn't wait to make her escape in the near future and spend a morning enjoying her favorite pastime, looking for seashells and pirate treasure.

"Hollan?"

"I'm sorry." She kept her gaze down and moved forward.

"Anyway, as I was saying, we have to discuss what will happen if the light-house inspector arrives and decides that we can't stay."

She froze. "Decides we can't stay? Why would he decide that?" The panic made her voice rise. She hadn't even thought about that possibility.

"The contract for the lighthouse is with your father, not with us. I don't know how that all works, but he might have someone else in mind to take over for your father—now that he is missing."

"Well, he can just wait." She set her jaw, daring him to disagree. "We have no— *proof* that my father isn't coming back. Until we do, we need to protect his job."

"You have a point. We'll keep that as our plan for now." He gently guided her face to look up into his. "But you have to keep in mind that we might need an alternate plan."

Hollan carefully avoided his gaze after one quick glimpse of his beautiful green eyes. She had to end this farce—tomorrow. She wanted one more day to savor the sights and Jacob's presence before telling him how drastically things had changed. He seemed genuine in his commitment, but he didn't have all the facts. "There'll be no plan other than the one that allows us to stay on this island."

"As you wish." He smirked. "I suppose we can always move into Amos's place. Quarters might be tight, but I think we could make do. I certainly could."

Hollan stared straight ahead, but she felt the flush wash over her features. *Close quarters* would be an understatement. "There would be bugs and snakes and other equally horrible things. I couldn't even imagine."

"I'd batten it down. I'll make sure they don't get you."

"We'd have no beds. We'd have to—" The blush continued. "We'd have no room to move around."

"I'd hold you close and keep you safe."

Hollan didn't know what to say to that. She'd love to have him hold her close at night and keep her safe. But she wasn't sure she was ready for all the changes that would bring to their relationship. They were married after all, but she hadn't kept up with all the changes as it was. She needed them to take things slow. But he'd slept inside the cottage—albeit in a chair—for the past three nights. He'd watched over her since the hurricane. She didn't want to send him back to the lighthouse now.

"That might be—tolerable."

"Tolerable?" He choked on a laugh, his profile showing his dimples.

She shrugged. "I'd do my best to adapt."

"Tell me, which part might be merely tolerable? Living in the cabin?" He stepped close behind her and whispered in her ear. "Or being held in my arms at night?"

Hollan shivered. "If necessity mandated such a situation, I'd probably survive both conditions."

"You'd *probably* survive them?" Jacob laughed out loud. "That's nice to know."

He spun her around and pulled her close. She knew he was going to kiss her. She closed her eyes. He planted several soft kisses on her lips, and she felt herself respond and kiss him back.

"I've missed you, Hollan."

She asked the question that had bothered her for so long. "Then why'd you leave?"

"It's complicated. But my decision to leave that night had nothing to do with my feelings for you. My love for you has never changed."

Hollan's heart swelled. "I'm glad to know that."

"I'd like to tell you about it soon."

"Maybe tonight at dinner?"

"I don't know. You've had a busy morning, and I want you to rest. I think we need to get lunch, you need to lie down, and we'll see what the evening brings later."

"You're avoiding me."

"I wouldn't say I'm avoiding you exactly. . . . I'm just trying to give you the time to heal. Besides your head injury, you've lost your father. I want to take things slow. We have our whole life ahead of us, and there's no reason to hurry while we're muddling through all the changes."

"I have faith that my father is alive. My head injury is fine." Hollan's good spirits began to slip away. He was echoing her thoughts from a moment earlier that they needed to take things slow, yet now she found herself pushing forward. "When you use the word *muddling* as you just did, it feels as if you think you're stuck here in this awful. . .*quagmire*. . .or something with me."

"I'm not *stuck* in anything with you, Hollan, and I'm sorry if it came across that way." She leaned against his chest, and he rested his chin on her head. "I know I'm where God led me to be. I'm perfectly content to be where I am. I love being married to you, and I can only hope that in a very short time we'll be living as a married couple in every way."

"Then why—?"

"I won't take advantage of you in a vulnerable state. I want to make sure you're coming to me freely when we make this marriage real. I'll sleep in the lighthouse for tonight, and we'll see what tomorrow brings—tomorrow."

Disappointment rolled over Hollan, but she knew he was right. They'd work things out as they went. But she knew she'd miss his presence in the cottage tonight.

They circled around toward the dunes in front of their home, and Jacob led her directly toward a piece of driftwood. She panicked. If she stepped over it, he'd know. If she had to trip, she'd feel like an idiot. It served her right for her deceit.

She slowed just as she reached the limb and bent down to fumble with her boot.

"Is everything all right?"

"Everything is fine, thank you."

"So we can continue on?"

"Yes."

At that slower pace, she had no trouble kicking her foot toward the driftwood. Jacob stopped her.

"There's a piece of wood in front of us. Come this way, and we'll go around it."

"Thanks," she mumbled.

"We need to head up to the cottage."

"Let's keep going." Hollan wanted to see it all. Everything she'd missed seeing for the past three years.

"No. You need to get back and rest. And I need to check the lighthouse." When she started to protest, he put a finger against her lips.

"You suffered a huge blow to the head. I don't want you to overtax yourself. We'll walk the other way in the morning." They continued in the direction of the dunes. "If you want us to save our post, we need to be ready and have things perfect at any given time."

"Good point." She sighed. "I'll come up with you." She couldn't wait to see the view from atop the lighthouse!

"You'll return to the cottage and sleep."

She made a disgruntled sound, and Jacob laughed. "You'll be up to par soon enough, wife. You need to have patience."

Wife. She grinned. "I'm up to par now. My tyrant of a husband just won't let me prove it."

Silence met her hasty retort, and she wondered if she had inadvertently offended him. Instead her eyes widened as Jacob leaned in for another gentle kiss. "I'm sure you have a lot to prove, wife, and I anticipate and look forward to each and every revelation."

He accentuated the word *revelation*. Was he insinuating something? Her guilt had her constantly returning to her deception. She stubbornly stood her ground. She liked things as they were. She didn't want to mess things up.

He captured her gaze with his own, and she swooned. She stepped backward. Jacob caught her by the arm. "Dizzy?"

"A—a bit maybe." She put a hand to her forehead and feigned exhaustion. No way would she admit that it was his kiss that threw her off balance. "I think you're right about my lying down."

"I'll get you settled then."

She ignored the laughter in his voice. She hadn't fooled him in the least.

Chapter 8

Hollan rose at dawn, determined to get an early start on her day. She figured the best way to effectively avoid Jacob would be to ease out the door well before their usual meeting time. He wouldn't be happy with her, but she needed some time alone. She wanted to be able to explore without hiding the fact that she could see. Today she'd tell him about the return of her vision—just as soon as she took this walk along the shore.

She had a feeling their relationship would take a turn for the better after she cleared the air. She looked forward to sharing her news. She hadn't liked sleeping alone in the cottage after having Jacob there the three nights before. She wanted their marriage to be real.

If Jacob felt she didn't need him anymore and he decided to move on, she'd work through the situation day by day, just as she'd dealt with every other challenge in her life. But she hoped and prayed he wouldn't decide that because she really did need him. She knew now that her love for him had never diminished; it had merely been buried somewhere deep inside.

Hollan stood before the mirror and smiled at her reflection. Today she could brush and style her auburn hair, and she would know what the end result actually looked like. She'd picked her favorite dress to wear and loved how the deep blue color she'd never seen before so perfectly matched the hue of the sea. Her brown eyes sparkled with excitement in the mirror's reflection. Soon she'd be walking along the beach, scouring the soft sand for shells. Seagulls called to her through the open cottage door. The waves pounded the shoreline in the distance, promising interesting treasure.

Mindful of the time, she hurried to prepare a batch of blueberry muffins. She arranged them on a plate and set a flowered bowl of butter and a matching one of jam beside them. Guilt had her scurrying to the garden for a pretty arrangement of flowers. Jacob likely wouldn't notice, but if he did, maybe he'd realize she'd taken the extra step to make her absence less harsh. Then again, he'd probably not even miss her and would be thrilled to have a morning meal without the awkwardness of their usual forced routine, though she had to admit their camaraderie felt more natural compared to before her accident. She now felt a certain comfort in the presence of her husband.

When she couldn't think of anything else to do, she hurried out the door.

Samson tried to follow, but she knew his barking would draw Jacob's attention. She blocked him with her leg and forced the door shut behind her. The dog would get even by leading Jacob straight to her side but hopefully not before she'd had plenty of time to savor the beauty of her surroundings. And when they arrived, she'd happily share her news with Jacob, and she'd ask him to move into the cottage so they could properly live like the married couple they were.

Hollan wasted no time moving past the lighthouse and let out a sigh of relief after she'd cleared the stone walls. Once on the beach, she breathed even easier. No voice called out to stop her. No footsteps pounded down the hard-packed sand walkway in her wake.

Her bare feet sank deep into the coolness of the powdery soft sand at the water's edge, and she laughed out loud, wiggling her toes in order to bury them deeper. She wanted to do so many different things. She wanted to swim, to explore, and to merely sit and savor. But first she had to make haste and get far away from here. She followed the shore in the direction they'd been heading the previous day. A tide pool usually formed just around the curve of the farthest dune, and she hoped to find it alive with crawling creatures. While she didn't care for most of the land-type creatures, she loved each and every one of the aquatic types.

And suddenly there it was—the tide pool—spread out before her, sparkling in the morning sun. From a distance the tidal pool looked placid, just a thin layer of water filling up the slight depression in the sand. But Hollan knew it would contain a whole underwater world full of sea creatures. Smiling, she dropped to her knees on the dry sand and studied the undersea world before her. She'd often wished in the past, as a little girl, that she could shrink down and be able to swim with the inhabitants. Now she was content just to be able to watch the miniature world. Everything she could see was a blessing and a privilege. She'd never take her vision for granted again.

Tiny coquina clams waved their siphons around, waiting for algae or plankton, not knowing they were a target themselves for the scavenging seagulls that flew overhead. Hermit crabs, their shells shiny and multicolored, glistened as they scurried across the bottom of the pool. A small blue crab lurked behind a rounded rock. A group of tiny fish swam together, twisting and turning with perfect precision. The scent of sea blew in on the breeze.

Hollan moved her fingers through the surface of the water, smiling as the clams pulled their siphons under the sand. The blue crab disappeared from sight when her hand's shadow moved too close. The hermit crabs pulled back into their shells. The fish darted away to the far side of the pool.

Something brushed against her foot, and she looked over to see a curious ghost crab hurrying away. It blended in with the color of the beach and disappeared down a tunnel dug into the sand nearby. She felt as if her favorite friends had all gathered to welcome her back. All these aquatic creatures she'd missed for so long. She sat and savored the sights.

Hollan settled onto her hip and curved her legs beneath her. She dug her fingers into the sand and let it sift through them as she breathed a heartfelt prayer of thanks for the return of her vision. She knew God had a purpose in returning her sight, but this moment defined why she personally valued the ability to see. Her entire world here at the beach revolved around the land and the creatures she loved so much.

She glanced up. Fluffy white clouds moved across the brilliant blue sky. The water wasn't quite as brown as it had been the day before. The sediment churned up by the storm was settling, allowing the water to return to its natural blue-green color.

Hollan wished she could throw caution to the wind and run out into the waves. But she wouldn't. Jacob would probably be along soon, looking for his errant wife.

Instead she stood slowly to her feet and began to move farther down the beach. She stayed close to the waterline, not wanting to miss a treasure. Though most shells lay in pieces, tossed and broken by the surf, a few choice shells made it through the treacherous waters. One particularly delicate-looking shell washed up at her feet. The wave flipped it upside down to show a perfect outer shell, the color bleached white by the sun.

Hollan picked it up, feeling a strange kinship with the item. She'd add it to her collection. She tucked the shell into her pocket. Several starfish and sea horses had washed in, too. She carefully lifted them and settled them back in the water. Most floated atop the water and drifted out to sea. But a few gave halfhearted efforts to swim before seeming to realize they were once again free to swim away to safety.

She was fully absorbed in her observations of the sea life at her feet. Hollan didn't notice the arrival of a large ship until the sound of men's voices carried to her from across the water. She stood watching the activity aboard ship, deciding it was likely a renegade privateer ship from the war. She knew from her father that a select few still sailed up and down the coast. Fascinated, she raised her hand to her forehead, shading her eyes so she could study the magnificent vessel.

"What have we here, gentlemen?"

Hollan jumped and swung around as a voice spoke close behind her. The hair stood up on the back of her neck.

A rough-looking man stood just to her right, and a bit farther back three others stood and leered at her. None of them looked like gentlemen as far as she was concerned.

She slowly backed away. She hadn't heard the arrival of the small boat that was now pulled up behind her down the shore. A shiver passed through her. For the first time that day, she prayed for Jacob to hurry and find her.

"I think we have a damsel in distress," one of the men muttered. "We need to *rescue* her."

They erupted into a semblance of laughter, the sound rusty, as if they hadn't laughed in a very long time. The grating sounds sent another round of shivers down her spine.

"Thank you, but I'm not in need of rescue." She turned and hurried in the opposite direction, on a path that would lead her directly back to Jacob. She wanted to run headlong into his strong embrace and never leave the warmth of his protective arms again. She wanted to tell him about the return of her vision. She wanted to say that she loved him. She suddenly realized that if a person waited too long, things could happen that would prevent those moments from ever happening. She prayed this wasn't one of them. She'd just regained her vision. She didn't want to lose her life.

A rough hand grasped her shoulder and spun her around. "It's rude to walk away from someone when they're talking."

"It's rude to place your hand upon a woman you've never met. Please release me at once," Hollan gritted out through her teeth.

"Ah, we've caught ourselves a spunky one, men."

They all laughed.

"You haven't *caught* me at all. I'm not a fish." Hollan fought off a wave of fear and held her ground.

"Ah, that's good! She's not a fish." The closest man mocked her.

Hollan tried to jerk from his grasp. "My husband will be along at any moment, and he won't be any too pleased to find you taking liberties with me."

If only it was true. She had no idea when Jacob would come looking for her, or even if he'd look at all.

"Then we'd best get back to the ship at once."

Her momentary relief turned into full-fledged panic when the closest man grabbed her roughly by the arm and dragged her toward their small wooden craft. She fought with everything she had, but that wasn't much. She might as well have been a feather for all the good it did.

She managed one more glance over her shoulder before they forced her into the boat, but the beach behind her remained empty.

❧

Jacob finished his morning chores and headed down for breakfast. He stopped by his tiny room, which was in dire need of cleaning, and hurried to freshen it up. He didn't think Hollan would mind if he took a few minutes to tidy things. And if he didn't take the time to clean it now, he knew she'd eventually make her way out and clean it for him. He made the small bed—the only item pushed against the north wall of the room—and gathered a few pieces of clothes into a pile. He went outside to dump the pitcher of water that had sat forgotten upon his small table on the opposite side of the room before returning to put everything else back in place. Hooks on the remaining wall—the one opposite the door—held the only other clothes he owned.

When he decided the room was clean enough, he bundled up the clothes to be washed and headed over to greet his wife. He needed to talk to her about several things. He laid his laundry down near the washtub. Hollan would insist on doing his laundry, but he'd insist just as hard on doing it himself. Until they lived in the same house as husband and wife, he wouldn't expect her to do his clothes. And that very topic was one he intended to bring up. He'd been lonely last night and wanted things to change.

His feelings for Hollan hadn't ever wavered. Though their marriage hadn't come about quite the way they'd planned, they were still married. It was silly to live apart as they were. He just hoped she returned his feelings.

If she didn't, he'd be patient and wait. In time she'd surely grow to love him the same way he loved her.

Samson barked from inside the cottage, and Jacob grinned. The dog had heard his arrival. Surprisingly, he didn't hear Hollan hush him as usual with her melodic lilting voice. He'd come to rely on the familiar sound at the start of his day.

The early morning sun beat down on his head. Though the autumn nights were cooling down, the days were staying warm. Judging by the way the sun heated his back, today would be a hot one. The cool interior of the cottage beckoned him.

Jacob knocked and pushed open the door. "Good morning."

Samson almost knocked him down in his hurry to get past and out into the yard, but Hollan didn't answer Jacob's greeting or bother to call Samson back.

With a whine, Samson wound himself around Jacob's legs.

"Hollan?" Jacob had a warning sensation that something wasn't right. He reached down and rubbed Samson on the head. "Where is she, boy?"

Samson glanced up at him with worried eyes.

Jacob moved into the empty room and let his eyes adjust to the dim interior. The table was set for one. The bed lay empty and neat. She'd taken time to pull the quilt up. She hadn't left in a hurry. The fire burned low, but she'd finished breakfast preparations before departing.

Maybe Fletcher had arrived early with the supply boat. Knowing Hollan, she'd have walked along with him to bring back supplies. Jacob glanced around.

The few times he'd seen Fletcher, he hadn't wasted time. If he'd arrived at Hollan's door, he'd have carried something along. No sign of packages or supplies sat anywhere nearby.

He sighed. More than likely Hollan had left early in order to be alone. He tended to be a tad overbearing when it came to her. He knew she didn't like to be coddled, but he couldn't help himself. He hadn't protected her three years earlier when he'd needed to, and he didn't ever want to mess up again.

"Ah, I see." Jacob put his hands on his hips and looked at Samson. "She snuck out and left us both behind, is that it?" He walked to the table and surveyed the arrangement. "Well, we might as well show our appreciation as long as she went to the trouble of setting it all out."

The aroma of fresh-baked muffins permeated the room.

Samson wagged his tail. Jacob slipped into a chair and held a muffin high over his head. Samson stood on his hind legs, begged for a moment, then tired of the game and jumped to snatch the delicacy from Jacob's hand. He hurried away to eat his prize at his favorite place near the fire.

Jacob frowned and spread some butter on his own muffin. It was lonely here without Hollan. Without her presence, he'd have preferred to eat outside. But the flowers on the table showed the care she'd put into making the table pretty for him, and he wouldn't chance moving out front only to have her return and jump to the wrong conclusion.

As he ate, he mulled over his thoughts. He was sure Hollan was hiding something from him, and he was pretty sure he knew what her secret was. Ever since she'd recovered from her storm injuries, she'd been skittish. Something in her eyes had changed. She'd looked right into his eyes a few times before catching herself and turning away. He didn't want to jump to conclusions, either, but he was pretty sure she'd regained her vision, at least partially.

Why she wouldn't tell him, he didn't know. He'd tried to figure it out, but he'd stopped trying to understand her years ago. Whatever her reason, he'd find out soon enough.

He wanted to go after her but decided to give her a little more time. She'd been through some hard times. He wanted her to feel free and comfortable enough to confide in him whenever she decided the time was right. He wanted to move forward and have a life and a future with her. But a part of him worried that she might be having second thoughts. Maybe the return of her sight had her thinking she didn't need Jacob at all. If so, they needed to talk things out. She needed him, and he'd be the first to explain that fact to her.

Jacob wasn't one to tiptoe around a delicate circumstance—he preferred to plunge headfirst into every situation that crossed his path. He wouldn't do anything different with this one.

While he waited for her to return, he decided to tend the garden. A little hard work would clear his mind and help him think. The growing season was almost over, and only a few vegetables remained on the vines. He picked the tomatoes that were ready and put them in a nearby bucket. He pulled the last few weeds. Next year he'd like to expand the garden's size. If there would be a next year.

The thought led him back to wondering about Hollan.

He put down the hoe and walked over to the dunes. Hollan's small footprints led down toward the beach. The impressions of her bare feet showed that, once again, she'd left her boots behind.

Enough was enough. It was time for Jacob to go after his wife. He wanted to feel her in his arms.

He walked over to the cottage's open door. Samson lay sprawled just inside the cool interior.

"C'mon, boy. Want to go with me to find Hollan?"

Samson almost bowled him over in his hurry to get outside. Obviously he didn't intend to be left behind again. They headed up the path. Jacob stopped at the lighthouse door.

"I need to check on something first, boy. Stay."

Samson whined again but stayed where Jacob pointed. Jacob hurried up to the top of the lighthouse, no easy feat with the multiple stairs he had to climb. He stepped onto the platform that circled the top and looked out over the island. Samson lay where he left him down below.

He didn't see any sign of Hollan, but he did see a large ship offshore. An uneasy feeling settled over him. He walked a bit farther around the platform to a better vantage point. His breath caught as he located Hollan. A small boat had been pulled ashore.

His wife was so enraptured by whatever lay at her feet that she didn't appear to notice the men coming up from behind her. From the stealthy way they walked, he sensed they were up to no good.

"Hollan!" His voice blew away on the breeze. He spun on his heel and rushed back to the stairs. He forced himself not to take them two at a time, a recipe for disaster. He couldn't afford to take a tumble. Hollan would be gone forever if that happened. She might be even as it was.

Samson stood at the ready, the hair on the nape of his neck standing on end.

"Go, boy, go to Hollan."

The dog tore away over the dunes and disappeared from sight. Jacob followed along as quickly as he could. The sand pulled at his heavy boots, slowing him even as he pushed to go faster. He didn't have a weapon, and he had no idea what he'd do once he reached her. But he'd do whatever was necessary to keep his wife safe.

God, please protect Hollan. Help me to reach her in time.

His feet slipped in the sand as he rounded the bend and approached the last place he'd seen his wife. He put his hand down to stop his tumble and landed on his knees. There was no sign of Hollan there now. The rowboat was halfway to the ship, too far away for him to have any hope of reaching it. From this distance, he couldn't tell if she was on board.

"Hollan!" No one aboard the small craft looked his way. The wind blew against him. They wouldn't hear him any more than Hollan had heard him from the lighthouse.

Samson stood chest deep at the water's edge and growled, confirming to Jacob what he already knew. Hollan was on the small boat.

Chapter 9

Hollan sat rigidly at the front of the small rowboat, glaring at her four captors. Two of them perched on the middle seat with their backs toward her while they rowed the small vessel closer to the large ship. The others sprawled on the remaining seat at the back of the boat, steadfastly glaring back at her. On closer observation she realized that one glared while the other tried his best to do the same through an obviously damaged eye. His left eye was swollen shut, and dark blue bruises spread outward from the edges.

She studied him, the smaller of the two, and winced. She vaguely remembered making the connection with her fist. "I'm truly sorry about your face."

An apology probably wouldn't make much difference at this time, but she figured she might as well try. She had no idea what awaited her aboard the ship, but surely arriving there after having assaulted one of the crew wouldn't work well in her favor.

The man didn't answer, but his good eye narrowed further.

"In my defense, you shouldn't sneak up behind a person like that. Surely you know the natural instinct is to swing around with a fist at the ready."

"I ne'er expected a lady to swing in such a way at all," the man muttered. He gingerly touched the area in question. "Or that a lady would connect with such accuracy."

"Because I'm a lady I'm supposed to just turn myself over to a bunch of scoundrels without a fight? Is that what you're saying?"

She folded her arms across her chest. Her bare foot tapped against the wooden floor with annoyance.

"It ain't polite to call people names, missy."

"It *isn't* polite to kidnap people, either." She raised one eyebrow and stared until he looked away.

The men in the middle rowed on without missing a beat. Each stroke brought them closer to their ship and farther away from Jacob. The methodical sound of their oars slapping against the water made Hollan want to scream. Every once in a while the wind would reverse and blow a whiff of their odor her way. She quickly figured out it was best to hold her breath under a direct assault and to breathe through her mouth the rest of the time.

Cloudless blue skies stretched high overhead. The sun shone down on the water, dappling on the tiny waves, just as it had when she was onshore. The gulls continued to scavenge for food. Nothing had changed, yet for her, nothing was the same.

While the injured man continued to look out over the water, the man beside him cleared his throat in an attempt to catch her attention. "Speakin' of faces, you're not sorry for mine?"

Hollan studied him for a moment and forced back the snide comment that first came to mind. She wasn't doing a very good job at keeping her thoughts kind. His perpetually bewildered expression wasn't likely any fault of his own. She noticed the bridge of his nose tilted at an odd angle, but she assumed it had been broken before. Then she noticed the trail of blood that led from his nose to his beard.

"Oh my." Her brows pulled close. "Did I do that to your nose, too?"

"You did."

"But when—?"

"You fought like a wildcat when we first grabbed you."

"Of course I did. Wouldn't you?"

"Then you snapped your head back into my nose."

"And I'm supposed to apologize to *you* for that? You grabbed me around the waist. Perhaps if you didn't snatch innocent women off beaches, you'd not end up injured."

"I told ya we should have left her there. She's gonna be nothin' but trouble." The man with the swollen eye returned his scowl to her.

"Couldn't leave her, Paxton. Cap'n gave us orders."

Hollan shook her head, trying to clear it. "He gave you orders to bring back a woman?"

"He gave us orders to bring back *you*." Swollen Eye—or Paxton—sneered.

"But how would he know about me?"

"Dunno. But he does, and you walked right into our arms."

"Hardly."

"Regardless, we didn't have any choice but to follow orders."

"You always have a choice," Hollan stated. "Are you nothing but slaves? This man—the captain—why would you allow him to order you around like that? Why would you want to do wrong on someone else's behalf?"

One of the men in the middle laughed. "It's his job to order us around." He glanced at the man beside him. "How dumb is this woman anyway?"

"I'm not dumb at all." Hollan tried to keep the hurt from her voice. "I'm only trying to understand why you'd choose to live this way."

Broken Nose gave her a sympathetic look. "There's no call to say mean things like that, Nate."

Hollan nodded. "Thank you. That was very kind."

He beamed at her. Nate sent her a glare.

"Look, if I had my way, you wouldn't be here at all. It's bad luck for a woman to go aboard ship. Just look at what's happened to Paxton and Jonathon." Nate nodded toward the men.

So the man with the broken nose is apparently named Jonathon. "If you believe that, then return me to shore."

Nate didn't answer. He just kept rowing toward the vessel. They were almost to the ship. If she wanted out of this situation, she needed to act fast.

"Paxton. Jonathon. Please. You seem like nice enough men."

They both looked away.

"Idiotic is more like it," Nate snarled. "Now sit tight and be quiet. You're going to see the captain, like it or not."

Panic threatened to overwhelm Hollan, but she forced it away. She had to keep her thoughts straight. She sat quietly, not moving until they bumped against the side of the larger vessel.

"Ladies first." Nate laughed. He stood and grabbed her by the arm, pulling her to her feet.

Hollan looked back at him, blank. "I'm sure I don't know what you mean."

He motioned at the rope ladder that dangled over the side of the ship. "See that ladder in front of you? Climb it."

"I will not." She sat back down and folded her arms.

"Oh, but you will." He grabbed her arm again.

"You're hurting me."

"I'll hurt you a lot worse if you don't do as I say and get up that ladder."

Tears of anger and frustration poured down Hollan's cheeks. She snatched at the ropes and began her ascent. The skirt of her dress, still drenched from her trek when they dragged her through the water, snagged at her feet. She'd made it halfway up when she lost her grip. With a scream of terror, she plunged to the boat below. The boat rocked wildly back and forth but didn't capsize.

"Miss, are you all right?" Jonathon helped her to her feet.

"I—I think so. Nate broke my fall." She turned to thank him, but he lay still on the bottom of the boat. "Nate?"

The other man, the only one she hadn't injured at this point, stared at her, speechless.

"Nate was right. You *are* bad luck."

She rolled her eyes. "There's no such thing as bad luck."

The man leaned away from her, fear filling his face. "I don't know about you two"—he glanced over at Paxton and Jonathon—"but I'm not sticking around to see what she does next."

"Matt, what about Nate?"

"Leave 'im."

Matt turned and scaled the ladder and disappeared from sight in a way that left Hollan envious.

"I didn't mean to hurt him."

She took a step toward Jonathon. He looked from her to Paxton.

Paxton took advantage of her inattention and followed Matt up the ladder. "Don't let her get away, Jonathon."

"But—I—" Hollan had no idea where they thought she would go.

Paxton made it up the ladder with surprising grace and disappeared from sight.

"I guess it's just you and me, Jonathon." Hollan put on her most charming smile.

"You, me, and the dead man." Jonathon eased around Nate and headed for the ladder.

Hollan huffed out a breath. "He's not dead; I just knocked him unconscious—or something."

"No offense, ma'am. Deep down you seem like a nice lady and all. But I don't intend to stick around and see how you hurt the next man."

"I don't intend to hurt anyone!"

"All the same, you seem to have a knack."

Hollan knew if she let him go, she'd be free and she could escape. But the currents were rolling offshore as the tide went out, and she knew she'd never have the strength on her own to get back safely. She'd be washed out to sea, which at the moment actually sounded appealing compared to the thought of whatever unknown situation awaited her aboard ship.

Before she could think things through, she was suggesting an idea to Jonathon. "If you help me get back to shore, I'll help you start a new life. You don't have to do this."

He stopped. "I'd never make it off your island alive."

"Yes, you would. My husband and I would protect you."

Jonathon hesitated.

"Please."

His bewildered face glanced from her to the ship's rail and back.

"What's going on down there?" a voice called from above. The muzzle of a rifle edged into sight from over the rail.

Hollan glanced at Jonathon. "The captain?"

Jonathon nodded.

"Get the prisoner up here at once!" the voice bellowed.

"We have to go. I'm sorry." Jonathon took her arm, his touch gentle.

Hollan felt the panic welling. "We still have time. We can push off and go ashore. My husband will be waiting."

"He's a very good shot, ma'am. I'm truly sorry. We hafta do as he says."

Hollan let silent tears fall in resignation as she put decorum aside and climbed the ladder to the top.

☙

A strong set of arms reached over the edge and pulled Hollan the last few feet up and over the top of the rail.

Hollan swung around and landed awkwardly on her hands and knees. "Thanks. I think."

"Welcome aboard the *Lucky Lady*."

"Funny choice of name for a boat since your entire crew begs to differ."

"Speaking of crew, it sounds like you might have an idea about what made them scatter."

The masculine voice sounded strangely familiar.

She ignored the offered hand and remained on her knees. She slowly raised her gaze. "David?"

"Indeed. Are you happy to see me?"

"I'm not sure." Would Jacob's brother show her favor? Had he changed his ways? Would he see to her safety, or would he continue his mutiny? She answered her own questions. He'd sent for her. And he certainly hadn't done so in order to congratulate her on her recent nuptials.

His laughter chilled her to the bone.

"Paxton!"

Paxton rounded a corner but kept his distance.

"Gather the rest of the men."

David didn't offer her further assistance. Hollan was content to remain on her knees—the more distance she could have between him and the rail, the better.

A few moments later her kidnappers reappeared.

David glanced at them and then looked again. "What happened to you?"

"*She* happened to us." Paxton pointed.

David stalked along the deck. "You're telling me this wisp of a woman gave one of you a black eye and the other a broken nose?"

"She did. And she kilt Nate." Jonathon sent her an apologetic look. "But I don't think she meant to do it."

"She killed—" David's eyes widened as he hurried to the side and peered down at the smaller craft where Nate still lay sprawled on the bottom of the boat. "But how?"

Hollan sighed. "I didn't kill him. He's merely unconscious." Her brows furrowed. "Or at least I think that's all it is."

66

THE LIGHTKEEPER'S DAUGHTER

"Well, don't just leave him down there. Someone bring him up."

"How we gonna do that, Cap'n?"

"Think of something."

Jonathon's studious expression made him look as if he was in pain. "We can wrap a rope around his neck and haul him up that way."

Hollan's eyes widened in horror.

Paxton rolled his own eyes. "That'd be called a noose, Jonathon. Wanna finish Nate off completely?"

"We'll tie it under his arms, then."

"That should work." Paxton glanced at Matt. "You climb down to the boat and tie the rope around him. Jonathon and I will pull him up."

David shook his head. "Or you *could* just raise the rowboat into place and then lift him over the side."

"Good idea, Cap'n. Makes more sense." Jonathon grimaced. "We can do that easy. We'll get right on it."

"See that you do." David stalked away toward the main deck, shaking his head. "And one of you take Hollan down below. Secure her in the hold."

"You go with her, Jonathon." Matt motioned her way. "Paxton and I will take care of Nate."

"Afraid to be alone with me, are you?" Hollan knew better than to goad Matt, but she couldn't resist. If the level of fear in his eyes when he looked at Hollan was any indication, the man still felt she had the ability to cause them all harm with nothing more than her presence.

"I'm not afraid of you, miss." Jonathon led the way. Hollan's moment of levity passed when she realized they were going below deck. The chances of escape were few, but if she remained below deck they'd be nonexistent.

"God is sufficient for all our needs, Hollan."

Hollan remembered Jacob's words from just before the hurricane. He'd been right then, and she felt sure God would bring her through this, too. A momentary sense of peace swept through her. Though this was a different kind of storm, the words couldn't be any truer.

Jonathon led the way, and Hollan stayed close at his heels. The ship's gloomy interior depressed her. It took a few minutes for her eyes to adjust. She could see the dim shapes of several other prisoners. Jonathon led her to a nearby pole and waited expectantly. Hollan stared back, not sure what it was he wanted her to do.

"You need to wrap your arms around the pole." Jonathon waved a piece of rope he'd snagged from a nearby hook. "I have to tie you up."

"Tie me—?" Hollan sputtered. Suddenly she realized the gravity of her situation. If she was tied up below deck and they set sail, Jacob would never find her. A sob forced its way through her terror. "But Jonathon—"

"I'm sorry, miss. I have to follow orders. I'll be back to check on you soon."

"Don't leave me in the dark. I've had nothing but darkness for so long. You don't understand."

"I really am sorry." He tied her hands around the pole and left to go above deck.

"Oh God, what am I to do?" Hollan whispered the words aloud. None of the emaciated men around her moved. She couldn't tell if they were dead or alive. Surely she hadn't been left alone in a room full of dead people. She shuddered. Based on the odors sifting around her, she wouldn't be surprised. Where was that sense of peace? It was as if she'd left it above deck before she descended. She felt as if she'd entered her own personal version of hell.

I will never forsake you. A gentle breeze caressed her hot skin. She looked around but saw nothing amiss. *God is here with me!* Hollan knew the fact as well as she knew her own name. She wasn't alone.

God had a plan for her. She didn't know what it was, but she rested in the knowledge that He'd led her here for a purpose.

"Hollan."

Had God spoken her name aloud?

She glanced around and saw movement to her right.

"Hollan." The raspy voice came again, stronger this time.

It couldn't be. Her mind must be playing tricks on her. But she hadn't imagined that voice.

"Papa?" Her voice broke. *Please, God, let it be so!*

"It's me, daughter."

Hollan pulled at her ties, but they only tightened.

"Papa!"

"Don't fight the ropes, Hollan. You'll only cause yourself pain."

"But, Papa, what are you doing here?"

"Same thing as you, apparently." His soft laugh flowed through her like a salve. "I've missed you so much. I know you had to worry."

"I knew you were alive." Hollan smiled into the darkness. God had indeed had a plan. He'd sent her to rescue her father.

Chapter 10

Jacob couldn't believe the mess his wife had gotten herself into this time. How could she not have seen the crew's arrival? He cringed as he thought through the words. Maybe her vision hadn't returned after all. And here he'd been thinking she was keeping something from him. He felt awful. He'd just found her again, and he wouldn't lose her now. He had to get her back.

The ship was too far out for him to swim to her, and though the tide was going out, he knew they'd never make it back to shore, even if he had their missing boat. The boat wouldn't have helped anyway. They kept it on the inland side of the island. He couldn't go after her. He'd never make it through the currents. He paced back and forth on the shore, trying to come up with a plan. Without his own boat, he had no choice but to watch as she floated away with the crew. He hadn't felt this helpless since the night his father and brothers had ransacked the town.

Samson remained at the water's edge, staring out over the ocean. Every once in a while he'd look at Jacob like, *Why aren't you doing something?*

Jacob returned to the dog's side and watched until the rowboat was too far away to see very well. Even if Hollan looked around, she wouldn't see him now.

He turned back and headed at a fast pace toward the lighthouse. Samson trotted alongside him. "We'll get her back, boy, don't worry."

Jacob sounded a lot more confident than he felt. He took the steps of the lighthouse two at a time. Maybe he couldn't go after her, but what he could do was keep watch, take notice of anything he could about the ship, and track their progress. When Fletcher came their way with the supply boat, Jacob would summon help.

The crew of the ship didn't appear to be in any hurry. They lingered offshore even as the sun set. The full moon tracked their progress as they curved around the end of the island and sailed toward the mouth of the river.

Jacob's heart skipped a beat. If the captain continued his present course, they'd soon be near the far side of the island. The channel narrowed on that side in a way that if Jacob left now, he might be able to get on board the ship.

❧

The thud of heavy feet lumbering down the stairs pulled Hollan from a restless sleep. She found herself curled up on the filthy floor.

"Jacob." Her voice was hoarse as she whispered his name. Perhaps he'd found a way to come for her. She peered through the darkness but knew immediately that Jacob would never arrive in such a noisy fashion. Her heart sank. He'd come in quietly, not wanting to rouse suspicion, and would sneak her—and her father—away without anyone the wiser. Whoever descended the stairs now had no concerns about drawing attention. Quite the contrary, from the noise the person made on the stairs, he wanted to alert everyone to his presence.

Her legs were numb from hours spent in an awkward position. Earlier, during the night when she couldn't bear the thought of sitting or lying on the slimy wood floor, she'd placed her forehead against the pole and settled into a squat. She hadn't slept well at all. The tormented moans of the other prisoners had her on edge. Throughout the night the sound of tiny claws skittering across the floor made her shudder. She could well imagine what type of creature the scurrying feet belonged to. And the cloying heat and putrid odors permeated every breath she took.

Each time she'd doze off, she'd fall forward, and the motion would jerk her back awake. Exhaustion had her on edge. She didn't even want to imagine what David had planned for her. And she hoped she'd never find out. He wouldn't have anything in store for her if she could help it. She only had to figure out an escape plan before the madman sent for her.

"Cap'n wants to see you on deck."

The escape plan would have to wait.

Paxton stood beside her. When she couldn't rise on her own, he grabbed her arm and pulled her roughly to her feet. Her legs tingled.

"You seem to take great pleasure in yanking me around by my arm." His bad eye made him look demented in the dimness.

"A lot of things bring me great pleasure. Dealing with you does not."

"Leave her alone!"

Papa.

Her father's voice brought her a measure of peace, even though he couldn't do anything to help her at the moment. She had to focus on a plan that would get them both away from here. In the meantime, it wouldn't hurt to pray.

Lord, I'm not sure what is in store for me while You have me on this ship, but I pray that You'll protect us. Please help Jacob to know where we are, and keep my father safe.

She turned her attention to Paxton. "What does David want with me?"

Paxton shrugged as he untied the knots in the rope that held her hands prisoner. Once he released her, she almost fell on her face.

"You'll get your sea legs in due time."

"I don't intend to be around long enough for that to happen."

Paxton laughed. "I don't see that you have a choice."

"I'll find a way out of here."

"You will, huh? We'll see about that."

He half-dragged her to the stairs. They exited the stairwell onto the main deck, and the bright early morning light shot a dagger of pain through Hollan's head. She closed her eyes briefly, let them adjust, and then squinted through them. Her vision remained clear. She eased her eyes open after a moment and located David at the ship's helm.

She left Paxton's grasp and plowed forward. "David."

"Ah, good morning, Hollan. I trust you slept well?"

She ignored his ridiculous question and instead asked one of her own, echoing her earlier one to Paxton. "What do you want with me?"

"It seems I need to go up the inland channel. In order to do so, I'll happen to need a guide."

Hollan couldn't hold back her smirk. He needed a guide, and he'd chosen the least able person to comply. "You do realize I lost my eyesight three years ago?"

He glanced at her, his forehead wrinkled. "You can't see at all? If that were true, you wouldn't have found your way so easily to me just now."

"Whether I can or can't see right now doesn't matter. What does matter is that I haven't seen this pass or much of anything else since. You've chosen and kidnapped the wrong person to help you."

"You can stop looking so amused." David's scowl deepened. "I'm sure the pass hasn't changed all that much over the past three years."

"Do you seriously believe that?" Hollan's jaw dropped. "Do you not remember the storms we get around here? Nothing ever remains the same."

Not in the least. The storms damaged everything. Her experiences attested to that.

"Then you'd better pray the storms haven't changed the pass."

Hollan started to refuse. She wouldn't guide him anywhere.

"If you don't abide by my terms, your father will pay the price for your rebellion."

That quieted her. She wouldn't do anything to bring more pain to her father.

An idea began to formulate in her mind. When they rounded the end of the island to enter the pass, Jacob would be at the closest point to help them. At least he would be if he knew she was aboard the ship and he'd been tracking their progress.

She couldn't stand the thought of the alternative. If he hadn't figured out where she'd disappeared to, why would he care about one more ship offshore? She hadn't a clue where her father had gone when he'd disappeared. Why would

Jacob have any idea about where she'd gone? Even if he went to look for her, she'd have disappeared just as completely as her father.

She decided that just in case Jacob hadn't figured out her whereabouts, her plan had to be something she could fulfill on her own. The pass was treacherous in the best of times. Maybe she could use that to her advantage.

"The currents are very strong at the mouth of the river."

"Thank you. We'll prepare for rougher waters. In the meantime, you'll remain below deck. I'll send for you when I'm ready."

Hollan thought hard. If she stayed above deck, she might have a chance to catch Jacob's attention. But if she went below, perhaps her father could help with suggestions to guide them through the channel. She didn't want to return to the stench of the dark, dank hold, but if she needed to, she'd make use of the option.

In the meantime, she'd try to stay above deck. "I'd prefer to remain up here if you don't mind."

"I don't recall giving you a choice."

"I'll stay out of the way." Hollan started for the rear of the ship. Maybe she'd spot Jacob and would at least be encouraged that he was looking for her. "I'll just settle in up there where I can observe the channel and the conditions."

A rough hand grabbed her arm. David leaned close. "You'll do as I say and go below."

His menacing blue eyes peered into hers. Hollan fought back a chill. The man's eyes were empty. He had no trace of heart or soul. The hold suddenly sounded inviting in light of this realization.

"Fine." She pulled her arm loose.

He pushed her forward toward Paxton. "Stow her below until we're ready."

The dirty hem of her dress tripped her as Paxton led the way downstairs.

Her father waited anxiously where she'd left him.

"Hollan. Are you well?"

"I'm fine, Papa."

He didn't speak again until Paxton had tied her wrists around the pole. As the man shuffled upstairs, her father leaned forward. "What did he want with you?"

"He wants me to guide him through the channel."

A soft chuckle carried over to her. "Did you explain?"

"I did. But, Papa—" She leaned nearer, wishing she could see him better in the darkness. "I can see clearly again. During the past couple of months, my vision would come and go, but now it stays."

"That's wonderful!"

"It is, but I'm not sure it'll help me guide the ship through the pass." She heard him change position. "Are *you* well, Father?"

"I'm fine." He shifted again. "Nothing the light of day won't fix, along with getting back to our island. I sorely miss your cooking."

Hollan laughed. "That says a lot, Papa. My cooking hasn't ever been all that great."

"I miss it all the same."

"Papa, what's going on? Why are you here?"

"David thought he could take me from my position as lightkeeper and use it to his advantage if he's captured. He wanted me to lead him through the inland waterway, but I refused." He let out a breath. "I refused to help the scoundrel. I had no idea he'd go after you next."

Her eyes had adjusted to the dim interior, but it was still pretty dark. "What are we going to do?"

"You're going to do exactly what they tell you. I don't want them angry with you. I don't want David to get violent. If he hurts you, you could lose your vision again—or worse. I won't have you risk that. Just do as he says, and let me figure something out."

Another figure stole quietly down the stairs. His furtive movements drew Hollan's attention. "Who is that, Papa?"

"I'm not sure. Keep quiet. Don't draw attention. I don't trust any of the crew around you."

Hollan settled low and huddled near the pole. The bulky figure carried a mop and moved through the men, stopping now and then to peer closely at each person as he passed. Hollan's heart beat quicker and sweat rolled down her face as the figure turned their way.

"Stay low, Hollan. Duck your head."

She did as her father instructed. The shadowy form loomed over her. He leaned close. Hollan kept her head down, praying she'd be left alone. The figure squatted down and leaned in close to her ear.

"Get away from her." Hollan's father's voice held a hint of panic.

Hollan knew it would kill him to watch if she was attacked and he couldn't do anything about it. She reacted instinctively, kicking the aggressor with her foot. A soft laugh rewarded her attempt.

"My darling wife. A bare foot does nothing to me. Though based on the stench of this hold, I might catch a nasty illness by connecting with your foot."

"Jacob?" A sob caught on Hollan's throat. "Is it really you?"

"It's me."

He wrapped his arms around her and held her close for a moment. She leaned nearer and drew in his scent. "You smell wonderful."

That comment drew a laugh out of him. "You seem to be in good humor. Are you all right?"

"I'm fine now that you're here." She savored the feel of his strong arms around her. She'd never take his presence or touch or encouragement for granted again.

"Want to tell me what you're doing here?"

"Rescuing him." She gestured toward her father in the dim light.

"Rescuing someone with your arms tied tightly around a pole. And whom would you be rescuing?"

"My father. He's alive, just as I said. What are *you* doing here?"

"Rescuing my wife and apparently helping her rescue her father."

Hollan laughed quietly. "I just about had my plan figured out."

Jacob trailed her arms to where they were tied around the post. "So I see. And your capture by the crew, that was all part of your plan?"

"Not exactly, but once it happened and I knew my father was here, I knew God brought me here for that purpose. I just needed to figure out what the plan was."

"Well I'm here now to help." Jacob put a finger against her lips. "Be quiet now; we don't want to draw any more attention our way. I'm going to be close, but I'll continue to pose as one of the crew until I get *my* plan figured out."

"Papa's right beside me, one pole over. He's a little worse for wear, but he says he's fine."

Jacob caressed Hollan's hair with a gentle hand before moving to her father's side. "Gunter? I'm so happy to see you're alive, sir."

Hollan grinned as she watched her two favorite men interact.

"I'm happy to see you, too. My daughter told me about your marriage and all that you've done for her. I appreciate that you took it upon yourself to watch out for her. It's not an easy task."

"Papa!"

"Well it's true. Now, Jacob, tell me what you've come up with to get us out of here."

"I haven't figured out the details on that myself. I saw the crew take Hollan, but I was too far away to do anything about it. I watched the ship from the lighthouse until I saw the present course. I was concentrating on getting aboard but didn't get far enough to figure out a rescue in the event I was successful. I've spent most of my time searching for your daughter aboard ship."

"Well son, you're aboard now and you've found my daughter, so you'd best get to figuring out our escape."

"Have you made friends with any of the other prisoners?"

"No. None of them have tried to communicate with me. I'm not even sure some of them are alive. From what I can tell, they're all worse off than I am. I think some of them are former crew members from whenever the present crew took over the ship."

"I see." Jacob moved back to Hollan's side and took her hand. "I'm going back up to have a look around. I'll return soon."

"Don't leave us."

Her father leaned forward. "They're coming for Hollan soon. They want her to lead them through the channel."

Jacob hesitated. "That might work."

"What might work?" Hollan didn't like his tone of voice.

"Hollan, if you're on deck, you'll be that much closer to escape."

"And if my eyesight falters?"

"We'll worry about that if and when it does."

"I won't leave without you and my father."

"We'll all go together. But I need you free and above deck." He turned to her father. "Do they check your ties often?"

"Never."

"Good. That'll work in our favor, too. I'm going to untie you. I don't want you to move until we're ready to go. Hollan, you'll have to get the ship stuck in a shallow, narrow part of the channel. Try to guide them close to the island. While they're unloading supplies in order to lighten the load, we'll make our move. I'll come down here to get your father. You get off ship and head for the cabin on the island."

"I won't leave without my father. I already told you that."

Papa motioned to her. "Hollan, you'll do as your husband says."

"But—"

"But nothing." Jacob's voice was calm but commanding. "If you're out of the way and safe, I can better help your father."

Hollan bit back her next words. They'd discuss this later. She watched as Jacob untied her father's hands.

"Try to stand. I want to see if you can walk."

Her father stood, but he wavered. Hollan wanted to cry. Her normally strong father was thin and very weak.

"I'll be fine. You go do what you need to do. I'll work on my stamina while you're gone."

"Hollan, I'll leave you tied up until the captain sends for you."

"Jacob." Hollan knew the next words wouldn't be easy for Jacob to hear.

Jacob paused.

"The captain—he's your brother. David."

"*David's* behind this?" Jacob spat. "Why am I not surprised?"

"Promise me you won't rush into anything."

"I won't worry about David until I have both you and your father safely ashore."

Hollan didn't like the innuendo behind his words. She had a feeling that as soon as Jacob had them safe, he'd risk his own life by going after his brother.

Chapter 11

Hollan didn't have to wait long before David summoned her. Paxton's heavy boots stomped down the stairs, echoing through the dim interior like a death sentence. She sent a frantic look at her father as the other man slopped through the muck and headed their way.

"It's going to be fine, Hollan. Jacob's watching out for you. God's on our side. Say your prayers and do what David says. Don't do anything dangerous. Let Jacob make the decisions that need to be made. Watch for him and be alert for any sign he sends you. He won't let anything happen to you."

"But if things don't go as we plan. . ."

"Our plans aren't what matter," her father interrupted her. "Do what you need to do, daughter. But above all else, keep your temper under control. Think before you act."

He lowered his voice as Paxton drew near. "Keep in mind what will happen to Jacob if you act in a rash manner. If he thinks you'll be hurt, he'll intervene before he's ready. The two of you are fully outnumbered by the crew. The timing for our escape needs to be perfect. If at all possible, do only what Jacob told you to do. Find a way to get the ship stuck on a sandbar and let him handle things from there. Remember what I've taught you about the currents. If you see your opportunity to get off the ship, take it and make your escape. Jacob and I will soon follow."

"But if you don't. . ."

"We will."

"*If* you don't. . . ?"

"Find a place to hide and watch for Fletcher to come."

"He's due back tomorrow."

"Then you'll go to him."

Paxton tripped over a body sprawled at his feet. He kicked at the immobile form.

Hollan glared at him as he continued his trek their way. The man was deplorable.

"Your emotions are written all over your face, Hollan, even in this dark place. Keep your thoughts hidden. If David thinks you're anything but compliant. . .it won't go well." Her father's quiet plea drifted her way. His gaunt face looked tortured for a moment. "Do this for your mother. David caused her to do what she did. I'll explain everything later. But we need to make things right. Do your part to get us safely off ship, and we'll talk when we meet back up."

Frustration edged through Hollan. She didn't know what the next few hours would bring, but she prayed they'd bring closure for all three of them.

"C'mon. Cap'n says it's time."

"Time for. . . ?" Hollan stalled.

"Let's go." Paxton ignored her comment and untied her. He reached for her arm.

Hollan scurried to her feet and backed away from him with her arms raised in defense. She knew her father would go after Paxton if he made any untoward moves. She couldn't let her father expose the fact that his hands were no longer tied.

"I'm ready. I don't need your assistance." The boat lurched, and Hollan pitched forward, plowing into him with her head.

Paxton let out his breath with a *whoosh*.

"Sorry. I didn't mean to." Hollan sent her father a quick glance and shrug. He remained in place, though his features were pained. "I lost my balance when the ship shifted."

"So I noticed," Paxton snapped. "See that you don't do it again."

"I'll do my best," Hollan snapped back.

She hadn't intended to get that close to the smelly man in the first place. As it was, she felt in dire need of a sweet-smelling bath. If she ever got out of here, she'd soak in an herb-filled bath for a full day. The hold's odors had permeated her nose and surely everything she wore. How her father had tolerated it for as long as he had she didn't know. It had to pain him to remain below deck, a free man, and not be able to do anything about it.

They exited the stairwell, and Hollan gasped for her first breath of fresh air topside. A gentle breeze blew her way, and even the fishy scent that rode along with it smelled pure after breathing in the stale air down below for the short time she'd been back down there. Now that the sun had risen higher in the sky, the day was clear and sunny. Inspiration bubbled up from deep inside. They had to make this work. Hollan wanted off the ship.

A movement to her left caught her attention. *Jacob*. He peeked up at her from beneath the rim of his hat. The bedraggled outfit he wore made him blend in perfectly with the crew. She twisted the corner of her mouth up in acknowledgment before diverting her gaze.

"What do you find so amusing?" Paxton glared around at the crew.

"There's nothing amusing about my situation. I'm simply rejoicing in the fact that I'm out of that pit for a time. Surely you can understand that."

Paxton scowled at her. "Don't try anything stupid. The captain doesn't tolerate anything close to what he considers mutiny."

Hollan didn't answer. She busied herself looking for Jonathon. Next to Jacob, he seemed her only ally. And though she wasn't sure his kindness would be enough to allow him to stand up against David and his crew, she had a feeling the man had a soft spot somewhere deep inside. If need be, she'd use that to both of their advantage.

"Are you ready?" David didn't waste time with pleasantries.

Hollan walked up beside him, shading her eyes with her hand as she scoured the water ahead of them. *How to best get the* Lucky Lady *stuck?* According to her father, it wouldn't be hard.

"We need to stay with the darker water. The path is narrow. Are you sure you don't want to turn around and go by sea?"

"What I want is for you to do as I ask. Don't question my decisions." He shifted his stance. "I have authorities looking for me on the open waters. I want to use this waterway to avoid a—shall we say—unpleasant outcome."

"You mean you want to avoid your imminent arrest." Hollan smiled up at him.

"I will not be arrested." His face turned purple. "I won't be captured alive."

She frowned. "Which means you'd prefer to be captured dead? But how will that benefit you or your crew? I'm not sure I understand."

"Must you always be talking?" He sighed with exasperation. "I don't intend to be captured at all. Now focus on the task before you."

Hollan laughed. "You sound like my father. That's his favorite thing to say."

David stared at her. "My crew doesn't dare to speak to me the way you do."

"Your crew? Is that what you call them? Better it be said that they are your slaves." She muttered the last part in a quieter voice, but he apparently heard her.

"Every man here has a right to leave anytime he chooses."

"Maybe—but only with a knife in his back or a bullet through his head."

David sputtered. "What gives you the right to speak to me like that? Your father has spoiled you. I'm not sure what my brother ever saw in a quick-tongued woman like you."

"Jacob saw my heart."

"And then, apparently, you drove him away."

"I didn't drive him away." His comment cut to her very soul. Jacob hadn't left her because of anything she'd done to him—had he? She shouldn't listen to this man. Her father told her to focus on the tasks set before her, and here she goaded the evil man instead of focusing on her responsibilities. She couldn't help spitting out one more remark. "That isn't true."

"Aw, have I hit a nerve?"

Hollan stared at the water ahead. "No, but you're about to hit that sandbar."

She pointed a finger straight out in front of them.

David swore and spun the wheel hard to the left. Hollan hid her impertinent smile. A cough slightly behind and to her left drew her attention. Jacob worked nearby, and she was sure he'd overheard their discussion.

"You did that on purpose," David snapped.

"I did. I pointed out the obvious. But next time you'd rather I allow you to hit the object we're heading for?"

"No!" He reached up to adjust his hat then glared her way. "You're trying to distract me so we'll run aground."

"I'm hardly *trying* to distract you. Do you think I enjoy your attention?" Hollan huffed out a breath of exasperation. "And if my intent was to distract you so that you'd run the ship aground, *why* would I warn you when I saw the sandbar coming?"

"I guess you have a point."

She pushed her hair out of her face and gave a distracted wave toward their left. "You'll want to steer hard to the left for a bit. The current here runs strong and pushes to the right." Strong enough to embed them securely just off the island's shore if things worked out as she planned. Hollan set her mouth in a pout and crossed her arms in front of her.

"You don't have to sound so offended."

"And why shouldn't I after I save the ship from going aground only to have you berate me?"

The ship missed the sandbar and gently drifted to the left. David relaxed his hold, and the wheel spun out of his grip. They picked up speed as the current forced them into the smaller channel. "Wha—?"

He frantically fought the wheel. "I thought you said the current pushes to the right!" His voice rose in pitch and shook with anger. His eyes held a hint of panic.

They headed toward the island at a fast pace. Hollan sidled over to grab hold of the ship's rail. "Did I say the current pushes to the right? I meant you'd need to steer right because the current pushes to the left. Sorry." She raised her voice to be heard. "You can correct the ship's course, right?"

"You did this on purpose!" David screeched. "All hands on deck—*now!*"

Strong hands grabbed Hollan from behind and dragged her away from the captain. "Get down!"

Jacob's voice.

Hollan did as he said. She hadn't quite hunkered all the way down when the ship went hard aground. Barrels and crew went tumbling across deck. David flew to the right, cracked his head on the rail, and landed facedown, motionless.

"I need to go to him. I did this." Hollan's breath caught in her throat. Had

79

her actions killed the man? She hadn't planned for anyone to get hurt. The ship listed heavily toward the mainland. "I didn't intend to hurt him."

"Well, he does intend to hurt you. Remember that. You're going nowhere but off this ship. As soon as you're clear, head for the cabin immediately." Jacob lifted her to her feet, and they took off across the deck at a run. He dodged both crew and debris as they went. No one looked their way with all the chaos. "David isn't worth your concern. Not right now."

"But my father."

"I'm sure your father is already on his way up here. I'll return to help him as soon as I get you safely on your way."

They reached the ladder. No one bothered with them as the crew frantically threw barrels and supplies off ship in an effort to stop her pitching.

Hollan peered cautiously over the side. "It's a long way down. Coming up was bad enough. My dress! The skirt will. . ."

Jacob snatched a knife from the sheath he wore around his waist and spun her around. He grabbed her skirt and hacked it off at the knees.

"Jacob!" Hollan sputtered.

"It's filthy and ruined. You'll move faster this way. Your skirt won't pull you under the water."

He resheathed the knife and eased her over the edge. "Hold the ladder tight. If you lose your grip, push off so you don't bump against the ship. Get away as quickly as possible in case she shifts. You don't want to be crushed beneath her."

"And there is a very pleasant thought with which to bid me good-bye."

"And a very likely scenario if you don't get out of the way." He hesitated and grasped her upper arms. "I love you, Hollan." He pulled her close for a quick peck on her lips. "Now go. Get out of sight. Move quickly."

She ducked below the ship's rail and headed carefully down the ladder. Her hands shook, and she prayed she'd not lose her grip. The ship's rounded sides made the endeavor awkward and hindered her descent. Her foot slipped, and she flailed for a moment before finding purchase again.

Just as she regained her footing, something large catapulted past her. She ducked with a scream. Another piece of her dress tore off as the large object shot past, but she was able to keep hold of the ladder.

Hollan lowered her foot again and felt for the next rope step. Something else fell from above, and again it barely missed her. A sob tore loose. Were they throwing things at her? Had they figured out the plan? Had someone noticed her missing?

She pushed herself to move faster but again lost her footing. This time her fingers slipped from their hold, too, and she plunged to the water below. The momentum sent her into a downward spiral under the water even as she fought to return to the surface. After a few panicked moments, her toes finally hit sand, and she pushed hard against the bottom. She broke through the surface of the water and gasped in a huge lungful of air.

A barrel splashed down beside her, barely missing her head. She swam in place and looked around for a safer location to wait out the barrage of debris. Only one area would offer her protection. She swam to the boat and hunkered down out of sight, slightly under the rounded side. If the ship shifted at all, she'd be crushed beneath it, just as Jacob had warned.

❦

Jacob hurried across the tilting deck and prepared to go below just as Gunter surfaced. A small man with a crooked nose assisted him. Jacob raised an eyebrow in question.

"It's all right. Jonathon here offered me his assistance. He said he failed Hollan when she needed him, and he wanted to make things right with me." Gunter looked around. "Where is she?"

"I've already helped her over the edge. She should be well on her way to the shore." Another glance at Gunter's helper reassured Jacob that the man didn't have any ulterior motives. The man nervously watched the actions of the crew but didn't try to draw attention. David still lay where they'd left him. "We need to get out of here before he comes around. He isn't going to be in a very good mood."

"Does the man *have* a good mood?" Gunter muttered.

"Not that I've ever seen, but we don't want to be here to see what he does when his perpetually bad mood gets worse."

They helped Gunter to the side of the ship where Jacob had last seen Hollan. He peered over and saw no sign of her. Hopefully that meant she'd made it to safety. Two members of the crew appeared, carrying a large barrel between them. They staggered up beside Jacob.

"Can you give us a hand in gettin' this over? It's mighty heavy," one of the men gasped.

"Set it down." Panic coursed through Jacob. "Have you thrown other things over this side?"

"Yep. We needed to lighten the load."

Jacob leaned over and again searched the water for any sign of Hollan. If a barrel had hit her. . .

He saw a piece of fabric from her dress floating on the water, but he didn't see any other physical signs of her. Surely if she'd been hit she'd still be in sight. He breathed easier and looked at the men. "Not on this side, you don't."

The man surveyed him suspiciously. "Why not?"

Jonathon stepped up beside him. "Ya see how the ship lists? Ya might knock a hole in the side."

"Oh. I hadn't thought about that."

"Head on over there with the barrel"—Jacob pointed to the far side—"and I'll be right behind you to help."

The two men struggled to lift the large container.

Jacob rolled his eyes. "Can I offer a suggestion?"

One looked at the other. "I guess."

"Roll the barrel to the other side. Don't carry it."

"That might work." The deckhand looked skeptical. "We can try."

They laid it on its side and pushed.

"No, you'll want to—" Jacob shook his head as the barrel picked up pace on its journey across the deck. It took out two men before slamming into the wooden rail on the far side. "Never mind."

The men took off at a run, and Jacob quickly turned around. "Come on, we need to get out of here before someone else comes along."

Jonathon helped lift Gunter over the side. Jacob looked at Jonathon. "Are you coming with us?"

"No. I'm needed here. You go. I'll keep watch as I work, and I'll offer a diversion if need be."

"We appreciate it, Jonathon."

"Tell Hollan I'm sorry. I couldn't help her before, but I hope she's safe now."

"Thank you."

Jacob glanced around, then slipped over the rail and followed Gunter down the ladder. He heard a soft *splash* below as Gunter entered the water. Jacob made quick work of dropping down beside him.

"Let's go. We need to get away from the ship."

"Jacob!"

Jacob glanced around and saw Hollan clinging to the large vessel's side.

"Woman! Don't you ever listen?"

"I *do* listen, but before I could get away, huge objects started raining down on me from above."

"I think we've stayed the falling objects. Let's get out of here."

They only had a short swim before their feet touched bottom. Jacob reached back and assisted Hollan until her feet reached solid ground.

"I'm fine, I'm fine. Go, go, go!" Hollan's panicked voice urged him on. She stepped up beside him and helped assist her father.

She started toward the shelter of the trees.

"Not that way. We need to stay in the water."

"They'll see us."

"Jonathon is helping from the ship. He won't let anyone approach this side. It's tilting away from us. The crew is busy on the other side, trying to lighten the load so the ship will rise off the sandbar."

"Why not go into the cover of the trees?"

"The foliage is too dense. We have to get to the path, but we need to stay in the water so they can't follow our tracks."

They reached a shallow creek and turned to follow it into the trees.

"We're safe for now, Hollan. Their guns won't reach this far. No one can see us."

Hollan's legs gave out. Jacob caught her and held her close.

"We're safe," he murmured again. "It's going to be okay."

"I need a quick rest." Gunter climbed out of the creek and sank to the ground nearby. He leaned against a tree. "What's the plan from here?"

"We'll go to Amos's cabin."

Hollan pulled her face away from Jacob's chest and looked up at him. Her eyes were smudged with exhaustion, but she stared directly at him. He watched her eyes soften as she surveyed his features. Her mouth broadened into a smile. "You're a sight for sore eyes."

"Your vision seemed to be intact the entire time we were on the ship. Is it fully restored?"

"At first it came back in bits and pieces, but yes, I can consistently see clearly now. And thank you."

"Why are you thanking me?"

"You came after me. You rescued us."

"You're my wife. I'll always come for you." He kissed the tip of her nose. "But about the return of your vision. . ."

She smirked and turned his words on him. "We'll discuss it later."

Gunter motioned for their attention. "If you two can try to concentrate, we do have some pretty angry men aboard that ship who would probably like to recapture us. I'd like to get some more space between them and us. I think I can walk some more now."

"Wait." Hollan looked up at Jacob. "You said the other day that the cabin looked like someone had been there."

"That would have been me," Gunter interrupted. "I cleaned it up and took shelter from a storm a short while back."

"I remember now." Hollan looked at her father. "You were gone all day, and I was so worried. If only I'd known then what the coming days would bring."

"Speaking of. . .we do need to move on," Jacob prompted.

Gunter stood to lead the way.

Jacob held Hollan back. "How long has it been since your vision returned? Since the day we walked around the island?"

"Before that." She frowned. "It was better when I woke up after hitting my head in the storm. I could see, but I wasn't sure my vision would stay."

"And you kept that from me? Why?" Jacob could hear the tremor in his voice. He wanted his wife to trust him, but apparently, after all he'd done in the past, she still didn't.

Hollan stared into his eyes. "I was afraid you'd think I didn't need you anymore. I was afraid you'd leave."

"So you trust me that little, even after I've told you repeatedly that I was here to stay."

"You did tell me that." Hollan nodded. "But that was when you thought I couldn't see. I wasn't sure things would stay the same if you knew. I needed more time."

"And when were you going to tell me?"

"The morning I was kidnapped."

"I see." Jacob stared back at her for a moment and then turned to stalk away up the path.

"That's it?" Hollan hurried to catch up with him. She grabbed his arm. "That's all you have to say?"

"I married you the moment I heard you were in need of a husband, Hollan. I stood by you through the hurricane, and I tended your injuries. I saved you from a ship full of rogues. If you don't trust me by now, after everything we've been through, I'm not sure I'll ever be able to regain your confidence."

Chapter 12

Jacob, wait!" Hollan's heart moved into her throat. She couldn't breathe. Her worst nightmare was coming true. Her deception had caused the exact scenario she'd wanted to avoid. She'd hurt Jacob, and now he didn't want to talk to her. "You kept saying you were here for me and that you wouldn't leave. But I wasn't sure if it was because you wanted to be here or because you had no choice."

"Not now, Hollan." Jacob continued to move ahead at a quick pace.

Hollan raised her voice. "I was afraid you'd leave if you knew I could see."

"I said not now." Jacob's words were clipped and cold.

Hollan dropped back and lagged behind. She could hardly see past her tears. She tried to tell herself it didn't matter, that with the return of her vision she'd be fine. She had her father back, and things could return to the way they'd been before this all happened. At least life would return to normal as soon as they figured out a way to rid themselves of David and his crew.

Hollan realized Jacob was right in that respect. This wasn't the time to worry about anything but their safety. They'd figure the rest out later. Even though she knew this all to be true, tears still forged their way down her cheeks.

The trio worked their way up the path, and Hollan wished for her boots. Chipped and broken shells lined the creek's bed, and the path wasn't any better. Hollan knew a cut from one of the shells could cause a serious infection. But she wasn't about to ask Jacob for his help. She hesitated and glanced around, trying to figure out a way to walk without causing injury or drawing Jacob's attention to her ineptness.

"Keep up, Hollan. We need to carry on."

Hollan snapped, "I have to find my way around the shells."

Jacob came back and abruptly swept her up into his arms. "You should have worn your boots."

"I'll try to remember that next time I walk the shore prior to getting unexpectedly kidnapped."

A vein throbbed in Jacob's throat, but he didn't comment further.

Still, her feet were scratched and sore by the time they reached the shack. Her tears of heartache had diminished, but the pain of Jacob's anger simmered under the surface.

Jacob set her down next to the small building in the clearing. Hollan wandered over to the edge of the stream and sat down, placing her sore feet in the cool water. She cupped some of the water into her hands to wash her face and scrubbed away all trace of her tears.

"I'm going inside to lie down." Her father's face was pale with exhaustion.

"I'll help you get settled." Hollan moved to stand, but her father waved her away.

"Let me be. I can manage to lie down without assistance. Rest your feet."

Jacob watched from a distance and waited until her father had entered the shack before coming up beside her. "You should have told me."

"About my feet or my vision?"

He squatted at her side. Hollan glanced up at him. The sun broke through the leaves, and one shaft highlighted the gold in his hair. His green eyes were lined with fatigue. "Both."

"I told you. I was going to tell you about my vision, but the crew got to me first."

"And your feet?"

"What good would it do to tell you? What could you have done? If I'd worn my boots, I wouldn't have had a problem. It was my problem alone to deal with, and my feet are fine." Her words sounded bitter, but he'd walked away from her. Why would she think to bother him with anything after that?

"To answer your second question, I would have done this"—his face took on a devious expression as he reached over and swept her up into his arms—"earlier than I did."

"Put me down!" she hissed while glancing at the shack.

"No."

"I'm a mess."

"You look fine to me."

"Then maybe we need to be concerned about *your* vision."

"My vision is fine."

"I just spent the night on a smelly ship."

"And you had a nice dunk in the water after. You look beautiful."

"*Beautiful?* My dress is torn and cut to pieces. My petticoats are in shreds. My feet are filthy, and my hair is a mess. How can you say such a thing?"

"I mean it. I went a lot of years without seeing you. I intend to enjoy every moment of seeing you now."

"You're finished being angry?"

"Do I look angry?" He raised his eyebrows up and down. "You aren't going to chase me away, Hollan."

Hollan rolled her eyes. "My father's going to come out and see us this way."

"Your father isn't coming out. He's exhausted." Jacob settled back against a tree with Hollan held securely in his arms. "And regardless, he's not going to take offense."

She laid her head on his shoulder and snuggled closer. Her heart felt full. "I didn't expect you to carry me through the woods. My feet hurt, but I'm fine. I would have dealt with sore feet."

"That's what I've been trying to tell you all along. Nothing—no problem—is yours to deal with alone. Not anymore. You have me to lean on now. I didn't marry you because you were blind. I didn't marry you because I felt sorry for you or because I felt there was no other choice. I married you because I love you. We'd planned to marry before I left. The pieces fell together when I returned, and I felt marriage to you was what God had brought me back here for. I'll carry you through any situation I need to."

Hollan stared at her reflection in the creek, afraid to meet his eyes. She knew she'd burst into tears. The stress of the past two weeks was taking its toll. She was exhausted from lack of sleep the night before and the anxiety caused by their escape. Her mind was a muddled mess.

"You need to rest. You barely recuperated from the blow to your head before you were taken. I'm sure you didn't sleep well on the ship."

The compassion in his voice was her undoing. A sob racked her body.

Jacob stroked her back. "I'm sorry," he crooned into her hair. "I didn't mean to make things worse."

"You didn't make things worse." She didn't want to talk. She just let him hold her while she stared into the water. The reflection there confirmed what she already knew. Her hair was a mess; her dress was dirty and torn. She looked awful. She likely smelled worse, even with her dip.

"You've made things so much better," she whispered.

"I haven't seen you cry before now."

"I haven't faced the reality of losing you before now."

He tilted her chin up. "I'm not leaving."

"You were so angry."

"Not angry, just frustrated."

His emerald eyes were so beautiful. He studied her.

"I don't want to make you frustrated."

He grinned. She'd forgotten about the way his dimples curved around his smile. "You've been making me frustrated since we were very young. I doubt anything's going to change in that respect."

"Oh."

He reached up to caress a strand of her hair.

She made a face and tried to swat him away.

His hand drifted down to her chin, and his thumb caressed her cheek.

"Hollan, I'm going to disappoint you. You're going to frustrate me. But none of that will change the fact that we'll always love each other. Can you live with that?"

"I can," she whispered.

He slid his hand back to comb through her hair. He gently tugged her toward him as he leaned in for a kiss. "I can, too, very happily."

They sat forehead to forehead.

She breathed him in. "I'm so glad you're back."

"Me, too." He kissed her again and pulled away. "You need to rest."

"Don't leave."

He set her aside and tried to stand. She tugged him back down and leaned against him. He stroked her hair.

"I have to leave. Samson must be going nuts in the cottage. If the men come ashore—and I'm sure they will—the cottage will be their first target. I need to get Sam out of there and salvage some of our things."

"Poor Samson. I wondered how you got away without him."

"I had to lock him up." He seemed as hesitant about leaving as she was about watching him go. "Anyway, we need some supplies. I'll run up to the cottage and bring Samson back with me. We'll need food and clean clothes." He sent her a pointed look. "And I'll grab your boots and some more salve, too."

She laughed. She wanted to go with him, but no way would her feet allow that. Nor would Jacob. The brambles in the path would tear her to shreds. "Thank you. I appreciate your consideration. Just stay safe and hurry back quickly."

"I'll always hurry back to you."

Hollan could only nod.

"Do you want me to help you into the shack?"

"I'll stay out here, thank you. I'll have enough of the cabin when we have to go in there at dark."

"I'll hold you close and keep you safe."

Hollan blushed. "I'm sure you will. And my father will be right there on the other side, with me sandwiched in between. Sounds like a wonderful way to spend the night."

"Oh yeah, I suppose your father will be right there." Jacob's laugh told her he hadn't forgotten her father. He was teasing her again. "But we will make an excellent shield for you, protecting you from all that lurks in the dark."

Hollan shivered. "And there could be plenty of things lurking with David's crew wandering about."

"Last time we were here, you were worried about gators and snakes. Are you sure you don't want to go in with your father?"

"It was dark and creepy that day if I remember correctly, or at least it seemed so back then. Now I know scarier things lurk in the area. Today the clearing feels brighter and sun dappled. I'll stay here."

"Sun dappled?"

"Sun dappled."

Jacob walked over to where he'd placed his coat and folded it into a square. He placed it on the ground and motioned for her to lie down. "Go to sleep. When you wake up, I'll be here."

"Sounds nice," she murmured. She was already drifting off.

Jacob hurried back to the cottage and heard Samson barking frantically from inside. He released the dog, and Samson ran in circles around his legs.

"She's fine, boy. I have her safely stashed away. We need to get you to safety as well."

Jacob hurried inside to gather some clothes for Hollan and her father. He stuffed a day's worth of food into the bag, too. He quickly grabbed anything he found of value and took it all to his room in the base of the lighthouse. Larger, less expensive items he hid as best he could in the outbuilding. He kept Gunter's rifle and ammunition with him.

"C'mon, boy, I need to make one more stop by the light house before I take you to Hollan."

Samson didn't need any encouragement.

Jacob hurried back into his room and added his clothes to the bag. He hefted it up and placed it outside.

"Stay." He pointed to the bag, and Samson sat beside it. "I'll only be a moment."

He'd come a long way since the day he'd watched the men take Hollan. He was back at the lighthouse. At least now he had Hollan safely tucked away and out of the grasp of David. Still, he needed to get back to her.

Jacob hurried up the stairs. The lighthouse gave him a full view of the stranded ship. The ship didn't list quite as badly and seemed to have stabilized, but it remained stuck on the sandbar. Perhaps his wife had done her job a bit too well.

He noticed the smaller boats from the ship were being lowered to the water. He searched the treetops for any sign of the shack, but it couldn't be found. They'd be safe as long as they could get to Fletcher before David and his crew got to them.

Jacob secured the lighthouse as well as he could and motioned for Samson to come. He didn't think the men would carry along the right tools to break into the tower, and he hid any of Gunter's tools he could find. He prayed the men would be too tired to try to gain entry to the lighthouse. The damage they could do in vengeance would be expensive to repair.

Jacob and Samson set off for the shack. They finally arrived, with Samson leading the way through the trees, into the small clearing. Hollan lay where Jacob had left her. He quietly opened the door to the shack and placed their supplies inside. Gunter's exhausted snores reverberated throughout the room.

Jacob closed the door and walked over to where Samson stood watch over Hollan. "I can take care of things from here, boy." He dropped down beside Hollan and pulled her close. He shut his eyes and listened to her breathe.

She shifted in his arms. "Jacob?"

"I told you I'd be back."

"I'm glad."

Samson nudged his way between them. Hollan laughed and petted him.

"I think I got everything we need."

"Good." She nestled against Jacob, still half asleep.

Jacob grinned.

"I think nothing short of the arrival of outlaws would wake you up right now."

Her auburn hair fell across her face, and he pushed it back. She squinted up at him, her brown eyes warm. "I'm awake."

"Ah, then you still must consider me an outlaw."

"Hardly." She tried to sit up. "More like a hero."

"Stay. We have nowhere to go." He captured her with his arm. "So I'm a hero now. I like that much better than being compared to my outlaw family."

"I apologize for that."

"You had reason to be upset."

"Perhaps just a bit of a reason." She changed the subject. "And what did my hero find out through his explorations?"

"The crew is just now leaving the ship." He felt her tense up. "They won't find us here. I knew where to look and couldn't see a thing. It'll be dusk before they reach the lighthouse. I'm pretty sure they'll head to the cottage for now. While I was up in the lighthouse, I tracked the path Fletcher's boat will travel if he shows up tomorrow. If they leave a man on watch, he'll see Fletcher coming this way."

"From the lighthouse?"

"Only if they can gain entry. I'm hoping they're too tired to try."

Jacob had left his hair down, and Hollan absentmindedly stroked it as she listened. Her touch made it hard to concentrate.

"We'll need to warn Fletcher."

"Yes. I figure if we can get an early start in the morning and stick close to the trees, we can intercept Fletcher before he makes it as far as the ship. We can hop aboard the supply boat and be out of here before David and his men get off the dune."

"That sounds fine."

He leaned on his lower arm, put his other hand against his heart, and feigned surprise. " 'That sounds fine'?" he mimicked. "You don't want to add to the plan or take something away?"

"Very funny." She pushed him back down and laid her head on his chest. Samson wiggled closer. "I trust you."

"You do?" Jacob sat halfway up again. "You trust me completely this time?"

"I do. We've been through a lot during the past week, and you've stuck by me through it all. You didn't have to risk your life to rescue me, but you did. I do trust you."

"Thank you, Hollan. Your trust means everything to me. I'll never break that trust again."

She settled back against him just as Samson let out a low growl.

Jacob glanced at him and saw the hair raised on the back of the dog's neck. The dog growled again.

A gravelly voice sounded from behind them. "What do we have here?"

Chapter 13

Samson barked.

"Samson, it's just Papa." Hollan laughed. "Your sudden appearance and hoarse voice must have startled him, Papa."

Samson jumped to his feet and wagged his tail as he sheepishly hurried over to his master.

Hollan surveyed her father. "Are you feeling better?"

He definitely looked better now that he'd had some sleep.

"I feel much better."

"Good." Hollan turned to Jacob. "You said you brought more of our clothes back with you?"

"They're in the shack." Jacob's voice was groggy. He hadn't moved from his place on the ground.

"I think I'll go a ways up the stream to bathe and change."

"Don't go far," Jacob warned. He yawned. "I'll rest while you're gone."

"Stay within calling range, Hollan." Her father's face creased with worry. "The men might come ashore."

"I'll be close by, Papa."

"Actually, I think I'll tag along and freshen up myself. That way I'll be nearby if you need me."

Hollan rolled her eyes. She might be a married woman now, but her father apparently didn't see her as such. "As you wish, Papa."

She knew he'd worry the whole time she was gone if he didn't accompany her. And truth be told, she didn't want her father far away after being apart from him in such a way.

They gathered their supplies and walked up the overgrown path. Hollan stopped and pointed out a small pool in the creek. "This looks like a perfect place. I'll stay here."

"Good. You'll be protected and safe. No one can get through this foliage. Jacob is just down the path behind us. And I'll go a bit ahead and stand guard from that angle."

"Thank you, Papa." She stopped and handed him a bar of lye soap. "I'm sure you can use some freshening up, too. You were on that ship longer than I."

"I can't wait to get in the water and then put on some fresh clothes. If we could light a fire, I'd burn these."

"Burying them will do just as well," Hollan teased.

Her father walked off, and Hollan savored the time alone. She slipped into the cool water and lathered up her hair. She scrubbed her body twice, just to make sure the filth of the ship was gone from her skin. Her skin tingled when she exited the water and dressed in fresh clothes.

She leaned back against a sun-warmed rock and contemplated the past few days while she waited for her father. She had her father back. The thought made her smile. More surprisingly, she had Jacob back. And for the first time, she felt confident that he meant it when he said he'd stay. He'd changed a lot during the past three years. They still needed to talk about why he'd left her in the first place. And she needed her father's explanation about what had happened to her mother.

The warmth of the late afternoon sun lulled her into a drowsy state. She listened to the sound of the birds in the trees. The wind rustled through the bushes. At least, Hollan hoped it was the wind. She knew the gators came out at dusk and willed her father to hurry.

She heard footsteps along the path and shrank down behind the rock.

"Hollan?"

"Papa? Oh, I'm glad you came back."

"Did something happen?" He glanced around.

"No." She smiled. "I'm just hearing things in the scrub. I'm ready to head back to Jacob. I don't want to meet up with an alligator any more than I want to meet up with David and his men."

Jacob woke up as they neared the small clearing and rubbed his eyes. "Is everything okay?"

"Just fine." Hollan smoothed her clean pink skirt and settled down beside him. He studied her fresh-scrubbed appearance. She couldn't help teasing him. "Everything meet your approval?"

"Indeed." He grinned. "I'm trying to figure out if you're the same woman who walked away from here a short while back."

"One and the same."

"I think I'd better follow suit." He hopped up to his feet. "Stay close to your father."

"You stay close to shore and make sure to be careful."

"What's the matter? You don't want me to end up as gator bait?"

She shuddered. "That's not exactly something to joke about."

"We have a bit of daylight left. I'll be fine."

"See that you are. I have some questions to ask when you return."

"Sounds serious."

"Maybe. But it's a conversation that's been a long time in coming."

"You're right." He nodded. "It has. We'll talk when I get back." He gathered his clothes and walked up the path from where they'd just come.

Hollan bent down and busied herself with cleaning and wrapping her sore feet.

"We need to talk, too, Hollan. Now's as good a time as any."

Hollan glanced back at her father. "About Mama?"

"Yes." He eased himself down beside her. "The night she—fell—from the lighthouse, something happened. Something bad."

"You don't have to tell me, Papa."

"I want to tell you. You need to know. You need to understand that she didn't do what she did to hurt you. She was hurting so badly, I don't think she gave anything else much thought."

"She'd just left the cottage. What could have happened?"

"David waited just outside, and he grabbed her. . . ." Her father stopped, his face both pained and angry.

"Papa, you don't have to do this."

"Yes, I do." He waved her words away. "David grabbed her, and he abused her. He—hurt—your mother. He violated her body. I was so close by, but I had no idea."

"Oh, Papa. I had no idea either."

"She didn't want you to know." He shook his head. "I was supposed to watch out for her, but I wasn't there for her in her time of greatest need."

"You didn't know."

"That doesn't change things in my mind."

"What happened next?"

"I went into a rage. I told her to go back inside, and I went after the vile man."

"But you didn't find him?"

"No. And I heard you calling, and I was afraid for you."

"Why would David want to hurt Mama?"

"I don't know. I'll never know. He and his brothers and their father hurt a lot of people that night, for no reason anyone has ever been able to figure out."

"I know what happened." Jacob stood at the edge of the path, his voice tortured. "I think I'm starting to understand."

They both spun around to look at him. He dropped his things beside the door of the shack and walked closer.

He sank down beside Hollan and took her hand. "He'd come to hurt you."

"But why? I didn't even really know him. Why would he want to hurt me?"

"Because hurting you would be the best way to hurt me." Jacob shook his head. "David hated that I was different from him and our father. He constantly

94

goaded me and tried to get me to go along with them as they destroyed everyone in their path. I wouldn't have any part of it, and I spent most of my time with your uncle and aunt."

"I knew your family was rough, but I had no idea they were that bad."

"I didn't want you to know."

"Oh."

"You were my refuge. You were the bright spot in my life. I didn't want to dirty that up with my family's reputation."

"It wouldn't have changed anything between us."

"I know. I just didn't want to sully what we had when we were together. Regardless, things weren't good at home. That last night, they'd decided to skip town. The law was coming down on them, and they knew it was time to move on. I heard them talking and planning. David asked me to go along, and I refused. I tried to talk them out of it, and I tried to tell them about my beliefs. I told them it wasn't too late to start fresh. David laughed in my face. They didn't want anything to do with any of it. I said I didn't want anything to do with their deeds. I had you, and I had my life there in town. I had no reason to run."

Hollan saw the muscle working in Jacob's jaw. "What happened next?"

He struggled for control. "David said he was going after you, that maybe he'd just take you with him instead. He hated that he couldn't control me. He hated that I was so different. He wanted to be in control of everything."

"Oh, Jacob." Hollan tried to grasp everything he was telling her. The raw emotion on his face clearly showed his pain. "What did you do?"

"I went into a rage, just like your father did later. I'm not proud of the fact. David has a tendency to bring out the worst in a man."

"But I don't blame you. You were totally justified."

"David laughed and said he didn't really want to take you with them. . .he'd just take what he wanted from you and would leave it at that."

He looked at her. Hollan continued to hold his arm.

"I went after David. All three of them, my dad and my other two brothers, jumped me while David hit me from behind."

Hollan closed her eyes against the horrific image of Jacob being held by his own father and brothers while another brother attacked him. "That's atrocious."

"They knocked me unconscious." He blew out a breath. "When I woke up, your uncle was bent over me and they were gone. It was daylight. My head was pretty messed up. I croaked out your name and your uncle said you'd been traumatized and it would be best if I left you alone for a bit."

He threw a small stone into the creek and watched the water ripple out from where it landed. Hollan remained quiet, figuring he needed time to gather his thoughts before continuing.

"I figured—based on his comment—that David had succeeded in getting what he was after. I figured your uncle's phrasing was his way of telling me to leave you alone."

"So you just left?"

"No, I couldn't travel. I was in and out of consciousness for a few more days, and your aunt and uncle cared for me. When I was finally well, I asked about you again."

He shrugged. "Your uncle again repeated that you needed some time. You'd been injured. The whole town had been wronged. I had to go after my brothers. I couldn't let them get away with what they'd done."

"I had been injured. Just not as you thought. The weather was awful, and my mother was standing at the edge of the platform on top of the lighthouse. I was afraid she'd fall. I tried to take hold of her arm, to pull her back, but she just shook me away like I didn't matter. I fell and hit my head. When I woke up, I couldn't see. We hoped it would only be for a short time, that maybe it was caused from the trauma of everything that happened, but after several days passed. . .we had to accept that the loss of vision might be permanent."

"I'm so sorry."

Hollan nodded. "What happened after my uncle told you I still needed time?"

"I decided I'd go after my father and brothers. I wanted to find my own justice."

"But you didn't. You went to the law."

"You're right, I did. As I rode after them, God shook some sense into me. He placed some good people in my path. I decided I would bring them to justice, but I'd do it the right way. I didn't want to become like them."

Hollan's voice was soft. "So, you didn't leave me because you didn't want me. You left because you thought you'd lost me."

"Exactly." He took her hand in his. "I never stopped loving you, Hollan. I just thought I'd lost you because of what my brother did. I thought when your uncle said to give you time, you didn't want to see me again."

"But David never came to me. . . ."

Her father spoke up. "Yes, he did."

Hollan was bewildered. "No, he didn't—"

"But he did. . . ."

She glanced back and forth between them. Realization dawned. Her breath hitched. "He got Mama instead."

Her father nodded.

"Mama wasn't his intended victim. He thought she was me. Then it was my fault David hurt her."

Jacob pulled her close. "No, it wasn't your fault at all."

She pushed him away. "It was! He'd come for me. Mama went out there...."

"And in the storm, she looked so much like you that David mistook her for you." Her father nodded again. "Hollan, your mother wouldn't have had it any other way. She told me as much. She said he kept saying your name, even as she fought him. She said she was glad it was her he'd found, not you. She didn't blame you, and you can't blame yourself."

Horrified tears poured down Hollan's cheeks. "Then why did she do what she did?"

"I don't know. She was hurt, angry, devastated. She begged me not to go after him. Not with the rage I was in. If I'd only stayed with her..."

"You can't blame yourself either, Papa." Hollan reached up to wipe her tears, but Jacob got to them first.

"Hollan, I don't think she jumped of her own free will. Now that we've all shared our views of that night, I think your mother must have gone up to the top of the lighthouse to get away from everything, to feel safe. You were in the cottage. She wouldn't want you to see how distraught she was. Your mother didn't leave you intentionally."

"I think you may be right." Hollan nodded slowly. She turned to her father. "Papa, if you won't let me blame myself, you can't take that blame either."

"None of us are to blame. It took me three years to realize that." Jacob caressed her fingers with his thumb. His golden hair glistened. He surveyed her, looking deep into her eyes. She couldn't pull her gaze away from his. "Only God can judge them for their sins. The law can try them for their crimes. Our responsibility is to forgive."

"It's hard."

"It is, but if you don't forgive...if you hold the anger and bitterness in... you'll become just like them. Don't let them win."

She turned to her father. "Papa?"

"Your husband is right, Hollan. As hard as it is to hear, Jacob speaks the truth. David needs to be brought to justice, but as soon as that's accomplished, we need to go on with our lives. We need to move forward. God has blessed us through all this."

"I guess He has, hasn't He? I'll still have to work through the anger toward David, but God restored my vision. He brought Jacob back to me." She smiled up at him.

"He led me back to you," Jacob agreed.

"And He allowed you both to find me," her father added.

"So we're all in agreement." Hollan stared back and forth between both men. "But what now? How do we bring David to justice?"

Her father considered her question. "We leave first thing in the morning and intercept Fletcher."

"What if he can't make it? What if he can't get away? The hurricane might have caused a lot of damage."

Jacob surveyed her expression. "You have something on your mind."

"Yes." She raised an eyebrow. "I do."

"I'm afraid to ask. . .but. . ." Her father's blue eyes twinkled. "Are you gonna fill us in?"

"David and his crew rowed ashore to get over here, right?"

"Right."

"They'd have to leave their boats onshore, wouldn't they?"

"I believe they would."

Jacob exchanged a look with her father. "Are you thinking what I'm thinking?"

Her father nodded. "I'm pretty sure I am."

They both looked back at her.

Jacob spoke first. "If they did leave the boats onshore, they'd surely have a guard."

"Guards can be bribed." Hollan shrugged. "Or overthrown."

Jacob laughed. "You say that like it's such a simple thing. And you're volunteering us for the job?"

"I'll do my part." Hollan tipped up her chin and dared him to cut her out of the plans.

"What did you have in mind?"

"I could sashay over and distract whoever it is while you two strike from behind."

"My wife is villainous!"

Hollan snorted. "I'm not. I'm just willing to do whatever needs to be done."

Gunter sat in contemplative silence.

"Papa?"

"I don't want to use you as bait. These men are very dangerous. Now they're both dangerous and angry."

"Do you have a better plan?"

"Well, I don't as of now, but I bet we can come up with one before dawn."

Jacob leaned forward and rested his arm on his knee. "They'll be watching for us. If we leave before daybreak, we'll have a better chance of getting away."

Hollan grabbed his sleeve. "And if we catch them off guard, maybe we can just slip away with one of the boats. David didn't seem to hire the brightest of men for his crew."

"That's because anyone with a lick of sense would have stayed far away from him."

"Jonathon actually has a heart," Hollan disagreed. "I don't know why he's with them."

They sat in silence for a few minutes.

"Jacob...Papa..."

Both men answered in unison. "What?"

"What if Jonathon volunteered for the watch?"

Jacob thought for a moment. "The odds are against that, Hollan."

"I know. But just think. God has protected us so far. What if He's put the next step into place by giving us Jonathon as a guard?"

"It could happen. And if not, I'm sure He has a plan for us to get out of here to safety."

"We won't know until we get there."

"You want to go now?"

"Why not? What better time? We've all slept. We'll sleep better if we get to the mainland. They won't expect us to act until morning. And they have to be exhausted, too. They worked hard all day trying to unload the ship. David told me he wanted to go up the inland canal because officials were looking for him. He won't want to stay around very long."

Gunter exchanged a look with Jacob. "I think the lady is on to something."

She smiled with relief. "So we act tonight? Now? I think I'll go crazy if we have to sit here any longer."

"You'll be okay walking through the area in the dark? I know you aren't real fond of it here, even in the daylight."

"I'm fonder of the thought of walking away than I am of spending the night here in that shack. And I have my boots on this time."

Jacob stood and pulled her to her feet. She dusted off her skirt. Gunter joined them.

"Let's get something to eat then see what the shoreline holds."

Chapter 14

The moon barely provided enough light through all the foliage for them to see as they walked down the overgrown path. Hollan stayed close to Jacob and clutched the hem of his shirt. Gunter followed close behind.

They neared the shore and walked quietly along the trees. Even Samson seemed to understand the gravity of the situation as he kept pace beside Hollan. She appreciated the solid warmth of his body as he pressed against her leg. She kept a firm hand on the nape of his neck. If anything lurked in the bushes, Samson would warn them in plenty of time.

They'd debated leaving him behind, but with no way to secure the shack's door, he'd break free and end up tagging along anyway. At least this way they had a semblance of control over the situation.

The large outline of David's ship loomed high against the horizon, its features eerie in the moonlight. The smaller boats were pulled up on shore, just as they'd hoped, and Hollan didn't see any sign of a watchman.

"No one seems to be around," Hollan whispered. "Maybe they're so cocky they don't expect us to steal—I mean, borrow—one."

"If so, it's more likely they were too tired or too drunk and they didn't give it a thought," Jacob interjected.

"Perhaps it's a mixture of both," her father agreed.

Jacob glanced back at Hollan, the moonlight highlighting the smirk on his face. "And surely my dear brother wouldn't have an issue with us borrowing one of his boats."

"Yes, he's so accommodating and thoughtful." The sarcasm rolled off Hollan's tongue.

They huddled at the edge of the trees.

"I've been wondering. How *did* David get a boat so quickly?" Hollan asked. "If you followed him here. . . ?"

"I told you I had to argue with God a bit before I headed back. David had time to secure the vessel. As to how, I'm sure it wasn't by legal means. The crew might belong to the ship—and it's a skeleton crew at that—but I doubt the ship belongs to my brother."

"Well said." Hollan was ready to leave the island. "Let's keep going."

They slowly crept along the edge of the curved beach that contained the rowboats. "If no one is here, we'll just hop in and go, is that the plan?" Hollan asked. "The area appears to be deserted." She couldn't wait to get out of there.

Samson let out a low growl.

"Then again, we could be wrong," Hollan hissed as the dark form of a man rose up from where he'd apparently been sleeping on the bottom of one of the boats.

They all ducked in unison.

"Who's out there?"

"It's Jonathon!" Hollan whispered, then stood and started to answer.

Jacob yanked her back down and shook his head then put a finger to his lips. Hollan nodded.

"We need to make sure he's alone."

"Of course. I'm sorry."

They waited in silence. No one else moved or answered. Jonathon stood and stepped out of the beached boat and headed for the trees. Samson growled again, and Hollan returned her hand to the nape of his neck.

"He's coming this way!" she hissed.

Jacob held up a hand. Hollan quieted. Her heart beat quickly in her chest as she watched her husband's actions. He crouched in the shadows and followed Jonathon's movements with scrutinizing eyes.

When Jonathon stood within reach of them, Jacob lunged forward and grabbed the man around the neck. He pulled him close against his chest.

"Jonathon. Don't make a sound. Is there anyone else here with you?" Jacob asked in a quiet voice.

"No, I'm in charge of the boats." Jonathon sounded rattled.

Hollan's heart went out to the man. "It's okay, Jonathon. It's just us."

Jacob loosened his grip, but Jonathon didn't move.

"You shouldn't oughta sneak up on a man like that," he groused. "A man could drop dead from fright. I didn't want to stay out here in the first place. It's spooky."

"Says the man who kidnapped me from a beach," Hollan pointed out.

"Fair enough." Jonathon shifted on his feet. He didn't exude any of the cockiness that David liked to portray. "I do apologize for that. But I couldn't go against the other men. They'd have killed me on the spot."

"I'm glad they didn't." Hollan's voice softened. She didn't blame Jonathon for not helping. But she did hope he'd help them now. "You can make it up to me, though."

"How's that?" His voice held a hint of distrust.

"You can let us have a boat, let us get away."

"Oh, I don't know. David would be so angry."

"Then go with us. We'll take you to safety."

"I don't think there's a place safe enough to get away from David."

"If we can get to the authorities, David will be captured by the law. You'll be safe. Think about it, Jonathon! Won't you feel good knowing you're on the right side of the law for a change?"

"I ain't never been on that side that I can remember. . . ." Jonathon sounded dubious.

"Jonathon. God put you here to help us. I'm sure of it. If you help us, we can help you."

"No offense, ma'am, but David's the one who put me here, not God."

"That's how it might look to you"—Hollan reached for his arm—"but I feel sure God put you here to help us. We can help each other. Come with us, help us paddle through the channel, and we'll hide you in a safe place when we get to town."

"I didn't know there was a town nearby."

"It isn't exactly a town, per se, but there's a small church and a building that's used as a general store. There's an acting sheriff. The townsfolk look out for each other. You'd be welcome there."

He hesitated.

"You don't want to let God down, do you? We need you to help us."

"You're sure I'll be safe?"

"Yes. But we need to leave right now."

"On the open water, at night? With a woman on board?"

"You can't possibly still blame *me* for all the problems after you kidnapped me. There's no such thing as bad luck. Everything that happened to you, Paxton, and Nate was caused by your own actions. And as for nighttime travel, there's enough moonlight to see pretty well. We know the waters, and this stretch won't be difficult at all. It's just a little ways away."

Jonathon didn't answer. Hollan didn't know what they'd do if he refused. She didn't want to see the man hurt and didn't know that Jacob and her father even had it in them to hurt a man. She had a feeling, though, that if pushed into a corner, when it came to her safety against Jonathon's, Jacob's protective instinct would kick in.

"Please? This would more than make up for the kidnapping." Hollan prayed for the right words. "If you help us escape now, the law will see that you assisted us. Otherwise, you might be charged with kidnapping along with the others when they're caught. And they will be caught, if not right now, then soon. David said the officials were after him."

"You're sure we'll get away?"

"Do you expect David or any of his men to come check on you tonight?"

"No, they won't be coming around till morning."

"Then we need to go now."

Jonathon nodded and led the way to the farthest boat. "If they catch us, I'll tell them you threatened me with that shotgun Jacob's carrying."

"Nice to know you have our backs," Hollan muttered.

Jacob bent down to help push the boat into the water. "I don't intend to let them catch us."

Hollan settled into the seat at the bow, the same place she'd sat when David's men first took her from shore. She patted the seat and with a whine Samson climbed in with her. He settled at Hollan's feet on the floor.

Jacob and Gunter took the middle seat, and Jonathon took the rear.

"Wait," Hollan hissed. "What about the men in the hold?"

"None of them made it," Jonathon said. "If it makes you feel better, they weren't much better than David and his crew. They were privateers during and after the war."

Hollan shuddered. "I'm not sure that makes me feel better, but thank you."

"Hollan, you'll have to watch for debris and sandbars," Jacob instructed. "We'll stay close to shore, but you'll have to guide us if you see anything coming our way."

Hollan shifted in her seat so she could see where they were going.

They traveled slowly. The gentle current worked with them. Hollan was glad Jonathon had come along. Though he wasn't a large man, he was burly, and his added strength as they rowed didn't hurt as they made progress.

"I have a confession to make." Jonathon's hesitant voice sounded loud in the silence. He laid his oar across his lap.

Jacob and her father stopped rowing, but they continued to drift along. They all stared at the man as they waited.

"We ran into a man on our way over this afternoon."

A chill passed through Hollan. "A man?"

"Yes. He came across on a flatboat just as we neared your island in our rowboats."

"A flatboat. . .like a supply boat?"

"Yes'm." Jonathon shifted nervously in his seat and set the boat to rocking.

"Sit still!" Jacob commanded. "What happened to this man?"

"David...um...well, he and some of the men sort of took advantage of him."

"Took advantage?" Hollan asked, confused.

"They beat him and stole his load from the boat."

Hollan's heart pounded. "Where is he?"

"I don't know. After stealing the supplies, they left him aboard his boat and sent it downstream. Last I saw him, the supply boat was floating this way."

"If the current caught Fletcher, he could be well on his way out to sea." The anger in Jacob's voice was palpable.

"I didn't do it," Jonathon defended.

"You might as well have if you just stood by and let it happen," Jacob accused.

Jonathon looked down and didn't say anything more.

Jacob ran a hand through his golden hair. "I'm sorry. You didn't have a choice. They would have just beaten you and added you to the boat with Fletcher or worse."

"We need to find him." Her father's voice was full of resolve. His comment was a command.

"We need to get closer to the other side. We've been fighting the same current his boat would have. It keeps pushing us to the east. The shapes of the vessels are different, so his boat would have flowed more smoothly across the water. There's a chance we'll pass him on the far side."

"If he didn't capsize or fall off."

"He was pretty well centered when they sent his boat off," Jonathon said quietly.

They crossed the channel and headed toward land. Hollan felt vulnerable out in the open, even though she knew no one could possibly be nearby. The moon glistened off the top of the water. She prayed Fletcher would be all right and that they would find him.

Though Hollan longed to dangle her fingers in the water, she knew better than to do it at night. She rested her elbow on her knee and put her chin on her fist as she watched the water for obstacles. She searched the shore for any sign of the supply boat. The lateness of the hour caught up with her, and she struggled to stay awake.

Lord, help me to focus and do my part. I'm so tired. I don't want to let the men down or fall asleep in my seat.

Just as she finished the prayer, a large shape rose up from the water and then rolled back down in front of her. Hollan smiled. A dolphin! She hadn't seen one in three years, and here this one was swimming in front of them as if directing their boat across the waters. Any thoughts of sleep drifted away as she watched the magnificent creature. Each time he ducked below, she hoped he'd surface again. As long as she could see him, she'd know there wasn't anything in front of them.

Finally the dolphin did a half turn and swam away from the boat. Hollan wanted to beg him to return. But as she looked up, she noticed a structure ahead of them.

"I see the dock! And Fletcher's boat is there." Hollan all but bounced on her seat as they neared their destination.

"Sit still, girl, before you swamp us," her father's good-natured voice called from the middle seat. "Looks like Fletcher made it back."

"What a relief."

"Strange," Jonathon said. "It looked like they did him in."

"Fletcher is a very strong man. He must have recovered from the blows and made his way back home," Jacob stated.

"I sure hope so. I'd feel a lot better."

"We'll know soon. We'll check on him as soon as we get in." Jacob dragged his oar in the water, spinning them around. The current pushed them closer to shore.

"Now to see how the town has fared."

They pulled the boat up against the dock. Jacob jumped out to secure it. He helped Hollan from the boat, and the other two men joined them. Samson ran happily from one end of the dock to the other.

Fletcher's boat was tied securely to the pier. There was no sign of the man on the dock or in the water nearby.

"Where do we go from here?" Jonathon asked nervously.

"We don't have far to go," Hollan assured him. "We'll go to my uncle's house. It's just up the road from here."

"It's the middle of the night. Will he be upset to find all of us at his door?"

Hollan grimaced. "He's the reverend of the church. He's used to late-night calls."

They trudged along the sandy path, the moonlight leading the way. Samson ran ahead. Every so often he'd return to check on them, and then off he'd go again. An alligator bellowed from the marsh to their right, and Hollan shivered. Jacob wrapped a reassuring arm around her shoulders.

Hollan let out a sigh of relief when they reached civilization, though the houses they passed were all dark. As they neared the row of buildings that composed the town, Jacob stopped. "I want to alert the sheriff. I doubt David would be so brass as to come here in the morning, but it's best not to take a chance."

"I'll head up the road. I'll wait for you there." Jonathon backed away.

"Nonsense." Hollan grabbed his arm. "You'll stay here with us."

She could feel his muscles tense when the sheriff opened the door.

"What's going on?" The gruff voice made her want to run, too, but she stood firm.

Jacob nodded toward Hollan. "Pastor Edward's niece here was kidnapped from the beach yesterday by my brother and his crew of men. They met with some misfortune and ran their boat ashore and have now moved into the cottage at the lighthouse."

"I see." The sheriff looked at each of them in turn. "Fletcher apparently met up with the same group on his way to your place. He made it back, but he's in pretty bad shape."

"Where is he?" Hollan asked.

"They took him to Doc when they first found him, but he's at his mother's now. We were going to put together a posse at first light and go over to check on you. At least now we can concentrate on the hurricane repairs. Where are you all headed?"

"We're headed for Edward's place, and we'll stay there for the night."

"I'll make sure to keep an eye out for anything suspicious."

"Thank you." Jacob reached out his hand, and the sheriff shook it. "When do you think you'll be able to secure the island? David said they were wanted. That's the reason he attempted the channel as it was."

"You said no one's in harm's way?"

"No, and David and his men aren't going anywhere fast. They're stuck there. Unless they decide to come over here."

"I'll set up watch, but I doubt David will come here. He's still a wanted man. We're still repairing damage from the storm. We need to secure the homes that are open to the elements. I'd guess we have about two to three more days, and then we'll gather up a posse."

"Three days?" Hollan asked in disbelief. "The cottage and lighthouse could be in shambles if you wait that long!"

"Hollan, it'll be fine." Her father laid a reassuring hand on her shoulder. "We're safe, and that's what matters most."

"What about the ships, Papa? Who will keep them safe? The lighthouse needs to guide them."

"Gunter? Is that you?" The sheriff leaned forward with his lantern.

"Yes, Sheriff Roberts, it's me."

"I'm glad to see you safe. Parson Edward said you were missing."

"David and his crew took me just before the storm hit. Hollan and Jacob came to my rescue."

"Only after they kidnapped me!" Hollan filled in. "But Jacob came for us both."

"I'm sorry this happened to you." The sheriff lifted his lantern and stared at Jonathon. "And who do we have here?"

"Jonathon, sir." Jonathon's voice quaked under the sheriff's perusal.

"That don't tell me much."

Hollan hurried to intervene. "He helped us escape. He's from the ship."

"Did you now? I'm glad to hear that. We'll need to talk in the morning. I'll have some questions for you."

"Yes, sir." Relief tinged Jonathon's words. "I'll be here."

Sheriff Roberts looked at Jacob. "Swan. It's good to have you home. Edward told me about the marriage. Congratulations to you both."

They thanked him.

"Go on with you now. We'll all get some sleep, and I'll see you in the morning."

They walked up the road toward Edward's place.

"Your uncle has room enough for all of us?" Jonathon asked.

"He does. He'll probably put you men up in the church, and I'll stay in their home."

"Will you be safe there?" Jonathon continued with his questions. "David is a dangerous man."

"Yes, she'll be safe," Jacob interrupted. "I intend to make sure of it."

"Jacob, you need to get some sleep. I'll be fine. David won't know where we are. He surely won't dare to come after us."

"I agree. Most likely he won't. But I'm not taking any chances. If I have to sit on Edward's front porch, I'll do so in order to know that you're safe."

"Then perhaps we'll all stay in their home. They have several extra rooms."

"We'll see what Edward says. But I can guarantee if you're staying in that house, I'll be right there with you."

Edward answered his door and welcomed them in. Ettie pulled Hollan into her arms and cried when she saw Gunter.

"My brother!" Edward's eyes moistened as he took in the sight of Gunter. "You're alive."

"I'm fine. Or I will be after a bit of rest."

"You look well, Hollan." Edward beamed. "Married life must agree with you."

Hollan smiled up at Jacob. "Much to my surprise, it does."

"And Jacob. Is island life everything you hoped it would be? Did you find it to be a balm to your weary soul?"

Hollan laughed out loud.

"You find the question amusing?" Her uncle looked confused.

Jacob looked at Hollan, and they shared another smile. "Life on the island has been interesting to say the least. Two things stand out at the moment, though. Hollan has her sight back, and Gunter is safe."

"Hollan!" Ettie's tears continued. "I'm so happy, sweetheart. Let me look at you."

"More importantly, Auntie, let *me* look at *you*."

"We have a lot to catch up on."

"Indeed we do."

Aunt Ettie turned to Hollan's father.

"Gunter"—she gave him a little poke—"you gave us all quite a scare."

Uncle Edward raised his hands. "I'm glad we've all had a moment to catch up, but I'm sure you didn't make your way out here in the middle of the night to share your good news."

Chapter 15

Gunter and Hollan were kidnapped by my brother David." The words rolled off Jacob's tongue.

A vein in Edward's neck began to throb. "Hasn't that boy caused y'all enough grief?"

"He's hardly a boy anymore, Ed," Ettie corrected. "But he does need to be stopped."

"Where is he now?"

Hollan answered, "He's on the island."

"Then we need to go after him. I'll get the sheriff."

"We've already talked to the sheriff, Uncle Edward. We're meeting him again first thing in the morning."

"Hmmph."

"There's more." Hollan knew her uncle and aunt were very close to Fletcher and Sylvia. "Fletcher apparently brought our supplies over about the same time David and his men came ashore. They stole everything he had, beat him, and left him for dead."

"Oh dear me." Ettie's hand was at her throat, and she fanned herself.

"Now, dear, sit down before you get yourself too worked up." Uncle Edward helped her over to the settee. "Where's Fletcher now?"

Jacob shifted on his feet. He looked tired enough to fall over. "According to the sheriff, he's home with Sylvia. We intend to go out there in the morning, too."

"I'll be going with you." Edward sighed. "Ettie and I were at the Black place all day. We had no idea."

"Poor Sylvia, dealing with this all alone." Ettie kept shaking her head.

"She's a strong woman, Ettie. I'm sure she's fine."

Hollan listened to them talk. "Well, I'm glad Sylvia was here to care for Fletcher." A plan began to formulate in Hollan's mind. If the menfolk were too busy to go over and capture an outlaw, she'd talk to Sylvia about flushing them out somehow. Surely the woman would be just as incensed as Hollan after what happened to her son. "She has to be furious at David."

"As well she should be," Ettie huffed.

Ah, yes. Hollan would surely have an ally in Sylvia. Ettie was upset, and it wasn't even her son hurt, though Hollan was like a daughter to her.

The simple facts were her father wasn't well, the lighthouse was unattended, and local seafarers were unsafe as long as they had no light to guide them. Hollan glanced at her father. He'd paled and now looked exhausted. She hurried to his side. "Papa?"

"I'm just tired. I suppose all the excitement of the past few weeks is catching up with me."

"Well, let's get you tucked into bed, then." Ettie was on her feet and acting as hostess, leading the weary Gunter to a room at the back of the house. "And you two take the room upstairs across from ours—Hollan's room when she stays here," she called as she retreated down the hallway.

Hollan darted her eyes to Jacob.

"If you don't mind, I'd rather stay down here where I can watch the door. Let Hollan sleep in the bed. She needs a good night's sleep."

"As do you," Hollan quipped. "You've lost several nights' sleep."

"I'll be fine. Like I told you before, between the war and the traveling, I've learned to sleep in snatches."

"Jonathon." Ettie's no-nonsense voice as she came up the hall made the man jump. "You'll settle into the room across from Gunter. Follow me to the back of the house, and I'll show you the way."

Jonathon blushed. "Oh no, ma'am. I'll be fine on the porch or in a shed if you have one out back. I haven't slept on the likes of a bed in longer than I can remember."

"Then it's high time you had a good night's sleep. Tonight you'll be blessed with a bed."

"I've already been blessed in many ways tonight." Jonathon glanced at Hollan.

She smiled back at him. "You deserve it, Jonathon. You helped save us. Tomorrow I'll make a celebration breakfast in your honor."

"I'm not sure I earned such an honor."

"You've more than earned it, Jonathon," Hollan encouraged.

"You brought our niece home safe and sound. We will celebrate."

Jonathon beamed.

Edward walked with Ettie and Jonathon as they headed for the back of the house, leaving Hollan and Jacob temporarily alone.

"Thank you for volunteering to stand watch. That saved us an awkward situation."

"I volunteered to stand watch because I want to know you're safe. Otherwise I would have grabbed Ettie's suggestion before you could have said anything about it."

"Oh," Hollan croaked.

He stepped closer, and his green eyes stared into hers with such intensity she figured he could read her deepest thoughts. "And when we get this all taken care of, I expect to start all over with this marriage. This time we'll do it right."

"I see."

Jacob laughed. "My wife appears to be tongue-tied for the first time ever."

Hollan mashed the toe of her boot into a knothole on the floor. "And what am I to say to such talk? I wonder. . . ."

"What?"

"Would it be possible to have our wedding ceremony over?" She felt silly asking. "I'd love to have Aunt Ettie there this time around. And our friends. . ."

"If that's what it takes to set this marriage straight."

"Your intensity embarrasses me." Hollan stepped away but laughed. She might as well get used to it.

He moved closer still. "It isn't my intent to embarrass you. But you should know my thoughts. We'll start our marriage again, and we'll do it right this time."

"I'd like that."

"Good." He grinned. "Now get up to bed. We have a busy day tomorrow."

🐚

Hollan woke later than she'd planned the next morning, after the long and tiring night. She couldn't wait to talk to Sylvia. She wanted to check on Fletcher. But she also wanted to ask for Sylvia's assistance in ridding their lives of David. If Jacob wouldn't go along with her, and the townsmen still wouldn't go after David after all that he'd done, she'd find a way to capture him herself. Surely after a night's sleep, Jacob, the sheriff, and the townspeople would agree this couldn't wait.

A few minutes later she listened as Jacob dashed her dreams of going home soon.

"We can't do this yet. The town needs to be secured, then we'll worry about the island. People will lose their life's belongings if we don't fix their roofs before the next storm rolls through."

"Jacob, why are you standing against me in this? Our life has been in turmoil far too long and all because of David."

"I'm not standing against you, Hollan. But we need to have a plan. David's not going anywhere. The ship is stuck for now."

"But I want to go home. I want our life to get back to normal. I want to enjoy the return of my vision in the place I love."

"Oh. . .and here I thought you were in a hurry to get back so you could officially start your life with me."

Hollan blushed. "You know I want that, too. But first we need to rid the island of David."

Jacob refused to budge.

She tried her ace in the hole. "The lighthouse is unattended. At least, it's unattended if they haven't broken into it yet. They've probably destroyed everything I hold of value. I could lose everything I own, too."

"I admit that bothers me." Jacob paced as he always did when stressed. "But the lighthouse is well secured, and I'm pretty sure they won't be able to get in. I'll replace anything we lose."

"You're 'pretty sure' they won't get in?" Hollan raised an eyebrow. "Do you realize how long it will take to replace the lens if they find a way to damage it?"

The scent of fried ham and eggs wafted into the room from the kitchen. Hollan's mouth watered, momentarily distracting her.

"Hollan. We can't go back until we put a plan in place. Gunter, Jonathon, and I will talk to the sheriff as soon as we've eaten breakfast. I want you to stay here and wait with Ettie. Understand?"

"I need to go see Sylvia."

Jacob's face lit up. "That's a wonderful plan. You spend your time with Sylvia and Fletcher while we menfolk come up with our plan."

Hollan scowled.

Jonathon walked into the room. He looked uncomfortable. "Good morning."

"Is everything all right?" Hollan hurried over to his side.

"I'm not used to waking up in a—home. It's unnerving."

Hollan smiled at Jacob. "I'm sure it is. Aunt Ettie has breakfast ready, and we were just heading that way. Do you want to clean up and meet us in the kitchen?"

Jonathon nodded and shuffled toward the back of the house while Hollan and Jacob headed for the kitchen.

Hollan hesitated in the doorway. "Aunt Ettie? If you don't mind, I'd like to go on over and see how Sylvia and Fletcher fared last night."

"Before you eat?" Jacob frowned.

Her aunt looked up from the biscuits she was pulling from the oven. "Can't you wait, dear? I'd planned to walk over with you."

"Father needs someone here. I'll stay if you'd like. . . ." She made her voice wistful.

"But you'd really rather go yourself." She sighed. "I know how important Sylvia is to you. I'll stay here with Gunter. You go on ahead."

"If you're sure. . ."

"Go on. Here"—Aunt Ettie grabbed a biscuit and smeared it with jam—"at least eat this on the way."

Hollan took the biscuit and gave her aunt a grateful look. She glanced at Jacob and tried to hide the guilt she was sure he could read in her eyes. "I'll be going then. I'll see you. . .after?"

"After? Oh, right. We'll talk to the sheriff and meet up with you later." He shrugged, though he still looked perplexed. Or did he look suspicious?

Most likely Hollan was merely feeling guilty.

She headed out the door and up the sandy path. The late morning sun beat down upon her back, and the day promised to be clear. The marshes on either side of the road were bustling with activity. Butterflies flitted from plant to plant. A lizard darted across the path right in front of her. A bit farther Hollan saw a snake slither through the tall reeds at her side.

The lizards and butterflies didn't bother her, but after the snake sighting, Hollan picked up her pace. It took the better part of an hour before Sylvia's small cabin was just around the bend.

"Hollan! What a pleasant surprise." Sylvia had been sitting on her front porch, sipping from a steaming mug, but now she hurried to her feet. She tilted her head and studied Hollan for a moment.

Hollan stared back and grinned.

The wind blew Sylvia's hair. Suddenly her hand flew to her chest. "You can see again."

"Yes, I can see again." She smiled at her friend for a moment then sobered. "I heard about Fletcher. How's he doing?"

A cloud passed over Sylvia's face. "He'll be fine, no thanks to whoever harmed him. We were so worried about you."

"I'm fine. . .and I know who did this to him."

Sylvia slapped her mug down with a *thump*. "You tell me, and I'll go after them on my own!"

"You don't have to go alone. I'd love to go with you." Hollan walked up the steps and placed a hand on Sylvia's arm. "The man responsible for hurting Fletcher kidnapped my father and me. He's also responsible for what happened to my mother."

"What a horrid person. How do you know?"

Hollan told her friend what had happened.

"We must put a stop to this."

"I agree, but Jacob says the town isn't in any shape to help us out. And he's right. People need a roof over their heads before the next storm hits."

"But a very dangerous man is lurking out there, waiting to hurt his next victim. We won't be safe until the authorities get him under control."

"I agree, but that isn't my only concern. The ships aren't safe without the lighthouse."

They exchanged a mischievous glance.

"Do you have a plan?" Sylvia took another sip from the mug. "You aren't thinking of going alone. . . ?"

"No–o–o," Hollan drawled. "But I *am* thinking of going over with help." She sent Sylvia a meaningful look.

"We don't want to put ourselves in danger."

"I know that island like the back of my hand."

"The menfolk will be so upset."

"I'm willing to take that chance. I'm pretty upset myself that we have to sit here and do nothing while those outlaws ruin what little I have left from my previous life."

"This isn't a decision to make lightly, dear."

"I'm not making it lightly." Hollan put her hands on her hips. "David has hurt too many people. If we don't act, someone else will be hurt. I saw the look in Jacob's eyes, Sylvia. He's telling me he has to wait to act, but I'm afraid he'll go alone and he'll confront David. I don't want him hurt on my behalf."

"Yet you're willing to be hurt on his behalf?"

"I don't intend to get hurt. But yes, I'd do anything for him. He's been here for me through everything we've endured of late. I owe him."

"But you don't think it'll upset him if something happens to you?"

"I don't intend for anything to happen to you or to me. I plan to use a little subterfuge. I'm not going to confront David."

Doubt crept across Sylvia's features. "Subterfuge?" She raised an eyebrow.

"I just want to set a bonfire as a warning to sailors entering the mouth of the river. We might not be able to use the lighthouse to show them the island's location, but we can light a huge fire on the beach that will serve the same purpose. They'll see the fire and know land is nearby."

"I don't know. Maybe we should just wait for the men to figure this out."

"And let Jacob sneak over on his own?" Hollan shook her head. "I won't chance that. We have to watch out for the sailors. At least help me set a warning fire on the shore. David said he and his crew are wanted. If men on ships are searching for them, I'd like to do my best to protect those men and lead them our way."

They stared at each other for a few more moments. Hollan prayed Sylvia would come along. "Please, Sylvia."

"Perhaps you just solved your own dilemma." Sylvia waved her hands and sighed. "I can't exactly sit by and let you do this alone."

"You're coming with me?"

"I suppose I am."

"And Fletcher will be all right if you leave him?"

"He'll be fine. He's sleeping. Let me run inside and make sure he has everything he needs. Then we'll make our plans. We don't want to get over there too early either. We need to do this under the protection of dusk."

"Sylvia—"

"Yes?" Hollan's friend stopped and turned around.

"Thank you."

"Sweetheart, I don't want you to take responsibility for what we're about to do. I'm doing this for you, yes, but also for your mother, Fletcher, and myself. I'm doing this for all of us. I want the man responsible for hurting my son behind bars."

Hollan smiled. "I understand. And I intend to do my best to see that happen, too."

Chapter 16

"We need to put in here," Hollan whispered. "We don't want David's crew to see us if anyone's on watch."

"I hardly think you need to whisper, Hollan. We're in the middle of a marsh."

"Must you remind me?" Hollan shuddered. If the reeds, taller than their boat, didn't clue her in, the stench of the stagnant water surely did. "Maybe I'm whispering so the creatures don't know we're here. Maybe it has nothing to do with David and his men hearing us."

Sylvia laughed. Hollan's nerves were shot, and she said crazy things when she was stressed and tired.

They'd commandeered Fletcher's supply boat for the trip. Sylvia was accustomed to piloting the flat-bottomed boat. She felt it would allow them to skirt the shallower water and hug the shore more closely. It would also hold the most supplies. Sylvia had been right on every count. Hollan knew she'd made the right decision when she invited the woman along.

They worked together to guide the front of the boat alongside the shore around the bend from where David's men had placed their boats. The watery ground was marshy. Hollan pushed back her fears of snakes and alligators and maneuvered the flatboat deep into the swaying reeds and grasses. They were able to secure the boat mostly out of sight. Hollan jumped into the water, saturating her boots, and tied the vessel to a low-lying tree.

"Tie both ends of the boat securely, dear. Otherwise it will swing back and forth and might work its way loose. We don't want it to be damaged."

Hollan shuddered. "You're right. I want to be sure we have a way off this island."

After doing what Sylvia told her, Hollan helped the older woman off the boat. They gathered their supplies. Sylvia had prepared well for the expedition. They were stocked with weapons, food, and various types of gear, the use of which Hollan didn't even understand.

The sun sat low on the horizon.

"Tell me what you have planned before we leave here," Sylvia requested. "We might not be able to talk as freely later."

"Well, I'd hoped to be here much earlier than this. But since you and I wasted time chatting—"

"Planning and preparing, dear. That wasn't a waste of time."

"Whatever you want to call it, it set us way off track," Hollan replied.

"Not necessarily. The dusk will keep us covered. They're drinking men. They should be well into their indulgences by now."

Which will put us into even greater danger if we get caught. Hollan felt responsible for Sylvia's well-being. It was one thing to deal with evil men. It was another thing entirely to deal with drunken evil men.

Hollan nodded. "I suppose we'd best be on our way."

"Let's pray first."

Sylvia said a quick prayer for their safety and for justice to be served. As soon as she finished, she motioned to Hollan with her hand. "Lead the way. I'd like to get out of here before nightfall."

"Me, too." Hollan didn't need to be asked twice. She was in her least favorite place on the island. The swampy, marshy grounds were home to all sorts of creatures she didn't want to think about, let alone meet. She avoided the area like the plague in broad daylight, so being here after dark was a nightmare.

They didn't talk; they just made haste while walking through the scrub. Hollan pushed through far more spiderwebs than she wanted to think about. Her skin crawled as she wondered about the spiders that lived in the webs. The cooler weather might have chased them off, but she couldn't be sure.

She did a little jig as she walked.

Sylvia's soft laugh flowed through the evening air. "You're fine, Hollan. I see no spiders on your dress or hair." She knew about Hollan's fear of spiders, and she also knew how much Hollan hated this area.

The older woman clucked her tongue. "Love certainly is a mysterious thing."

"Pardon?" Hollan called over her shoulder, not slowing her pace.

"I know how you feel about this area. Yet you're willing to brave it for Jacob."

"I'm braving it in order to right the wrongs David has brought upon our families."

"How far do you plan to go?" Sylvia was out of breath. Hollan needed to slow her pace for the older woman.

"Not much farther. We're nearly at the end of the island now."

"And what are we doing here?"

Hollan stopped a few feet away. "We'll set up a bonfire." She moved her arms in an arc, gesturing toward the beach. The moon was climbing upward, reflecting off the water. Stars studded the sky. The only sound was that of the water lapping gently against the shore.

"Why here?" Sylvia frowned.

"We're at the bay end of the island. If any ships come through here tonight, they'll be able to see where we are. Even better, the outlaws shouldn't be able to see us. We might not have use of the lighthouse, but we can warn the ships' captains of the island's danger from here."

"Good idea."

They busied themselves with gathering all the driftwood they could find.

"I want the fire to be big so it can be seen and so the outlaws can't easily put it out if they do see it."

"Another good idea."

They placed Spanish moss throughout the wood, and Hollan set it on fire. The fire flared, dimmed, and as she held her breath, flared again. Suddenly it caught and made its way through the pile of wood.

"It's magnificent!" Hollan trilled. "And the warmth feels wonderful against the night's chill."

"Indeed it does." Sylvia stared out over the darkened beach. "Only one problem comes to mind."

"What's that?" Hollan asked, turning to look at Sylvia with a smile. No problem could possibly dim her satisfaction now. She'd reached her goal to warn the sailors. Anyone drifting along the shore would see the bonfire and veer away from the land. Their main task had been accomplished.

"A large and very angry group of men seems to be headed our way."

Hollan looked up, and her heart leaped into her throat. Sylvia spoke the truth, and they didn't have time to hide. The men carried torches, and according to their well-defined silhouettes, they also carried very big guns.

＊

Jacob couldn't wait to get his hands on Hollan. He glanced at her father, wondering how the man had ever survived her. "I specifically told her to stay with Sylvia."

"Yes, you said to stay with Sylvia, which is exactly what she did." Gunter's forehead was creased with worry, but admiration for his daughter's spunk put a spark in his eyes. "In time, son, you'll learn to be more careful when choosing your words."

"I chose my words carefully this morning. Hollan deliberately chose to ignore them and twist them to her own benefit."

"Yes."

"Yes? That's all you have to say about it?" Jacob stomped along the path. The group of men walking with them tailed behind. They couldn't hear the conversation between Gunter and Jacob.

"You should know Hollan well enough by now to know she doesn't take well to direct commands."

"I'm her husband."

"And I'm her father. Apparently those two facts don't mean a lot to her when the time comes to make her decisions. Hollan has always acted first and thought later."

"We'll be changing that as soon as I have her safe."

Gunter's only response was an annoying chuckle. "We'll see about that, Jacob. The girl has a mind of her own."

Jacob sighed and pushed his hair back from his face. "I know. And I love her for it. I just don't like it when she puts herself in danger."

"God has His hand on you both. He won't fail Hollan—or us—now."

"You're right." Jacob sighed. "It's just that she makes me crazy with worry when she pulls a stunt like this. I want her home safe, knitting or sewing like a normal woman, but here she is ready to take on a band of roving privateers!"

"I would imagine that when Hollan continues to see her faith is safe with you, Jacob, she'll learn to settle down and let you lead."

"I certainly hope so, sir. I can't take much more of this."

"Meaning?" Gunter raised an eyebrow.

"Meaning, I want my wife safe at home."

"I understand. And I think we'll get her there tonight."

The sheriff walked up to join them. "Any idea what Hollan and Sylvia would have planned?"

"I know she was worried about the lighthouse not being lit. She wanted the seafarers to remain safe. She hated that the light was off during most of the war. She was also worried the men would destroy the cottage and everything in it."

They continued to work their way along the beach. The boats were pulled ashore just as they'd been the night before. It didn't seem as if Jonathon had been replaced by another guard.

Jacob glanced at Hollan's father. The man was pale but hanging in there. "Gunter, what do you think the chances are that David hasn't even missed Jonathon?"

"Pretty fair, I'd say, based on the fact that no one's been sent in his place."

They wove around the boats and continued along the shore, heading for the far end of the island.

The sheriff looked at Jacob again. "Which concern of your wife's would be the priority?"

"I think she'd worry first about the safety of others. My guess is she'll take care of the lighthouse situation first."

"Would she try to get into the lighthouse? Surely she'd know she'd be trapped inside as soon as the light was lit."

Jacob's heart dropped to his toes. What if his brother recreated the situation he'd been in with Hollan's mother? Jacob would throttle Hollan if she survived this! He'd never felt so much concern for another person. He couldn't lose her.

Not now. Not after everything they'd been through. Not ever.

"You look ready to take on the outlaws single-handedly," Gunter observed.

"I feel like I could do just that. If they hurt Hollan. . ."

"She'll be fine, son. We're here now, and we'll find them. And although Hollan is contrary and impetuous, she's also very smart. She won't allow herself to be boxed into a corner."

"So how do you think she'll protect the lighthouse without endangering herself?" Jacob hoped with everything in him that Gunter was right.

"I believe—if I know my daughter—she'll set a bonfire on the beach."

"A bonfire, huh?" Sheriff Roberts rubbed his chin. "The fire would warn any captain of the island's dangers."

Jacob pointed ahead. "And it would lead my brother directly to Hollan's side."

⯌

"What do we do now?" Hollan panicked. "My plan was that we'd set the fire and then move away the other direction. We'd go into hiding and make the next plan."

"I think we better figure out another plan and fast." Sylvia's voice was shaky.

They'd left their weapons in the trees. They couldn't get them now. In unison, they began to back away.

"We could always turn around and run for it."

Sylvia's laugh held no humor. "Yes, we'd run with a throng of angry men chasing after us with guns. We'd not likely get very far."

"Then we stand tall and go out fighting."

"I don't much like that plan either. Don't you have anything else?"

"No. I have nothing."

The men were getting closer. Hollan reached over and took Sylvia's hand. Not the most heroic gesture, but she drew comfort from her friend's presence.

"We need to pray!" The urgency in Sylvia's voice sent a chill down Hollan's spine.

Hollan heard Sylvia whisper a prayer for their safety. The words had no meaning in Hollan's terrified brain. She didn't want to be in David's custody again, especially now. He'd surely be angry about the ship going aground and about their escape.

The men continued to move closer.

"I'm starting to think we made a really bad decision in coming here."

The sneers on the men's faces scared Hollan to her toes.

"You're just starting to think that? I came to that conclusion when we first saw the throng of men coming our way."

The men neared the far side of the bonfire. Suddenly, as quickly as they'd appeared, they stopped and started to back away.

"Pray again, Sylvia, I think your prayers are working."

"I've already said my prayer, Hollan. I don't need to repeat myself to God."

The men looked wary and then alarmed. They turned heel and began to run.

"I don't understand."

"Me, either." Sylvia laughed. "But I like it!"

"I do, too." Hollan grinned with relief. "If and when we get out of this situation, let's not ever get ourselves into another."

A deep male voice whispered into Hollan's ear, "Is that a promise?"

Hollan screamed.

Jacob leaned around her. "Don't be afraid, Hollan. It's only me."

"You?" Hollan spun around. Her father, the sheriff, Uncle Edward—and almost every man from town—formed a line that stretched across the beach.

"Papa." Her father grinned at her. He didn't seem too angry. Jacob, on the other hand—he seemed angry enough for the both of them. He was possibly angry enough for the entire group.

"Well, I guess now we know why they turned and ran."

"Hollan. We'll discuss this later."

"That's all right," Hollan hedged. "We don't really have to discuss it at all. Let's just let bygones be bygones and start fresh like you said."

"We *will* discuss this." The fire reflected in his eyes and intensified the emerald-green color. His golden hair hung loose in wild curls that danced across his shoulders. He towered over her, looking every bit the outlaw rogue she'd imagined him to be on their wedding day.

A commotion up ahead interrupted their conversation.

"What is it?" Hollan stood on her tiptoes but still couldn't see. Some of the men who had gone ahead returned.

"It seems the bonfire offered a much-needed diversion for the naval patrol. They were able to make landfall and sneak in behind David and his men. They're rounding them up as we speak."

A cheer rose up from Hollan's friends.

"But how—?"

The sheriff walked up with a huge grin on his face. "They knew where David was all along. They only needed the perfect break to come in and overwhelm them. Hollan, your bonfire created that diversion."

Hollan smirked at Jacob.

He quirked up the corner of his mouth and shrugged his shoulder.

Most of the men were drifting back the other direction. They were ready to head home.

Her father, Sylvia, and the sheriff walked ahead. Jacob and Hollan followed at a more leisurely pace.

"You know what this means." Jacob took Hollan's hand in his own.

"We can go home." Tears filled Hollan's eyes as she said the words. "Finally, after everything that's happened, we can go home."

"I like the sound of that, wife."

"That is, if we have a home left to go back to."

"Our cottage is tougher than a few crusty outlaws." Jacob smiled. "Our home will withstand more than that." He stopped and pulled her into his arms. "More importantly. . .home for me is wherever you are."

"Oh Jacob, that's so sweet." Hollan considered his words. "But it's also very true. I feel the same exact way."

Epilogue

O nce again Hollan faced Jacob on a dune overlooking the ocean. This time nothing about the situation felt surreal. The wedding *was* the wedding of her dreams. And the man who stood beside her was as familiar to her as her own face. All of her loved ones stood alongside them to witness the event.

Their house—now put back in order after their adventure—and the untouched lighthouse stood sentry behind them. Samson ran between all the people, savoring their attention and happy to be back home.

The afternoon couldn't have been more perfect for their ceremony. The seagulls serenaded as they flew overhead. The ever-present sound of the waves crashing onshore brought a familiar comforting reassurance. Hollan would never tire of the roar of the surf from the Atlantic Ocean. She couldn't wait to wade along the tide line with her husband.

She turned her attention to the man at her side. She saw him clearly. She drank in his dimpled smile, his sparkling green eyes, and the way his golden hair blew in the wind. The sun silhouetted his broad shoulders and proved he wasn't the skinny boy who'd left three years before. The planes of Jacob's face had indeed changed with the years, but the changes were all for the better. And Hollan knew from recent experience that Jacob still didn't like to stay indoors any more than necessary, which accounted for his sun-kissed skin.

Her uncle's voice intruded on her musings. "Hollan. Jacob. I think we're all about ready. Let's do this ceremony right."

"We're ready, too," Jacob said with a grin. He gently squeezed Hollan's hand. She nodded.

Uncle Edward smiled at her. "No regrets?"

"Never. Not a one."

"Jacob, has life on the island been everything you thought it would be?" Uncle Edward asked.

For a moment, Jacob could only laugh. Hollan watched him with a frown.

"Edward, we've been through a hurricane, I saved Hollan's life—more than once. I watched her captured at the hands of outlaws. I helped her escape. We slept outside with all the bugs on the Georgia coast and the various creepy-crawlies and reptiles. We found out about Fletcher's attack and were chased again by the outlaws. . . ."

"When you put it that way"—Hollan's heart plummeted—"I'm not even sure why you'd want to stay. Why *did* you keep coming for me, even when I put us in danger?"

"My unending love and protection of you is similar to God's unending love and sacrifice for us. Hollan, as long as God allows me the privilege, I'll be right here to pull you away from any danger that comes our way."

Hollan smiled.

"And Edward, to answer your question—" Jacob looked at them both, but his eyes settled on Hollan. The look of love he sent her filled her heart to bursting. "This experience has been everything I imagined and more."

"I'm glad to hear it, son." Uncle Edward slapped Jacob on the back and turned to welcome their guests.

Again he made quick work of the ceremony.

"Jacob, you may now kiss your bride."

Hollan grinned up at him. This was the perfect moment.

Jacob leaned forward and touched his lips to hers in the most gentle of kisses. Hollan's heart soared.

THE DISPLACED
BELLE

Dedication

For our newest "Belle," Ashton Mackenzie!
We love you so much!

Chapter 1

Outskirts of Atlanta, Georgia, 1870

Y ou aren't going in the saloon, Shane." Gabriel clutched his ever-present Bible and held it tight against his chest. The sun's slanted rays shone against the black leather of the worn book. "We have things to do."

Shane wanted to grab the Good Book, thump it upside Gabriel's tilted head, and remove his friend's smug expression.

Instead of acting on the tempting—but inappropriate—thought, Shane raised an eyebrow and glared at his annoyingly self-righteous friend. "I'm not going to the saloon, you say?" He settled back against the plank wall of the storefront, crossed his arms, and glared. The aroma of fried chicken from the kitchen of the boardinghouse two doors behind him wafted by and momentarily distracted him, setting his mouth to watering. He struggled to keep his focus on Gabriel while his stomach rumbled in protest.

Gabriel's eyes widened as he stared Shane down, the whites a stark contrast to his dark features. He shifted his stance and held his ground. "No. You're not going to the saloon. You have two little girls waiting for you, Shane. We need to get home to them."

"Those little girls probably don't even know I'm coming. One more night won't hurt them. And it's not like we can go without grabbing a bite to eat." He pushed off from the wall of the general store with a grin, problem solved. "We'll head out first thing in the morning and fetch 'em."

"Smelling of liquor and smoke," Gabriel muttered. He stepped between Shane and the saloon, effectively blocking his path. "Those sweet little girls don't need their older brother coming home reeking of cheap perfume."

"I'm going in to play a few hands of cards, Gabriel. Nothing more." Shane tightened his hands into fists and released them. He shifted to the left. If he moved fast, he could duck around Gabriel and be halfway down the walkway before Gabriel knew what happened. One thing Gabriel hated was making a scene. This little interlude had to be unnerving his friend as it was.

Gabriel watched and countered, his eyes narrowing. He straightened the fingers of his free hand and wiggled them, a telltale sign of his frustration. His eyes were alert for Shane's next move.

Shane stepped back to the right. All he wanted was an evening in the saloon. Just one, before he fetched the girls. He needed to feel the papery texture of the cards in his hands. He needed to smell the reassuring aromas of the saloon. He wouldn't imbibe, but he'd think about it. Imagine it. Dream about it. The saloon was his refuge, Gabriel his ubiquitous thorn in the flesh.

When Shane had befriended the skinny little misfit outside the school-house twenty years earlier, he'd had no idea the frail boy would make it his life's purpose to "protect" Shane from himself.

Back then Gabriel had been the one who'd needed protecting. As a boy, Gabe would sneak up to the schoolhouse door and listen in on the lessons—something Shane found intriguing. Shane did everything he could to get kicked *out* of the schoolroom.

Gabriel's determination impressed Shane in some way, and he'd secured Gabriel a slate. He defended Gabriel when the other kids caught him listening in and taunted him.

Shane shook off the memories. Those were hard days for both of them. "No women, no liquor, just cards, Gabe. Is that so much to ask? After we get the girls, I won't have a chance to do anything like this until I find them another place to live." His voice trailed off. The girls were a handful. Placing them with a new family wouldn't be an easy task. "And we both know finding them another home could take a while."

"They've been with everyone we know, Shane. You're out of options. The girls wouldn't be nearly as challenging if you would take responsibility and raise them yourself as you should. They need their big brother. They want to be with you."

"I love the way you go from 'we' to 'you' when it comes to my options with the girls."

"Like I said, they need you." Gabriel shrugged and turned away, his attitude saying he'd won and there was no suitable response to his final comment.

"Oh come on, Gabe. You've been trying that whole back-to-the-world stance since we were boys. You should know by now it doesn't work on me."

"Nothing works on you, Shane," Gabe tossed over his shoulder. "You're unchangeable. I don't even know why I put up with you. You can't keep living your life this way."

Shane's laugh drew the attention of a group of women who also stood in front of the general store, the side nearer the saloon. One woman, a pretty blond, appraised him for a long moment. She turned back to her friends, but not before he'd sent her his charming trademark grin.

"Did you hear me?" Gabriel's voice interrupted the moment. "I'm talking to you, Shane."

"The question is, Gabriel, did you see her? She's breathtaking." Shane lounged back against the wall and watched her as she spoke to the other women.

"Your breath hasn't been taken. You're still talking to me." Gabriel remained where he was, facing the women's direction while keeping his back to Shane.

"Don't be so literal. Look at her." Arms folded, Shane tipped his head back against the wall, trying to see past Gabriel's silhouette. "She's different from the other women around here."

"You haven't been around 'here' for a while. How would you know what the women are like? You discerned that from her dismissive glance? You haven't even met her, Shane."

"So you did get a look at her. Her glance wasn't dismissive. She was flirting with me. Did you see her little smile?"

"No, but I did see her little boy. Or did you miss him? The little lad standing beside her and pulling at her skirts? Did you happen to notice *him*, Shane?"

"A child?" Shane shuddered and hurried to stand upright, peering at the child from over Gabriel's shoulder. "Well, that's that, then. We'd best be moving on."

"To get your sisters?"

"No. To get to the saloon."

Shane had tired of their sparring. He pushed past Gabriel just as the swinging doors of the saloon burst open. The wooden doors slammed back against the rough plank wall of the building as two men tumbled through. Patrons poured out from the saloon, yelling and inciting the fighting men.

The three women outside the general store screamed at the ruckus and scattered as the belligerent men punched and stumbled their way.

Shane moved through the chaos, grasped the larger man by the collar, and yanked him out of the brawl. As drunk as the man was, he was no match for Shane's agile moves. Shane settled him on a nearby bench while the smaller man stepped back and wiped at his bloody lip.

"Thank you, sir. I owe you one."

"You don't owe me anything. If that ring on your finger is any indication, you owe someone else your presence. You have better places to be. Just get on home to your family and stay away from here." Shane caught the blond woman's eye and smiled. "The saloon isn't the place for a family man."

He heard Gabriel's judgmental intake of breath from slightly behind him. He ignored the insinuation. Shane wasn't a family man and planned to keep it that way.

"Oh my, did you *see* him, Lydia?" one of the older two women gushed from a few feet away. "That handsome man just stepped right in and ended the skirmish without as much as a thought for his own safety or well-being."

"Indeed, Lydie, have you ever seen such a brave, brave man?" a second voice joined in. "And to send that other man home to his family. Precious. You don't come across men like him very often these days."

Gabriel snorted.

Shane glanced over his shoulder. Judging by the location of the blond, she hadn't been one to speak. Instead she stood slightly to the side, surveying him through guarded eyes. This time he didn't miss the presence of the small boy who clung to her skirts in fear.

Shane tipped his hat at the trio and turned back to the drunk in front of him. "Let's get you inside and see if we can sober you up before you head home."

"Oh. Just a *perfect* gentleman," the first woman crooned. She tsked her tongue. "I need to marry a man like him."

The older women exchanged amused glances. They were having a great time at Shane's expense.

Marriage. Not a concept Shane wanted to think about. He preferred to move through life alone. It was bad enough Gabriel had attached himself to Shane's side, but after tomorrow he'd temporarily be saddled with his two little sisters as well.

"Help me out here, Gabe. This man has drawn enough attention for the day." Shane couldn't resist one more glance over his shoulder at the blond. Her green eyes widened as their gazes met, and without thinking he grinned at her and winked.

He'd *winked.* His spontaneous reaction startled him. He rubbed at his eye like he had a tic. He'd never winked at a proper woman—let alone one that was hitched—in all his life. Especially one with a watchful lad by her side. He saved that sort of nonsense for the nameless girls in the saloons. He was losing his touch. He turned and snatched the man off the bench with a bit more force than he'd meant to use and hauled him through the saloon doors.

❧

"Did you *see* that, Mavis? That darling man winked at our Lydia here."

"I don't think anyone with eyes missed that wink, Beatrice," Mavis tittered. "I thought my heart was going to melt right then and there. It was beautiful. Absolutely beautiful. And he couldn't take his eyes off her."

"Oh I don't think he winked," Lydia corrected. Judging by the warmth in her cheeks, her face had to be red with embarrassment. "He merely had something in his eye. Didn't you see him rub it after? I'm sure it meant nothing. Poor fellow had his hands full with that inebriated man."

And Lydia had no tolerance for inebriated men. Her stepfather was one drunk too many as far as she was concerned. And speaking of. . .they needed to get going before he took issue with the length of time they'd been gone. "Come along, Wyatt. We need to finish our shopping and get home."

Wyatt resisted. "Aw, Lydie! I wanna watch the men fight some more. It just got interesting out here."

Lydia dropped to his level. "Wyatt. Men like that aren't interesting. They're pathetic. I wish you hadn't seen that interlude, and I want you to forget about it."

"Do I have to forget about the man who broke up the fight? Did you see him, Lydie? He just grabbed up that big, fat man and put him on that bench like it was nothin'."

"Nothing," Lydia corrected.

"I know! He was brave, Lydia. And he winked at you. I wanna learn to wink like that." Wyatt's face contorted, and his nose wrinkled as he squished both eyes tightly shut. "Did I wink at you like he did?"

Mavis and Beatrice laughed.

Lydia's face burned. "That's enough, Wyatt. He didn't wink at me. I told you… he had something in his eye."

Had he winked? Against her will, her heart beat a little faster at the thought. He was most definitely handsome, and she couldn't deny—to herself at least— that she enjoyed his attentions. She shook off her silly musings. Her stepfather's actions during the past decade had taught her that just because a man looked nice, didn't mean he was.

"I sure wish I coulda grabbed that fat man and put him on the bench like that. Bam! Sit there, you bad guy!"

Mavis and Beatrice's laughter abruptly stopped as they gasped at the vehemence in Wyatt's voice. Mavis's hand moved to her heart, and Beatrice fanned her face.

"Wyatt!" Lydia sent the two women an apologetic smile. "Children do say the silliest things, don't they?"

She turned to the small boy. "We mustn't talk like that about other people, Wy. You need to speak with respect, even if someone isn't making the best choice. And I don't want you to ever go near a man like that. It isn't proper. Promise me?"

Wyatt looked confused. "Then how can we go home to Daddy?"

Lydia closed her eyes. Her precocious brother was too perceptive for both of their own good. "It's different with Daddy. We'll talk about it on the way home. Right now, though, we need to go and gather up our supplies."

Wyatt shrugged, already moving on. "Do I still get my peppermint stick?"

"I don't know." Lydia laughed. "Are you *still* going to behave?"

"I always do, don't I?" He grinned.

They both knew that wasn't true. Wyatt could find more mischief than time to fit it all in.

Lydia couldn't help but notice that his grin contained all of the charm the flirtatious man at the saloon had exuded and then some—the man who most surely did wink at her. And here was Wyatt, bent on mimicking the man. Lydia could think of worse men for Wyatt to imitate, his own father topping the list.

131

Still, she planned to raise Wyatt to be a steadfast, hardworking, and trustworthy man, not a flirt who tried to turn a woman's head. And to flirt with a woman who had a child hanging on her skirts at that! Surely such a thing would make most men think twice about her availability.

Lord, I'm going to need everything You've put in my arsenal when it comes to raising this one! Please help me prevent Wyatt from growing up to become anything like the charmer who walked into the saloon next door.

Lydia glanced down at her younger brother and sighed. He grinned up at her. With his golden ringlets and guileless blue eyes, she didn't stand a chance. He was a natural-born charmer.

❧

"You've brought yourself to a new low, Shane," Gabriel started in the minute they cleared the saloon's door. "You've deceived a lot of people in your life, but to act like you were only coming in here to sober that man up. . ." He clucked his tongue. "It's just wrong, Shane."

"I tried to get him to take the coffee. He wasn't interested." Shane glanced at the man who had pushed Shane away and had then collapsed just inside the saloon's doorway. He now lay curled on his side, snoring peacefully. "He looks content enough to me."

"That's not the point, and you know it. And you sent that other man home to his wife, then turned right around and got all flirty with that married woman on the walkway."

"I didn't flirt."

"You winked at her."

"I had something in my eye."

"I'm sure you did. Lust for another man's wife is what you had in your eye."

"It wasn't like that, and you know it." Gabriel was definitely getting on Shane's nerves. He needed this last night to forget the responsibilities waiting for him at the little farm on the outskirts of town.

"Do I? And how would I know that? I can only go by what I—along with the whole town—saw."

"Look, Gabriel. We're both tired from our trip. Why don't you head on over and secure a couple of rooms at the hotel while I unwind a bit? I'll catch up with you later."

"I'm not leaving you here, Shane. I'll just stand here and wait."

Shane managed to tamp down his groan. He turned around to hide his frustration. He closed his eyes and analyzed how to get Gabriel to give him a moment's peace.

"There are mirrors everywhere in here, Shane. I can see your expression. And I'm still not leaving."

"Suit yourself."

Shane had already garnered the attention of two pretty ladies who now headed his way.

"Can we get you anything, handsome?"

"A bit of good luck with my card game." Shane crooked his arms, and they each grabbed hold. He worked his way over to a table where three men played a round of poker. Gabriel trailed along. "Y'all have room for one more?"

"You ever played before?"

He shrugged. "A couple of times."

"A couple of times, you say?" The men exchanged glances that insinuated they had a greenhorn joining their game.

"Yes, sir."

"What about your friend there?"

"He doesn't play."

"Good enough for me. Have a seat."

Shane slid into the fourth chair, and the pretty saloon girls stood on either side of him, tussling for the closest spot. Tomorrow might bring a whole slew of headaches into Shane's life, but from where he sat at the moment, life looked pretty good.

Chapter 2

L ydia, that nice young man hasn't exited the saloon yet." Bea gawked out the front window of Thompson's General Store, almost tipping over from her awkward angle as she tried to see the front of the saloon down the way. "If you hurry, dear, you might be able to arrange another *tête-à-tête* on the walkway."

Mavis snorted. "Ignore her, Lydia. She's been reading French literature again. The endeavor always gives her new words to try out and fills her head with silly romantic notions. Why she thinks any of it would be of use to us here in the Georgia wilds is surely beyond my understanding."

"I'm standing right here, Mavis. I can peer out the window and hear at the same time."

"I just don't understand why you'd waste your time that way. The time spent on those books is purely a waste."

"Educating your mind is never a waste, Mave, dear. Letting your mind languish is a waste."

Hiding her smile, Lydia glanced away from the bolts of fabric she'd been perusing and looked over at the sisters. "I'm afraid it doesn't bode well for the man's character, Bea, if he's still in the saloon. Surely it doesn't take this long to settle a man in his chair."

"Perhaps the inebriated gentleman put up a struggle. Your knight in shining armor might be in need of assistance himself at this very moment."

"My knight?" Lydia glanced over at Wyatt and lowered her voice. The boy sat by the door and sucked his peppermint stick, but his hearing tended to be quite sharp, even when it seemed he wasn't paying attention. "I believe he saved us all from being plowed down during that horrible skirmish."

"But he only had eyes for you."

"Nonsense." Lydia turned back to her shopping.

She needed to pick out the fabric for Natalie's birthday dress and finish tallying her purchases. She'd spent too much time in town as it was. She found delicate pink linen that suited Natalie's fair complexion and pulled it from the shelf.

"That's a beautiful fabric," Mrs. Thompson said as she came around the counter near the back of the store.

Lydia ran her fingers over the fine cloth. "It is. It's for my sister's birthday. She'll love it."

"I'm sure she will." The woman made quick work of cutting and packaging the material and other supplies Lydia requested.

"I also need the same amount of your finest white silk."

Mrs. Thompson stopped and looked at Lydia. She peered over her glasses and smiled, an act that softened her features. "Is there a wedding on the horizon?"

Lydia blanched. She surely hoped not. Her stepfather had stepped up his comments pertaining to Lydia's own approaching birthday that hovered on the far-too-close horizon. He'd insisted on the white silk for Natalie, a special eighteenth-birthday surprise, he'd said, but the move seemed much too calculated, even for him.

She almost canceled the request for the silk. It was true enough that they attended the expected parties at neighboring plantations, always the perfect little family. But the white silk was far too rich for even the fanciest of their neighbors' soirees.

Lydia heard the door open and close, but didn't bother to turn around. The last thing she needed was to get drawn into another conversation that would cause her a further delay. The plantation and its myriad of chores awaited them, and her stepfather didn't appreciate tardiness.

"Here's your parcel, honey." Mrs. Thompson handed over the brown paper-wrapped package. Lydia sighed with relief. "William already loaded your other supplies on your wagon. Anything else I can get for you?"

"No, thank you." Lydia looked around for Wyatt. He wasn't in his chair. He must have dropped down to play on the floor. She smiled at the proprietor and headed for the front of the store. "Wyatt? We need to get going, sweetheart."

No response.

"Wyatt, Daddy's expecting us. We need to get home."

His peppermint stick lay abandoned on the floor by the wooden chair, but Wyatt wasn't anywhere in sight. With a sigh, she picked up the candy and glanced around. She didn't want to rush back to the plantation any more than he did, but they really needed to be on their way.

She tamped down her frustration. At the tender age of six, he didn't understand all the complexities that came along with a trip to town. She made sure of it. She'd have to play along. She began their signature game of hide-and-seek.

"I wonder where Wyatt could be." She peeked around shelves and under tables stacked with goods as she walked toward the back of the store. Mrs. Thompson had returned to the back room, leaving Lydia alone with Beatrice and Mavis. The two women huddled near the front of the store, talking quietly.

Lydia's heart picked up pace as she neared them with few hiding places left and no Wyatt in sight. She remembered hearing the door open and realized no new patron wandered amidst the dry goods.

"Bea? Mavis? Have you seen Wyatt?"

Mavis smiled. "Why yes, dear, he wandered outside just a few minutes ago."

And you thought I was playing hide-and-seek by myself for the fun of it? Lydia seethed. She knew the two spinsters had no experience with small children, but surely even they knew it wasn't safe for a young boy to wander around the walkway without proper supervision.

"Thank you." Lydia pasted on a smile and forced the words through clenched teeth. "Have a good evening."

"You, too, dear."

Lydia exited the store and clutched the parcel with one arm. Stray strands of hair blew across her face, and she held them back with her free hand. Wyatt wasn't anywhere in sight. She could hear the early evening ruckus from the saloon, but other than that, the town was pretty quiet. She glanced back at the saloon. What if Wyatt had gone in search of his newest hero?

She shivered. *Surely not.*

But if not, where else would her little brother have gone?

❧

Shane held his cards close to his chest and tried not to gloat. Finally, he held the perfect hand. The one he'd been waiting for since he'd entered the establishment. After too many thrown games, he now held the coveted royal flush. It wasn't often his cards aligned so perfectly and at such an opportune time.

He debated how to pursue his win. He'd pretend beginner's luck was on his side, he'd play the cards, and then he'd collect his winnings and head over to the hotel to call it an early night.

Shane grinned up at Gabriel. His friend had been shifting from one foot to the other and sighing for the better part of the hour they'd been here. He'd be more than happy to be on their way. Gabriel glared back at Shane. Or perhaps not. He'd have been happier not to have entered the place he referred to as "the devil's den" in the first place.

"Shane, we really need to go."

"In a minute. Let me play one more hand."

"No, Shane. Now."

"Oh c'mon, let him play his cards." The fidgety man across the table from him obviously enjoyed the fact that Shane had lost every hand he'd played so far. It would serve the man right when Shane won the round, a win that would be followed by Gabriel's customary lecture about tricking innocent men. As if any innocent men would be playing cards in the saloon.

Shane knew what Gabriel was up to. Gabriel was trying his best to prevent

Shane from playing his winning hand and taking all the money. But it wasn't like Shane was cheating. He'd played fair and square. He just hadn't played his best. Until now.

He forced a yawn.

"I'm tired. I think I'll finish things up by betting it all." Shane prepared to push his remaining chips into the center of the table, then hesitated. "I think I'll give it all up."

"You're well on your way," one of the men said under his breath. The other two snickered. Shane pretended not to hear.

"Shane, Savannah's waiting for you to come home."

He ignored Gabriel, too.

"Savannah?" One of the women who'd been draped over his shoulder jumped to her feet, planting her hands on her hips.

The other followed suit. "You have a girl waiting for you at home? I didn't figure you for the type."

"Two girls, actually." Gabriel's tone was entirely too smug. "Both sweet little things, anxiously awaiting his return."

"*Two* girls?" The redhead hit Shane's arm.

He rubbed it with his free hand. For such a little thing, she could pack a punch.

"So you sent that family man home for getting in a ruckus, but then you decided to come in yourself." The brunette tossed her hair.

"They don't mind that I'm here. Why should you?"

The women gaped and shook their heads in unison.

"You're despicable." They turned as one and stalked off toward the back room.

"It's not what you think, ladies." Shane narrowed his eyes at Gabriel as the women stomped away. He called after them, "They're just young'uns. They really don't care that I stopped by!"

Gabriel had the audacity to chuckle. "I don't think you're helping matters, Shane."

"Let's just finish up this round and be on our way, shall we?"

"If you say so." Gabriel seemed more than happy to wait now that he'd disrupted Shane's pleasant camaraderie with the ladies. Gabe hugged his Bible tight—the faded words HOLY BIBLE facing out toward Shane—his lips moving in silent prayer. The other men continued to ignore the dark, soft-spoken man as they had for the better part of the past hour.

"You first," the shifty man said. "You were going for the win?"

Shane drew the moment out. This was the part of the game he enjoyed most. The three men at the table positively glowed with their excitement, mentally counting their winnings as they waited. He'd feel guiltier for duping them if they weren't so giddy at doing the same to a man they considered a beginner. Shane couldn't wait to see the shocked looks that would fill their features when he played his perfect winning hand.

"Me first, huh?" He stalled, hand on chips. "Alrighty then. Let me think a moment."

The other men leaned in, practically panting at the pile of chips about to be thrown.

"I *think* this is a good hand. . .but maybe I should wait and play one more before putting it all in. . . ."

"Don't hold off on our account," Shifty said.

"Well—" Shane drummed his fingers on the table, one breath away from making his play. He felt something brush against his arm.

"Ace, king, queen, jack, and ten!" a small voice shouted from next to Shane's left elbow. "That's a really great hand, mister!"

"Argh!" Shane's garbled words stuck in his throat as he spun around to see the young, towheaded lad from the walkway standing beside him—the one who'd clung to his mother's skirts before Shane had entered the saloon. "What are you doing in here? *Where* is your mother?"

"Dead." The boy stated matter-of-factly. "Where's yours?"

"Dead," Shane spat out. "But that's beside the point. I'm an adult. My mother doesn't travel with me."

"Then I guess I'm a 'dult, too, cause my mama don't travel with me, neither."

Shane forced a strained smile and looked over at the gamblers. "Kid doesn't know his aces from his twos, but he's an adult." He turned back to the wisp of a boy and sent him a pointed look. "Go along now and play outside. The saloon isn't the place for a kid."

"I thought you said the saloon ain't a place for a family man."

"It isn't."

"I'm confused."

"It doesn't matter. What matters is you shouldn't be in here. Now go. Scat." The boy scowled. "I don't wanna."

"Well, you're gonna." Shane shook his head. Now he was talking like the kid. Shane carefully laid his cards on the table, face down, and snagged the boy by the collar. "Come along."

The boy futilely swung his arms. "I wanna watch you play cards."

"And I wanna watch you walk out that set of swinging doors. Now."

"No."

"Yes."

"You can't make me."

"Wanna bet?"

"Really? You mean it?" The boy's eyes lit up. "Like you was gonna bet with those three men?"

"No." Shane lifted the boy by his overall straps and held him in midair, his small body dangling two feet off the ground. The boy sent him a childish grin. Shane ignored it. "Now you gonna leave?"

"I can't. My feet don't reach the floor." He gave a few halfhearted kicks, which made him swing like a puppet in Shane's hands.

Shane lowered him until he was almost touching the rough-hewn planks below his feet. "There. Now I'm going to put you down, and you're going to get on back to whoever should be watching you."

"No!" The boy gave a well-aimed kick, and Shane dropped him the rest of the way to the floor with a groan.

"Why you little…" He sank into his chair, but still managed to reach out and snag the kid by the overalls again.

"Now you listen here—"

"No, *you* listen to *me*!" The pretty blond from outside the store appeared beside him, furious. "Get your slimy hands off my little brother."

"Hey, he started it." Shane kept his grip on the boy's overalls with one hand. He held his other hand up in a gesture of innocence.

"And I'm finishing it." Two bright spots of red colored her cheeks. The heightened color made her eyes appear greener than ever. She was even prettier when angry than she had been when out on the walkway.

Shane shook off the ridiculous thought. "I can explain."

"No need. Just unhand my brother, and we'll be on our way."

"Your *brother* just cost me the card game."

"I couldn't care less," she stated, nose in the air. "Serves you right for indulging in such a foolish and wasteful endeavor. Come along, Wyatt."

Wyatt dug in his heels. "But, Lydie!"

"*Now*." She tried to drag him out.

"Listen—Miss Lydie—" Shane held tight, wanting compensation.

The woman glared.

Shane narrowed his eyes and settled in. He'd stand his ground until the woman offered a solution to even things up. Truth be told, he didn't want compensation. He was enjoying their little standoff, and he wanted a few more moments of her company. She was mad as a wet hen. He tipped back in his chair with a cocky smile and pulled the boy close, resting an arm on the boy's bony shoulder. He whispered in an aside. "Your sister sure is a spitfire. You know that, Wyatt?"

"How's this for a spitfire?"

The words had barely cleared his mouth when her foot swung out and clipped the back leg of his tipped chair, knocking the legs clean out from under him.

Shane fell to the floor, flat on his back, before he knew what hit him. Speechless, he lay in shock, stunned and staring, as a look of horror crept across her delicate features.

Wyatt had fallen to the floor along with Shane, and a deep belly laugh rose from within him. The rest of the patrons were already laughing when Shane joined in. The little boy's mirth was contagious.

Lydie's blush went from bright red to deep crimson. "If we're through here, I'll be on my way. Wyatt. Come along. Immediately." She spun on her heels and headed for the door.

Gabriel helped Shane to his feet. Shane tugged Wyatt up beside him and hurried in her wake.

"Lydie. Miss—I'm sorry, I don't even know your last name."

"And I'd like to keep it that way," she spat over her shoulder. "There's no need whatsoever for you to know my last name. Wyatt?"

"I'm here, Lydie." Obviously a smart boy, Wyatt hurried forward and grabbed her hand without a backward glance.

"For what it's worth. . .I'm truly sorry for what happened back there."

She didn't acknowledge him or give any indication that she'd heard his heartfelt apology. Shane stood in the middle of the road, feeling bereft as she walked away.

Gabriel appeared beside him. "She really got to you, huh? I've never seen you so taken by a woman."

Shane didn't respond.

Gabriel looked from Lydie to Shane and back. "If it makes you feel any better, the men said that was the best entertainment they've had in a long time and they'd share the winnings with you if you want to go back inside and claim them."

Shane didn't take his eyes off Lydie's retreating back. He watched as she loaded Wyatt in a wagon at the far end of the street, climbed up beside him, and turned the corner to ride out of sight.

Chapter 3

Lydia tossed and turned, but she couldn't settle down enough to sleep. The trip to town had unnerved her, especially her altercation with the man from the saloon. She couldn't get him out of her head, even after finding out what a scoundrel he really was. Mavis and Beatrice thought him the perfect gentleman, bless their hearts. Lydia was glad they'd still been in the store when she had her exchange with the man.

A noise from the hallway interrupted her musings. She rose up on her arm and tilted her head to listen. The movement disrupted her covers, and cool air slithered underneath her blankets, causing Lydia to shiver. The fire in the hearth on the opposite side of the room had died down to embers, leaving the bedchamber's air chilly.

The floor squeaked outside her door, just before the doorknob turned and the door inched open.

"Lydie?" Wyatt's quiet whimper drifted through the silence.

"I'm here." Lydia wondered if he'd had another nightmare. "Come on in."

She hoped Joseph hadn't heard Wyatt in the hall.

The door opened some more, and she heard the shuffle of Wyatt's feet as he hurried to her bedside. "I'm cold."

The full moon highlighted his slight figure. Lydia lifted the covers. "Climb in bed with me. We'll keep each other warm."

"I had a bad dream." Wyatt's voice dropped to a whisper. "And I'm wet."

His shame carried through the space separating them.

"Oh sweetie. No wonder you're cold. Let's get you dressed in a dry gown." She reached over in the dark and felt around for the gown she kept nearby for him. "We'll get you fixed right up."

"I'm sorry."

Lydia's heart broke for her little brother. His father had humiliated him into thinking he was somehow at fault for soiling his bedclothes at night. Lydia knew the opposite was true. Her stepfather's harsh nature caused Wyatt's nighttime terrors and frustrations.

She made quick work of getting him freshened up and into dry clothes. She pulled back the bedcovers, and he hurried to slip under them. She slid in beside him, allowing him the warm spot where she'd lain several minutes earlier.

His shivering stopped after a few moments, and he snuggled close as she tucked them both securely into her bed.

"Let's both try to get some sleep now."

As soon as the words left her lips, a bright light illuminated the hallway. Lydia whispered a quick prayer, knowing what would happen next. As expected, the bedroom door slammed open. Her stepfather filled the doorway. He held up his lantern, leaned against the frame, and leered at her.

"Isn't this a cozy sight? I wonder what could possibly bring young Wyatt running to your bedside."

Wyatt's shivers returned, this time from fear. His tiny body quaked as he pushed closer against her. Lydia placed a reassuring hand against his leg. "He's fine. He just had a nightmare."

"A nightmare, huh?" Never one to wait for an invitation, her stepfather walked farther into the room. He snagged Wyatt's wet nightclothes with his toe and kicked them up into Lydia's face. "Then why is *this* lying on the floor?"

Lydia had a hard time not hating the man. "Please don't do this. Let's let Wyatt go to sleep."

"Don't do what?" His words slurred. He'd been drinking, as usual.

"You know exactly what I'm talking about." Lydia fought to keep the anger from her words. It didn't do any good to provoke him.

"If we can't talk about the boy," he laughed, "then why don't we talk about us."

It was Lydia's turn to shiver. "There isn't any 'us.'"

His crazed laugh filled the room, and Wyatt began to cry.

"There will be soon enough. I noticed you bought the fabric for your wedding dress this afternoon. You'll look mighty pretty in that fancy white silk."

Lydia felt like she was going to be sick. "You told me to buy the fabric for Natalie's birthday."

"That I did. Brilliant, don't you think? I knew if I told you what it was really for, you'd never oblige."

"You're right. And I'm still not going to oblige."

He reached out and grabbed her arm. He jerked her upright to a sitting position in the bed. "You *will* oblige me. Our wedding will be right after your twenty-first birthday. I've waited long enough."

"It's not right. You were married to my mother."

"And your mother is dead. You're no kin of mine. I can marry you if I choose."

"I have no say in the matter?"

"None whatsoever."

"And what if I refuse?"

"Is that what you're doing?" He jerked her arm and squeezed. She'd have bruises in the morning. "Are you *refusing* me?"

"I am." Her voice came out as a whisper, but she had to say it.

He laughed again. "Do you really think you have a choice? You will marry me. And since you have such a disrespectful attitude, I'll move our wedding day up. You'll become my bride first thing in the morning."

Lydia panicked. "No."

"Yes." He released her arm, then shoved her back on the bed. He stalked to the door, but couldn't leave without one more caustic comment to his son. "Enjoy your last night sleeping with your sister, Wyatt. From now on you'll deal with your soiled clothes and your nightmares alone. I won't have you in my bed."

He slammed the door as he went out. Darkness surrounded them.

"Lydie?"

"I'm here, sweetheart." She pulled Wyatt close and closed her eyes, resting her cheek against his baby-soft hair and savoring his little-boy scent. How could someone so precious be related to someone so evil?

"What are we gonna do?"

Lydia sighed. "I don't know."

"You'd make a good mama."

"Thank you, Wyatt. You know I love you with all my heart. Being your mama wouldn't make me love you any more because I already love you with everything I have."

Wyatt giggled. "I know."

"I'm the happiest big sister in the world because I have you."

"And I'm the happiest little brother in the world because I have you." Her little brother finished out the routine with a yawn.

Wyatt's security was the sole reason that almost tempted Lydia to marry the despicable man. But she knew if she married him, nothing would change for the better, and everything would change for the worse.

"Wyatt?"

"What?" His tired voice came out a whisper.

"Things might get rough for a while. But no matter what happens, I want you to be strong. All right?"

"Aw' right."

"I might have to leave for a few days. If I do, I'll come back for you."

"I don't want you to leave!" His voice rose in pitch, and he clung to her.

She held him tight against her. "I don't want to leave either, but if I do, Natalie and Nathan will be here to watch over you. If you have a bad dream or anything, go to one of them. I need you to be strong."

"Okay."

"Promise me?"

"If you promise me you'll come back."

"I will."

Lydia rubbed his back until Wyatt's soft sobs turned into steady breaths of deep sleep. She needed to figure out a way to avoid the wedding. She could take Wyatt and leave, but where would she go? What would happen to her other siblings? The twins would probably do fine. They'd be eighteen in a few weeks. Nathan would take care of Natalie.

But where would Lydia go? Perhaps Mavis and Beatrice would take them in, but that would only be a temporary fix. Word would get out soon enough that Lydia had taken Wyatt without his father's permission, and she'd be forced to return him. Joseph put on a good front when it came to dealings with the community. It was very unlikely anyone would ever believe her.

Joseph hadn't been this way when her mother had first married him, at least not that he'd let on. But as the years went by, they'd begun to see another side to him. When the war ended, he refused to comply with the mandatory release of his slaves. He kept several of the men in shackles in the barn and outbuildings and used the well-being of their loved ones to keep them compliant.

Lydia began to pray, and immediately Ben came to mind. She hated to put his family in jeopardy, but she knew he'd come through for her. She could release Ben, and he could go for help. He had connections with other freed slaves, and she knew he was in the process of arranging for his own release.

But the wedding was tomorrow. She didn't have any more time. If they worked together, perhaps she and her siblings could go away with Ben tonight. They'd have to take Sadie, Ben's wife, along, too. It would be too dangerous to leave her behind. Her hopes sank. They'd make a large entourage in their quest for escape. Not the best of plans, but she had nothing else in mind.

Lydia waited until she was sure Wyatt had fallen into a deep sleep before slipping out of bed. She donned the outfit she'd worn to town, pulled on thick wool leggings, and laced up her boots. She threw a warm wrap over her shoulders before making her way silently down the long upper hall. Her stepfather's loud snores drowned out any noise she created. She made her way through the lower level of the house and stepped into the kitchen. It took her a moment to locate the key to Ben's shackles and remove it from its hiding place. She clasped it tightly in her hand. A moment later she slipped through the back door and stepped out into the cold night air.

Her boots crunched on the frozen ground as she made her way to the barn. Ben was highly regarded by the other slaves. To counteract any chance of rebellion, Joseph kept him separated from them. The looming structure looked sinister in the darkness. Lydia ran her hand along the rough wood until she came to the entrance. The large door squeaked loudly as she carefully tugged it open.

"Who's there?" Ben's deep voice called through the darkness.

"It's me, Ben. Lydia. I'm in trouble."

"Get out of the cold, child, and close the door." Ben's chains clanked as he closed the gap between them. "What kind a trouble you in, girl? You and me both be in a heap o' trouble if the master finds you out here wit' me."

"I know, Ben, and I'm sorry to drag you into this. It's just that I don't have any other options."

"What you need me to do?"

Lydia wanted to hug the man. He'd been her ally since she first moved to the plantation, and she knew she could trust him now. "Joseph just announced that he intends to marry me tomorrow." The words rushed out on a sob. "I can't marry him, Ben."

"Of course ya can't. What we gonna do 'bout it? Do ya have a plan?"

"No. I know you've been making plans, and I'm hoping you can take us along with you. Just me, Wyatt, Natalie, and Nathan."

"The plans aren't fully in place, Miss Lydie, and that'd be quite a group."

"I know, but maybe you could hurry the plans along? We could all leave now. I'll sneak back in and get the others." She was pleading now. "Please, Ben."

"Let me think." Ben shuffled back and forth in the darkness between them. "Joseph will come after us if we take your kin. Especially if we wuz to take Wyatt. You have no right to him."

"We can't leave him behind. Joseph doesn't care about him, and you know it."

"He takes pure pride in his ownership, Miss Lydie. I can attest to that."

"I know, Ben."

"Joseph'll make an issue if we takes Wyatt, sure as he'll throw charges 'gainst me."

"He has to find us first." The first ray of hope shot through Lydia. "Stop pacing. I brought the key to unlock your shackles. Let me release them."

Ben froze in place. Lydia felt her way through the darkness and dropped to her knees. She reached forward and felt her way along the cold steel of his chains. She hated her stepfather for treating Ben this way. She felt a certain satisfaction in rebelling against Joseph.

"Ya do realize what'll happen to us if we gets caught, Miz Lydie—to all of us if ya bring your kin along."

Ben's dire words hung in the air.

"It's a risk I'm willing to take. Staying here is no longer an option." She hesitated. "But I don't want to drag you into my mess unless you're sure, Ben."

"My days be numbered, too. I might as well go along with ya." It was his turn to hesitate. "They took my Sadie away earlier this afternoon, Miz Lydie. Master Joseph done sent her away."

"Sadie? No. I saw her before I went into town."

"And after ya left, Master Joseph had a visitor, and that visitor left with my Sadie. She sat in his wagon, tears rollin' down her face. I couldn' do nothin' 'bout it."

"Are you sure?" Lydia's heart sank. Sadie worked for them in the kitchen. She'd made their breakfast that morning. As long as Ben did as he was told, Joseph left them both alone. "Why would he let Sadie go? Maybe she's gone off to help someone in need."

"I don't know why he'd let her go unless he somehow got wind of my plans. But she be gone for sure. She don't cry like that 'cause she's off to help someone in need. He done knowed about my plans."

"He'd have made an example of you if he did." Another shiver rocked Lydia's body. "But with Sadie gone, you have nothing to lose by leaving."

"That be true, Miz Lydie."

"I'm going for the others. We'll meet you back here." Lydia headed for the door. "Be careful, Ben."

"I be careful and then some, Miss Lydie. You be careful, too."

Even though Lydia inched the door open this time, it still creaked loudly.

"Lydia?" Her stepfather's voice bellowed across the yard.

Terror moved through Lydia.

"Ben, go lie down and pretend to be asleep. I'll act like I was just going in, not leaving. If I don't come back down with the others in thirty minutes, go for help on your own."

"Lydia!" Her stepfather yelled. "I hear you over by the barn."

"I'm here, Joseph."

Ben's chains clanked as he gathered them up, then he rustled his way back to his sleeping area at the back of the barn. She heard his soft snores as her stepfather drew near.

"What do you think you're doing out here in the dark? You think you can get away from me?"

The moonlight shone down and distorted his angry face. He looked more menacing than ever.

"And leave Wyatt and the others behind? Do you really think I'd do that?"

"Then what are you doing out here, sneaking around in the dark?"

"I heard a noise and came out to investigate."

"What made the noise?"

"I don't know. It must have been the animals. All seems well from what I can see."

Joseph stepped closer to the slightly open door. They could hear Ben's snores loud and clear.

"Get yourself on back inside."

"Yes, sir." Lydia forced her tonality to be civil and hoped he saw her obedience as acquiescence. She took a few more steps. Suddenly the rough hands of one of Joseph's men grabbed her from behind. Lydia fought but couldn't get free. Her stepfather's harsh laugh sounded from a few feet away.

"How stupid do you think I am, Lydia?"

Lydia froze. She was sure the question was rhetorical, though she longed to answer in full honesty.

Instead she hedged. "I'm afraid I don't know what you mean."

"You know exactly what I mean. You have no intention of marrying me in the morning. You're sneaking around out here trying to find a way out of our nuptials."

All coherent thought fled from Lydia's mind. "No—I—"

He slapped her hard against the face.

She whipped her head up and glared at him. "Fine, so what if I was? You can't make me marry you against my will. The preacher will never allow it."

Joseph's face was full of hatred.

"Fine. We won't marry."

It was too easy. He never gave in without punishment.

"What are you going to do?"

"I'm giving you your freedom."

Maybe she'd misread him. Maybe he had some decency left in him after all. "My freedom?"

"Yes. Your freedom. I'm sending you away. I'll marry Natalie instead. I'm sure she'll be much more open to the idea than you were, once she hears what happened to you when you refused me."

"Why you evil, hateful. . ." Lydia fought hard against the hands that held her. "I hate you."

The person behind her jerked hard, making her teeth rattle and slam down on her tongue. She tasted blood.

Joseph laughed at her. "The feeling is mutual."

She lowered her head. She couldn't let him send her away like this. She needed to protect her siblings. "Fine. I'll stay. I'm sorry. I'll marry you. Please." Lydia's voice sounded panicked, even to her own ears. "Please. Give me another chance."

He waved her off. "Too late. Do what you want with her, boys, but get her as far away from here as possible before dumping her body. I have no further need for the girl."

Chapter 4

If you had listened to me and headed for the cabin last night, Shane, you wouldn't have lost all that money at the saloon," Gabriel scolded. "And you wouldn't have had to pay for the hotel. We'd be eating breakfast with your sisters and making our plans for the day."

He'd been yammering about Shane's choice ever since they'd left the hotel an hour earlier.

"And we'd have spent a long, chilly night on the hard, cold floor of the cabin," Shane threw back over his shoulder. "Or worse, we'd have slept in the barn with the horses and the cows. Wasn't the expense for a hotel room worth it for that? Now we've had a good night's sleep, and we're fresh to deal with the girls. We need to figure out where to place them next."

Gabriel shook his head. "I still don't understand why you won't settle down and raise Lucy and Savannah on your own."

"For the hundredth time, Gabriel, I'm not meant to be a family man. Haven't I seen that proved time and again? I lost my parents, my fiancée set her sights on another man and ran off with him, the war took both my brothers—trust me, the girls are better off with a loving family than they are with a bitter old brother like me."

"Better off? They're so unruly and resentful at being left that they get sent away from every home you place them in so you'll come back for them. They're both determined to fight for your love and affection and security. They want to be with you. And you're hardly old."

"I feel like I am. I know you fancy the idea of me raising the girls, but it's not gonna happen, Gabe. You—along with Savannah and Lucy—might as well accept that as fact. As soon as I figure out the girls' next placement, I'll be on my way. Alone."

"Oh no you don't. You aren't going to leave me behind."

"Watch me."

"You've tried to lose me over and over through the years and haven't ever succeeded. You don't want to leave me behind. I think it's time you realize you depend on me."

"I depend on you? You follow my heels at every turn, making my life—" Shane's voice stopped abruptly as they topped the hill that led to the cabin.

"Making your life what, Shane?" Gabriel, a few paces behind him, couldn't see what Shane saw.

Shane yanked his horse to a standstill, speechless, as Gabriel rode up beside him. The scene in the valley set his stomach to churning. His breath came in quick gasps as he tried to take it all in.

"Shane?" Gabriel looked from Shane's horror-struck expression to the ruins that lay before them.

"The girls. The cabin. This is my fault." Small wisps of smoke rose from the burned rubble that had once been the house where his sisters had lived. "I could have prevented this."

"Shane."

"No." The tortured word slipped past Shane's lips. "What have I done? You're right. We could have been here last night, just like you said. That's fresh damage. If we had come last night, we could have saved them. Surely God wouldn't take my sisters, too."

"Maybe they're in the barn."

Shane took off at a hard gallop, leaving Gabriel to follow behind. He headed straight for the barn, calling Savannah's name. As he neared the open door, he yanked hard on the reins and hit the ground at a run. He entered the eerie quiet of the barn.

"Vannah?" An unnatural silence met his ears, dashing his hopes and confirming his worst fears. "The animals are gone."

"Maybe Maria took them to a neighbor's after the fire started."

"Always the optimist, aren't you, Gabriel? Look around you. Does it look like they cleared out and went to a neighbor's? Would they have abandoned the farm like this?" Shane stalked toward the skeletal remains of the cabin. "I suppose they loaded up their chickens and cows and horses and took them along with them while the house burned down. Why would they do that, knowing they'd be back to try to salvage the house? Where are the neighbors? Wouldn't they have come right over to help?"

Gabriel stood silent and let Shane lash out. His eyes reflected Shane's heartache.

"Where else would the animals be, Shane? They didn't get out on their own."

The acrid stench of burned lumber blew toward them on the breeze. Shane moved closer.

Gabriel touched his arm. "Don't, Shane. Let me."

"No, it's my fault. I want to look in the face of the damage I've caused."

"It's not your fault."

Shane froze in place and watched his friend walk toward the debris. He tried to convince himself that the burning sensation behind his eyes was caused by the blowing ash.

He clenched his hands. He reared his head back and roared. "Lucy! Savannah!"

Gabriel jumped, but no childish voices responded. Gabriel continued his trek into the debris.

Shane shook his fist at the sky. "You did this to me! Why? One miracle, is that so much to ask? I just need one chance for things to go right."

Fact was, Shane hadn't wanted the girls, and God had taken them away. Shane had chance after chance to care for them, and he'd chosen to place them anywhere but in his own protective care. It was his fault, not God's. He hadn't even said good-bye the last time he'd left them.

Lucy always cried and hung on his hem while Savannah gave him the silent treatment when he'd prepare to leave. They'd wanted to be with him, and self-ishly he'd convinced himself that he needed to earn their keep by gambling, an occupation that didn't allow him to drag along two small girls. The last time he'd left, he'd snuck out in the middle of the night in order to avoid the tantrums.

If he could do it all again, he would do things so much differently. He'd stay with them. He'd find a way to be the man they needed him to be.

"Shane. There's something over here you need to see."

Shane's stomach churned. He didn't want to see whatever Gabriel had to show him, but he deserved it. While he'd lain all cozy in the warm, soft bed at the hotel, his sisters had faced—this inferno.

He sluggishly moved forward. "What is it?"

"Nothing."

"You called me over to see nothing?"

"I don't see any—remains."

"Maybe the fire burned too hot."

"I don't think so. Everything else is here, charred, but intact. The bed frame, the dressing table, the kitchen table. A hot fire would have reduced it all to dust."

Shane saw something pink by the woodbox. A small, simmering pile of rubble on the far side of the cabin popped. He walked over and picked up the pink-clad object. He started to laugh, the sound harsh. "Lucy's doll."

The smoke-damaged doll had survived the fire. The doll he'd brought her as a peace offering the last time he'd seen them. Just before he'd left them with Maria.

"A stupid cloth doll made it through the fire. The woodbox full of kindling made it through intact."

He glanced around at all the stray pieces of firewood scattered around the plank floor. "Why didn't this wood catch fire?"

"Looks like the fire blew the other way. It seems to have started in the corner by the bed."

"Lot of good that did the girls."

"Based on the blankets here in the corner nearest the woodbox, the girls slept in this corner of the cabin."

"While I slept in my nice hotel bed."

Shane picked up a random piece of wood and flung it forcefully at the woodbox. The loud clatter and vibrations caused the wood inside the box to shift.

Gabriel didn't answer. He just stood there, staring at Shane. "We should go."

Shane glared at the woodbox. The stupid thing stood there untouched. It should have burned. "Remember when Savannah climbed in the one at home while they were playing hide-and-seek?"

"I do." Gabriel's eyes pleaded for Shane to stop talking and start walking.

Shane knew Gabriel wanted to keep him away from the pain the memories would bring up.

Gabriel took a deep breath. "She was bit by a snake and swore she'd never go near another woodbox again."

"She was so sick from the bite. We didn't think she'd make it."

"But she did." Gabriel grinned. "She's a little fighter." His grin disappeared just as quickly as he realized what he'd said. "I'm sorry."

Shane picked up another large piece of wood and threw it at the box. "If she hadn't been so terrified of the snakes, maybe she would have crawled inside and survived."

"Shane—" Gabriel flinched as Shane hurled a third log with all his might at the wooden structure.

Shane didn't care. He picked up two more and hurled them in the same direction before he stalked toward his horse.

He swung up on Pal's back and spurred him into action. He heard Gabriel behind him as he hurried to keep up. Blinding tears flowed freely. He'd made it to the edge of the barn when a piercing shriek stopped him.

At first he thought Gabriel had taken his grief to the extreme, but when Shane spun around, Gabriel looked as startled as he felt.

"Did you hear that?"

Shane nodded. He slid his shotgun from the saddle as Gabriel did the same with his rifle. They turned their horses and rode over to the woodbox.

The scream sounded again, louder than before. Shane jumped down and tripped as he scrambled to get back to the woodbox. He steadied himself with a hand in the dirt and kept going. Gabriel rode up close behind him. Shane flung the lid open with his free hand and looked down into Savannah's precious, angry, soot-covered face.

Tears coursed through the black, leaving trails down her cheeks. Shane followed the motion of her terrified eyes and saw a piece of wood that resembled a snake, coiled like it was hissing, on the top layer of wood beside her. The wood, knocked off balance when Shane had thrown the logs, had pinned Savannah in place.

"It's okay, sweetheart. Look here, it's just a piece of wood."

Shane quickly dropped his shotgun. He pulled Savannah from the box and hugged her against his chest.

His eight-year-old sister shoved him away. "'Bout time y'all *finally* decided to get here."

A wave of relief rolled through Shane. With her perpetual scowl in place, it seemed Savannah would be just fine. He pulled her close again. "Where's Lucy?"

"Shane. I can't breathe." She struggled to push him away again, her complaint muffled against the front of his shirt.

He relaxed his hold, but didn't let go. Her warm, safe little body felt so good in his arms.

"Lucy's still in there." She pointed behind her toward the woodbox. "She's scared."

Shane picked Savannah up and walked over to look into the box.

Lucy lay curled in the farthest corner, motionless, her eyes wide with fear.

Shane kissed Savannah's head before handing her off to Gabriel. Gabriel wrapped her in his arms, his face crinkled with concern. Shane saw the unspoken question in his eyes. *Why wasn't Lucy making some sort of noise? Had she been injured by the falling wood?*

"Luce." Choked up, Shane reached inside for his youngest sister. He gingerly lifted her out, pulling her warm body against him with relief.

"She's alive." He caught Gabe's eye and laughed. "They're both alive, Gabe!"

"So I see." Gabe's smile was every bit as big as Shane's as he hugged Savannah close. Savannah snuggled into her brother's friend's secure embrace, her narrowed eyes following Shane's every move.

"Let's get them over to that tree." Shane motioned toward the large Spanish moss–draped oak tree that grew tall against the barn. "Something isn't right with Lucy. We need to check them both for injuries."

"Shane?"

"Yes, Vannah?"

"Emma's in there, too."

"What?" Shane wasn't sure he'd heard her right. Emma was Maria's four-year-old daughter, same age as Lucy. Savannah had to be mistaken. They'd been through a rough night. He hadn't seen anyone else in the box.

"Emma's still in there, Shane. I could feel Lucy breathing, but Emma didn't move at all. Is she all right?"

Gabriel let Savannah slide to the ground and reached for Lucy. Savannah clung to Gabe's side. Shane handed Lucy over and hesitantly peeked into the woodbox. He saw another small body nestled in the closest corner. The only possible way for all three girls to fit was for Savannah to have pushed her way up near the piece of wood that she thought was a snake. Shane had received his miracle. His sisters were safe.

Emma shifted when he touched her.

"It's all right, honey. I'm going to get you out of there."

She didn't respond, and his heart sank. He reached down to pick her up. Her body also felt warm. A bit too warm. He glanced over at Savannah. "She's just sleeping."

Relief filled her eyes. "There wasn't much room. I tried to get the lid open, but I couldn't." Her tears started again. She angrily swiped at them with the back of her hand.

Shane adjusted Emma in his arms and reached to pull his traumatized sister close. "Let's get out of here."

They guided the girls to the nearby tree and settled them in the grass.

"Did the shifting wood hurt anyone?"

"No." Savannah pushed her dark hair away from her face. "I was closest and kept the little girls below me."

"You did good, Vannah. I'm really proud."

Her blue eyes, so similar to his, stared up at him. Her hesitant smile lit his heart.

Shane glanced over at Emma. "We need to check the little girls, and then I'll look you over, okay?"

"I'm fine."

"All the same, I'll feel better if I make sure."

Savannah nodded.

Gabriel brought over the horses and removed some packages from the saddlebags. "Who wants something to eat?"

With Savannah distracted by the snack, Shane gave the younger girls his full attention. Lucy appeared to be sleeping, but Shane feared she might have been hurt by one of the logs. He carefully removed her clothes and checked her for any signs of bruising. Her too-thin frame bothered him. He threw her soot-covered clothes into a pile and covered her with a blanket.

He did the same with Emma. No signs of a mark on her either, but she felt a little warm.

"Savannah, has Emma been sick?"

Worry creased Savannah's face. "Yes. She got sick before Maria."

"Maria was sick?"

"Yes."

Shane had to listen close to hear her grief-stricken words.

"I guess I kilt her. I helped Maria take care of Emma, and Emma started to get better. But then Maria got sick, too. I did the same things for her, but she didn't get better. I brought her tea. I made cool cloths for her forehead. But the last two days, she didn't move."

"What happened last night, Van?"

"Some men came. One wanted Maria to marry him, but he wasn't very nice. I was scared. They banged on the door so I made the little girls get in the wood-box through the little inside door. Lucy cried, but I told her we had to be quiet and brave. Emma was sleeping so I put her in first, then I got in and thought I heard snakes. I told Lucy I'd get closest to them and protect her. I had her hand, and she dropped her doll. I made her get in without the doll. Lucy got mad at me and didn't talk to me again."

"That's okay, Van. I have the doll. We found it in the cabin."

Savannah's deep blue eyes twinkled. "She'll be happy to know that. You should wake her up and tell her."

"Let's let her sleep a bit longer. I think she's really tired. What happened next after you got in the box?"

"The men banged around a bit. They said Maria was dead and they'd need to bury her. They said they'd split the animals between them. They were banging stuff around and said something caught on fire. Then I thought I heard snakes and was too scared to move."

"Maria's sickness caused her demise, Van. You didn't kill Maria. You kept the little girls safe. That's all that matters."

"I fell asleep and didn't wake up until I heard something banging on the woodbox. I think it was giant snakes trying to get us."

"No, Van, I was the one who was banging. That was only me. I thought I'd lost you, and I got angry and threw several logs at the box. I didn't know you were in there. I'm sorry I scared you."

"You didn't know." She shrugged and pinned him with her gaze. "But now that you have us back, you'll have to keep us. Right?"

Shane evaded her question. Savannah narrowed her dark blue eyes and stared him down, a perfect imitation of Gabriel's glare. Gabriel loudly cleared his throat before stomping off to the pump. Now he'd have both of them petitioning him to settle down. Shane turned to Emma.

"Emma." He gently shook the little girl. "Emma, wake up."

Emma opened her eyes, focused, and began to wail. Shane held her close and rocked her until she quieted.

Gabriel returned with a piece of cloth he'd dampened at the pump. "You sure look like a family man to me."

Shane ignored him and cleaned Emma's face before pulling two new dresses and fresh sets of underclothes from one of the packages he'd brought along for the girls—this trip's peace offering. He'd brought the clothes for Lucy, but Emma needed something to wear, too.

"Look here at these pretty dresses, Em. Which one do you like?"

Emma pointed to the light blue dress.

"Vannah, can you come over here and help Emma get dressed while I take care of Lucy?"

Savannah flipped her disheveled hair over her shoulder and eyed the new dresses as she moved to Emma's side.

"I have a package for you, too, Van."

She shrugged. Now that she felt secure, she was going to give Shane her indifferent side. It happened every time he returned. He always arrived bearing gifts, and she always acted like she didn't care.

According to Gabriel, she really didn't care. On the heels of the thought, Gabriel leaned close. "She wants you, not the gifts, Shane."

Shane reached for Lucy. He freshened her up and slipped the pink dress over her head. His large fingers had a hard time fastening the tiny buttons. She could pass as Emma's twin with her blond hair and blue eyes. Eyes he wanted to see right now. He shook her shoulder. "Luce. Wake up."

Lucy shrugged his hand away and burrowed deeper against Shane's chest. He grinned and persisted. "Luce."

She wriggled in his arms and finally opened her eyes and looked up at him. She mouthed his name, but no sound came out.

"You need a drink? Is your throat sore?"

She nodded.

"I'll get her a drink." Gabe was on his feet and hurrying back toward the pump.

She clung to Shane, and he held her close for a few minutes.

"Luce, I'm going to leave you with Gabe and check on Savannah."

Lucy glanced over at Gabriel, who'd arrived with the water, and reached up to cling to Shane.

"I'll ready the horses." Gabriel walked away to give them some privacy.

Savannah looked up from her package of clothes. She yanked her new hairbrush through her tangled hair. "I told you I'm fine."

Shane settled Lucy beside him on the blanket. "I know you did."

With a sigh she scooted closer. Shane held up a blanket, and she stripped down to her underclothes. He checked her back and neck specifically, still not believing she hadn't been hurt. "There's nothing here."

"I told you."

He wrapped the blanket around her. "Why don't you slip over there to the barn and put on your new clothes? Bring the sooty ones back so we can wash them down the road."

She grabbed her package and scampered off with the blanket held tight around her.

"God gave you your miracle. Are you going to throw it in His face?" Gabriel called out.

"No, I'm not going to throw it in His face, Gabe. I haven't said a thing about what I'm going to do."

"We should go back to town."

Shane contemplated his next words carefully. "I'm thinking we should return to the family homestead."

Gabriel nervously cleared his throat. "The, um, *the* family homestead? As in *your* family homestead?"

"Yes, Gabriel. My family homestead. Who else's homestead would I return to?"

"This is unexpected."

Shane leaned around and looked up at his friend. "You have a problem with us going back? I thought this was what you've been wanting."

"Well, it is. But after all this time I didn't think you'd really consider it."

"What am I missing, Gabe? Is there something I need to know?"

"No. It's just, the house—"

"I know how things grow around here. The house is probably buried beneath a layer of vines. It's not like I expect the house to be as I left it."

Gabriel muttered. "That's an understatement."

"I'm not worried about the house, Gabe. We need a place where we can settle in while we figure out what we'll do next. I want to be with the girls. I still don't feel like I'm cut out to be a family man, but I don't want to leave them."

Their conversation was interrupted by the arrival of a dark, emaciated man.

Chapter 5

The man's slow, shuffling footsteps were muffled by the dirt road. Gabriel hurried over to help him. His dust-coated bare feet and torn, filthy clothes told of a long journey or at the very least, hard days of neglect.

The man waved him off. "I's a slave from the Maxwell Plantation. I need help searchin' for my mistress. She be in trouble."

Shane and Gabriel exchanged glances.

Gabriel laid a gentle hand on the man's arm. "With all due respect, the war is over and has been for several years. Slavery has been outlawed."

"Tell my owner." The man raised his pant leg and showed the deep scars from years in shackles, some of the abrasions quite fresh.

"That's just wrong." Gabriel's voice shook with outrage.

The man's agitation continued. "I'm Ben. My master done sent my wife away yesterday. Last night, he say he gonna force marriage on his wife's oldest daughter."

"His stepdaughter?" Shane tried to follow the man's frantic words.

The man nodded.

"I take it she wasn't agreeable with the choice of groom?"

"No suh. My master be the groom of choice."

"I see." Shane remembered what happened to his mother after her sorry choice of a spouse. His father had left her alone with Shane and his brothers while he continued his travels on the gambling circuit. He'd returned a total of two times, those two visits producing Savannah and Lucy. After Lucy's birth, they'd never heard from him again. Shane was sure he was cut from the same cloth and hoped he could do right by the girls. "What happened next?"

"She done refused him. She run out in the dark o' night to get my help. She unlocked my shackles, but her father, he caught her."

"He knew she released you?" That didn't bode well. If the man was corrupt enough to keep slaves after the law declared it illegal, he'd not hesitate in correcting his rebellious stepdaughter.

"No. She told a story to divert his attentions. He act like he gonna go along with it, but then two of his men, they grab her, and he send her off wit' them."

Shane's jaw clenched. He didn't sit well with anyone who mishandled a woman or child. "Sent her off where?"

"I dunno, suh. I waited till I wuz sure it be safe, and I came fo' help. You the first people I seen." He glanced at the remains of the smoldering cabin. "And it look like you down on yo' luck, too."

A couple of thoughts warred in Shane's mind. He'd made it clear that he wasn't a family man, nor did he want anyone to rely on him. Despite that fact, he had Gabriel, Savannah, Lucy, and Emma to deal with. Now this man showed up needing help, not only for himself, but for someone else.

Yet Shane couldn't deny he'd been given a second chance with his sisters. If they needed help and he wasn't around, he hoped someone would step in to help them. It only took a moment for Shane to act.

"We only have two horses for six people. It'll be slow going." He looked at the man's weak body and sore feet. "We can take turns riding and walking."

"Or," Savannah piped in for the first time, "we can round up Twister and take him along with us."

"Twister?" Shane motioned toward the barn. "All the animals are gone."

"I doubt Twister is." Savannah's smile quirked up at the corner. "You know how Twister hates strangers. When the men tried to get him last night, I heard one scream that the palomino had bit him. There's no way Twister let that man capture him."

"Twister." Shane grinned. "Ornery old boy. Where is he?"

"Most likely in the trees behind the barn. He never goes far."

"Hurry and round him up, and we'll be on our way."

Savannah's mount was as stubborn as his young owner. They made a great pair, Twister not doing any better with strangers than Savannah. For the first time ever, Shane was grateful for the willful horse's trait.

Gabriel looked at Emma, who now sat quietly on the blanket, watching the men as they talked. He lowered his voice. "What are we going to do with Emma?"

Shane raised a shoulder. "We're taking her with us. What choice do we have? Maria was a widow who had no relatives or close friends. The girls are the closest thing Emma has to family. She's my responsibility as much as the other girls are."

A flash of humor passed through Gabriel's eyes, but the man was smart enough to stay quiet. Shane spun on his heels and went to help Savannah round up her wayward horse.

They made quite a sight as they rode out. Gabriel rode Twister, the cantankerous creature taking up all his attention as they took the lead. Savannah sat beside Shane on the seat of the old buckboard the marauders had left untouched in the barn. Pal, along with some help from Gabriel's horse Chester, pulled the wagon.

Lucy and Emma curled up on Gabriel's bedroll in the back of the wagon. They quickly dropped off to sleep. Ben rode along with them. The exhausted and emaciated man was in no condition to fight high-spirited horses like Pal and Twister. He let down his guard and settled in. He was asleep almost as quick as the little girls.

Shane sighed as he surveyed the group of people scattered around him.

God, I told You I wasn't worth anything to anyone and I didn't want to be respon-sible for a family. Yet You've placed one person after the next in my care. I'll do my best to handle things as they are, but I'd be mighty obliged if You'd take these burdens from me as soon as possible.

❧

Lydia had survived the long night, no thanks to her horrible stepfather and his cruel intentions.

She welcomed the stillness and thanked God that a few hours earlier, when the men had dumped her into the brush at the edge of the road, she'd been dumped without the men taking any liberties. She had no idea where she was. When they left the plantation, they'd taken the dirt road that led from the fam-ily estate and turned the opposite direction from town. She'd lost track of their travels when they took a fork in the road that led to higher ground. The plan— at least according to their detailed conversation as they traveled—had been for them to toss her off the side of the mountain. A chilly rain pushed their hand, and they'd pulled her off the wagon earlier than expected in their hurry to get back to the plantation.

Lydia felt the cold and was aware that lying here on the damp ground might not be the best idea. But for the moment, she remained there and savored the fact that she was safe and free from the despicable men who had taken her from the plantation.

The breezy morning air permeated the cloth of her dress, and she snuggled deeper into her wrap, a part of her willing the comforting darkness to return while the other part of her knew she needed to go for help and get back to her siblings on the plantation. No way would she leave them in her stepfather's care a moment longer than necessary. An internal prompting to move had her pushing up on her elbows. Her head throbbed. Her eyes squinted against the brightness as she took in her surroundings. The effort was rewarded with shooting pain that cascaded through her temples.

Thick, overgrown trees above her and the partially overcast sky blocked her direct view of the morning sun, preventing her from figuring out the time. Based on the slant, though, she thought it was midmorning. She listened for a moment, suddenly afraid to tarry. What if her stepfather had second thoughts and decided to come back for her? Or maybe he'd send his men back to fetch her. Or worse, perhaps they'd return to make sure their plan had worked and if they found her alive—they'd feel the need to remedy the situation.

Lydia had no idea if Ben had made it off the plantation. He might have decided to reattach the shackles and stay put. She wouldn't blame him if he did. Her situation proved Joseph had no qualms when it came to showing his evil nature.

She needed to find help on her own. She couldn't rely on anyone else. If Ben had managed to safely escape the plantation, her siblings didn't know where she was—and who knew what story Joseph would concoct for them. Nathan was already wary of the man, and if he had any suspicion that Joseph had orchestrated Lydia's disappearance—Nathan's wrath would equal or surpass Joseph's. She couldn't stand the thought of Nathan getting hurt.

Dear Lord, please keep Joseph away from me as I work my way home. Please watch over Wyatt, Natalie, and Nathan. Please keep Ben safe, too. Protect them all until I can think of a way to help them. Please let me find help and a trustworthy friend—soon.

The whispered prayer uttered under the tranquil morning light brought her a small measure of peace. Lydia couldn't get over the serenity and quiet of the area surrounding her. Even the local creatures were still, her presence putting them on alert.

Her head hurt, and she debated staying in place a bit longer or trying to get up and go for help. The cool air muddled her mind. Or maybe it was the head wound that muddled her thoughts. The wooziness overcame her determination to find help. She closed her eyes and tried to drift off, but thoughts of her stepfather's return prevented sleep from returning.

She pushed to her feet, glad she'd taken the time to pull on the wool leggings before heading out to request Ben's assistance. Though her feet were cold, she wasn't in jeopardy of suffering from frostbite from the early spring night spent out in the elements. She stood on shaky legs and tried to ignore the throbbing in her head and aches and pains of her body.

The men had discussed their choices for her demise in depth and had argued about the best way to go about it, but in the end the dropping temperature, rain, and late hour had won out, and they'd decided to dump her over the side of the road. In the dark they'd chosen the wrong spot, and instead of falling to her demise, she'd only suffered a hard wallop to her head. She'd fought them, and they'd kicked and hit until they were able to push her off the wagon. With a scream, she'd flown backward into the darkness. Her head struck a tree or something just as unforgiving and that was all she remembered until she'd awakened, miraculously alive.

She felt sure God had used the weather conditions to spare her from further abuse and death, and to get her away from Joseph, but her siblings weren't as fortunate. They weren't safe as long as Joseph was with them.

Lydia had to get back to Wyatt and the twins. She had to get home before Natalie's eighteenth birthday. In two short weeks, they'd celebrate, and Joseph would announce his plans. She took a step and stumbled. Dizziness set her head to swirling. She paused, leaning against the rough bark of a nearby tree with a shaky hand.

The gambler's face chose that moment to appear in her thoughts, and she semismiled. He'd seemed so confident on the walkway while taking care of the inebriated man. He'd seemed so thoughtful and charming when he looked her way and winked and left to take the man inside. She'd love to have the aid of someone like him right about now.

Reason pushed that thought away. He'd also snagged her brother by the shirt when Wyatt made him lose his nefarious card game. The scoundrel. Lydia frowned. He hadn't actually hurt the boy. In fact, in light of the seriousness of what Wyatt did, the man had been amazingly patient with her brother. Wyatt thought him the perfect hero. Lydia needed a hero. She needed a knight in shining armor to ride in and save her. The handsome gambler would be perfect for the feat. She sighed and smiled another dreamy smile.

If he were there, she'd swoon and peer into his handsome face. He'd catch her and grin, his smile charming. His long, dark hair would fall into his face, and she'd gently push it away, tucking it behind his ear so she could better see his deep blue eyes.

Lydia put a hand to her head and forced away the irrational musings. Her head wound must be worse than she thought. The last thing she needed was a gambler—an untrustworthy man of any sort—invading her life. And to stand here while her mind wandered wasn't doing anyone any good.

Though Wyatt thought the man was the answer to all life's woes, Lydia knew better. She closed her eyes and leaned her forehead against the tree until the dizziness—and crazy notions—passed.

She pushed herself to carry on. She stepped over roots, slipped on the furry green moss that surrounded them, and pulled her way up the rocky incline until she reached the road. She half crawled onto the unkempt road and stood to survey her situation.

Spanish moss–draped oak trees and huge magnolias flanked both sides of the dirt road that stretched out before her. She didn't see any sign of a cabin or family home in either direction.

A barely discernable trail worked its way through the trees a few yards to her left. She could stay on the main road and hope she picked the right direction to reach the closest dwelling, or she could follow the trail and hope it led to someone's homestead. If she took the road, she could run into Joseph or his men. Though she'd kept track of the switchbacks as well as she could, the beating they'd given her just before they tossed her off the side of the mountain muddled her thoughts. She figured if she headed down the mountain, she'd eventually hit the road that led back to her home.

The protective safety of the brush-surrounded trail won out. Lydia began to hike, holding on to the trees and stopping to rest whenever she felt light-headed. Her entire body ached. Several times she swooned, sure she'd lose consciousness on the trail, but each time she rallied and made her way forward after the dizziness passed. She felt safe and protected as she walked through the wild palmettos, vines, and scrub that were on the verge of overtaking the path.

When she reached the end of the trail, she faced another open road instead of the cabin she'd hoped for. Tears of frustration blurred her vision. She wasn't sure if it was the original road the men had traveled the night before or one of the switchbacks, but it was better than being lost in the woods. Nothing looked familiar. The sun peeked out from behind the clouds and warmed her back.

Lydia had walked downhill the entire time. Chances were it was the same road they'd traveled up into the hills. That is, if they'd zigzagged up the mountain more than if they'd traveled around it. For all she knew, she could be on the far side of the mountain, walking away from home and farther into the wilderness. Panic threatened to overtake her. She forced herself to proceed with the thought she hadn't traveled that far away from home.

She tried to focus. If town was to the west of their plantation, she'd be east of home, based on the original direction they'd taken when leaving. If she was on the right path, she'd need to follow the sun's lead and head west. For now, the sun was directly overhead. She'd have to wait a bit to see which way the sun moved before she'd know which direction she'd need to travel. Of course if the sun didn't move parallel to the roadway, she'd know she was completely and hopelessly lost. She prayed the sun would move parallel to the road. Regardless, the road had to lead somewhere. She'd find her way in time.

Lydia released her breath with that thought and headed over to a soft patch of grass that surrounded a large magnolia. She settled beneath it, letting the sun warm her body through the branches. Her head pounded, and she knew she'd overdone it. The head injury should have taken precedence when she set her pace. She leaned back against the sturdy tree, closed her eyes, and contemplated her choices.

Unbidden, the image of the handsome man from the saloon returned to fill her head. He'd set her heart to fluttering out there on the walkway, there was no denying that. But she apparently had her mother's aptitude when it came to choosing men because the scoundrel had shown another side when she saw him in the saloon. She couldn't keep dwelling on him.

Scowling, she pushed the image away. She didn't need help from a man like him. As a matter of fact, she couldn't think of one single male she'd trust to help her. Most of the men on the neighboring plantations were loyal friends to her stepfather. They'd never believe her story. Frustrated, she tried to come up with a man-free plan. Maybe if she could get Nathan's attention out in the fields, they could work together to come up with a plan. Though he was male, he was trustworthy. If she caught him in the light of day, instead of in a panic in the middle of the night, perhaps he'd be reasonable and not act rashly. Returning to the plantation on her own seemed to be her best option.

Lydia's stomach rumbled, reminding her she hadn't eaten since the day before. She ignored it and tried to focus on her travels.

She felt it best to stick to the road. If Joseph or his men were going to come back to see how she'd fared after last night's venture, they surely would have been there by now. She felt a bit safer taking that route this time around. She didn't want to get caught in the woods later in the day when darkness fell. She'd feel safer sleeping—or at least trying to fall asleep—if she were near the road.

A lizard ran across her ankle, and she stifled her scream. Lizards she could deal with. Snakes she could not. She scoured the surrounding area, making sure no other living creature waited to catch her off guard. The effort distracted her. She wasn't paying attention to her surroundings and didn't hear the arrival of company until they were almost upon her.

Voices carried her way from up the road. In her panic that the newcomers would include Joseph or his hands—and after her past twenty-four hours, she wasn't about to take the time to see who was coming—she looked up and saw the low branches of the tree above her made a perfect climbing perch. She worked her way up into the tree, trying to keep the dizziness at bay, and waited.

Chapter 6

Shane scanned the road ahead. They needed to take a break. The little girls needed to stretch their legs, and everyone needed to eat. He saw an open grassy patch under a tree just ahead.

He called out to Gabe. "Let's pull off in that grassy spot." He motioned toward the side of the road.

Savannah sighed. "Why're we stopping so soon? There'll be plenty of chances to rest after we get home."

"We won't be long." Shane glanced over at her. "What's your hurry anyway?"

"I just wanna make sure we get there before you go changin' your mind about keepin' us."

"I'm not changing my mind. I have no one else to take you to right now, Van."

"Thanks. That's reassuring." Sarcasm dripped from her words.

"Listen, I'm not going anywhere. God just gave you back to me. I'm not letting you go anytime soon. I'm keeping you. Got it?" He felt her relax and rest her cheek against his arm.

For all her bravado and posturing, she was such a tiny thing. It suddenly dawned on him that when he'd left her behind, she'd been forced to be the strong one for Lucy. She'd picked up where he'd left off, just like their mother had when abandoned by his father.

"You ever realize how much you're like our ma?"

"I hardly remember her." Savannah shrugged. Her next words, quietly spoken, betrayed her attempt to feign indifference. "In what way? I mean, how d'you suppose I'm like her?"

"Mama had grit. Spunk. She found a way to survive, even when life was hard." And for her, life was always hard.

"What happened to our pa?"

"He didn't stick around long after Lucy was born."

"So I guess that makes you a lot like him."

Her words didn't sit well with Shane. All through the years he'd wondered why card games held so much more power over their father than his desire to be with his loved ones. As soon as Shane was old enough, he'd gone straight out to find the answer. He'd found that he had a knack for cards and learned cards had the same power over him.

Savannah was right. He'd let the cards become more important to him than the little sisters who needed him more than ever without their ma. "I'm sorry, Vannah. I don't want to be like him in that way."

"But our ma, she was a good person?"

"She was." Shane smiled. "She was a very good person. The best. She worked hard to provide for us."

At first he'd assured himself he was only playing the cards so he'd have money to send back to his ma. He'd been able to make her life easier in those last few years. But the cards had taken precedence over everything else. He should have been there for the girls, just as their pa should have been there for their ma.

"You know, if you found us a new ma, you wouldn't hafta be herdin' us all over Georgia."

Savannah's words almost made him fall off the wagon. He choked. "A ma? Where do you get such thoughts?"

"I've been thinkin'. If you found us a ma, we could go home and settle back in."

"We're going home now, Vannah. Isn't that what I've been saying?" Shane reiterated. Again. "And I haven't exactly sent you all over Georgia. Georgia covers a lot of area. Haven't you ever seen a map before? Our little area is only a small part of the whole."

"Sure, I learnt all about maps and Georgia in school." Savannah huffed. "Oh, wait, maybe I haven't learnt about it after all because I ain't never been to school."

Shane cringed. She had a point. He'd moved them around so much he hadn't really given the girls' schooling much thought. Gabriel had pressed him about the importance of Savannah's education a couple of years earlier, but Shane hadn't realized how quickly time had passed. He glanced back at her.

"Your lack of education is obvious in your choice of words. Since when have you used 'ain't' and 'learnt' anyway?"

He arrived at the tree. He jumped down from the wagon and reached up for Savannah. She ignored him and clambered to the ground. Lucy and Emma woke up, reached for Shane, and wandered around after he lifted them to the ground. Gabriel and Ben tended to the horses.

"I guess I learnt it since we lived with Maria. She talked like that all the time. I got used to hearin' it, and I guess I started sayin' it."

"Well, Mama raised you better. We'll work on proper language while we're at the house." And he'd make sure to pick more appropriate caretakers in the future, a feat that would add further challenge to their search.

"*While we're at the house.*" Savannah glared and dropped to a sitting position on the ground. "I knew it wouldn't last."

"We're going home, Savannah. Why can't that be enough? Let's take one day at a time and see what happens." Shane sank down beside her.

"I want to *stay* at home." Savannah's voice broke. "I heard you talkin' to Gabriel. You only plan to settle in long enough to figure out another place to send us."

"It's not practical to keep you with me. I have to work."

"You could find us a ma. She could watch us while you work. You could marry her and could stay home and be our pa. We'd be a family again."

"We're still a family, Van."

"I want a ma."

"And I'm not going to find you one. Settling down like that isn't in my plans, Savannah." A niggling thought made him pause. If he thought about it, planting his feet at home called to his heart. The thought scared him. "Listen, I'm doing the best I can. You're proving the fact I don't have a clue on the best way to raise you."

"If you found us a ma, she'd know how to raise us."

He leaned against the trunk of the tree and stretched his legs out in front of him. He crossed his ankles with an air of nonchalance. He held out his arms. "Fine, Savannah. I'll tell you what. If God wants me to find a wife and make her a ma for you girls, He'll have to drop her on my lap."

"You know that won't happen." Savannah narrowed her eyes and pinned him with a glare. Her nose wrinkled as she growled at him. "Don't make fun of me."

They froze in a standoff of wills. Shane wanted to laugh. His sister couldn't be any more like him in nature. He raised his eyebrow to egg her on, his arms still outstretched. Savannah slapped her arms into a folded position across her chest and resumed her pout.

"Sorry, sis, I guess it isn't meant to be." Shane wiggled his outstretched fingers. "If He'd wanted me to have a wife, she'd surely be here by now."

Savannah looked away.

He closed his eyes. "Are You sure, God? Vannah really wants a ma." He opened his eyes to see Savannah staring at him, her blue eyes questioning his sincerity. He felt a pang of guilt. Gabriel would be so disappointed in him.

I'm sorry, Lord, I didn't mean to be sarcastic or disrespectful. The wisp of a prayer surprised him.

"I'm sorry, Savannah. Gabriel has tried to teach me about God and His love for us. Sometimes I do stupid things without thinking." Shane relaxed his arms on his legs, palms up in a partial shrug. "That right there was a perfect example. If a person is going to talk to God, he should do it with respect and reverence."

Gabriel picked that moment to walk up.

"Shane, there's something I need to tell you—" He perused Shane's upturned arms. "What are you doing?"

"I was waiting for God to drop a ma for Vannah on my lap."

"I see." Gabriel shook his head, used to Shane's oddities. "As I was saying—"

166

A shrill scream filled the air, and a bedraggled woman fell from above, landing perfectly in Shane's relaxed arms.

"Aaaieee!" Shane jerked upright, the motion allowing the woman to settle fully onto his lap. "Wahh. . . ? How. . . ?"

Savannah screamed and scurried out of the way. Shane wanted to do the same, but remained frozen in place.

Emma and Lucy stood a few feet away and echoed Savannah's screams. They simultaneously burst into tears. Ben and Gabriel hurried over to scoop the girls up. Emma had been standoffish with the dark-skinned man earlier in the day, but now she buried her face against Ben's solid chest, her fear of the situation overtaking her fear of the now-familiar, kind man.

Gabriel stared, waiting for an explanation. "Shane?"

Shane shook his head. "Wh–wh—I don't understand."

"I do." Savannah had stopped screaming and crawled closer to Shane and the mysterious unconscious woman, seemingly over her initial shock. Her voice dropped to a reverent whisper. "You prayed for a ma for us girls, and God sent us one!"

"God sent us a ma?" Emma peeked around at the disheveled woman. Her face crumpled. "I want a clean ma like my last one. This one's all dirty and messy. I want my other ma back." She began to cry.

Lucy kept her head on Gabriel's shoulder, sucking on her thumb and watching with horrified eyes.

"You prayed for a ma for the girls, Shane? *That's* what you meant a moment ago?" Gabriel's voice was laced with disgust. "I hope you meant it from the heart because God doesn't want us taking prayer—"

"I already apologized to both God and Van, Gabe. And I sure didn't know God would answer! Not like this." Shane gently placed the woman on the soft grass and backed a safe distance away. "Not exactly anyway. I was just trying to prove a point to Savannah. Van said she wanted me to find them a ma and then settle in as the girls' pa. I said God would have to drop a ma for them on my lap."

"And He did." Savannah looked at Shane, her eyes full of wonderment. The wonderment changed to confusion, and her mouth dropped into a frown. "But I wanted a ma that could take care of us. Seems God sent us a broken-down one instead."

"He sure enough did answer that prayer, Savannah, whether Shane's words were heartfelt or not." Gabriel raised an eyebrow and sent Shane a pointed glare. He wrapped his arm around Savannah's shoulder. "God works in mysterious ways."

"My words were heartfelt," Shane muttered. He felt a certain level of satisfaction for placing the startled look on Gabriel's face.

Gabriel recovered quickly and leaned forward and peered at the woman. "She does look a bit worse for wear. Is she breathing?"

Worry crinkled Savannah's features. "She's all right, isn't she, Shane? Our new ma ain't already dead, is she?"

Shane didn't want to go near the woman. The past five minutes had taken at least a decade off his life. The whole day was something nightmares were made of—everything from finding the girls' home burned down to suddenly having six people in his care. He wanted nothing more at the moment than to hop on his mount and ride off into the sunset—alone. "I'm sure she's fine. She was breathing when I held her."

"You mean when God *dropped her on your lap*?" Gabriel inserted. "I'm telling you, Shane, God's trying to get your attention. I suggest you listen to Him."

"I'd listen to Him, too." Savannah nodded in agreement. "He sure enough did drop our ma right down, just as Shane asked Him to. She done fell straight out of the sky."

Ben had remained silent throughout the exchange. Shane looked over at him. Ben clutched Emma tight against him, looking like he'd seen a ghost.

"You okay, Ben? I'm sure she's fine, whoever she is."

"How'd she drop down from the sky like that?" Ben's words came in gasps. He slowly moved forward and deposited Emma next to Shane. "I ain't never seen nothin' like that in all my days."

"I don't figure she fell from the sky. More likely she was in the tree above us for some reason. She probably screamed because she lost her grip, and then she fainted from the fright." Shane motioned to Gabriel to come and sit with the girls. Gabriel brought Lucy and settled down between Emma and Savannah as Shane reluctantly moved forward to check on their new arrival.

The woman's face was hidden by her untidy hair. Shane gently pushed it back. She had a nasty gash on her forehead and several bruises on her face. "She's had a rough time."

Figures God would send me a misfit to mother the girls. Shane didn't deserve any better. His intentions the past few years hadn't exactly been the best when it came to a relationship with his heavenly Father. A sense of shame flowed through him. He'd told Savannah that their ma had taught her better when it came to her words and speech. Well, their ma had taught *him* better when it came to loving the Lord.

Shane felt compelled to whisper a heartfelt prayer for the woman, his first in a long, long time. God had blessed him through the well-being of his sisters. He'd allowed Emma to pull through the same illness that took her ma away from her. He'd answered Shane's sarcastic prayer for a ma for the girls in the most surprising manner. And Shane wondered if He'd possibly answered this broken and abused woman's prayer by sending them to help her.

Lord, it's been a long time since I've talked to You, and I'm sorry. I'm sorry for drifting away in anger. Instead of turning to You in my grief the past few years, I shut You out. You've tried to get my attention through Gabe, and I've continued to shut You out. I want the peace that he has. Please forgive me and take the lead in my life as I move forward. I want You at the reins wherever I go. I give You my heart, my future, and my will. I'll even give up my—he stuttered a bit on the next few words. They came hard for him—*my cards. I'll give them up for You. Amen.*

In that moment, as he stared down at the quiet form in front of him, Shane felt a powerful tug on his heart. All these years, everything Gabriel had told him, all his preaching and teaching—the words and the verses and the parables—now wrapped around him like a comforting cloak. He felt God's presence in a very real way, a presence he'd never felt before. He knew everything would work out for the best, for all of them, this strange woman included.

"This woman"—Ben's voice cut through Shane's wonderment—"she's my mistress—from the plantation."

Shane's focus had fully been on God and the miracle the past few minutes had worked in Shane's heart. He knew he had a long way to go, but this was a good start. Shane longed to explore the revelations more fully. He glanced up at the newcomer. "I'm sorry, Ben. What did you say?"

"The woman. She be my mistress from the plantation, Miz Lydia. And from the look o' things, those wicked men who took her sure did give her a beatin'." Anger laced his words.

A shock rolled through Shane's body. He pinched himself. Surely he was dreaming. The moment couldn't get any stranger. "Did you say—Lydia?"

"Yes, suh."

Shane tilted his head for a better look. Though beaten and dirty, he could see the similarities to the bright, clean, spunky woman he'd met in town, the one who had turned his head. His heart broke a little as he stared down at her. What horrors had she been through since she'd stood on the walkway in town the previous day? He was disappointed that on the heels of his reunion with God, white-hot anger like he'd never known roiled through his soul.

I'm sorry, Lord, but if I ever get my hands on the men who did this to her, I won't be able to control myself. I'm sorry for my thoughts and anger, but I hope righteous anger is acceptable.

Later he'd discuss his conflicting feelings and confusion with Gabriel. For now he needed to tend to the broken woman that God had laid before him. After that he'd go and set things to rights with her poor excuse of a stepfather.

He flinched as her eyes flickered. After their meeting in the saloon, she'd likely come after him like a wildcat.

Chapter 7

L ydia felt her world shift and tried to open her eyes. She peered up into a circle of faces, the nearest one vaguely familiar, the others a blur. She smiled at the man who leaned over her, then sighed as she cupped his cheek. "My hero. You came for me. You're my answer to prayer."

Shock filled the man's handsome features. His blue eyes widened as his hands waved out in front of him. "Huh-uh. You've got it all wrong. I'm nobody's hero. I'm far from a hero."

Judging by his reaction, of all the words he'd expected her to utter, those hadn't been anywhere close to the ones he'd conjured in his mind.

He scowled. "And I've never been called anyone's answer to prayer. I don't think that's right."

"You're wrong," Lydia argued. She caressed his rough cheek with her thumb. "I prayed for you, and here you are. God sent you here. You are the answer to my prayer."

A young voice agreed from somewhere behind him. "She's right, Shane."

The man momentarily closed his eyes as he cupped his hand over hers, holding the palm of her hand against his face for a moment longer.

Lydia could feel her heart beating loud and strong. Her hand tingled where his strong hand touched it. She wondered if he felt the strange sensations, too. He suddenly pulled her hand away from his face and cleared his throat. "You're hurt. What hurts the most?"

She grimaced. "Everything."

"Do you feel like anything's broken?" His reassuring grip on her elbow calmed her racing heart. He stared into her eyes.

"N–no." She had a hard time focusing when he stared at her like that.

"Can you stand?"

His intense gaze made her feel weaker than she was, but she wasn't about to admit that. "1 walked here. I think I'm only bruised and sore. I don't think anything's broken. Unless—"

"Unless?" His forehead creased.

"Unless I suffered a new injury after my fall from the tree." She raised her eyes to look above her and frowned. "I felt dizzy, and before I could move to a more secure position, I felt myself tipping off the branch, but I couldn't react in time to stop myself. Everything went black. How'd I—?"

"I caught you." Shane grinned. "It's a long story."

"Well, the short of it, Miz Lydie, is you be safe." Ben stepped forward, catching her by surprise, a huge grin brightening his dark features.

"Ben!" She reached up to hug him. "You're safe. I've been so worried."

She sat forward and struggled to stand. "We have to get back and save the children."

"Whoa, whoa, whoa!" Shane raised his arms and waved them in a bid for attention. "You just survived a fall from a tree and, from the looks of things, a serious beating. You aren't going anywhere for now."

Daggers flew from her eyes as she settled back on her elbows. "I'll do as I please. My siblings need me. I'll not tarry when they still reside under the roof of a madman."

"Mister Shane's right, Mistress. We be goin' back fo' the others, but not till we know you be okay."

Lydia raised an eyebrow. "Ben, please don't ever call me 'mistress' again. I've never been your mistress, nor will I ever be. You're a free man. We're simply friends from here on out."

"Yes'm." Ben dipped his head in a submissive gesture.

Lydia sighed. Lifelong habits were hard to break. She'd work with him on that later.

She made another attempt at sitting up. Shane took her arms and assisted her to a sitting position, though she sat more by his strength than any of her own. She enjoyed the sensation. She wished she could lean against him like she had in her earlier musings.

Shane introduced her to several cute little girls and his friend Gabriel before motioning for her to relax. "We were about to eat the noonday meal when you—dropped in. It's a bit late, but we've been traveling, too. Why don't you join us? As soon as we're finished, we'll head out. We're going to our homestead, which isn't too far away. I'm afraid it'll be in poor condition after being neglected for the past few years, but a little work will set it to rights soon enough." He hesitated. "You'll be safe there."

"About that, Shane. . ." The man called Gabriel looked nervous.

Shane frowned. "You don't think she'll be safe?"

"It's not that, it's just—"

"Anything else can wait." Shane waved him off. He looked back at Lydia. "Do you think you can travel a bit farther today?"

Lydia nodded. "I'll be fine as soon as I eat. As a matter of fact, I'm fine with eating as we go."

"We'll eat here."

"But—" Lydia bristled. She didn't like to be bossed around by anyone, and she had one goal in life—to get to her brothers and sister. Her argument died on her lips. Shane had already moved away to get their food.

≈

"What happened to our brothers, Shane? I don't remember them."

Savannah sat on the far side of Lydia, flanking her on the wagon's bench. Lydia leaned against Shane's arm. The rhythm of the horses' hooves had quickly lulled her into a deep sleep.

"They left for the war right before you were born. I stayed behind to take care of Ma."

"Weren't you old enough to go?"

He nodded. "In theory, yes. There were boys younger than me who'd joined the cause, though many of them lied about their age. I'd just turned fifteen when our brothers left, but Ma needed me at home."

Savannah looked surprised. "You stayed behind to help Ma?"

"I haven't always been a rambling, no-account, Van."

"I never thought you were a no-account." She played with her skirt.

Shane glanced down at Lydia. She hadn't moved. Ben sat in the back of the wagon, entertaining the little girls with his chatter.

"What happened to our brothers?"

"Edward was killed in battle a few months before the war ended."

"I'm sorry."

Shane smiled to see this sensitive side of his sister. Edward was just as much her brother as he was his, but she didn't see it that way. He hadn't been close to his brothers by the time they'd left, but Savannah had never known them.

"Thanks."

"What happened to the other one?"

"Lucas made it through the war and returned home."

"And something happened to him, too?"

"Yes." The wagon jerked as they started to climb. The road wound upward into the tree-clad mountainside. This last little bit of the journey would take them uphill. His anticipation grew as he suddenly realized he was going home. For the first time in four years, he looked forward to seeing their old place.

"What *happened* to him, Shane?" Exasperated, Savannah kicked her feet against the front of the wagon.

Lydia shifted beside him.

"He made it through the war, tough as can be, but after he left the homestead, he took ill and died without us ever knowing it'd happened. Apparently, he'd been injured in the war, and infection weakened him and took his life."

"How did you find out?"

"His pastor friend sent us a note. He said Lucas had died but that he'd asked the Lord to be his Savior on his deathbed." Shane watched as Gabriel dropped back to ride beside them.

"You never got to say good-bye?"

"No, I was busy helping Ma with you, and then Pa came home for a bit, and next thing I knew, we had Lucy to care for. Ma was sickly after Lucy came, and then she passed away, too."

"You've lost a lot of people you love. No wonder you sent us away."

Shane tilted his head sideways and observed her. Did she really comprehend him that well? The fact that he'd lost so much, he was afraid to hold too tight to the girls in case he lost them, too? "You think I sent you away so I'd not feel hurt again if something happened to you?"

Savannah giggled. "No, I figured you sent us away because you seem to have bad luck when it comes to lovin' somebody, and you didn't want to bring that bad luck on us."

Shane reached over and tugged her black braid. "You really believe in bad luck?"

"No." She tugged her braid from his grasp. "But I sure do love teasing you." She settled back on her seat. "I think you'll do a fine job keeping us safe, just as you always have."

His heart hitched. He didn't feel like he'd done such a good job of late. "Well, it's good that you feel that way, Van, because I intend to be around for a long, long time. I'll be around so long I'll handpick your beaus and pull my shotgun on any of the boys that come around so I can send them scurrying."

Savannah raised an eyebrow. "You'll have to get past me first, 'cause any boy comes callin' on me and I'll have my shotgun out before you ever see him. I don't take kindly to any boys wantin' to court me."

"Promise?"

"Promise!"

Shane laughed out loud. "That's my girl." Now if only she'd hold to that grand promise for another twenty years or so, it'd be fine with him.

They rode in silence for a bit. Vines and overgrowth crowded the rugged road. They jarred and bumped along the ruts. The breezes carried with them the smell of spring mixed in with freshly kicked-up dust. The road had narrowed considerably from when they'd started, and Shane wondered if they'd be able to make the full trip in the wagon. Gabriel rode alongside them, a feat that wouldn't be possible if the road narrowed further.

Shane nodded ahead. "You think we can make it all the way in?"

"I don't think it narrows much more after this. I thought I'd ride ahead and look things over."

"That might be a good idea."

Gabriel spurred Twister to move ahead. The huge beast hurried to obey. The other horses seemed to make him nervous. Shane watched as they rounded a curve and disappeared from sight.

"I came in from the path and followed the road 'bout here," Ben's voice called from the back. "I seen it as I walked through the woods, and it looked to be about the same up 'head from what I saw."

"Thanks, Ben." Shane looked at the overgrowth and understood a bit more why Ben's ankles were so torn up. The shackles had done their damage, but the weeds, roots, and branches he'd walked through hadn't helped.

"Why's it getting so rugged anyways?" Savannah asked. "Don't nobody live out here no more?"

"Anybody," Shane corrected.

"Don't anybody live out this way?" Savannah tried again.

"Doesn't anybody?"

Savannah leaned around Lydia, staring at him in confusion. "That's what I asked you."

"You say it like this, 'Doesn't anybody live out here anymore?'"

Savannah carefully enunciated her next few words. "Doesn't anybody live out this way no more?"

Lydia, awakened now that the road had roughened, laughed. Shane found himself grinning along with her—until she lifted her head from his shoulder. He frowned at that and wanted to pull her back against him. With effort, he refrained.

She glanced around. "Where are we?"

"We're getting pretty close to the homestead. We haven't been there for several years. The buildings should be intact, but I'm sure we'll have some cleaning up to do to make them habitable. We'll make quick work of it, though, don't you worry."

"I'm not worried." Her expression clouded. "Not about that anyway."

"What are you worried about?"

"My stepfather finding Ben and me. My sister and brothers being hurt while I'm away."

"We're going to get them out of there."

She nodded, but didn't look convinced. She'd pulled her hair back from her face and secured it at the nape of her neck with one of the new ribbons he'd brought for Savannah. The bruises on the soft skin of her face reinforced the reason for her concern.

"We haven't passed anyone, have we? While I was sleeping?"

"No, and we won't this far out. This road circles out from town and backs up on a private mountain. My father's family owned the mountain for as far back as anyone remembers. I suppose it belongs to the girls and me now, though I've not really given it much thought until now."

"We own a whole mountain?" Savannah bounced on the seat.

"I reckon we do."

Lydia contemplated that. "And what lies on the far side of your homestead? Does your family own whatever is there, too?"

"No. The land beside us isn't worth much. It's all trees and hills and rocks. Ma didn't talk much about that, and my pa was so seldom home, I didn't ask who owned it."

"There's a good chance it back up on yo' place, Miz Lydie," Ben piped up from the back of the wagon where he'd been telling the stories that so wonderfully entertained Emma and Lucy. "Yo' pa's land run right back to the mountain, and this here's the same mountain it backs up on. Unless I's wrong, we done circled around to the back of the plantation."

"We're heading toward the plantation?" Lydia's words came in a panicked burst.

Shane nodded. "I suppose so, but in a roundabout way. The road from town heads east, and we rode out and headed north to get to Emma, Lucy, and Savannah." They hadn't filled Lydia in on that part of their day. "Now we're heading west again. If your place backs up to the mountain, we're heading that way now. But we're talking a no-man's-land. The land between our homesteads is wild and overgrown."

"That it is," Ben muttered.

Lydia leaned forward, her knuckles going white where she clutched the bench. "We need to go back, Ben. We need to get you out of here. What if Joseph's men find you?"

"I be safe out here, Miz Lydie. I done told you I had some friends working to help me and my missus escape. They live right back here on this edge of the plantation."

Shane frowned. "I'm afraid you've got that wrong, Ben, unless we're at a different angle from where the plantation backs up to the mountain. Our place is the only homestead out here. Maria was our nearest neighbor."

"I had no idea we were so close to home!" Savannah pouted. "If Maria lived so close, why was she the last one you left us with?"

"I suppose I felt the need to keep you girls far away from the homestead, Van. I can't rightly say why, but obviously it doesn't matter anymore 'cause just around that bend we'll see home again."

Chapter 8

They rounded the bend, and Lydia leaned forward for her first glimpse of her new temporary home. She glanced sideways and raised an eyebrow at Shane. "Your homestead doesn't look nearly as bad as you presented it."

Shane reined in the horses. "This can't be right."

Savannah mimicked Lydia's movements, leaning forward and holding a few dark strands of stray hair out of her face. "Why can't it be right? Is this our house or ain't it?"

"Isn't it," Shane corrected, his brows furrowed. "It's our place, but it should be well on its way to being buried in weeds by now. We've been gone four years. When we lived here, it was a constant battle to keep the foliage from growing back and taking over the grounds."

A two-story home with covered porches wrapping around the front and both sides stood proudly in the center of a crisp clearing. Flowers circled the base of the house, circled each of the trees that stood sentry out front, and lined up in a neat row along the walkway. Spanish moss hung from the huge trees that flanked both sides of the yard. More moss-laden trees filled the land as far as the eye could see. Gray curls of smoke curled from the chimney and wafted their way on the breeze. The comforting scent of woodsmoke tickled Lydia's nose and welcomed her to the spread.

In the distance, freshly planted fields stretched out along the base of the mountain.

Ben and the little girls sat quietly in the back of the wagon.

"Someone most definitely lives here, Shane." Lydia's heart fell. She'd been ready for a good night's sleep in a soft bed so they could wake up fresh and ready to figure out a way to save her sister and brothers.

"I can only think of one explanation." A muscle worked in Shane's jaw. "We have squatters."

"Bold ones at that." Lydia felt a chill race up her spine. What if the squatters were Joseph's people?

"What're squatters?" Savannah asked, her voice serious as she reached across Lydia and placed her hand on Shane's leg. Lydia wrapped a reassuring arm around the thin girl's shoulders. "Does that mean we don't have a home after all?"

"Squatters are people who try to take over someone else's home." Shane growled. He squeezed Savannah's hand. "I'm not having you lose two homes in one day, Van. The squatters are the ones who'll lose their home this time around, not us."

This was a side of Shane Lydia hadn't seen at the saloon. He'd been angry, but fair with her younger brother. Wyatt had apparently caused Shane to lose a good amount of money and shouldn't have been in the saloon in the first place. Other men would have been far harsher. He'd been kind to her younger brother despite the money lost. This irritated side of Shane was ready to take matters into his own hands no matter what the outcome. Yet he didn't show any of the raw anger Joseph always displayed. Lydia still felt safe in his care, even though he was angry.

"Where's Gabe?" Savannah glanced around, her question momentarily distracting Shane and wiping the scowl from his face.

Realization dawned on his features. "Good question, Savannah. Where *is* Gabe? Seems he was in a mighty big hurry to get over here before we did."

"And he kept trying to tell you something after you said we were coming home. He looked worried."

"Hmm, he did, didn't he? I should have paid more attention." He shrugged, once again the easygoing man she'd first met. "Maybe we don't have squatters after all. Let's find out what's going on."

Lydia touched his arm. "Maybe Ben and I should remain in the wagon until you do know who's living here."

"You'll be fine." Shane shook the reins and set the wagon in motion.

Lydia glared and pulled her shoulder away from where it touched his. She crossed her arms in front of her to further prevent contact. A moment earlier she'd enjoyed the strong security his closeness represented; now his closeness annoyed her.

He sighed. "If there'd been a problem, Gabriel would have warned us. Savannah has a point. Whoever is living here is staying with Gabriel's blessing."

"You're sure?" Lydia wasn't. Again she wished Shane wasn't so authoritative. This was the Shane from the saloon—confident and cocky.

At that moment, Gabriel and two other dark-skinned people exited the front door of the home. They stood on the porch as Shane pulled the wagon to a stop and jumped to the ground. He motioned for the others to stay put.

"Gabe?"

"I'd, um, like you to meet your caretakers, Matilda—"

"Please," inserted the dark-skinned woman. She stood regal and tall. A scarf covered most of her short gray hair. "Call me Tildy."

Shane nodded. "Tildy."

Lydia almost laughed at Shane's confused expression. She felt safe. The couple wasn't one she'd ever seen before, and Gabriel did indeed seem to know them.

The light breeze blew a strand of hair across Lydia's face. She pushed it back and inhaled the sweet scent of jasmine. The intoxicating fragrance made her want to curl up on one of the comfortable chairs on the porch while sipping a cup of sweet tea.

Gabriel motioned toward the man. "And this is Tildy's husband, Isaac."

Strong and muscular, Isaac had the look of a man who was used to hard work. "Pleased to meet you, suh."

Again Shane nodded.

Lydia watched in fascination. These people were strangers in his home, yet Shane spoke to them with complete respect. Lydia couldn't help but compare his reaction to the way Joseph treated the people he came in contact with.

Shane worked his hat in his hand for a moment, the only sign of his inner turmoil. "Gabriel, could I speak to you in private?"

Gabriel looked around as if searching for an escape, like he'd rather do anything but speak with Shane at that moment.

With no escape in sight, he moved forward and down the porch stairs. "Um, sure."

Isaac motioned toward the house. "We'll just step inside and prepare something for you all to eat. Join us whenever you're ready." He hesitated and looked over at the wagon. "If you want help with your bags—"

"We're fine for now, thank you, Isaac," Gabriel interjected.

"If you're sure—"

Gabe nodded.

Shane and Gabe walked to the far side of the wagon.

"I have *caretakers*, Gabe? Since when?"

"Since you up and abandoned the place, Shane. This is a good spread. I wasn't about to let you lose it. Savannah and Lucy deserve to have their home intact."

"So you let strangers move in?"

"They aren't exactly strangers." Gabriel looked out over the fields.

"Suppose you tell me who they are, then." Shane crossed his arms and stared Gabriel down.

Gabriel looked uncomfortable. "My Aunt Tildy and my Uncle Isaac."

Lydia listened with interest. Gabriel had apparently hired on staff without talking to Shane, and Shane took it in stride. Her stepfather would have injured people over such a thing. Shane's only reaction was to lean back against the wagon and fold his arms across his chest.

"You didn't think this was something I needed to know?"

"I knew you'd say no."

Lydia's eyes widened.

"So you did it anyway." Shane just sighed. "Care to fill me in on the details?"

"They needed a place to stay after leaving their former home. They worked inside the house of a wealthy couple, Isaac managed the outdoor laborers and doubled as a butler, and Tildy managed the house staff. They had wonderful skills, but once they lost their positions, they had nowhere to go. The homestead was sitting here, abandoned. I told Isaac he could live here in exchange for working the land and keeping things fixed up."

"You did, did you?" Shane scowled. "And where do you propose we all sleep now that we've arrived to find the place full of people?"

"It's hardly full of people. There's plenty of room for everyone."

"I be fine sleepin' in the cabin out back if it helps, or even in the barn," Ben piped up from the back of the wagon.

Shane turned to look at him. "The cabin?"

"Yes, suh." Ben glanced at Lydia as if for reassurance. Confused, Lydia nodded for Ben to go on.

"Tildy and Isaac be the folks who wuz aidin' Sadie and me in gettin' away from Master Joseph." He lowered his eyes. "I's sorry, Miz Lydie, but we knowed that what Master Joseph wuz doin' wasn't right. We had a right to be free. We wanted to move on. Only the master got rid of Sadie 'fore we could follow through."

"I completely understand, Ben."

"They say there be a cabin in the hills for us to stay in."

"Tildy and Isaac are running an underground railroad out here?"

Gabriel rolled his eyes. "No, Shane. You know there aren't slaves anymore. Not legally anyway. Tildy and Isaac were just offering a place for people like Ben and his wife to go when they needed to get—away. They'd remain here until they could find a place to become established."

Lydia couldn't see Shane's face, but from Gabriel's reaction and the way he took a step backward, she was glad. She reached over and took Savannah's hand in hers. Surely Shane wouldn't cause a scene with the children present, but that had never stopped her stepfather.

"Okay." Shane shook his head again and pushed away from the wagon. "And what cabin are you referring to?"

"Ben's referring to your folks' original place up in the hills, the one your ancestors built. The cabin they moved into after they married. It's up the mountain a bit."

"That old place? Is it habitable?"

"It is now. Isaac and Tildy stay there most of the time. He said it's just as nice as this place."

Tildy exited the door and motioned them in. Shane reached up to help Lydia from the wagon. She tottered at the edge of the wagon when a shaft of pain shot through her head. She was still unsteady on her feet. Shane caught her and swept her up in his arms. Gabriel moved forward and reached for Savannah. She leaped into his open arms. Gabriel lowered her to the ground, then lifted Emma and Lucy from the back. They ran around in circles, following along at Savannah's heels.

"Can we see out back?"

"Just for a few minutes. Listen for me to call." Shane's face transformed, and a gentle smile formed on his mouth as he watched the little girls scamper off with childish enthusiasm.

"I be waitin' out here." Ben moved to settle back on his pallet.

"Nonsense." Shane tipped his head toward the house. "We all go in together." Ben looked surprised, but he nodded in agreement.

Tears filled Lydia's eyes. Ben had never been allowed to enter their plantation home, even when his wife Sadie had been working in the kitchen. Joseph hadn't treated Ben any better than his animals. In fact, the animals were often offered better respect and care than Ben.

Gabriel started to help him down, but Isaac called out to them to wait.

"Gabriel told me who you have there. Joseph came around this mornin'. He brought his dogs along and asked if we'd seen Ben. Ben shouldn't have his scent on the ground just in case he comes around again."

Ben and Lydia exchanged glances. Shane shifted her in his arms and frowned as he contemplated Isaac's words.

"Gabe, bring the wagon as close to the porch as you can. Ben can step down from there onto the porch steps."

Gabe did as Shane said. Ben shakily mounted the stairs and walked across the porch. His ankles were swollen. They looked infected. Lydia would tend to his wounds once they were all inside—that is, if Shane ever put her down.

"I'm perfectly able to walk," she chastised. Though she guessed it wouldn't do to have her scent on the ground anymore than Ben's if Joseph and his men were snooping around.

"I saw that you were able to walk, right before you swooned and fell into my arms."

"I didn't 'swoon and fall into your arms.' I merely—"

"Merely?" He smirked. "Merely what?"

She wasn't making things better. "I had a moment of dizziness, but it's passed. I'm sure I can make my way inside on my own."

"I'd rather not take any chances." He ignored her expression and followed the others onto the cozy porch and through the door.

Chapter 9

They stepped into the home and followed Tildy down the entry hall and into a warm kitchen at the back of the house. The room looked out toward an open space that was flanked by a large barn. Lydia saw Gabriel pull the wagon around into the open space and on into the barn.

Isaac hurried out the back door and down the steps to help Gabriel with the horses.

Tildy stared at Ben's sore ankles after they'd entered the room and, with a frown, motioned him to a seat at the large rectangular table. Ben eased into the wooden chair.

Shane didn't make any move to set Lydia on her feet.

Uncomfortable with Tildy's assessing stare, Lydia said, "Shane, I think I can make it from here."

"What?" Shane pulled his attention from the clearing behind the house where the girls ran free and only then seemed to realize he still held Lydia in his arms. "Oh, I'm sorry."

He carried her to the table and settled her down beside Ben.

"Y'all look a bit worse for wear," Tildy chided. "Gabriel filled us in a bit on what you have been through."

"I'm sure we'll be fine, now that we're here." Lydia smiled. She didn't want to cause the kind woman any worry. "After a good night's sleep, we can head over to the plantation and collect my brothers and sister."

Shane had moved to stand close to her side, and now he sank down into the empty chair to her right, the opposite from where Ben rested. "You aren't going anywhere fast, Lydia. You can't run off without a plan, or you'll end up worse off than you are now. We'll all sit down together and talk this through and figure out the best way to get the children as soon as we've all had a time to rest." He sent her a pointed look. "And to recuperate."

"Now's as good a time as any to make plans." Shane's reticence to hurry forward with the rescue frustrated Lydia. If it were his little sisters that were held captive, she doubted he'd even have bothered to stop by the homestead. She told him as much.

"I'd make sure I had the proper supplies and could do the rescue right the first time, Lydie. I wouldn't run off half-cocked."

"I'm not running off 'half-cocked,'" she huffed. Her heart skipped a beat at his intimate use of her nickname. "I've had plenty of time to think things through as I walked here."

Shane leaned back in his chair. "All right, then fill us in. What's the plan?"

Lydia hesitated, not sure her plan was a good one now that she had to share it. "I wanted to get them while they're out in the fields. If we don't hurry, they'll be going in for dinner. Joseph had all of us work in the fields alongside the others."

"I'm listening." Shane looked intrigued. "He doesn't have anyone watching over them?"

His interest encouraged her to go on. "That's the only problem. The men who took me away and dumped me over the side of the road sit on their horses with shotguns strategically placed on their laps and watch over the fields as everyone works. Their presence is supposed to intimidate the hands into staying on. They're grooming my brother Nathan to help."

"And how do you propose we get around these men?"

A small trill ran through her at his use of "we," but her shoulders drooped as she answered his question. "I haven't figured that part out yet."

"See? Half-cocked. That's not the type of thing you figure out when you're charging into battle, not if you don't have to." He held up a hand to still her protest. "And in this case, you don't have to."

Tildy stood at the stove dipping up bowls of savory-smelling soup. She shook her head as they talked.

Ben joined the conversation. "I can help. I don't have no suggestions 'bout gettin' rid of the foremen, but I get respect from the other workers. They be trustin' ya if ya take me along."

"Ben, I can't ask you to take that risk," Lydia hurried to say.

"But—"

She interrupted. "I can only imagine what Joseph would do if his men catch you. It's too dangerous." She motioned to his ankles. "And you can't walk that far anyway. Not until your ankles heal."

"If y'all will wash up, you can eat," Tildy said as she placed a serving of soup in front of each of them. "And I'll have a look at that ankle, Ben, as soon as you have your fill of dinner."

She crossed the room to the door and called for the girls. As they came giggling into the room, she carried a basket of cornbread and a bowl of creamy butter over to the table.

"Gabriel and Isaac will join us in a moment." She took a seat across from Ben.

The little girls settled into the two chairs beside Tildy, and Savannah glanced at the two chairs that flanked each end.

"Just choose one, child. We don't stand on formality around here."

Savannah took the chair at the end, which placed her between Emma and Shane. Lucy stared up at Tildy with a grin. "I like it here. You have a pretty house."

The grown-ups smiled as Tildy looked at Shane. Her eyes sparkled with amusement. "This is y'alls house, little one. We just been watchin' over it for you."

Lucy tilted her cherubic blond head, her blue eyes serious. "We 'preciate that." Everyone laughed.

Lydia watched Shane's expression change from one of concern to an expression of gentle pride as he watched the interaction. He noticed Lydia watching, and the corner of his mouth quirked up.

"She's so sweet," Lydia whispered.

"I've been worried about her," he explained quietly. "Those are the first words she's spoken since her trauma in the woodbox."

"That makes it all the sweeter." Lydia said a quiet prayer of thanks for Lucy's recovery and prayed for a similar outcome for Wyatt.

Gabriel and Isaac entered the kitchen, their hands dripping with water from the outdoor pump. Tildy motioned them to a towel that hung on a hook on the wall.

"Smells mighty good in here, Aunt Tildy," Gabriel said.

Tildy motioned to the seat at the end. "Have a seat, Gabriel. We'll get another chair for Isaac." She started to stand.

"Sit yourself back down, woman." Isaac waved her back. "I can find myself a chair."

He left the room and hurried back, carrying a wooden bench.

"I wanna sit on the bench!" Emma bounced in her seat, almost falling off in her exuberance.

"Me, too!" Lucy chimed in.

"Girls—" Shane intervened, but Isaac ignored him and lifted the small girls from their chairs.

He pushed one chair back toward the window and moved the other to the far end of the row and placed it next to his wife. The bench for the girls was slid into place, and Isaac lifted the girls onto it.

"Are we all set then?" he asked.

Both girls covered their mouths and giggled.

Isaac's smile filled his face. "I'll take that as a yes." He moved to take his seat next to Tildy.

Shane thanked him.

Isaac beamed. "We're so glad y'all are here and that we finally get to meet you."

Lydia couldn't tell if Isaac knew this had all come as a huge surprise to Shane.

Before Shane could speak, Tildy motioned toward the food. "Why don't we say a prayer over the food and get to eatin' before the soup gets cold."

She reached for Gabriel's and Isaac's hands, and the others followed suit. Lydia's hand felt small in Shane's strong grip. Her fingers tingled at his touch. The prayer ended, and she was sure Shane gave her hand a gentle squeeze. She blushed and stared into her bowl of soup. Everyone began to talk.

Lydia's headache had returned. Her throbbing temples prevented her from entering into the discussion. She closed her eyes to fight off a bout of nausea.

"Miss Lydie, you look like you're about to fall asleep in your dinner." Tildy's concerned voice carried over the others' conversation.

Lydia startled. "I'm sorry. It's been a long day, and my head is starting to rebel. I'm sure a good night's sleep will remedy things."

She could feel Shane's intense stare as he studied her. "I think it's more than that, Tildy. Lydia took a pretty good beating at the hands of Joseph and his men. She has a head injury and a cut up under her hairline."

"Oh child, why didn't you tell me before we ate?" Tildy stood.

"Finish your meal, please," Lydia insisted. She didn't like being the center of attention. "I'm fine, just a bit tired."

"Well I'll let you eat, but as soon as you're finished, we're going to get you cleaned up and tucked into bed."

Lydia would have argued, but the proposition sounded too good to resist.

"Thanks, Tildy." Shane nodded toward Lydia. "This one needs a firm hand. She can be a bit oppositional."

"I beg your pardon!" Lydia fumed.

He grinned. "As I was saying."

The others laughed.

Gabriel smiled. "It's true you knocked the chair clean out from under him in the saloon, Miss Lydia."

Her face flamed. She could only imagine what Isaac and Tildy were thinking about her after that statement. "Just call me Lydie, Gabriel."

Gabriel turned to his aunt and uncle. "Lydia's little brother wandered into the saloon just as Shane prepared to play his winning hand." He paused and sent Shane a condescending look.

Shane rolled his eyes in response.

"The lad called out the numbers and named each face card."

"Oh my." Isaac's soft chuckle filled the moment.

Tildy raised her eyebrows as she slathered butter onto a piece of cornbread. "No offense, Mr. Shane, but serves you right for being in a saloon."

Lydia snickered. "That's pretty much what I told him."

"Shane grabbed the youngster by the collar," Gabriel continued. "Just about the time Lydia came through the door."

Tildy gasped. "Oh my. I can only imagine what you felt when you walked in on that."

"I was steaming angry."

"Tsk, tsk." The woman shook her head. "I would be, too. So you walked over and knocked him flat?"

Gabriel laughed. "Oh did she ever. She swung her leg out faster than Shane could say, 'Howdy, ma'am,' and there he was, sprawled on the floor with all the patrons of the saloon looking on. His expression was one I'd never seen before, complete and utter shock."

"It wasn't like I'd lift a hand against a woman," Shane drawled. "I could have stopped her, but I didn't want to cause a scene."

Gabriel guffawed. "Didn't want to cause a scene? What was it you did, then, if not cause a scene? Face it—you didn't have a chance to react. Lydie was too fast for you."

"I'm glad you're enjoying this, Gabe."

"Oh, I am, Shane. It's not often someone bests you. Lydia seems to catch you off guard in a way no one else ever has."

"All right then." Shane finished his last bite of soup and changed the subject. He leaned back in his chair. "What do you say we get on with fixing Lydia and Ben up?"

Gabriel sent one last grin across the table. "Aunt Tildy will fix them up in no time. She's a natural-born healer and has medicinal herbs for just about anything you can imagine."

"That's good to hear."

Isaac looked over at Lydia. "If you think you can make it a bit longer, Tildy can take care of Ben, and then I can get him settled up at the cabin while she cares for you."

"I'm fine with that." Lydie felt better after eating the satisfying meal.

"I have some cookies for the girls to enjoy in the meantime." Tildy got up and served two cookies to each little girl. They squealed with delight.

"You're going to spoil them." Shane's smile softened his words.

Tildy didn't falter; she just returned his smile. "And I'll enjoy every minute of it." Tildy poured cups of milk for each girl, then left the room to gather her supplies.

"I'll just wait here in the chair—"

"We'll wait out front on the swing," Shane corrected. "Can you walk, or do you want me to carry you?"

"I could have walked the first time. You *insisted* on carrying me."

"Fine, but if you wobble at all, I'm sweeping you off your feet and up into my arms." He seemed hesitant to let her walk and said the words with all sincerity.

Her wayward emotions heard them a different way, and she imagined what it would be like if he'd meant the words in a romantic sense. She almost swooned at the thought. Fighting the dizzying emotions, she forced one foot in front of the other and made her way up the front hall. At the door he did the very thing he'd threatened and swept her off her feet.

"I didn't even swoon!" she cried as he pulled her close against him.

Her heart pounded against her chest as she clung to his arms in surprise. His arms were strong and muscular as he gripped her in a secure embrace and walked across the wood planks.

"Shane!" Her voice was breathless, and she was glad when he shushed her. She didn't trust her voice not to break or give away her whirling emotions.

He carried her over to the wooden seat. The chains creaked as he lowered her down into place. He settled close beside her and placed his arm across the back of the seat. "I don't want your scent on the porch, just in case Joseph brings his dogs up here." His eyes twinkled.

Lydia narrowed her own eyes and stared. Shane shrugged. Lydia had a hard time believing him when he looked so amused.

His words sank in, and she appreciated the warmth and solidity of his strong body close beside her. "What if Joseph does come? Perhaps we should move inside—"

"He won't come this close to evening. It would get dark before he ever made it home. The land between your place and ours is too rough to travel at night on a whim."

Lydia settled back and leaned her head against the high wood back of the swing. Shane moved his arm to cushion it.

"If we lived so close, why didn't we ever meet?"

"I don't know." Shane started the swing into motion with his foot. Lydia closed her eyes, the motion soothing. "I suppose that even though our land touches, the roughness of the terrain in between prevented much exploring. My brothers and I spent most of our time up on the mountain."

"And we were expected to stay close to home and help out." Her voice quieted. "I wish I were there right now. I can't help but wonder what Wyatt's been thinking. He probably thinks I abandoned him. I want to be there with him."

"I know you do." Shane cupped her shoulder and gave it a quick squeeze before returning his hand to the back of the swing. "But would you truly want to be there, knowing your wedding to Joseph was imminent?"

She sighed. "If it meant my siblings were safe, then yes."

A shudder passed through her.

"Your body says differently." His words were soft. "I'm not happy that you were hurt, but I'm glad you aren't there anymore. I'm glad you found us. We'll find a way to get the others out. I promise."

"You didn't seem so sure about my presence when I dropped onto your lap."

"I'd had a hard day." He grinned. "I'm a loner, and I had just been saddled with three little girls, and then Ben, and then you. That's a lot of companionship for a man to take all at once."

"You were *saddled* with us all?!" Lydia tried to pull away.

Shane wrapped his arm around her shoulder and held her tight against him. "That's how it felt at the time."

"But now?"

"Now, I'm kind of liking things as they are." He thought a moment. "I know if Savannah or Lucy or Emma were in a situation similar to yours, I'd do anything in my power to get to them and to rectify the situation. I can't do anything less for you and Wyatt. I kind of like the kid, even though he did cost me a small fortune."

Lydia punched him in the arm.

Chapter 10

Dusk fell as Shane and Lydia sat in quiet contemplation. Locusts filled the night with music. The scent of jasmine lingered in the cooling air. Lydia felt much too comfortable snuggled up as she was next to Shane. She shifted and started to move away.

"Don't move." Shane cupped her shoulder.

"I don't want anyone thinking us improper."

"Improper according to whom? There's only you and I out here." Shane tightened his hold on her arm. "Besides, I own the place."

"I don't want Tildy or Gabe or Ben to think ill of us or to get the wrong impression. And we need to consider the little girls—"

"I guess I have a lot to learn about what folks consider improper. We're not doing anything untoward, Lydia. And if I let go of you in your present state, you'll likely tumble onto the porch. I doubt anyone would think that a proper action to allow from a gentleman like me. Stop worrying and let someone take care of you for a change. Relax."

Shane had a point. Lydia hadn't had an opportunity to have someone else care for her, not in a long, long time. She thought about it a moment. Not since her mother had passed away. Sadie had tried to mother them, but Joseph always intervened, trying to keep her away.

Lydia allowed her mind to drift. She wondered what it would be like to know Wyatt and the twins were tucked safely away inside Shane's house along with Emma, Lucy, and Savannah. She considered how nice it would be to spend each evening with Shane in a similar manner to this, swaying on the swing, the two of them discussing their accomplishments at the end of the day, and then planning together for the day that would follow.

The swing creaked as Shane toed it along, and Lydia closed her eyes. She savored the magical thought and wished the moment could last forever. She might not ever enjoy such a pleasant routine in her daily life, but she could certainly take pleasure in the experience while she had it. At Shane's side, she felt protected and safe.

"I'm ready for you, Miss Lydie." Tildy's cheerful voice interfered with Lydia's musings and shattered them, ruining the moment as suddenly as she stepped onto the porch. She hesitated. "Oh dear, I'm sorry. Did she fall asleep?"

"I think she might ha—" Shane started.

"No, Tildy, I'm awake," Lydia interrupted, her voice groggy. Maybe she had fallen asleep.

Shane stayed her with his hand. "Let me help you inside. Joseph's dogs, remember?"

Lydia remembered all too well.

He carried her into the foyer. "I'll go out back and check in with Isaac and Gabriel. We'll come up with a basic plan." He set her down just inside the front door.

She felt bereft. "I want in on the discussion."

He was shaking his head before she finished. "You need to let Tildy tend to that cut. You get cleaned up, and we'll fill you in on our plans come morning."

Tildy nodded her agreement and nudged Lydia toward the kitchen. Shane passed through the kitchen and exited the back door. Lydia longed to go with him.

"Go sit on that chair, and I'll be right with you." Tildy walked over to the stove. "I hope you don't mind, but I took a bit of extra time to clean the young'uns and tuck them into bed before comin' for you."

Lydia didn't mind. It allowed her more time with Shane. "I wasn't going anywhere."

"So I noticed. You and Mister Shane sure looked cozy on that swing."

"Oh—I didn't mean to act inappropria—"

Tildy shushed her. "You didn't do anything wrong, child. Seems to me you could use some pamperin'. From what Gabe told me, you've not had much in the way of leisure with that awful stepfather of yours. And with that said, it's my turn to pamper you. For a long time I've not had anyone but Isaac to fuss over, and he doesn't take very well to fussin'."

"I can imagine." Lydia sank gratefully into the chair. Everything felt woozy. "Fuss away."

"I enjoyed cleanin' up the little girls and tuckin' them into the fresh clothes Gabriel fetched for me. The poor little things were asleep before I left the room. The water from their bath was dirtier than bathwater from Isaac after he works in the fields! I had fresh water drawn for you."

"Thank you."

A warm bath sounded heavenly, even though Lydia had nothing clean to put on after. She glanced over and saw that someone had dragged a large tub into place in front of the roaring fire. Hot water steamed on the stove. Tildy dipped some and placed it into another, smaller pan and placed it on the table next to a white cloth. "We'll start with the gash on your head. Let me take a look."

Tildy's small intake of breath let Lydia know the gash wasn't a small one. "Is it bad?"

"I don't know how you've managed to stand on your feet after a knock like this. It's a miracle pure and simple that you were able to think clearly enough to get up and find help as you did."

"Thank you, Lord," Lydia mumbled.

"That's exactly right. Um-hmm. Thank the good Lord indeed. He was watchin' over you, child. Watchin' over all of you it seems. He has a plan in motion and must have had it goin' for a long time to pull you all together like this. Each one of you seems to need the other."

Lydia felt her face warm. "Oh, I don't know about that."

"Well I do. And those little girls need a family," Tildy stated as she gently cleaned the area around the wound. "I can see the beauty of His plan as clear as I can see the pretty little nose on your face."

Lydia resisted the urge to roll her eyes.

Tildy continued talking. "You all were meant to be together. That man out there is smitten by you, and I'm thinkin' you have similar feelings for him. I'm gonna enjoy sittin' back and watchin' the Lord work His miracles in both of your lives."

"Tildy, please! You're making me blush."

"Well hold on tight to that chair, honey, because now I'm about to make you yell in pain."

Even pain sounded like a good diversion from where their conversation had been heading. Lydia rethought that statement a few moments later. Tildy didn't hold back when she scrubbed the filthy wounds.

"I don't want this wound to get infected so I have to clean it well. I know it hurts."

At one point Lydia cried out, and footsteps pounded up the back steps. "Everything all right in there?"

Tildy snickered. "We're doin' just fine, Mister Shane. You go on and don't worry about this pretty lady none. She's in good hands with me."

"Lydia?"

Tildy raised her eyebrows and sent Lydia a knowing look.

The heat crept back up Lydia's cheeks. "I'm fine, Shane. Thanks for asking."

"Told you he has it bad for you," Tildy said in a quiet voice. "He's been sittin' out there on that porch just waitin' for a chance to check up on you, and you've only been out of his sight for a few minutes." She grinned. "Um-hum, he's got it bad for sure."

Lydia tried to fight off the small smile that threatened to turn into a full-fledged grin. "He probably doesn't want me to bleed all over his nice, clean kitchen."

"Oh I think the man knows I can clean the kitchen and put it back to rights whether you bleed all over or not. It was a wreck when we got here, and I got it to looking like this. I reckon I can do it again."

Though she listened hard, Lydia didn't hear the sound of Shane's boots thumping down the steps.

"He's gonna sit out there and wait until he knows you're all right." Tildy shook her head. "We gonna have to hurry and fix you up so he can get on with his plans."

With the worst of the cleaning over, Lydia was able to relax against the chair. Tildy made quick work of the other small cuts and then directed Lydia toward the bath.

"You can go now, Mister Shane."

Lydia jumped as Tildy yelled through the door.

"We're just fine in here. You can be on your way. Miss Lydia sat through my abuse to her cuts brave as can be, but now she's about to climb into a warm bath. You're free to go on out and get some work done now."

Shane's chuckle drifted through the closed door. "Thanks for the update, Tildy. I suppose I'll do just that."

Lydia buried her mortified face in her hands.

❧

Shane stalked off toward the barn. He couldn't believe he'd been so obvious sitting outside the door like that. What had gotten into him? Lydia wasn't exactly the damsel-in-distress type. She'd been a force to be reckoned with at the saloon! Granted, the head injury made her appear more vulnerable and had put her in a weakened state, but he had no doubt the ferocious woman he'd first met was waiting just below the surface.

If he gave her half a chance, she'd probably lay him flat again as soon as she recuperated. And he'd enjoy every moment. That thought made his mind go in all the wrong directions. He pushed away the image of him pulling her down along with him and forced his wayward thoughts in another, more proper direction.

Truth of it was, Lydia had gotten under his skin—something no other woman had ever been able to accomplish. He'd always been more of a love-'em-and-leave-'em type of a man, but Lydia lingered in his thoughts, and she'd even invaded his dreams the previous night at the hotel.

The woman he'd met in town seemed reserved and aloof. This version of Lydia was warm and in need of his protection. He wondered which was the real Lydia. Perhaps she was a bit of both. He moseyed in the general direction of the barn, walking slowly to savor the moment of aloneness.

Twister, Pal, and Chester waited in the corral beside the barn. Shane could hear their grunts and whickers as he passed by.

He walked over to the recently reinforced fence and leaned against it to reach his hand toward Pal. Pal walked over and let Shane rub his nose. The large moon reflected off his brown eyes.

"How ya doin', Pal? Does it feel good to be home? No livery, no hitchin' post—just you and your buddies relaxing in the fresh evening air."

Pal tossed his head and snorted.

"I'm kind of enjoying it, too, buddy. Much more than I expected."

Of course it helped to come home to a warm, inviting house instead of the mess of a place he'd envisioned. This life beckoned to him, begged him to step back in. He found himself wondering why he'd ever left in the first place.

He'd felt lost after his father and brothers left. That part he knew. He'd wanted to look around and see if he found a better fit for himself outside the homestead. He'd given in to wanderlust, wanting to know if he was like his father, only to discover he didn't find peace on the trail. Yet he'd had it here at the house. The closer they had come, the closer he'd felt to God. Had Shane chased all over the state for something that was here all along?

He knew he wasn't his father. He wasn't his brothers. He actually liked working the earth and seeing the fruits of his labor pay off when fresh green plants pushed their way through the soil and reached toward the warm sun. Why had it taken four long years for that realization to dawn?

He found himself looking back toward the house.

Maybe he'd needed a gentle prod. A few years earlier, he hadn't felt fit to raise Savannah, let alone a baby. He was exhausted after caring for his mother, the homestead, and the two little girls. He'd made the decision to place his sisters in a home where they could get a mother's love. Instead, Savannah had done her best to thwart his every plan, only wanting to come home. He owed them both an apology.

He'd been selfish to abandon them and take away the only security they had left. He'd only thought of himself when he'd hit the trail. And in the mix, he'd almost lost the girls, too. The only family he had left.

Again, he realized what a miracle it was that they'd survived the fire and were back in his care. He wouldn't blow it again. No matter what decision he made for the future, he'd make sure the plan worked with the three little girls by his side.

He figured he'd dawdled long enough and walked into the barn. The sweet scent of fresh hay tickled his nose. He drew it in, savoring the familiar fragrance.

Gabriel and Isaac were hard at work inside the large structure. Shane didn't have the heart to make them sit down to a meeting this late when they were all tired. The discussion and planning could wait until tomorrow. That way Lydia could join in, too.

"'Bout time you decided to join us," Gabriel teased. "I thought you were going to sit on the porch all night like a little lovesick puppy." He paused before adding, "A lovesick puppy who has been relegated to the back yard for the night."

Shane threw a handful of hay at Gabriel, and Gabriel ducked.

Shane had never seen this side of his friend. The Gabriel he knew tagged along on Shane's heels, going wherever Shane chose to go, nagging and preaching at him along the way. This Gabriel wore his sleeves rolled high on his elbows and was filthy dirty and apparently enjoyed every moment of it. He'd regained his sense of humor.

"Hard work seems to agree with you, Gabe."

Gabe and Isaac were cleaning out the unused stalls and preparing them for the horses.

"Seems I remember you being a lot happier when you were working the land, too. I can't believe it's taken us four years to get back here."

"I can't either."

Gabriel stared at him with wide eyes. "You're actually thinking of staying?"

"I think I am." Shane smiled. "I gave up cards in an offer to God for Savannah and Lucy's safety. God gave me my answer, with Emma thrown in as a bonus."

"You have a fever or something, Shane?" Gabriel looked over at Isaac who wore a grin on his face while still shoveling hay. "I can't believe you just said an extra child to care for is a bonus when you haven't even wanted to care for your sisters."

Shane flinched. "I don't have a fever, and I mean it, Gabe. God got my attention at the cabin, and I think now He's calling me home."

"G—God?" Gabe's dark face paled a shade. "Ca—calling you home?"

Shane laughed. "Not in that way, Gabriel. Calling me back to the homestead. Calling me home to stay here."

"Whew." Gabe's eyes lit up with hope, and he wiped his forehead with his arm. "I thought for a minute there I was going to be raising three orphaned girls on my own."

Isaac called from the next stall. "You know Tildy and I would have helped, Gabe."

"I appreciate that, Uncle Isaac." Gabe leaned on his shovel and looked at Shane.

"Sorry, guys, I plan to stay around and see to that job myself."

Isaac leaned against the top of the stall and looked Shane over. "You know, it never hurts to have a few extra hands wieldin' shotguns when you're raisin' pretty little fillies like those three in the house."

Gabriel chortled.

Shane threw back his head and joined in. "Isn't that the truth! I'll surely take you up on that offer. I'd be mighty obliged, Isaac, if you'd stay and continue with what you've been doing here."

"I was hopin' you'd say that." Isaac beamed. "I do enjoy working this place. The three of us workin' together will surely make it better."

Chapter 11

Lydia woke the next morning to a brilliant beam of sunlight shining in her face from across the room. She glanced around at the unfamiliar space and tried to gather her bearings. White curtains were pulled across the windows, but they didn't do much to prevent the sun's glare at this late morning hour. A small table to the left of her bed held a ceramic pitcher of water, a bowl, and a crisp white towel.

The small dresser that flanked the window opposite the bed remained empty. Lydia didn't have any clothing to fill it, nothing to place in the drawers. She smoothed her hand down the soft gown Tildy had loaned her and gingerly moved to a sitting position, relieved to find that her head ached far less than it had on the previous day.

Lydia walked to the window and threw back the curtains. The sunny day lifted her spirits and made her smile. She'd slept later than she'd intended, but after the previous night of very little sleep and the hard morning of walking, she'd enjoyed the cozy warmth of the soft bed.

She turned to survey the room, wondering where Tildy had put her dress. A splash of color near the door drew her attention. A delicate pink dress with a tiny floral design was draped carefully over a nearby chair that sat between the bed and the door. She moved closer to look at it. The dress hadn't been there the night before when she'd gone to bed. Tildy must have brought it in after Lydia had fallen asleep.

The fabric looked crisp and new. Lydia knew Tildy couldn't have whipped it up while Lydia had slept. She'd ask her new friend where the dress had come from when she next saw her. She slipped it over her head and, though it was a bit loose on the sides, it skirted the floor perfectly.

She sat to put on her freshly cleaned boots before walking over to the small vanity. A brush and a few hair accessories lay centered on top. She drew the brush through her hair, pulled her hair back, and fastened it at the nape of her neck. She quickly splashed water on her face and dried it with the waiting towel. It was so strange to find everything at the ready and not to have staged items there the night before. She was used to doing for herself. With a smile, she headed out the door.

She found Tildy hard at work in the kitchen. A lone plate and a set of silverware rested on the table in front of the farthest seat.

Tildy motioned her over to the chair. "Sit down and I'll serve your breakfast in a moment."

"Nonsense." Lydia joined her at the stove. "I can make my own breakfast. Just show me where everything is, and tell me what to make."

"You tryin' to take my job away from me?" Tildy waved a spatula in her face. "You'll have your hands full in the coming days, so take a load off your feet while you can."

"My hands full?" Lydia asked in confusion. "With what?"

"Well, you plan to gather up your siblings and get them out of your stepfather's clutches, don't you?"

"I do." Lydia hadn't given much thought to where they'd go after she collected them. The thought of bringing them back here put a lift in Lydia's spirits. Her new friend was talking as if the event would occur in the very near future! Lydia surely hoped so.

"And if you're stayin' here, you'll also have your hands full keepin' up with Emma, Lucy, and Savannah."

"I will, won't I?" Lydia loved the thought of staying and taking care of the three darling girls. But she knew Tildy was up to the task and would enjoy every minute of mothering them after her comment the night before. "You don't want to raise them?"

"I'm not goin' anywhere. But you're the one who'll be in charge if you stay."

"No one's asked me to stay." Her spirits plummeted. "Shane has only agreed to help me free Wyatt, Natalie, and Nathan. Nothing's been said about what will happen after."

"I've only just met Shane, but I've known Gabriel his whole life. I can promise you those two aren't going to put you out on your own. You'll be an asset to them if they decide to stay on, and based on what Isaac told me last night, they're plannin' to stay on."

"What a lovely thought." Lydia wandered over to the table and settled into her seat. She stared out the window and saw the men working near the barn. The little girls played nearby in the shade under a tree. She smiled. "You placed my table setting where I could best see the view. Thank you."

Tildy smiled and continued cracking eggs into a skillet. Bacon sizzled in the same large pan. The aroma set Lydia's mouth to watering. She busied herself watching Shane work. He'd donned work clothes and wore his sleeves rolled high above his elbows, much like Gabriel and Isaac. The three men appeared to work well together.

"Shane said for me to send you out to him as soon as you're finished eating." Tildy carried the frying pan over and slipped the bacon and eggs on Lydia's plate.

Lydia started to stand. "I'll go now. I can eat later. I don't want to keep Shane waiting."

"You'll do nothing of the sort." Tildy patted her shoulder. "He also said to let you sleep as long as you needed. He's in no hurry."

"I don't want him to think I'm a pampered princess. I want to do my part."

Tildy snorted. "No one thinks you're anything near a pampered princess."

"I can carry my weight and that of my siblings."

"No one doubts that, Miss Lydie. But you suffered a severe blow to the head and a very traumatic experience. We want you to heal. You won't do anyone any good if you collapse from exhaustion."

Lydia's forehead furrowed into a worried frown. "You're sure?"

Tildy sank into the chair beside her. "Positive. We talked over breakfast. Shane said you're the strongest woman he's ever met. The most stubborn, too. He wants you to rest now because he knows you won't in the future."

"He called me stubborn?" Lydia started to stand. She'd show him stubborn.

"And strong." Tildy laughed, pressing her back into her seat. "Stubborn isn't exactly an insult. It shows you have stamina and perseverance. Something every woman needs here in the foothills of the Georgia mountains."

Lydia picked up her fork and moved her eggs around on her plate. "You have to admit, 'stubborn' isn't the most romantic description he could make when speaking of me."

"Ah, you want him to speak romantic words about you?" Tildy's face lit up. "I can tell you that man isn't gonna say romantic words about you around Isaac, the girls, or me. He'll save his sweet nothin's to say to you in private."

"Tildy!" Lydia rested her elbow on the table and dropped her forehead to the palm of her hand. "It isn't like that with us."

"Maybe it isn't yet, but that day is fast a'comin'. I see it in his eyes. In your eyes, too, if truth be known."

"If so, I can do without that truth being known." Lydia laughed. "Shane whispering romantic words to me? It isn't going to happen." Though she found herself wishing it would.

"Too late for that, dearie. Your feelin's are written all over your face, plain as day."

"What feelings are written on Lydia's face?"

Lydia jumped. Shane stood in the doorway, hat in hands. His laughing blue eyes appraised her as he leaned against the doorframe. The way he grinned, Lydia figured he knew exactly what Tildy had said.

"We didn't hear you coming."

"I kind of gathered that by the startled look on your face."

Lydia forced herself to look away from his beautiful eyes and instead lowered her own and studied the way his dark hair curled against his collar. He looked larger than he had before, lounging like he was in the doorway. His broad shoulders were relaxed, his left leg crossed casually over his right ankle. He tossed his hat on a nearby hook and folded his arms. He looked as if he had all the time in the world to stand and stare at her. She continued to push her food around the plate.

"You gonna eat that food, or are you gonna just sit there and torture it?" he asked with a soft laugh.

"I've lost my appetite."

"Nonsense." He pulled out the chair at the far end of the table from her, as if moving closer would put him in harm's way. He seemed to prefer having the table between them. He gripped it with both hands.

Tildy discreetly slipped out the door that led to the hall. The coward.

"You look much better today. Does the dress suit you?"

"It does." Lydia reached down to finger the soft fabric. "You brought it for me?"

"I gave it to Tildy. She brought it into your room. It was my mother's. I hope you don't mind."

"No, it's beautiful. Thank you."

"I have several others if you'll have them. Tildy washed them and placed them in a trunk in the loft of the barn. I'll take you up later to look if you'd like."

I'd like. Lydia shivered at the thought of being alone with him in the loft. Going through a trunk of clothes with him. The experience would feel intimate.

A thought occurred to her. "Maybe you should save the dresses for Savannah. She'll be wearing them before you know it, and she might want the memory of her mother."

"I can buy her new clothes." He frowned. "Unless you'd rather I get you new ones? Not now of course, but when this is all over—when we get to town."

"You have no obligation to buy me new clothes." She couldn't meet his eyes. This whole conversation felt so strange. "If we can get back to the plantation, I'll have access to my own clothes." She glanced up at him. His intense stare made it hard for Lydia to breathe.

Shane's frown deepened. "Is that your plan? To return to the plantation and go on as if nothing happened?" He sounded angry. "You think your stepfather will welcome you back with open arms?"

His harsh tone caught her off guard, and angry tears formed in her eyes. She dropped her gaze to hide them. "I don't expect him to welcome me at all, and I surely don't intend to live there with him." What must he think of her if he'd expect such a thing?

She dropped her fork onto her plate and dropped her hands to hug around her waist. She clutched a handful of fabric in each fist. Could Shane possibly think any less of her? Tildy was way off when it came to Shane engaging in thoughts of romance. He apparently didn't think much of her at all if he thought she'd choose to go back to that life and future.

Disappointment flooded through her. "I hadn't heard your plan yet, Shane. I merely meant I could gather my things when I gathered my siblings. I didn't see any reason why you'd be obligated to clothe me. I'm not your responsibility."

Despite her attempt to hide the angry tears, her voice cracked with emotion. "I'd appreciate your help, but as soon as I have the kids safely in my care, I'll move out of your life." She'd been way off in her daydreams. And apparently making a home here had been just that—a dream. Shane lumped her in with all the others he'd become responsible for. He only saw her as a needy orphan like Emma. Someone to provide for.

Shane was out of his chair and by her side in an instant. He knelt down on one knee and rested his elbow on the edge of the table. "I'm sorry, Lydie. I didn't mean to make you cry."

He pushed a strand of hair away from her face with his free hand. She longed for him to cup her cheek and kiss her tears away. The ridiculous thought angered her further. She'd barely known him a day, and he was toying with her emotions. And she was feeding into all the silliness. She never acted like this. Maybe her head injury wasn't as healed as she'd thought.

She glared at him. "I'm not crying." She swiped at a tear and dropped her arm back down to hug her waist. She leaned against the back of the chair to gain distance. His closeness and warm breath on her face did funny things to her stomach. "How could you even think I'd go back to him? To Joseph. He left me for dead. He told his men to do what they wanted with me."

"You said they didn't hurt you." Shane grasped her arm, his grip gentle. Nothing in him resembled the roughness of Joseph's men.

"They didn't. Not that way." Her voice broke. "But Joseph gave them permission. How could you think so little of me that you'd think I'd go back to—to—that or to what he expects of me?"

"I don't know. But you turned down my offer for clothes and mentioned what you had at the plantation. It sounded like—" He sighed. "Will you accept my apology? I'm not good in situations like this. I'm sorry."

Lydia stared up at him through tear-filled eyes. "Situations like this?"

"That romantic talk you were discussin' with Tildy. The kind of stuff you're expectin' from me. I'm much better at this type of thing—makin' a woman steamin' mad at me."

"I don't expect romantic talk from you!" Mortified that she wanted just that, Lydia punched him in the arm. Denying the very thing she wanted the most felt much better than admitting it to him. Her voice rose as she sputtered, "I wasn't talking about us—about you—about—"

His lips were inches from hers, and she forgot what she wanted to say. "About—um—" His eyes were such a deep, intense blue. They reflected his thoughts, and right now they were searching her eyes with a pleading apology. What was it she'd been trying to say?

She didn't know how to respond to his unspoken question. *Forgive me?* He moved closer, brushing her lips with his own. Her thoughts were a muddled mess. She closed her eyes.

Shane's lips returned to close over hers, making her forget about finding her forgotten words.

He moved a breath away. "Are you going to stop yelling now?"

"I wasn't yelling." She didn't recognize the breathless voice that answered him. She opened her eyes. Surely the voice wasn't hers. She sounded so—addled.

He brushed her lips again, addling her further. "Are you finished denying everything that's true?"

"I'm not denying—argh!"

This time Shane framed her face with his hands and pulled her tight against him. He kissed all sense out of her—that is, if she had any to begin with. And at this point, she wasn't really sure.

She swooned, grasping Shane's upper arms with her hands. She opened her eyes to see Shane staring at her in consternation.

"You surely are the most frustrating woman I've ever met. Definitely the most frustrating in the state of Georgia." He jumped fluidly to his feet, walked to the door, snatched his hat off the hook, and sent her one last look. His expression bordered on terror as he turned and stalked out the door.

Lydia looked up to see Tildy standing in the doorway fanning her face with her hands.

"Oh honey, if that wasn't romantic, I don't know what is."

"You were *watching*?" Lydia squeaked.

"Not by choice. I heard his chair scrape back, and I thought he'd left." She fanned her face again. "I was wrong."

"Obviously. Well, maybe you can tell me what that was all about?" Lydia watched through the window as he made his way to the barn. "He's angry at me."

"Oh no. Ain't no way he's angry after that passionate of a kiss, Miss Lydie. You need to learn the difference between angry and smitten."

"I don't understand. If he's smitten, why'd he get up and stomp out of here like that?"

"He doesn't understand his emotions. Isaac acted the same way. Got all fired up and stomped around till he finally demanded I marry him."

Lydia giggled, resting her fingertips on her tingling lips. "Just like that?"

"Pretty much." Tildy rolled her eyes. "He's lucky I ever said yes, but he made up for it later. He's been a wonderful husband ever since. Some men just don't understand all the emotions that come with attraction and love."

"Love? Whoa, Tildy, slow down. We only met two days ago. We barely know each other."

"Sometimes love doesn't wait for the emotions to catch up. Y'all have it about as bad as I've ever seen it."

"As bad as you've seen what?"

"Love."

Lydia gave up trying to eat breakfast and stood.

"Where are you going?"

She looked toward the barn. "I suppose I should go out there and find out what plans the men came up with." She wiped her damp, shaky palms on the skirt of her dress.

Tildy's laugh made Lydia jump. "You look like you're walking out to face a firing squad instead of three gentlehearted men."

"Did you *see* what just happened between Shane and me?" She waved a hand in front of her, pointing toward the barn and then back at herself. Her heart pounded at the memory, and she glanced down to see if the front of her dress moved with the rhythm. It didn't. "That can't happen again."

"Oh honey, it isn't a matter of it not happenin' again. It's just a matter of when."

Chapter 12

Shane heard a noise and looked out through the open barn doors. He watched as Lydia exited the house and headed his way. From the expression on her face, she meant business. He wished for an easy escape but instead looked around for something to busy his hands.

Gabriel entered the side door from the corral, glanced out front, saw Lydia coming with her storm-filled expression, and headed right back out the same door.

Little girl squeals erupted from the large shade tree, and Lydia stopped in her tracks. She put a hand up to her forehead to shade her eyes, and her lips formed into a soft smile. She called out to the girls. "What are y'all up to?"

The transformation from irritated southern belle to doting female was instantaneous. The little girls obviously adored her, and according to Lydia's reaction, the feeling was mutual. The realization caused a hitch in Shane's breathing.

Savannah threw her arms around Lydia. "We're having a tea party. We found some of my old toys. Miss Tildy made us some cookies and lemonade, and later we're going to help her make more cookies!"

"Sounds wonderful." Lydia placed a hand against her heart and feigned shock. "But a tea party at this early hour? And just before we gather for lunch? Whatever was Tildy thinking?"

The younger two girls caught up with Savannah, giggling. They each took one of Lydia's hands and began tugging her arm. "C'mon. C'mon! You're just in time to fix our hair and read us a story."

"A story, huh?" Lydia looked over at the barn, and Shane backed into the shadows. "Well, I suppose I have time to join you for that. I can't resist a good story."

"You'll hafta read it to us 'cause none of us can read." Savannah sounded wistful.

It was all Shane's fault. He hadn't paid enough attention to Savannah's schooling. The years had passed so quickly! He'd make her schooling his number-one concern after he helped Lydia free her siblings.

Shane moved forward and peeked around the barn door just as Lydia sank down onto the blanket. The three girls crowded around—Savannah and Emma on either side and Lucy standing behind, her arms wrapped around Lydia's neck as she peered over her shoulder.

Lydia started reading, and the girls quietly listened. As soon as the story ended, Lydia glanced over at Savannah. Her words carried clearly. "I've been working with my younger brother, Wyatt, and he's learning to read. I can work with you, too, Savannah, if we come back here after. . ." Her voice drifted off.

"After what, Miss Lydie?" Savannah tilted her head in anticipation. Her eyes had brightened at the prospect of learning to read.

Lydia's shoulders lifted and drooped with a sigh. "We need to get my little brother and bring him back here. Shane's supposed to help me."

"Is your brother in trouble?"

"I hope not. I pray for his safety and well-being every day. I have another brother and sister I pray for, too. They're both seventeen. I'm sure they're watching out for Wyatt."

"We can pray for them right now if you want to."

Lydia's face lit up. "Thank you, Savannah!"

They bowed their heads, and Shane found himself doing the same. He said a quick prayer for the kids' safety and that they'd be able to get them off the plantation without too much trouble. He returned his gaze to the foursome under the tree. They looked so serene sitting in the magnolia's shade. The blue sky made a beautiful backdrop to the tree's green leaves. Fresh green grass covered the ground around the blanket. The pastel hues of the girls' dresses added splashes of color to the scene.

Lydia busied herself with fixing the girls' hair into fancy twists and braids.

Shane watched as Savannah gave Lydia a spontaneous hug and then placed a hand on Lydia's arm. "You don't have to worry about Wyatt and the others, Miss Lydie. Shane will get your brother back. He'll get your other brother and sister back, too, if you want him to. Shane can do anything in the world. He's strong and smart and fixes everything."

Lydia smiled. "He does, does he?" She glanced over at the barn.

Shane stepped back again.

"Yes." He could barely hear Savannah's quiet statement. He leaned around for a better view and so he could hear better. "I tend to get in a lot of trouble. Shane always comes when I need him. He always fixes things and makes them right."

"He loves you very much." Lydia hugged her and then stood, dusting off her skirt. "Each and every one of you."

"Even me?" Emma asked softly.

Lydia squatted and took Emma's hand. "Of course he loves you. I love you, too. You're a wonderful little girl and a perfect sister for Lucy and Savannah."

Emma beamed. "And you're a wonderful mama for all three of us."

Shane cringed as Lucy and Savannah nodded in exuberant agreement.

Lydia's only response was a laugh. "You girls better get back to the tea party before the ants invite themselves to your cookies." Her expression turned apprehensive. "I suppose I should go talk to Shane about fixing my situation." She started toward the barn.

"He'll fix it, you'll see," Savannah called after her.

Shane's young sister had total faith in his ability. He sure hoped he measured up.

He hurried to a dark corner of the barn, snatched up a tangled harness, and laid low. He prayed Lydia would peek in and go back into the house. He wasn't ready to explain the kiss. He didn't understand the kiss. But he knew she wanted to talk about the plan.

He needed a chance to talk to Gabriel and Isaac before talking to her about a plan. He hadn't come up with one and didn't know what to tell her. Her kisses had muddled his mind. He turned his back and fought harder with the tangled leather harness strap—the strap that had only tangled in the first place because earlier, after kissing Lydia so thoroughly, he couldn't get his thoughts away from her or force his concentration to cooperate.

And here she walked around the yard all composed and sensible, reading stories to the girls and fixing their hair as if nothing had ever happened.

"You never did get around to telling me about the plan."

He jumped when her voice sounded right behind him. So much for hoping she'd go back to the house.

Shane stilled his hands but kept his back toward her. "That's because we were too busy—" He paused. What was he going to say? *We were too busy kissing to talk about much of anything at all?*

He abruptly changed direction. "We—Gabriel, Isaac, and I—were too busy last night to discuss today's plans. We had to prepare the stalls for the horses."

"Oh."

Shane tried to ignore the disappointment in Lydia's voice. She wanted a plan, and she wanted her brothers and sister safely away from Joseph. He couldn't blame her. He'd always hurried to Savannah and Lucy's side as soon as a summons would come.

"We'll get to it today. I promise. I plan to ride over and look the situation over this afternoon."

"Really?"

He turned to her with a frown. "You sound surprised. I've already told you I'd help."

"I know, but that was before—well—you know. Before what happened in the kitchen."

"We kissed. Why would anything change just because of that?" He tried not to scowl.

"The way you stomped out of there, I figured I'd done something wrong. I didn't ask to be kissed, but you seemed to regret it the moment you moved away."

She thought she'd done something wrong? The only thing he regretted was that he couldn't stay and kiss her again. But he couldn't tell her that.

He told her the opposite. "The kiss was a mistake. It can't happen again." He didn't want to hurt her, but they'd only just met, and he had a lot on his mind. He couldn't be slowed down by a budding romance. Now to convince his heart of that fact.

"There was more than one kiss, actually. Plural. Kisses. But I fully agree. No more kissing. That was most definitely a mistake."

She agreed way too fast. She actually sounded relieved. The thought grated on Shane's nerves.

Now he scowled. "You agree?"

Why did it matter to him that she so easily brushed off his kisses? So what if the most wonderful kisses of his life were being diminished to a silly mistake? After all, he was the one who used the stupid term *mistake*. At least now she wouldn't be making demands of him.

"Of course I agree." She moved closer.

He couldn't help but notice the way her skirt swayed daintily with each step. The sun shone through the slats of the barn and highlighted her blond hair. Her eyes sparkled as she neared.

"We've been through a lot together in the short time since we've met, Shane. It's only natural that we'd turn to each other for comfort in a weak moment."

"You found our kisses to be *comforting*?"

That didn't sit well with him at all. His entire world had been turned upside down by their kisses in a way he'd never experienced before. He'd been so muddled that he'd completely tangled the harness he was supposed to be fixing. *Comforting* was the last word he'd use to describe their kisses.

"Yes, I found the kisses to be comforting." Lydia laughed and lifted her arms in a shrug, confusion lurking in her green eyes. "What else would the kisses mean if not comfort? We barely know each other."

"You have a good point." Shane stalked across the barn. He needed to get away from her before he took her in his arms and kissed her until she admitted his kisses were much more than a means of *comfort*.

She remained where he'd left her. "About our plans—"

He had no reason to be on the far side of the barn. He fussed with a stall door before walking back to her. "*We* have no plans."

"Not true." She grinned. "We just made plans not to kiss."

She had a point, though he was trying to get his mind off kissing her. "We have no plans beyond that. I said *I'd* ride out and survey the situation at Joseph's place. You'll remain here with the girls."

"What about Ben? You'll take him along, won't you?"

He was shaking his head before she even finished. "No. I can't risk putting him in danger. He's safe at the cabin. I want to leave him there."

"Then you need to take Gabe or Isaac. I don't want you to go alone."

Maybe she cared after all.

They heard a scuffling sound in the yard. Several dogs barked in the distance. A look of terror washed over Lydia's face.

"Joseph's dogs. Hunting dogs." Lydia enunciated each word as she looked up at Shane.

He hated the fear that lurked in her eyes. The fear this Joseph had put there.

"I walked here from the house. I left a scent for the dogs to follow. I wasn't thinking—"

Panic washed over Shane. He didn't have his gun. He had no way to defend Lydia. He'd let himself get distracted by her, and he'd let down his guard. "You'll be okay. Let me think."

The dogs were closer. Isaac and Gabriel ran from the corral and quickly herded the little girls into the safety of the house. Shane didn't have the privilege of doing the same with Lydia.

"I have an idea. Trust me." He hurried forward and swept her off her feet. He held her close as he carried her toward the ladder that led to the loft. He couldn't resist giving her the slightest of kisses. Lydia resisted, pushing hard against him.

"Put me down." Her words were angry. "You said this couldn't happen again, that kissing me was a mistake, and then you choose a time like this to sweep me up in your arms? Joseph wanted me dead. If he finds out I'm alive—" Her words were lost in a sob.

"Hush, woman. I said I have a plan." As he said it, he lifted her to the highest rung of the ladder he could reach. "I've lifted you as high as I can. Grab the ladder and get to the far back corner of the loft and stay quiet."

Lydia nodded. She hurried to do as he'd asked. She secured her boots on the rung, grasped the side of the ladder, and scurried out of sight.

Chapter 13

Lydia held her skirts high so she wouldn't trip and quietly moved to a better vantage point. She peered through a knot in the wood and saw Joseph and his men enter the clearing behind the house. Her heart began to pound. Isaac walked out to greet him, his demeanor casual. There was nothing casual about the rifle clutched in his hand and held at the ready. The dogs were going wild, running in circles and sniffing the ground.

"What can I do for you gentlemen?" Isaac called out, sounding like the perfect neighbor, not a hint of nerves apparent in his voice. Lydia was impressed.

Joseph had a hard time keeping his focus on Isaac. He frowned and watched as the dogs ran in frantic circles toward the barn. He studied the barn, and Lydia felt like he could see straight through it and see her cowering in the loft. Her heart pounded harder in her chest. Though Joseph watched the dogs, he made no move to follow. He returned his attention to Isaac.

"I know I've come around before, but I thought maybe I'd come back and explain a bit more about my situation."

Isaac leaned casually against the porch rail, but his grip on his rifle didn't waver. Lydia had a feeling he was completely confident and wouldn't hesitate to use the weapon in his hand. "Sure. I'm here to listen. What can I do for you?"

"Well, a couple of nights ago one of my sla—I mean, one of my workers took off with my oldest daughter."

"I'm sorry to hear that. It had to be upsetting."

"It was, in more ways than one. I've been nothing but good to Ben, and it hurts to have him turn on me like that."

He played up his hurt, shaking his head in disappointment. Lydia's stomach churned. How convenient for him. He was pinning her disappearance on Ben! If Lydia turned up dead, Ben would be tried and hanged for her murder. Joseph and his men would walk away, free of any wrongdoing. She wanted to surprise them by bursting out of the barn. She wanted to see the look on Joseph's cocky face.

"Stay put, Lydia. Let me take care of this." Shane's quiet voice carried up from below.

How'd he know what she'd been thinking?

"As you can imagine, I love my girl. I don't want to see her to come to harm," continued Joseph.

"He's lying through his teeth!" she called down to Shane in a loud whisper.

"I know he is, but we don't want an altercation right now. Not here. Ben's safely tucked away at the cabin. We'll take care of him. We need to do this right."

The dogs circled closer.

"They've picked up my scent."

"Stay put and trust me."

"I am. I do."

Joseph resumed speaking. "I don't suppose you've seen the murderous fool around here—or have you?"

"Can't say that I have. Ain't been no murderin' fools out this way that I've noticed."

"I can think of at least one," Lydia hissed.

"Lydia. Quiet!"

"Sorry."

Joseph watched the dogs circle the yard. They were waiting for Joseph to give them permission to move on.

"The dogs seem to think otherwise. They seem to have picked up a scent."

Shane stepped into the clearing. "You think so? You're calling these people liars? From what I've seen, they haven't been anything but neighborly to you."

Joseph spun on his heels and raised his rifle. He stared at Shane for a moment. "Who are you? Are these people your workers?"

"Actually, the opposite is true. I showed up yesterday, and Isaac put me to work."

Disgust and disrespect filled Joseph's face. He'd never understand or respect a white man who worked for ex-slaves. Lydia wanted to hug Shane.

Joseph turned his back on Isaac, dismissing him, and faced Shane. "Mind if I have a look around? The dogs never make a mistake when they smell a familiar scent. Either Ben or Lydia is hiding in your barn."

Shane shrugged. "I don't mind you looking around, but that decision is up to my boss." He nodded his head toward Isaac.

Isaac played along. "Fine by me. Let me know what you find."

Lydia's heart pounded. Were Shane and Isaac going to hand her over just like that?

Joseph gave the command for the dogs to move forward, and they headed full-speed for the barn. Joseph hurried to follow them. They circled around inside and made their way back out to Shane. They sniffed and circled again. After several passes, they focused on Shane and howled their find.

"Seems to me they've found what they were looking for." Shane laughed. "Which do I resemble most, your worker or your daughter?"

Joseph glared. "I don't understand. They've never been wrong before. Get over here, you stupid dogs."

The dogs ran to him, and he swiped at them with the butt of his rifle. The dogs skirted away from him and headed for home.

Joseph lifted his rifle and pointed it at Shane. "I don't know what you have going on here, but I'll be back again soon."

Shane didn't say a word.

"Drop the rifle." Isaac's words were loud and commanding. He stood at the ready with his own rifle pointed directly at Joseph. "You aren't welcome back here in your present state. If you do come back, it better be in a neighborly fashion and without the dogs and weapon. I don't take kindly to people showin' up and pointin' a gun at my friends."

Joseph lowered his weapon, but he didn't acknowledge Isaac's command.

He motioned for his men to leave and followed them from the yard. He stopped and sent one hostile glare back that encompassed both men. Isaac waited until Joseph was well on his way before walking back inside.

Lydia sat frozen in place. She pulled her knees against her chest and wrapped her arms around them. She leaned against the wall for support, too scared to climb down from the protection of the loft. What if she did climb down and Joseph was lying in wait?

"Lydie? It's safe to come down."

"No." Her voice wavered. "Not right now. I'll come down in a bit. I want to make sure they're gone."

Wood creaked as Shane made his way up the ladder. He walked over to her side. "Are you okay?"

Tears of anger and fear overflowed from her eyes. "I hate him so much. He's turned this around and is putting all the blame on Ben. Ben wouldn't hurt anyone. He's the most gentlehearted man I've ever met. He's taken care of me, and he'd never hurt me."

Shane sank down beside her. His strong presence made her feel safe and protected. The soothing aroma of fresh hay wafted her way as he settled in place.

Lydia looked up at him. "What if they find the cabin? Ben won't have a chance."

"They won't find him at the cabin. It's too remote. Just to show you how remote, I'll take you there after lunch. We'll check on Ben so you know he's okay."

"What about my brothers and sister?"

"After meeting your stepfather and his men, I think it's best if I meet him with the sheriff at my side. I'll send Gabriel to fetch him while we ride up the mountain."

"If the sheriff goes along, you'll be able to bring the children back with you for sure, won't you?"

"I can't make any promises that we'll get them right away, but I'll do the best I can. We can't break any laws in the process. I will get them back to you. We just have to tread carefully. The sheriff will know what to do."

A sense of peace flowed over her at his words. "I believe you. I'm going to pray that God provides a way for you to get them tomorrow."

"Your faith is inspiring." Shane stared at her from his place in the dusky loft. "I'm new to all this. Gabriel has explained enough to me, but I still don't understand it all. With everything that's happened to you, how have you kept your faith?"

"How could you not have kept yours?" Lydia countered. "With everything that's happened over the past few days, how can you not see God's hand in things?"

Shane smiled. "You have a good point. I'll contemplate that."

The sun shone through the cracks in the wood, highlighting the dust that floated between them.

She changed the subject. "You kissed me again just before you sent me up here."

"I did."

"You were the one saying we couldn't do that again."

"I know."

"Then why'd you do the opposite? And at such an inopportune time?"

"I kissed you so your scent would be on my clothes. The ruse worked. The dogs were thoroughly confused. They followed your scent in the barn, but it ended with me."

Lydia laughed. "I guess that's true. What a brilliant idea! I wondered what all that was about."

"Well now you know."

"Thank you." She wanted him to kiss her again. "For everything."

"You're welcome." Shane stared at her for a moment, then looked away. "I have a confession to make."

Lydia settled back against the rough-hewn wall and waited. She hoped he wasn't about to say he'd changed his mind about helping her. Though she had to admit, now that he'd seen Joseph in action, he had reason to rethink his involvement.

"What?" she asked warily.

He grinned at her. "I don't consider our kisses a mistake."

"Oh. You—don't?"

"No. I don't."

"What changed your mind?"

"I didn't have to kiss you before you climbed up in the loft. Your scent was already on my clothes from me holding you in my arms. I just wanted to check my emotions and see if kissing you really was a mistake or if it was something I enjoyed."

She raised an eyebrow. "You couldn't tell that from the kisses in the kitchen?"

"I wanted to be sure." He laughed. He ducked as she dropped a handful of hay on top of his dark curls.

"In all seriousness—why did you kiss me again?"

"I like kissing you. It's as simple as that." He settled back into place. "I'm not used to feeling that way. You have to understand. My father was a horrible husband to my mother, but my mother was a wonderful wife to him. The last time my father came home, he gave me a piece of advice, the only advice I ever remember him giving."

Lydia waited a moment, and when he didn't speak, she prompted him. "What was the advice?"

Shane looked at her long and hard. "He said for me to find a woman as good as my mother to marry and for me to stay away from his wandering ways."

"And you ignored him on both counts."

"I did." He nodded. "Right up until the other day when I saw you standing on the walkway in town. Something about you had my father's words coming back to me. You showed the same spirit as my mom. You were beautiful, intelligent, and courageous. You were fiercely protective of Wyatt. My mother would have been the same way. As a matter of fact, she would have cheered you on when you knocked that chair out from under me."

Lydia laughed in spite of her stress. "Oh, I doubt that."

"No, she absolutely would have. Then she would have grabbed me by the ear and hauled me out of the saloon."

He looked down. "My choice to follow my father into gambling would have been the biggest disappointment of her life."

Lydia was glad he couldn't see her face. She wasn't sure what to say in light of his confessions. "I doubt that would have been her biggest disappointment. Your father had to have broken her heart."

"And I would have broken it all over again."

"But you didn't. And now you're here, taking care of your sisters. The choice might have come late, but you've been given a second chance. It seems to me you're bent on taking it."

"I am." He sighed and pushed to his feet. He reached down to help her up. "I suppose we should go down now before tongues start wagging."

"I suppose you're right."

"Though if they're going to talk anyway, we might as well share one more kiss."

211

"You're incorrigible!" Lydia moved toward the ladder.

Shane grabbed her arm. "In the stories—stories like the one you just read to the girls—the fair maiden always rewards her rescuer with a kiss."

"I've already rewarded you with a few kisses too many."

"But this is a completely new rescue." He leaned nearer, and her heart did flips in her chest.

She leaned forward, too, and dropped her voice to a whisper. "And what would your mother have to say about you being alone in the loft with a woman who isn't your wife—*without* the benefit of a chaperone?"

He was close enough that she could feel his breath. "She'd probably tell me to do the proper thing and make the woman my wife."

Her heart skipped a beat. "And would you listen to her?"

"I'd probably listen to her about as well as I listened to my father."

The kiss never came. He smirked and moved away from her and easily down the ladder.

The loft felt lonely without his presence. She hurried to follow him.

"As I said before"—he leaned close to her ear as she finished her descent—"no more kisses."

She buried her face in her hands and groaned. "You're the one who said I owed you a kiss!"

His blue eyes twinkled, teasing her. "And I think you might agree."

She thought she might agree, too. If she needed rescuing, which seemed to be quite often of late, Shane was the perfect hero to do so.

"Shane?" Gabriel's voice called from just outside the door.

They jumped guiltily apart.

"In here." Shane sent her an apologetic grin.

Gabriel entered the dim interior and looked back and forth between them. "It's safe to come out. I've been watching Joseph and his men from the attic. They headed back down to the plantation."

Shane stood in the doorway. "He's not happy."

"No, he isn't. We need to do something and fast."

"Lydia and I were just talking about options. I want to send for the sheriff."

Gabriel looked over at Lydia. She nodded her agreement.

"You need to stay here, Shane, in case they come back. I'll ride for the sheriff. Tildy has lunch on the table. She sent me to fetch you two."

"My thoughts exactly. I appreciate it, Gabe." Shane motioned for them to lead the way toward the house. He fell in behind them. "I'm taking Lydia up to visit Ben as soon as we've eaten. If you bring back the sheriff, we'll have everything in order, and we can ride out first thing in the morning."

Chapter 14

Lunch had been a quiet affair. No one wanted to talk about Joseph's visit with the children present. As soon as the girls excused themselves and ran out the back door, Shane leaned back in his chair. "They sure seem to be in a hurry to get outside."

"I told you they love it here." Gabriel smiled, watching them through the window. "It's the kind of place every child needs to grow up in. Plenty of fresh air. Lots of space. A nice, safe house."

"I get your point, Gabe." Shane softened his words with a partial smile. "And I agree. The girls love it here. I plan for them to stay."

Lydia's heart melted. She wanted the same for Wyatt. He'd thrive in a place like this. Though the plantation was roomy and had every comfort imaginable, it lacked the warmth of the homestead. And for the most part, no one but Joseph was allowed to enjoy the comforts. Wyatt's days were filled with chores and work in the fields. Joseph used every bit of help at his disposal, even the help of his children. Everyone at the plantation carried their weight—everyone but Joseph. Joseph paraded around and berated or disciplined anyone who didn't work up to his or her potential.

Shane placed his cloth napkin on the table. "Lydia and I are going to head up to the cabin and check on Ben. I want to make sure he has everything he needs."

"I'll put a basket together for him." Tildy hurried to her feet and began gathering supplies.

Lydia walked over to help her.

"I'll ready the horses." Shane headed out the back door with Isaac and Gabriel on his heels.

The two women worked side by side and packed the basket full of muffins, eggs, jam, two loaves of bread, some butter, and a variety of cured meat. Tildy added a container of milk. "I hope he isn't lonely up there all alone."

"I would imagine he's relishing the quiet. Ben was born into slavery. He's never had the luxury of choosing how to spend his day." Lydia grew thoughtful. "Though I'm sure he'd enjoy it more if Sadie was at his side. He won't rest until he has her with him."

"I can't imagine being separated from Isaac." Tildy clucked. "We worked the

213

same plantation together, grew up side by side. We had a kind master who let us marry and live as husband and wife. He gave us our freedom, but most of us chose to stay on and continue as we were."

"What changed?" Lydia couldn't imagine slave owners who were so kind. She'd only known the harsh ways of her stepfather and his friends. "What made you leave?"

"Our master passed away, and his wife wanted to sell. She gave us plenty of warnin', though, and we were able to contact Gabe. He suggested we come here and take care of Shane's place for him." She smiled. "It was in horrible disarray. We both worked long, hard days and enjoyed every minute. The first structure we rebuilt was the cabin—the one Ben's living in now."

"I look forward to seeing it."

"I believe you'll enjoy its charm. We lived there while fixing up the house and barn." She wiped her hands on the skirt of her apron and glanced around the kitchen. "I suppose we have everything Ben will need for now."

"He'll think this a feast fit for a king. As you've seen, my stepfather wasn't a good man. His slaves—his *workers*," she said, her voice laced with sarcasm, "weren't treated very well, and they were fed even worse. Ben and the others have lived a very harsh life. There wasn't anything I could do to make things better."

"I can imagine." Tildy laid her hand on Lydia's shoulder. "His choices aren't your burdens to carry."

Lydia sighed. "I know. But it's hard to let go of a lifetime of guilt. While I walked around in my beautiful clothes, Joseph treated us all horribly, but we had to make a good impression on his friends who would drop by without warning—the other girls my age on the plantation wore nothing but rags. We ate till our bellies were full, even though the best food went to Joseph. We never went hungry like the slaves."

"That was Joseph's choice, child, and he alone will pay the price for his sins."

"I suppose you're right."

"I am and don't you forget it." She cupped Lydia's cheek and grinned. "You get on up there and take your friend his food."

"Yes'm." Lydia picked up the basket. "And you have fun with the girls."

"I fully intend to. We have cookies to make."

"They'll love that, Tildy." Lydia looked out the window where Isaac was hanging a swing made of ropes and a board on a sturdy branch in the girls' favorite tree. All three clapped their hands with excitement and anticipation.

"We've only been here two days, and already the girls are blooming."

"Um-hum. I'd imagine we're in for some tough times with Emma after the new wears off and she starts missing her mama." Tildy tsked at the thought. "But we'll rally and be here for her when that time comes."

"We will," Lydia agreed. "I mean, if I get to stay on."

"Shane ain't sendin' you nowhere, Miss Lydie."

"I hope you're right. This place is as soothing for my soul as it seems to be for theirs."

They watched Isaac put Lucy on the swing and gently give it a push. She squealed with terrified glee. Savannah and Emma jumped up and down, vying for a turn. Isaac helped Lucy off, and Emma took her place. Savannah bounced with excited energy. When Savannah finally got her turn, Gabe and Shane walked toward the house with Chester and Pal.

"Looks like it's time for me to go."

"Have fun, Lydia. You deserve to."

"I'll have fun after I get my family to safety."

"Your siblings' situation ain't gonna change just because you're mopin' around worryin' about them. Have some fun. There's nothin' you can do for them right now. Enjoy this time with Shane."

"That's a good way to look at it, Tildy." Lydia gave the older woman a spontaneous hug. "You give good advice. Thank you. I know our arrival must have turned your peaceful world upside down. Yet you've been nothing but kind and gracious to us."

"I love my Isaac and his company, Miss Lydie, but when y'all arrived here yesterday, our whole world lit up like the sunrise. We've been mighty lonely after all this time on our own. We grew up in the company of friends, and we're more than ready to share our time with others." She swatted at Lydia with her towel. "Now go on with ya while I try to compete with Isaac and the swing for the girls' company."

Lydia stepped out the door and was greeted by Shane's crooked smile. "Ready?"

"I think so. Tildy and I packed enough food to feed a family for a week."

Tildy opened the door. "I slipped a couple of sandwiches in so y'all could have a picnic if you're late gettin' home."

Lydia flushed. Tildy didn't even try to be subtle.

Shane helped her up onto Chester, secured the basket of food, and swung up onto Pal. "Let's go."

He took off at a trot, and Lydia fell into place behind him. She studied him as they rode. He sat tall and straight in the saddle. His black hair peeked out from under his hat and curled at his collar. From the back he looked like an Indian warrior sitting confidently atop his palomino.

They headed into the woods at the base of the mountain and began to climb. The trail was barely noticeable, and if Shane hadn't been in the lead, Lydia would never have seen it. The branches and scrub tugged at their clothes. Shane stopped and thoughtfully held back the longest of limbs so Lydia wouldn't be hurt by their backlash, protecting her just as he had in the barn.

She'd badly misjudged him at the saloon. The man she'd met that day had been hurting and trying to find his way, just as she'd tried to find hers all these years while under Joseph's hand. Now they were both free to discover who they were. Shane had found his place by returning home while Lydia found hers by leaving.

The trail began to climb, and Lydia focused on her surroundings. The rugged hillside beauty was nothing like the flatter land of her home. She'd seen the mountains from afar, but never had she found the time to go exploring.

A bubbling stream flanked the trail for a time, and Lydia slowed when the trail widened. She drifted over to the beautiful space and stopped in the middle of a clearing. She wanted nothing more than to settle down on the luscious grass that grew beside the brook and watch the water rush over the pebbles.

"You'll have plenty of time to linger after we visit Ben and rescue Wyatt." Shane's chuckle from behind her caused her to start.

She glanced back at him. "The only time I've ever been in the hills was when my stepfather ordered the men to leave me two nights ago. It's so beautiful here. I never even knew something like this existed."

Shane looked at her, contemplative.

"What?" She grew self-conscious.

He turned his horse back to the trail. "Follow me. I want to show you something."

She urged Chester to follow him. Their trail wound around the side of the mountain now. After another mile, Shane swung to the ground. He secured the horses to a nearby branch where they could reach the stream for a drink or snack on the abundant grass.

"We have to walk from here." He reached for her hand.

"To get to the cabin?"

"No, to get to the place I want to show you."

She took his hand, and they worked their way through the dense underbrush for what seemed an eternity. Lydia couldn't imagine what was worth the scratches and rough terrain.

Finally they stepped into an open space that ended in a ledge. Lydia looked out over the expanse, and the view took her breath away. "It's—it's absolutely beautiful."

"It is. I thought you'd like it."

The valley spread below them, and in the far distance she could see the plantation home where she'd grown up. Tears filled her eyes. "Wyatt's down there somewhere, wondering where I've gone, wondering why I've abandoned him."

Shane pulled her into his arms. "I bet he's tougher than you think. He knows you'll return for him." His strong hands caressed her hair.

Lydia laid her head on his shoulder and let him hold her close. She pulled strength from his nearness. "This is what you wanted to show me?"

"Yes." He moved away from her and led her closer to the edge. "I spent so many boyhood hours in this place. I loved the view from here, and I'd often imagine who the people were that lived in such a magnificent house."

"Our house."

"Yes." He stood with arms crossed and feet spread. He looked like he owned the world. "You said back at the stream that you'd grown up here and had never known the beauty of the mountains."

"Right."

He sent her a smile. "I grew up in the mountains and never knew the beauty growing up in the house I'd watched over from afar."

"Oh. Um—" Lydia didn't know how to respond to such a blatant compliment. "Thank you."

"You're welcome."

They stood and studied the plantation for a few more moments.

"We need to be going." Shane took her elbow and turned her from the view.

She looked over her shoulder for one last glance, wishing she could see Wyatt. "Thank you for sharing this with me."

"I have a lot of other things I'd love to show you and experience with you after all of this is over. That is, if you'll let me."

"You have to ask? I'd love to have you show me all of it!" Her heart trilled. He wanted to see her after he helped her. "Wyatt would love it up here."

"Then we'll start by bringing the kids for a picnic here on the ledge. Maybe let them have a swim in the stream."

"Wyatt has never experienced such a thing. We've had impromptu picnics in our yard, back when my mother was alive—on the rare occasions when Joseph would go to town. I'm not sure about him being up here with the ledge, though. He's so impulsive."

"So was I, Mama Bear. He'll be fine. I'll make sure of it."

"All right."

"You're gonna love it here, Lydia. It's a great place for a boy like Wyatt to grow up." He took her hand, and his deep blue eyes peered into hers. "I hope you'll stay on after we get the kids, at least for a while, once Joseph is taken care of. I'll understand if you want to return home at some point if Joseph ends up in jail. But I want you to know that Wyatt, Nathan, and Natalie are welcome to stay with us for as long as you want."

Lydia blinked back the tears that threatened to fall. It was official. They had a place to go, a place that wasn't the plantation. "I'll never want to go back there if I have a choice."

"You have a choice."

"Thank you. I'd like to stay, at least for a while."

His eyes clouded for a moment. "I know we've just met, but I hope you'll consider staying on for more than a while. Take the time you need to heal. Take the time to figure out where you want to be." He leaned down to give her a gentle kiss. A kiss that carried a world of promise. "It took me four long years to realize I'd already been to the place I wanted to be. I had to explore the countryside to appreciate what I had here at home."

"I can already tell you I don't need to go anywhere else. It's beautiful and peaceful here." Peaceful was the only requirement she had.

Shane laughed. "Peaceful? With three little girls and Wyatt on the way? Throw in the twins and you'll have anything but peaceful."

"Peaceful and quiet are two different things, Shane. I never said it would be quiet. Peaceful is a place deep inside your soul. A place deep within my soul anyway. I've never experienced it before now."

His expression turned teasing. "I think that's what I felt right up until you fell out of that tree and landed on my lap. Savannah had been nagging me about finding a wife and settling down so we could stay at the homestead." He glanced at her. "If you haven't noticed, she's very persistent."

"I've noticed."

"I told her if God wanted me to have a wife, He'd have to drop her on my lap."

"And there I was."

"Yes. There you were. There's no stopping Savannah now. She's sure God sent you to us."

Lydia turned back to the view. "And what do you think?"

He was silent for so long she turned around to make sure he still stood beside her. "I think God has a plan for all of us, and I think God's central to that plan."

"I agree. I've always had faith. I don't know how I'd have made it through the past few years without it. But you—your faith is new, isn't it?"

He nodded. "I was raised up to have faith, but I pushed it away after I lost my mother. Gabriel made it his life's quest to bring me back to that faith."

"It worked."

"It did. In an unexpected way and when I least expected it."

"That's how God works." Lydia gave him an impish smile. "And how life works, too. If you aren't careful, you'll be stuck with us forever."

"I can think of worse things than that."

"Wyatt can be a handful. I know you've seen that, but he can really take a toll on a person's nerves."

"Sounds like me when I was young."

Lydia laughed. "I can only imagine."

Chapter 15

They walked back to the waiting horses and continued their climb. The path turned and zigzagged the opposite direction until they entered another clearing. A small cabin sat in the midst of the open area. A cozy porch ran across the front of the house.

Lydia hurried Chester forward and slid down from his back. "Ben!"

She expected the front door to burst open, but it didn't. She continued forward, leading Chester along behind her. Shane pulled up and reached for the reins.

"Thank you." She smiled at him and hurried up the steps. "Ben?" She knocked on the door.

Heavy footsteps moved across the room from the other side of the door.

"Ben, it's me, Lydia."

The door opened wide, and a huge grin spread across his wrinkled face.

"Miz Lydie! You be lookin' much better than last time I saw ya."

Lydia laughed. "It's hasn't been such a long time. Only a day."

"You still be lookin' better. You rested, and the bruises done faded."

"She was worried about you." Shane stepped up beside her, having secured the horses.

"Now Miz Lydie, why you go worryin' 'bout an ole man like me?"

Lydia looked at Shane.

He nodded and pointed at the chairs that stood in a row on the porch. "Let's sit down."

"Joseph came to the homestead today."

Ben's features wrinkled with concern. "He didn't find out you wuz there?"

"No," she hurried to reassure him. "But he was angry, and he's pinning my whole disappearance on you. He told Shane and Isaac that you kidnapped me and disappeared. Ben, you have to be careful. If they find you—"

"I've done had my taste of freedom, Miz Lydie. The only place I'm goin' when I leave this mountain is to find my precious Sadie. Joseph and his men ain't gonna stop me."

"Gabriel has gone for the sheriff. Let us take care of Joseph before you leave here. I don't want to take any chances. Joseph's men had a lot of guns today. You wouldn't stand a chance if you ran into them. They'd shoot first and explain later. We need you alive and well."

Ben started to disagree.

"Sadie needs you alive and well," said Shane.

Ben couldn't argue with that. Lydia sent Shane a thankful smile and turned back to Ben. "We brought you some food."

Shane went down the steps two at a time and retrieved the basket.

Ben shook his head. "Tildy done packed me a hamper yesterday. I ain't begun to eat it. How can she expect me to eat all this food? Have y'all eaten?"

Shane nodded. "We did before we started up here, but I'll take a muffin."

"Miz Lydie? You wanna a muffin?"

"Sure."

Lydia figured if they kept him distracted, he'd forget about going after Sadie. She picked a muffin from the basket and leaned back to nibble on it while the men talked. It was the first time she'd paid attention to the view from the porch.

"Oh Shane, it's beautiful up here." She stopped with the muffin half raised to her lips, mesmerized. They were halfway up the mountain, and the cleared trees allowed a view that looked out over the distant mountains. Rolling hill after rolling hill went on for as far as she could see. "I feel like I can see all the way to Atlanta!"

Shane laughed. "You could if we were facing south. We've traveled around enough that we're actually facing northwest. These are small hills compared to the mountains north of us, but they do make for a pretty view, don't they?"

"Breathtaking. I had no idea. I could sit on this porch forever."

"That works fine for me, Miz Lydie. You sit up here and stay safe while enjoyin' the view, and I'll go down the mountain with Shane to settle things up with Joseph and his men. I s'pose it'll do him good to see me face-to-face while he's telling the sheriff his lies."

Lydia sat up straight in her chair, the muffin dangling in her fingers. "You'll do no such thing! And neither shall I. I refuse to sit here while everyone else is down there fighting my battle."

"It's my battle, too, Miz Lydie," Ben said quietly. "Joseph made this my battle the day slavery ended and he didn't give us our freedom. He made it another battle when he took away my Sadie. Now he's settin' me up for a kidnappin' charge I never committed."

Tears filled Lydia's eyes. "I understand, but I don't like it."

"I don't much like it either, child, but we be all right. We have the good Lord on our side, and ain't no one gonna hurt us. I got to go along. Joseph'll have his guns and men, but we also be havin' guns and men. If I's there, we be gettin' the cooperation of the others. They need me, Lydie."

The tears rolled freely down Lydia's cheeks. It was the first time he'd sounded grandfatherly. The chains that had bound his spirit were falling off.

"I see that they do, Ben." She wiped at the tears with the palm of her hand. "But I'm going down the mountain, too. As beautiful as it is up here, I'm not staying alone. Shane's already said I can't go along to the plantation, but I want to be as close to the action as I can. If y'all bring Wyatt back, I want to be there to hold him."

"You watch for us, Miz Lydie. I'll bring Wyatt back to you. You know he'll come with me."

"That he will."

Shane stood and paced the length of the porch. "We plan to bring everyone back if we can, Ben—the workers, Wyatt, and the twins. We won't know the details until we get back to the house."

"Do you think Gabe and the sheriff are back?" Lydia wanted to get going if so. The nearer they were to making the final plan, the nearer they were to getting Wyatt safely in her arms.

"I doubt it. Gabe took the shorter route through the back side of the plantation, but it'll take him the better part of the afternoon and evening to get there and back. There's no road, but the path should get him there fast enough."

Ben intervened. "What 'bout Joseph's men? They patrol the back end o' the farthest cotton field."

"He'll stay on our property. Joseph's men won't catch him."

"I don't see no reason for us to sit up here talkin' when we can make our way down the mountain." Ben stood. "I'll grab my things, and we be ready to go."

Lydia joined Shane and rested her forearms on the porch rail. "It's unbelievably beautiful. I didn't think it could get any prettier than down at the stream. Then you showed me the ledge—now this."

"The beauty is unending."

Lydia looked up at him, ready to agree, but she realized he was staring at her. Her mouth quirked in a self-conscious grin. "Are we talking about the same thing? The beauty of the mountainside?"

"More or less." He laughed. "I'm learning there are many different kinds of beauty in these hills."

"Hmm." She glanced back out over the valley, furrowing her forehead.

"We'll come back up here with the children, too. They'll like it. Savannah and Lucy don't remember any of this. I'll enjoy seeing our mountain through their eyes."

"Maybe Wyatt won't be so wild if he has all this within reach. I bet we can tire him out really well."

"I'd imagine, now that you mention it, that's the exact reason why my mother allowed us boys to run the hills so much in our youth."

"I'm sure you're right."

"I'm glad she got to enjoy Savannah for the first four years of her life. Mama had her hands full of us boys."

🙠

Shane enjoyed the trip down the mountain enough that he again chose the longer route. Ben started to question him as they rode out, but Shane silenced him with a nod. Ben looked at Lydia, who sat in front of Shane on Pal, and gave him a knowing grin.

Shane knew Lydia would find out about the more direct route down to the homestead soon enough, but he'd enjoyed their trip up, and he intended to prolong their trip down. Gabe wouldn't be back until just before nightfall, so they had no reason to rush.

He savored the scent of her sun-warmed hair. She smelled fresh like spring. He wished the bruises and cut would fade away so he'd not be reminded of the trauma she'd experienced after he met her in town. He wished he could wipe it all away. He remembered standing in the middle of the street in town, watching her walk away, watching as she climbed onto the wagon with Wyatt, and watching her round the corner.

He'd wanted to go after her. Gabriel had walked up and in one look had known Shane had lost his heart.

"I should have gone after you." He whispered the words into her hair.

"What?" Lydia turned a bit in his arms.

"That day in town, after we left the saloon, I wanted to chase you down."

"Oh."

He didn't blame her for the surprise in her voice. "You were so angry, and I didn't like the way it made me feel. I watched you stalk away. I wanted to make you come back, to make things right. I didn't want you upset with me."

"You didn't even know me."

"My heart did. Somehow. Though I didn't understand it then."

They were nearing the main path to the house. Ben moved around them and headed in as Shane slowed. "I know it's only been a couple of days. But that moment, standing there on the dirt of the road, I might as well have been hit by a bolt of lightning. That's how mesmerizing the moment was for me."

"I'd just knocked you flat on your back." Lydia laughed. "You must have hit your head."

"No. My senses were fully intact." He enjoyed her sense of humor.

"And then I fell on your lap from the tree. Are you sure you can stand having me around? It could prove to be very dangerous."

Dangerous to my foolish heart, he thought.

"After facing off with Joseph tomorrow, spending time getting to know you will be most enjoyable." He laughed.

"I'm glad you think so."

Ben was heading into the stable as they rode into the yard. Shane swung off Pal and reached up to help Lydia.

"Lydie! Lydie! Lydie!" A chorus of voices called out moments before the girls burst through the back door. They threw their arms around her.

"We missed you." Lucy's words were muffled against the skirt of Lydia's dress.

Lydia pulled the other two girls slightly away so the child could breathe as she looked laughingly over at Shane. "So I see."

"You were gone a long time," Emma said solemnly.

"Not really," Lydia corrected. "We were only gone for the better part of the afternoon. You haven't even had the evening meal, have you?"

"No."

"What about me?" Shane inserted, wanting to give Lydia a break. "Didn't anyone miss me?"

Savannah rolled her eyes. "We've always had you around."

Shane raised his eyebrows. "Oh really? That wasn't what you said when I saw you yesterday morning! You said it was about time I'd come back to get you. And"—he moved slowly forward—"I believe it's about time I get you right now."

A moment later realization dawned on Savannah's face. "No!"

She tripped backward in her hurry to get away from him. Emma and Lucy clung to Lydia's skirt, their faces apprehensive. He winked at them. Lucy gave him a shy smile, but Emma still looked worried. Lydia swung her up into her arms.

"Yes." He crept closer.

Savannah was scrambling backward on her hands and feet and laughing. She couldn't move fast enough to get away from him. He dove forward and tickled her until she could hardly breathe.

"Tickle me! Tickle me!" Lucy jumped on his back. He swung around on his hands and knees, spinning until she lost her grip. Her giggles were contagious. Even Emma joined in the laughter. He caught Lucy with his arm and used the other to tickle Savannah some more.

"Miss me now, Van?"

"No! Not when you're tickling me!"

"Admit it, you like the attention."

Emma wiggled down and crept closer. Lydia stayed close to her side. Shane reached up and tickled the little girl until she laughed out loud. She jumped on his back, and the other two joined in, trying to hold him down. In the end he let them win.

They ran off to the swing, and he sat on his knees watching them, breathing hard. Isaac had come for Pal while Shane played with the girls.

"You just gained Emma's trust." Lydia smiled.

"I believe you're right. And Savannah let her guard down."

Lydia held out a hand to help him to his feet. "She was pretty upset with you from what I understood. She's missed you."

"I don't know what I was thinking. I've missed so much of their lives."

"And now you'll be here to experience so much more."

"You always see the good, don't you?"

"I try."

Gabe rode into the yard with a stranger. He hadn't brought the sheriff. Shane dusted off his clothes as he walked over to greet them.

"Shane, this is Duncan." Shane shook the man's hand and waited for Gabe's explanation. "The sheriff couldn't come, he has a problem in town, but he deputized Duncan a while back and sent him in his place."

"This won't be easy—"

"Gabriel filled us in on everything," Duncan interrupted. "I've worked with the sheriff on several other occasions. I feel confident I'll be able to handle things."

"Good." Relief washed over Shane. He didn't want their plans to fall apart. "I'm glad to meet you, Deputy."

"Duncan is fine."

Tildy called everyone in for supper. Shane looked over at the girls. "You girls want to have a picnic?"

They ran inside to wash up while Lydia went in for a blanket. Tildy said she'd plate up their meals. Shane saw the lilt in Lydia's step as she carried the blanket over to the girls. She shook it, and the ends of the linen flew high into the air. It drifted slowly to the ground. Lydia bent to smooth the edges.

Shane felt like the piece of linen. Lydie's arrival had shaken him up, too, and now her presence smoothed his rough edges. Tomorrow would end Lydia's trauma, and hopefully by the end of the day, Wyatt would be safely in her arms. His displaced belle might change her mind and be more than happy to stay at the plantation after everything leveled out. He wouldn't blame her if she changed her mind. With Joseph safely behind bars—the best scenario for him—Lydie might realize her place is in her family home. Shane knew she wouldn't be far, even if she did decide to return to her family home. Their boundaries touched, and he could court her from afar. But he desperately hoped she'd decide to stay with them. Regardless, the deputy's arrival had set the plan into motion.

Chapter 16

Shane sat on his horse and surveyed the five ladies lined up before him. He had a feeling this image would be forever burned into his memory. He'd already told the women to stay alert and to keep their weapons within reach.

Lydia held Emma on her hip. Lydia's features were strained and her eyes full of concern. He tried to convey through his confidence that everything would be fine. Emma lay with her head on Lydia's shoulder. Though young, she obviously felt the nervous tension. Tildy held Lucy, who was reaching and crying for Shane. The older woman rocked his little sister in her arms, crooning softly in her ear.

Tildy nodded her head at Shane and waved him on, assuring him she had everything under control. Savannah, looking half-grown, stood between the two women, courage and concern warring across her features. Shane knew she wanted to be strong for him, but at the same time he could see she wanted nothing more than to throw herself into his arms.

"I'm going to be fine, Van. We'll come home as soon as we can."

A lone tear rolled down Savannah's cheek as concern won out. She nodded, her voice lost in a sob.

Tildy wrapped her free arm around Savannah's shoulder at the same time that Lydia took the little girl's hand.

"We know you're goin' to be fine." Tildy voiced her faith. "We're goin' to be prayin' the entire time y'all are gone, aren't we girls?"

"I'm glad to hear it." Shane looked them over one last time and turned his horse to follow the other men. The deputy led the way into the trees, the others falling in single file. Shane brought up the rear.

"I love you, Shane!" Savannah's panicked voice suddenly broke the silence as she chased him into the trees.

He pulled his horse to a stop and turned around. "I know you do, Van. I love you, too."

A tiny smile shaped her mouth as she nodded. Lydia called her back, and Savannah hurried to obey.

The ride to the plantation was a quiet one. No one wanted to chance warning Joseph's men of their arrival. They'd discussed it the night before and felt catching everyone off guard would be the best way to go.

Ben motioned for them to stop. "This here is the outskirts of the western corner."

The deputy nodded and slowly moved forward. They stopped just inside the tree line to study the situation.

Shane pulled up alongside the deputy. After a few moments, he quietly asked, "What do you think?"

Pal shifted beneath him, his movements antsy. Two horses down, Chester snorted.

Duncan adjusted the front of his hat. "I think we should ride out of the trees as we are. Keep your rifles at the ready, but don't point them at anyone unless necessary. Let me take the lead and listen for my direction."

The men murmured in agreement.

"Let's go."

They moved casually from the trees, and for a couple of minutes, no one noticed their arrival.

Shane scoured the field, locating Wyatt at once. He bent over the crop right alongside everyone else, his features tired and strained. A younger version of Lydia worked at his side. Natalie. She reached over and caressed the little boy's head. Wyatt appeared to be in good hands.

One of the hands on horseback started their way. The others fell in behind him.

"Can I help you?" This boy was just shy of adulthood. His size and features put him at the right age to be Lydia's other brother, Nathan.

"We're here to talk to Joseph."

"He's not available at the moment, but you can talk to me."

"We really need to talk to Joseph."

The men behind Nathan nervously shifted their shotguns.

A burly man pushed ahead of Nathan. "The boy's made it clear Joseph isn't here. Y'all need to be on your way."

Nathan scowled, not happy with the man's pushiness. "I'm handling things."

"We can wait." Duncan wasn't going to be put off. "We'll head over to the plantation house and make ourselves at home."

Shane noticed one of the riders had moved away and was now riding full speed toward the house. He nodded toward the rider. "Looks like someone is going to get Joseph for us."

The other men looked over their shoulders, and the burly man swore.

Wyatt was looking their way, and Shane pulled his hat lower over his face. The last thing he needed was for the boy to recognize him from town and make a scene. The workers had stopped their progress. Natalie nervously wiped her hands on her skirt, staring their way. Shane saw her mouth Ben's name. Her face hardened. Shane wondered if Joseph had spread the same rumors about Ben to Lydia's family and the workers. If so, it would be harder to gain their trust.

Two riders were heading their direction from the far side of the field. Shane recognized Joseph as they neared.

"What are you men doing on my property?" he bellowed.

"Same thing you were doing on their property when you paid them your friendly little visit yesterday," Duncan drawled. "The way I hear it, you threatened these folks and said you'd return."

"I just asked them some questions," Joseph hedged. He glanced along the line of men and noticed Ben. His eyes went wide as he pointed a shaky finger in Ben's direction. "If you want to question someone, why don't you ask that man right there what he did with my daughter?"

"This man didn't have anything to do with your daughter's disappearance."

Ben's quiet voice joined in. "But I can tell you who did." He looked over at the burly man and his partner.

The burly man paled. "You can't prove anything with your empty threats."

"I shore enough can, and Miz Lydia will testify, too."

"She survived?" The smaller man backed his horse away. "I don't want no trouble. We was only followin' orders. Joseph ordered us to take her away."

"Shut up!" Joseph snarled. "They're bluffing. They don't know where Lydia is any more than we do."

The man cringed, wrapping his fingers nervously into his horse's mane.

"If that's true, why are you blaming Ben for her disappearance? Your man there pretty much gave me a confession just now."

"Idiot," Joseph snarled under his breath. His words slurred.

The numbers were pretty even. Besides Joseph, Nathan, the burly man, and his scrawny partner, there were only two others. Shane calculated their odds if everyone went for their weapons.

Nathan, according to Lydia, wouldn't engage in any shooting. Not unless he was sure he was fighting on the right side. From his expression of distaste, he didn't think the right side would include Joseph.

Joseph would shoot, but based on his slurred speech and his alcohol-scented aroma, his aim would be poor due to drinking. The scrawny man was shaking too hard to pull a trigger. That left the burly man and the two others to their five.

"Ben, did you have anything you wanted to say?" Duncan asked.

"I do." He looked over at the workers. "Joseph sent Lydia away with these two"—he waved toward the culprits with two fingers—"two days ago. He instructed them to do whatever they wanted with her, as long as they made sure she didn't ever return."

Nathan's eyes narrowed. "Is this true?"

Joseph's laugh was sinister. "None of your business, boy."

"It is my business."

Duncan moved closer to Joseph.

An instant later, paranoia swept across Joseph's features. "You ain't taking me away. I have family and responsibilities to tend to. Y'all get off my property and don't bother coming back."

Duncan looked over at the workers. "Are any of you working of your own volition? Are you here by choice?" A few of the workers glanced at each other, but most merely looked down at the ground. "If you're being held here by force, I'm giving you the chance to leave right now."

A few of the faces filled with hope.

Shane noticed that Natalie had moved closer, her hand protectively on Wyatt's shoulder. Both had fresh bruises on their faces. Shane looked at Nathan and noticed he favored his left arm. Joseph had been a very busy man. And a very angry man.

Ben looked over his people. "Please. You'll be safe with us if you leave right now. Joseph can't hurt you now that the law is involved."

Shane saw desire war with terror, but finally several of the workers stepped forward.

"Is it true?" Wyatt's quiet voice asked. "Is Lydia with you?" Wyatt looked hopeful, then burst into tears. "I want Lydie!"

Natalie pulled him close against her skirt.

"It's true," Shane stated. "Lydia's fine. She sent us to get you."

"You ain't takin' my kids anywhere."

Duncan raised a hand. "I'm taking them. I have a responsibility to see to their safety, and with the fresh signs of abuse on their faces, I'm taking them with us."

"You can't do that!" Joseph's expression was wild.

None of the workers dared move.

"I can, and I am."

"It's not legal."

"We can figure all that out in town at the sheriff's office."

"You ain't taking me to any sheriff." He spun his horse around and looked at his men. "Take care of them!"

He hurried off, but Duncan didn't show any sign of chasing him. Instead he targeted the other four men with his glare.

"I ain't doing nothin'," the scrawny one said. He threw his rifle to the ground. "He don't pay us enough for the things he wants us to do."

"I agree." The burly one kept his firearm, but he spun around and headed toward the far side of the property, away from both the plantation and Shane's spread. The scrawny guy followed along. It only took a moment for the last two to follow suit.

"Nathan?" Duncan asked.

"Yes, sir."

"Are you going to 'take care of us'?"

"I am, sir." He turned his horse to face his sister and brother. "Natalie? Wyatt? Prepare to ride out with the men here."

Duncan laughed. "I'm not sure that's exactly what your stepfather had in mind."

Nathan's grin matched the deputy's. "I don't reckon it is, but it's what we're doing."

Wyatt's face lit up. "You're the man from the saloon!"

Shane cringed. "I am, but I'm not ever stepping foot in a saloon again. God and Lydia have changed my ways."

"I wanna ride with the brave man. Please, Nathan? Lydie knocked him flat on his back. He was really mad."

Nathan's eyes narrowed.

"It's a long story," Shane hurried to say. "I can assure you, your sister has made her peace with me."

"Um-hum, according to Tildy, she sure has." Isaac spoke for the first time.

Gabriel's mouth dropped open, and he stared from Isaac to Shane. "What haven't you told me, Shane? What's all this, 'Um-hum, she sure has' stuff?"

"Tildy caught them kissing in the kitchen yesterday morning."

"You kissed my sister?" Nathan's gun raised a notch. "After only knowing her one day?"

Shane wondered if Lydia had underestimated her younger brother.

"It's not how it sounds. I can explain. But this is hardly the place."

"He's right," Duncan interrupted. "We need to be going. I want to get the kids settled in before dark."

"Lydia's going to be worried if we don't hurry up and get back to her. We'll explain everything when we get there."

Natalie reached up to touch Nathan's leg. "Please, Nathan. I don't want to spend another night here. Let's get going."

Her plea seemed to center him. "Okay, Wyatt, you ride with—what did you say your name is?"

"I didn't. The name's Shane. I own the land behind the plantation and the better part of that mountain." Shane reached down, and Wyatt grabbed his hand. Shane pulled him up and settled him in the circle of Shane's arms.

"Good to meet you." Nathan reached a hand to Natalie and swung her up onto the horse behind him. "I'm Nathan, and this is my sister, Natalie."

"Lydia's told us all about you."

"Let's get out of here," Duncan said. He looked over at the workers. "We'll move slowly, and you all can keep up on foot. I'm sorry we don't have a better way. It's not safe for you to remain behind."

"They are good people," Ben reassured. "Let 'em help you."

"What about Joseph and the men who left Miss Lydie to—" Isaac glanced over at Wyatt and tempered his words as he voiced the question everyone had to have on their mind. "Who left Miss Lydia in the woods? Shouldn't we go after them?"

"No, the sheriff told me to get the kids and workers to safety. He said he'd put a posse together if he needed to and would round up whoever needed roundin'."

Duncan turned to Shane and Nathan. "You two ride ahead and give the women some peace. They're going to worry until they have news. You'll have time to reunite everyone and to let Tildy know there'll be about a dozen extra people for dinner before we arrive at the house."

Shane looked over at Gabe and Isaac. Both nodded their agreement.

"Don't do anything crazy," Shane admonished them. "I don't want to face Tildy or Lydia's wrath if something happens to either one of you."

"Nothing's going to happen, Shane. We'll be fine." Gabriel grinned. It wasn't often he got to stay around for the finale while Shane missed out. Shane usually *was* the finale.

"I'll bring up the rear. If Joseph tries anything, he'll have me to deal with," stated Duncan.

Shane felt secure knowing Duncan had everything under control.

❧

Lydia paced the clearing. She'd circled the open area at least a hundred times while keeping an eye on the girls. Tildy stayed inside the house, cooking up a storm. She said she had complete faith that God would protect and bring the entire plantation's worth of workers home.

Lydia had explained that the plantation only had a handful of workers. She passed by the back door. Tildy opened the door and stepped out onto the porch. "No sign yet?"

"Nothing." She wrapped her arms around her waist. "What's keeping them, Tildy? It's been longer than they expected. What if—"

"Huh-uh, honey. You aren't goin' there. We aren't going to think the worst. We're gonna keep on prayin' and wait to see how God answers. His ways are always best, right?"

"You're right." Lydia sighed. "I guess I'll continue to—"

"Shane!" Savannah screeched.

Lydia spun around to see the three girls running toward the trees. Shane rode their way with Wyatt nestled in his arms. Lydia pressed her shaking hands over her mouth as tears poured down her face. "Wyatt!"

The words were barely a whispered sob, too soft for Wyatt to hear.

"Is that your other brother and sister behind him? God's answered our prayers, Lydia. He's brought your family home."

Lydia nodded, still not able to speak. She moved forward toward the happy group. The two littlest girls danced dangerously close to Pal's legs. Shane shooed them away, but they didn't listen. They wanted to be close to Shane.

Shane gave up. He stopped the horse and waited for Lydia to join them. She was crying so hard she could barely walk.

"I told you I'd bring them home."

"Lydie!" Wyatt's and Natalie's voices merged. Nathan sat on his horse and grinned at her.

"I've missed you all so much!" Lydia reached for Wyatt and wrapped him in her embrace. He clung to her neck and cried. "I told you I'd come back. I came this far and couldn't get to the plantation, so Shane volunteered to go the rest of the way for me."

"I told you he was brave." Wyatt sniffled.

"You were right." She exchanged a happy, watery smile with Shane. She turned to her sister. "Natalie. Nathan. I'm so glad you got away." Nathan and Natalie jumped down, and they all hugged.

"Where are the others?" she asked Shane as they walked toward the house. The little girls had already snagged Natalie and were dragging her over to the tree. Wyatt wouldn't leave Lydia's arms, and she was glad. She wasn't ready to let go of his warm little body.

"They're coming up behind us," Shane explained. "Or at least they were. They're with the workers who are traveling here on foot."

They stopped at the porch steps.

"Tildy, we'll have another dozen or so people for dinner. I was told to warn you."

"Oh my goodness. I'd best get back to work."

"I'll help." Lydia started up the steps.

"Nonsense." Tildy waved her towel. "You'll go visit with your family. You know I have things under control."

Nathan took his horse and Pal to the barn. Natalie went in to help him. The girls trailed at her heels.

"Your family settles right in." Shane led her to a bench.

"They do. You'll like them. Nathan's a hard worker, and Natalie will love helping Tildy in the kitchen." Wyatt rested on her shoulder. Lydia could feel his sweet breath blowing against her neck. "He's exhausted. And he has a bruise on his cheek."

"I saw."

"What did they do with Joseph?"

Shane hesitated.

"Tell me."

"He ran off. Duncan said the sheriff will put together a posse to find him and the two men who left you in the woods."

Panic flared. "He'll not give up, Shane. He hates to lose. He'll come back for us."

"He won't get you. Duncan's staying over, and we'll have a barn full of men to help. We'll assign people to watch over the yard in shifts as everyone else sleeps. We won't let anything happen to you."

Lydia knew she wouldn't sleep a wink. She'd make sure her siblings slept in the room with her. She knew Nathan would insist on doing his share of the watch.

"Duncan told me last night that once they have everything finished up here, they'll locate Sadie and bring her back to Ben."

"I'm glad to hear that."

Gabe interrupted, bursting from the trees at a fast pace. He saw Lydia and tried to gain his composure. "I need to speak to you, Shane."

Lydia stayed Shane with her hand. "Please, Shane. I need to hear what he has to say."

"If you don't mind, Lydia, I'd rather not say this in front of you."

"Gabriel, you're scaring me." Lydia stood, holding Wyatt against her. "Do we need to hide?"

His expression was guarded. "No."

Shane intervened. "Just tell us, Gabe. What happened?"

Gabriel looked from Shane to Lydia and back again. "Joseph ambushed us on the trail."

Lydia gasped. "Was anyone hurt?"

"Only one person."

"Ben or Isaac? Duncan?"

"No—o—o." He stopped. "Shane, I'd really rather discuss this in private."

"I'm not leaving," Lydia snapped. "Tell us what happened, Gabe. Please."

"If you're sure."

Lydia nodded.

"Duncan wasn't kidding when he said he had things under control." Gabe glanced over at Natalie and Nathan who had just exited the barn.

Lydia waved them over. Tildy came to the kitchen door and called the little girls in.

"Joseph came up behind us, riding fast. Duncan whipped around with his rifle raised and told him to stop."

"He didn't stop."

"No."

"Did Duncan shoot him?"

"That's where things got strange. Before Duncan could fire off a shot, Joseph ran headlong into a tree and fell from his horse."

"How bad is he?" Lydia wished she could work up some sympathy, but she couldn't. The man was nothing but evil.

"Duncan went back to check on him. Joseph hit the tree hard. We all saw it. He wasn't breathing. Joseph is—well, he's dead, Lydia."

Lydia was stunned.

Natalie buried her face in Nathan's shoulder. Nathan led her over to Lydia and Wyatt. "He can't hurt us anymore."

"No," Lydia whispered. "Just like that."

Gabriel frowned.

"I know we sound callous, Gabe, but you saw Joseph. He was horrible to us. I don't know what he was like when our mother first met him, but from my earliest memory, he was horrible to her and horrible to us."

"We saw." Shane laid a supportive hand on Lydia's arm.

"I'm sad for the person he could have been, but he never was that person."

Gabriel nodded. "Duncan sent me ahead. Ben is waiting with the others. Isaac and Duncan stayed back with Joseph. Duncan wants me to return and tell him your preferences."

Lydia shivered. "I don't want him anywhere near us, even in death."

"I'll go." Nathan started back to get his horse. "Someone will need to tend to the livestock."

"Nathan, wait." Lydia allowed Shane to take Wyatt. "I don't want you over there alone."

"I'll be fine." He smiled. "I'll check in first thing tomorrow."

"Ben told me he'd like to go back and care for the livestock," Gabriel inserted. "The workers want to go with him."

"Oh." Nathan seemed undecided.

"I need you here, Nathan. Ben needs to do this. Let him go. It'll give him something to do while he waits for Sadie."

Nathan nodded. "Gabriel? Tell him to make himself at home inside the plantation house. Tell him I'll be over in the morning to help. As for Joseph, tell Duncan we don't have a preference other than he take the body well away from here."

"Will do." Gabriel headed out.

Lydia shivered again. The words were eerily similar to the ones Joseph had said a few nights earlier about her.

"You two go on in. We'll join you in a few minutes." Shane took Lydia by the arm and held her back.

Nathan led Natalie toward the kitchen.

Shane led Lydia around to sit on the front porch swing where they'd talked their first night at the house. "I'm sorry about Joseph."

He sat down beside her and settled Wyatt in her arms. She nestled her face in Wyatt's soft curls.

"I'm not sure how to feel. I mostly feel relieved."

"I don't blame you." He put his arm around her, and she rested her head on his shoulder. "I'm sure you'll all go through some mixed emotions while you're sorting everything out."

"Nathan won't be back after tomorrow. He'll stay on to run the plantation."

"Is that a bad thing?"

"No. He loves it there and does a good job. He's a hard worker. He'll make a good plantation owner."

"What about Natalie?"

"I think she'll stay around for a while. I'm not sure she'll want to return to the place that holds so many bad memories, at least for a while." She shuddered. "At least that's how I feel."

"You know you have a place here."

She nodded against his sleeve. "She and Nathan are close. She'll return at some point, but she'll want to be here with me, too. She'll bounce back and forth until she finds her place."

"She's welcome here, too. All of you are."

"I know, and I thank you for that."

"Lydie?" Shane stopped the swing.

Lydia raised her head to look at him.

"Like I said, I know it'll take a while for you to sort everything out."

"Right. I understand."

"I just want you to know that I'm here for you while you're sorting."

She laughed. "I know that, too. And I appreciate it."

He sighed. "What I'm trying to say is, take your time grieving, adjusting, and making whatever decisions that need to be made. I'm going to be right here, waiting until things settle. After that, I'd like you to consider a future with me."

She nestled back in his arms. "I think I'm going to enjoy the settling process."

He kissed the top of her head and pulled her close. "Me, too, Lydie. Me, too."

THE RELUCTANT
OUTLAW

Dedication

To my good friend Jennifer Sexton. It isn't often that a friendship lasts through the decades. I'm so glad to have you as that kind of friend!

Chapter 1

North Georgia Mountains, 1873

Bella narrowed her eyes and resisted the urge to turn the squint into a full-fledged glare as her arrogant brother rode his horse back and forth on the hard-packed ground in front of her. It wouldn't serve any purpose to make him mad. The corner of her mouth turned up in a hard smile. He was already halfway to mad, much like their deceased father, and because of that she didn't need to make him angry. She forced her mouth into a straight line and focused on the tufts of dust that rose into the air from Wayne's huge horse's prancing. She tried hard to control her anger. She didn't want to be like them. She wanted out. She no longer wanted to be part of her brothers' gang. She never had wanted to be part of it, not that her opinion had ever been asked.

Bella sat high in her saddle listening to Wayne's lecture, determined to hold her ground. His eyes gleamed in a fanatical way, one she'd come to recognize as a prelude to a tangent, his stature full of self-importance. His moods were becoming more unpredictable every day. Bella refused to let him get to her. She'd had it with his attempts at intimidation. Her brother was most definitely turning into a madman. Or maybe he already was one. With her rough family history, at least after her mother passed away, it was difficult to tell.

"You *girls*"—Wayne accentuated the term with syrupy contempt, wanting Bella and her younger sister, Andria, to know their place—"need to ride down the mountain today. Be prepared to go into town tomorrow at first light. Don't dally, and don't draw attention to yourselves. I want you to check around and see if they're gettin' ready to send another posse up here anytime soon."

Charlie, the older brother closest to Bella in age, snorted.

Wayne swung around to face him. "You got a problem with something I said, Charlie?"

"There ain't no way these two are gonna go into town and not draw attention. You happen to look at 'em lately? I mean *really* look at 'em?"

Wayne stared from Bella to Andria and back again. "They look all right to me."

"They look more than all right, Wayne. They ain't little girls no more. Them single men in town will take one look and will be after them to stay. Fights'll break out in their wake. I've seen it happen with plainer women, and these two ain't plain."

Wayne sneered. "Well, they *ain't gonna* stay on—you hear that, Bella? Andria? You won't be stayin' in town. You get in there, do your business, and get out."

Bella heard all right. Staying in town was the last thing she wanted. "I hardly plan to ride into town and get myself hitched, Wayne. Settlin' down with any man is the last thing on my mind."

Her father and brothers made that decision easy. As far as she was concerned, she'd stay unhitched forever if the concept meant being tied up for life with a man who resembled the likes of her brothers. And since she'd never before seen a man who acted otherwise, she had no intention of getting hitched at all. Ever.

Bella's secret wish was to be a schoolteacher, but she doubted that would ever happen. Single women were preferred when it came to teaching, so the arrangement would be just about perfect. She doubted any school would hire a member of one of the most notorious outlaw gangs in the area, but she could always dream. Her participation in the gang might be reluctant on her end, but no one would see it that way if they were caught.

Wayne continued his lecture. "Good. No weddin's for either of you, and don't you forget it." Wayne rode closer and leaned into Bella's face. She could feel the brim of his hat against her forehead as he stared into her soul with empty, hard eyes. "Speakin' of, what *is* on your mind, little sister? You been awfully quiet these past few days. You better not be thinkin' about tryin' somethin'."

Bella met his gaze for several long moments before deciding it was best not to answer him. She was thinking of trying something all right, but she wasn't about to tell Wayne that. And she refused to tell a lie, even to the likes of him. She raised an eyebrow and lifted one shoulder before turning her horse away from him.

Before she could move away, Wayne hit her hard from behind, knocking her from her place on the saddle. "Don't *ever* turn your back on me, you hear?"

The motion swept her sideways, and though she grasped for a hold on the saddle horn, she lost her grip and arced through the air.

Andria screamed as Bella sprawled flat on her back on the hard, dusty ground. Everything faded to black, though Bella could still hear the horses as they shuffled their hooves nervously beside her, far too close to her head. She panicked when she realized she couldn't pull a breath into her lungs. She fought to take in air. She couldn't die like this—not now. Andria needed her.

"Now look what you've gone and done!" Charlie yelled as he swung down from his own mount and knelt at her side. Bella felt his knee brush against her as he gingerly tilted her up into his arms. "She can't breathe. You done broke her back, you stupid idiot!"

"Her back ain't broke. I just knocked the wind out of her." Wayne spat a thread of tobacco. From the sound of it, the disgusting substance landed mere inches from Bella's face.

Charlie shifted her again, and fresh air gushed into Bella's lungs. She took a deep draw of the life-sustaining air before giving in to the anger that simmered deep inside. Her vision cleared, and she located Wayne. He remained where he was, straddling his horse, but now he leaned forward, one arm resting cockily on his thigh as he peered down at her with a hateful smirk on his face. She pushed up and lunged for him. "How—dare—you—"

Charlie held her back. "Not now, Bella. Let it go."

His words were quiet, for her ears only.

Her breath came in short, fast bursts as she watched Wayne ride away. He glanced back over his shoulder, and she fought again, futilely, against Charlie's hold.

Inappropriate humor danced in Wayne's eyes as he surveyed her. After a brief moment, he emotionally discarded her with an expression of disdain. He pulled his hat low on his forehead, a defensive move that cast his eyes into dark shadowed orbs. Bella shivered.

"Remember, ride in. Ride out. Don't draw attention. Attend to business and return home. That's an order."

"You might as well order the wind to stop blowing. Like Charlie said, we can't help but draw attention." Bella hissed the words, not caring if he heard or not. "How often do you think two mountain women ride alone into that tiny ole town?"

Wayne either didn't hear her or chose to ignore her statements. "See ya when you get back. I'll be waitin'." He slowly turned his horse and rode toward the high trail that looked out over the valley.

Bella watched him go. Wayne had reached a new low when he'd knocked her from the saddle.

"I hate him, Charlie." Bella felt something crack deep inside as she uttered the statement. "I hate him."

Pain stabbed through her heart as she stated the words. She'd never felt such wrath, hadn't ever hated anyone before now. She'd hated circumstances and situations, she'd hated certain days and experiences, but never had she hated another person with such passion. The realization scared her. If she continued on this path, she'd end up as mean and full of hate as Wayne. She had to get out of the gang, and she needed to take her younger sister with her.

Charlie scratched his head in frustration. "Bella, you gotta speak to Wayne with respect from now on. This new attitude of yours ain't gonna do no one no good."

"I'm the one with a new attitude?" Bella asked, incredulous. "Did you see what Wayne just did to me? *He's* the one who's out of control."

Concern filled Charlie's eyes. He was no saint, but he wasn't as bad as Wayne. "Ain't gonna do no good if you keep challengin' him, Belle. You just gotta do as he says."

She'd do nothing of the kind, but she wouldn't admit that to Charlie. He was in too deep and fully under his older brother's control.

"I understand, Charlie."

"I hope you do. He ain't stable right now."

He hasn't been stable in a long, long time.

A short time later, Bella thought about Charlie's comment as she guided her horse down the steep mountain trail at as fast a pace as she dared. She was still filled with anger—anger that Wayne had ignited deep inside her. *Stable, hmph.* Wayne hadn't been stable since as far back as she could remember. Even when their mother had been alive, Bella could remember him challenging her every request. Many times Bella had seen fear move into the gentle-natured woman's eyes when she'd attempted to reprimand her son. To Bella's recollection, Wayne had never been anything near stable.

Even though Bella was angry, she still proceeded down the mountain with a heightened level of awareness. She knew the pitfalls that could await her and her sister on the unseen parts of the path. They moved stealthily with purpose, yet also with caution. Her brother wasn't the only weasel who lived and rode in these mountains.

The path widened and opened into a small meadow, which allowed Andria to ride up beside her. "Wayne shouldn'ta talked to you that way, Belle. It ain't right. And he sure shouldn't have hit you."

"I didn't exactly ask him to talk to me like that or to hit me, Andria. If you noticed, I ended up flat on my back."

"I noticed all right." Andria's voice was laced with anger. "The question is, what are we gonna do about it?"

"*We* aren't gonna do anything about it. For now we'll go into town like we were told. We'll let this die down a bit, and then I'll come up with a plan. Wayne'll expect somethin' from us now, so we'll wait till we can catch him off guard. When the time is right, we'll put my plan into motion."

Chapter 2

Duncan slowed his horse as he rounded the last bend in the trail. He tilted his head and listened for the voices he thought he'd heard a few moments earlier. He'd diverted from the main trail—taking to a side path so he could water his horse—but the unexpected sounds in the brush up ahead caused him to slow his progress. Duncan knew enough from past experience to use caution when catching people unaware, especially out here on the less-frequented trails.

Sure enough, the rustle of fabric and the sound of harsh feminine laughter drifted his way on the breeze. They weren't the usual noises one would expect to hear while riding the trail, but they weren't completely uncommon either. Erring on the side of caution, he slipped his rifle from its place at the side of his saddle and rested it atop his legs as he quietly urged his horse to move forward. The laughter sounded again. It sounded anything but menacing, more self-deprecating, but Duncan wasn't taking any chances. The voices grew louder as he slowly rode closer.

"I wish you could see how funny you look." The speaker sounded young, her voice full of barely contained laughter.

"I'm glad you find this amusin'," a second voice chimed in, this one sounding older, less patient, and a bit more serious. "It's not like you don't have to follow suit. Whoever invented women's clothin' must have done so as a method of torture for someone they loathed."

Interesting. A woman complaining about wearing women's clothing? That was something Duncan hadn't heard before. The situation grew more intriguing by the moment.

Duncan reined his horse to a stop as the first female laughed out loud. He didn't exactly want to ride up and surprise whoever appeared to be in the process of changing clothes on the other side of the trees. If he had the choice of another watering hole before heading back to town, he'd turn around and head in that direction. But since turning around wasn't an option considering the narrowness of the trail behind him, he figured he'd bide his time until they were finished, then he'd water his horse and move along when he could. It wasn't like he was hard-pressed to be anywhere specific at the moment anyway.

"Argh." More rustling of bushes as the more serious speaker shifted around. "I give up! Let's stay as we are, find a place closer to our destination where we can settle in for the night, and then we can change into these ridiculous clothes right before we walk into town tomorrow mornin'."

"Fine by me. You know I'm not happy about wearin' that awful dress in the first place. The less time I have to suffer through the experience, the better. I still don't see why Wayne wants us to wear the horrid things. He's only our brother. Why should we listen to him? Especially after what he did to you this mornin'."

"We'll do it because he told us to, Andria. I don't want you hurt. You know what he said; he wants us to blend in and not look like we just rode down the mountain. It's best for now that we do as he says. You have to stop fightin' the way things are, at least for now. Don't try to fight my battle for me."

Did they mean "hurt" physically? Or are they just talking about hurt feelings from an older brother's overprotective attitude? Duncan sure hoped it was the latter.

"Blend in?" the younger voice stated. "In these hideous things? How do you plan to do that?"

"We need to wear the dresses, Andria. We need Wayne to think we're in agreement with him. Our future plans depend on it."

From what Duncan could hear, these two couldn't "blend in" no matter how hard they tried. They were obviously from the hills, and judging from their conversation, they didn't often wear women's clothing. Their brother most likely wanted them to dress like ladies before their courting days began. Duncan smiled. He could only imagine what a handful two sisters like this would be for an older brother. Though he was curious to know what this older brother had done to his sister earlier in the day.

Duncan wanted to wait until they were dressed and then ride around the bend and introduce himself, but he was sure the women who were making the outrageous comments wouldn't appreciate his appearance. He'd wondered at times about the ridiculous outfits some women insisted on putting together, but he'd never considered that there were womenfolk who felt the same way—not that he thought about it often. As far as he knew, it was their lot in life to dress as they did, and none of them ever considered doing anything different.

These anonymous speakers taught him otherwise. Instead of approaching them, he figured he should find a way to turn around and head back along the trail that meandered through the trees. Perhaps if he could back the horse up a few feet, he could find a wider area and make his turn.

Instead of leaving, though, something compelled him to remain where he was. He heard more rustling, a few frustrated grunts, then two matching sighs of relief.

"Much better!" the older voice exclaimed. He heard the soft whinny of a horse. "I know one thing for sure. I completely prefer to wear pants over dresses.

How do women get anything done in those things?"

"I dunno."

"Seems they'd be trippin' over their own skirts all the time. I certainly would be."

"Bella, about what you said—I'm not 'fightin'' things," the younger woman stated, her voice taking a hard edge. "I want to be more involved. I want more responsibility. Our brothers use us to do their biddin', yet they show us no respect. They'll learn to respect me before all is said and done." She paused. "And you'd do well to make them respect you as well."

Duncan leaned forward on his saddle. A warning sounded in his head. If these two women were in danger, he needed to intervene and at least offer up his help.

Bella didn't comment for a few moments, but when she did, her voice was tinged with resentment. "They'll never respect us, Andi. You'd do well to accept and understand *that*. What our brothers do—it ain't right. One of these days their actions will catch up with them, and I for one intend to be far away when that day comes."

"And how do you plan to get away? You have no money. The only time they let us out of their sight is to go up to Momma's place or when they come down here to a nearby town. This is the first time they've allowed us to come to town alone, and we have a tight timeline to work with. Without money, how do you ever plan to escape?"

Duncan hung back, wondering who Wayne was and why he treated his sisters so poorly. As the local parson, he wanted to help these hurting ladies. But he didn't want to burst in on their private moment. He assumed they wouldn't be receptive of his offer to help. As it was, he shouldn't have been eavesdropping on their conversation for as long as he had been. Maybe he could talk to the sheriff and together they'd be able to figure out a solution to provide for the women's safety.

He whispered a quick prayer for direction and was disappointed when he didn't feel led to interrupt their private discussion. God was clarifying what Duncan already knew. He needed to leave them alone for now.

The two women would head into town the next morning. He'd watch for them and have a plan in place when they arrived. For now, he needed to be on his way. They'd reach the trail at any moment, and he didn't want to be caught listening in. He looked around and noticed another, smaller trail forking off at an angle from the way he'd come. He decided to take the trail and see if it led to another watering hole farther downstream. In the meantime, he'd continue to pray for the women. He could still hear their voices as he backed his horse to the mouth of the smaller trail and moved away.

"Andria, I'll figure somethin' out. Just be patient and wait until I have a solid plan. We won't be under our brothers' control much longer."

"Well, I plan to be *in* control before much longer."

The voices still carried through the trees at his new angle. Duncan stopped again.

"Andria, don't say that! You'll only be hurt. There's no way our brothers will ever take orders from a mere *woman*. No one will ever force our brothers to change their ways. They're dangerous. Please promise me you'll listen and you'll wait for my lead before doing anything reckless."

Duncan debated going back. If he offered his help, maybe he could provide a way for the two women to get away from their seemingly unstable brothers.

"What if I have a plan laid out before you come up with one?" Cockiness oozed through Andria's words.

"A plan to break away from the boys?"

"Maybe."

"Tell me before you act on it. We have a better chance of gettin' away if we work together."

"I'll tell you when the time is right."

"Andria—"

Duncan heard the younger woman's laugh as she urged her horse into action and burst through the trees behind him. He couldn't turn around on the narrow path but looked over his shoulder to see if he could identify the rider. He missed the first rider but saw a brief flash of auburn hair as the second rider gave chase. If he hadn't heard their feminine voices, he'd have been sure the riders were male based on their attire. He followed the new path until it opened up in a small clearing alongside the stream. He led Blaze toward the watering hole and offered up a prayer of thanks for God's provision, then added a petition for the safety of the two women he'd overheard.

After he'd watered his horse, Duncan followed the overgrown path to its end where it intersected with his original trail a good ways down the mountain from where he'd diverted to head for the water. He smiled, happy to know of another, quicker way to get through the area. He studied the mouth of the path that had all but disappeared once he'd cleared it. The surrounding landmarks would remind him of the path's presence in the future. Duncan's early days as an outlaw had taught him to watch for alternate trails. Back in his wilder days, he'd never known when he'd need a secondary escape plan. It was always best to have an alternate plan in place.

The old habit died hard and suited the life of a preacher just as well as it did a hardened outlaw. He glanced forward and noticed another rider approaching from the direction of town.

Duncan greeted the familiar man. "Afternoon, Jack."

"Howdy." Jack pulled his hat from his head and wiped his brow. The sun beat down hot on Duncan's back now that he had moved away from the trees. "Sheriff's looking for you, Duncan. I told him I'd pass the word along if I saw you on my way out."

"I appreciate it, Jack. I'm heading that way now. Anything serious?"

"Naw." Amusement passed through Jack's eyes. "I think he needs you to talk to a young prisoner."

"Ethan in trouble again?"

"Something like that." Jack put his hat back in place and firmed his grip on the reins, preparing to ride on. "He seemed pretty distraught."

"Ethan or his father?" The sheriff had his hands full with his young, errant son.

"Both."

"I can imagine. It's kind of hard for the sheriff to uphold the law when his own son thrives on breaking it."

"And it's hard for the boy to figure out how to spread his wings when his father's bent on clipping them."

"That's very true." Duncan's focus was on the unruly boy he'd grown so fond of when two riders flew around the bend of the main trail and startled both Jack's and Duncan's horses. The men fought to retain control of the scared beasts as the approaching riders skidded to a stop, fighting their own mounts as they reared backward.

"I'm so sorry," the farthest rider gasped. "We were in a hurry and didn't think about the fact that someone might be sittin' on the trail ahead of us."

Duncan recognized the voice and bright auburn hair. Bella. The nearer woman, the one Duncan guessed to be Andria, scowled.

As usual, God's providence caught Duncan by surprise. Even now, after all his training as a pastor, he was often awed by God's unfolding plans. He didn't know where this particular plan would lead, but he did know the shortcut had allowed Duncan to bypass the women when they'd taken the more visible upper trail.

He exchanged a curious look with Jack and shrugged. "No apology necessary. You're right. No one would expect to come upon someone sitting on the trail like we were. This isn't the place to be having a conversation."

"No harm done." The woman's smile was tight. She didn't allow time for introductions. "Come along, Andi."

Andria continued to scowl as they rode past.

"I'm—" Jack held up a hand but let his words die out as the women picked up their pace and hurried on down the trail. "Interesting pair."

Duncan watched them go. Even though he'd seen them face-to-face, he didn't know that he'd be able to identify them in town. They wore their hair pulled back in braids, and their faces were dusty from the trail. Their hats were pulled low on their foreheads. Intriguingly, they looked very much like two women who had a lot to hide.

Chapter 3

Bella McLeod rode into a small clearing and motioned for her younger sister to stop. She figured this was as good a place as any to set up camp for the night. A bubbling brook beckoned from the other side of the trees, and the greenery and scrub formed a protective canopy over their heads. The cozy area lured her in, promising a peaceful experience that Bella often dreamed about but never quite achieved. Not with her brothers around, anyway.

"We'll stop here. In the mornin' we'll get up early, dress proper-like, and walk the rest of the way into town."

"You want to walk?" Andria shrugged and dismounted. "I s'pose that'll work. I still don't understand why we can't just ride the rest of the way in tonight, dressed as we are. We'd have an extra night to enjoy the sights before we take care of business. As a matter of fact, it would be the *perfect* time to take care of business."

"You mean you'd have an extra night to get into trouble." Bella shook her head. "I hardly think that's a good idea. You heard Wayne. He wants us to go in lookin' presentable, go about our business, and get out. He doesn't want us drawin' attention to ourselves by hangin' out in the saloon."

"You don't think we'll draw attention tryin' to look all ladylike when we're used to wearing men's pants and ridin' around on horses?" Andria challenged. "I'll probably trip on my skirt and fall flat on my face, just as you said before. And I'll likely take you down with me."

"You'll do no such thing. Don't talk like that. If you're focused on fallin' and get yourself all worked up about it, you'll fall sure enough."

"But people relax more in the evenin'. They let their guard down. I might be able to loosen a tongue or two over at the saloon and find out when the next posse'll ride out our way. Why waste a whole day eavesdroppin' around town when a simple question asked at the right time in the right place will do the job as well?"

Bella swung her leg over her horse and dropped down beside her sister. She busied herself with pulling items she'd need from the saddlebags that were slung over Steadfast's back. "The saloon is forbidden, Andi. You'll not step foot inside that place. We'll do as Wayne said, and we'll go about our business with our ears open. Nothin' more. Promise me you'll stick to the plan. I can't have you causin' trouble."

Andria stared at Bella, her expression calculating. Bella raised her eyebrows and stared back, daring Andria to challenge her. Her sister was fast gaining the reputation of a rebel, and Bella didn't like it.

"Andria, please. I want to keep you safe, and I can't do that if you run off and get into trouble."

"I can handle myself." Andria's eyes sparkled, and at the moment, Bella saw a little too much of Wayne in her younger sister.

Andria had something on her mind, and Bella wasn't sure she'd like it.

"Belle—I think I have a way to fix things."

"I'm sure you can handle yourself, but we need to do this together. We need to work as a team. We'll fix things *together*." Bella sighed, wondering how much she should share with her sister. "The boys are dabblin' in things they shouldn't be—"

"Nothin' new there. They've always dabbled in all the wrong things. It's not like I don't already know that."

"Maybe not, but they're changin' for the worse. Wayne's drinkin' more and actin' stranger than ever, and Charlie's bent on staying on his heels. Somethin' ain't right, and I don't like it. Until I know what's going on, we need to be careful."

"All right." Andria took up both horses' reins and led them toward the trees. The sound of running water bubbled from somewhere in the near distance. She stopped at the edge of the trees and glanced back. "You better promise me you'll tell me what's going on as soon as you figure it out."

"I promise." Bella smiled in relief and nodded. Her sister might be getting a stubborn attitude, but when she gave her word, she kept it. "You'll be the first to know."

Andria hesitated at the edge of the clearing, as if she wasn't completely sure she wanted to play whatever card she held. After a moment she blurted, "Bella, there's somethin' I need to tell you. Something that's gonna help us out." Her eyes sparkled with anticipation.

"Tell me now." Bella placed the items she'd been gathering on a nearby tree trunk.

Andria looked around. "Not here. Back by the water where no one can overhear."

Bella sighed. What was Andria up to? Her younger sister, the youngest of the McLeod clan, always seemed to get herself into fixes, but she never sounded as serious about any of the past offenses as she did about this.

They led the horses to the bubbling brook, a place Bella would find magical if she wasn't so worried about Andria's upcoming confession. The large oak trees closed in behind them to form a private oasis. Spanish moss drifted over the oaks' strong limbs. Birds serenaded from the treetops. Bella wondered what other secrets had been whispered under the protective branches of the trees.

The shallow stream to the right of them rushed over rounded rocks, each one polished smooth by years of tumbling water. The scent of jasmine filled the air. The water beckoned Bella, urging her to slip in and soak away the dirt and grime from the trail. Instead, she turned her focus on her sister.

"What have you done?" Bella knew she sounded judgmental, but years of experience led her to constantly question her sister's actions.

"I didn't *do* anythin'. I found somethin'. Somethin' wonderful." Excitement, fear, and wonder chased across Andria's features.

Bella frowned. "What did you find?"

"A treasure, Bella. Lots of it." She hesitated and licked her lips. "Bella—you and me—we're rich."

"Rich?" Confused, Bella studied her sister. She didn't seem to be teasing. But she doubted her sister knew what "rich" was. "How do you figure?"

"I was ridin' around up by the caves a few weeks ago—"

"The caves?" Bella shrieked. "You know you aren't allowed up there! It's dangerous. Wayne has repeatedly told us both to steer clear, unless the boys needed us and were nearby to offer protection."

No doubt about it, Bella needed to keep better track of her wayward younger sister. But Bella had her own responsibilities to tend to, which made it hard to keep track of Andria. Bella kept busy, and Andria was wily.

"Wayne needed me, Bella. I was on my way back home—"

"Wayne asked you to help with somethin' but didn't bother to ask me? Where was I?" Bella didn't like the implication of this. She'd talked to Wayne about making some changes a few times of late and had broached the topic of pulling out of the "family trade" and moving into something more reputable, but Wayne had laughed in her face.

She'd begged him, even suggesting doing something a bit more reputable like running moonshine, but Wayne would hear nothing of it. And now he'd cut Bella out of a situation and had used Andria by herself instead? Bella had a feeling she'd underestimated the depth of Wayne's anger.

"When was this?"

"It was when you went to gather Ma's dresses for this trip to town."

Wayne had sent Bella to their other cabin—Momma's place—while he used Andria to do his bidding. This couldn't be good. Bella had a really bad feeling about the whole situation.

"Andria, we need to get out. I don't like that Wayne's separatin' us. Next time he suggests this, I want you to tell me right away." Bella didn't want to think about what could have happened to Andi. "What did you find?"

"Gold and lots of it. It was hidden way back in one of the smaller caves. One we've never gone in before."

"The one I've told you to stay out of because of its instability?"

Andria had the grace to blush. "Yes. But nothin' happened. As you can see, I came out just fine." She motioned toward her intact body.

"But something could have happened and we'd have never known where you were. You can't just run off and do things like this, Andria. You mustn't be so impulsive."

Andria's expression changed to one of rebellion when she saw the flash of Bella's anger. Bella tamped down her frustration and changed her tone. "Okay, what's done is done, tell me more about the treasure."

"I went deep into the cavern, deeper than we've gone into the other caverns. . . ." Her voice drifted off as she watched for Bella's reaction.

Bella bit her tongue and fought to keep her lecture at bay.

"I had to light a lantern—it was really dark that far in. I'd decided to turn around and go back to the opening when I found these bags, they were just sittin' there against a wall."

She glanced over at Bella, and Bella nodded for her to continue.

"At that point I got scared. I realized someone else had been there, and whoever it was could either still be there or could come back at any time. Then I saw a skeleton. It scared me to death."

"So you decided to do the smart thing and get out of there?" Bella couldn't resist asking.

"Yes, as soon as I'd seen what was in the bags."

Bella rolled her eyes. "And?"

"Each bag was full of gold, Bella. They weren't huge bags, but it was a lot of gold just the same."

The thumping in Bella's head increased. "This is important, Andria. Did you tell Wayne or anyone else about the gold?"

Andria's eyes flicked away and back. She bit her lip. "No, you're the only one in the family that I've told."

"Andi. . ."

"I don't recall tellin' anyone else. Wayne for sure doesn't know. He'd gone off the other direction after tellin' me to head on home."

Bella had a feeling that Andria wasn't telling the whole truth, but there were more important matters at hand.

"Where is the treasure now?"

"I left it where it was. I couldn't carry it on my own, but I did grab a few pieces so I could show them to you." Andria slipped her hand into her pants pocket and pulled it out again.

Bella leaned forward as Andria gently unfurled her fist. Several small chunks of gold rested on Andi's open palm. The shafts of sunlight filtering through the trees glinted off the gold, making Bella's eyes hurt.

"Wow, you weren't kiddin'. It's beautiful."

"What do we do next? You'll help me get it, right, Bella?" Andria closed her hand and slipped the nuggets back into her pocket. She reached out and placed her hand on Bella's upper arm. "We can use the money to start over far away from here. We can get away from the boys. We can be free to live as normal folk, rich ones at that."

"We can't rush into anythin'." Bella chose her words carefully. Her heart was jumping at the thought of moving on. The possibility the gold offered them for a fresh start was enticing indeed. "We don't know who the gold belongs to, and we could get in a lot of trouble if we're caught with it."

"We could get into a lot of trouble by being caught with our brothers, too. I thought you wanted out?"

She had a point. Bella sighed. "I do want out. I just don't want to work ourselves into a worse situation in the meantime."

"How can it get any worse? If anyone finds out what our brothers do up in the hills, we'll be arrested right along with them. We *know* some of what they do up there, Belle, but we don't know all of it. You said so yourself. If we know about them robbin' and stealin' from people who pass through, what *don't* they want us to know? Why are they always sendin' us off before they join us back at the homestead?"

Bella had wondered about that many times herself, but she hadn't been able to sort things out. She always had Andi to consider and didn't want to put either of them at risk. When the boys told them to hole up at Momma's cabin, they did just that. Many times she'd been tempted to double back and watch to see what the boys were up to, but she knew Andi would be right on her heels and Bella couldn't take the chance.

Already, Andria seemed too enthralled with the boys' actions. She hated being left out of the mix. Bella tried to fight her sister's attraction to the outlaw ways, but if Bella didn't get her out soon, she knew it was only a matter of time before Andi gave herself over to that way of life completely. This was the first time Andria had insinuated she wanted a fresh start.

"If we work together to start fresh, you promise you'll change your ways?"

"I don't want to be a part of what the boys do. I want to live right, but if we're going to stay in, I want to be in control."

If the gold allowed them the opportunity to start a new life, who was Bella to say no? Who knew how long the treasure had been there. Bella couldn't let this opportunity get away. She'd sneak over to the cave and take a look at the situation herself before deciding, but if the gold looked to have been there for a while, she was taking it and her sister and leaving the hills to make a new beginning. She'd take personal satisfaction in the fact that her brothers had ruthlessly robbed people at gunpoint for so many years while the true treasure rested in their own backyard.

Bella nodded. "You have a point. We need to take action now. Let's do what we came to do and then after we're back home, we'll talk about it some more and finalize our plans."

"The boys will likely send us to Momma's cabin after we tell them whether or not a posse will be arriving soon." Andria's expression was calculating.

"Yes."

"We can finalize our plans up there."

Bella sighed with relief. "Yes, we can."

Relief flooded Andria's features, too. Bella felt herself soften inside. Maybe Andria's rebellion of late had been her way of dealing with the desire to get out of the gang, not a desire to get further in.

With that thought in mind, Bella determined to get her sister safely away from the gang before she got in any deeper.

The decision to wait bought them some time. Bella could do some checking around before they walked into an even worse situation than they were already in. Maybe while they were in town she'd be able to find out if there had been a recent robbery nearby—one that involved a lot of gold.

Chapter 4

The problem with trying to be somethin' you aren't"—Bella stated as she pulled the voluminous amount of blue flower–adorned white cotton fabric over her head for the second time in as many days—"is the huge possibility that you'll get caught out of sheer stupidity. I still can't figure out top from bottom in this thing! How hard can it be to put on a simple dress? Other women do it on a daily basis."

Andria's contagious giggle carried through her own layers of fabric and over to Bella. Her entire mood had lifted since she'd shared about the gold. "Apparently, when you aren't used to wearin' them, it can be very hard. I'm afraid I'm permanently lost in here. How *do* women do this every day? I'd surely suffocate myself at some point. As a matter of fact, I think that's a huge possibility right now. It's so hot in here!"

Bella shifted her dress and pushed her head in another direction. The effort was for naught. Another barricade. "I don't see hide nor hair of daylight. What about you?"

"No." Andria's laughter still flavored her words. "I'm afraid I'm stuck somewhere between the linin' and the actual dress. I've taken a wrong turn somewhere."

Bella found the comment funny. "There *aren't* any linings in these dresses, Andria."

"Oh."

Andria's huffs and puffs of effort carried on the wind. Or maybe it was Bella's younger sister's attempt to breathe while stuck in a mix of frothy pastel pink fabric that made her sound so breathless.

"Belle, if someone stumbles upon us while we're like this, we're in trouble. We can't shoot while we're all tangled up in this constrictin' fabric. We should have dressed one at a time while the other stood guard."

The comment jolted Bella and urged her to find the right outlet for her head. "Fine time to realize such a thing, Andi! Why didn't you think of that a few minutes earlier? But who'd have thought we'd have so much trouble getting into the confounded things? We're women. By our very nature we should be able to dress in feminine attire."

At least they'd chosen the private area beside the stream to dress. It was less likely someone would stumble upon them way back here. Though if someone noticed their horses where they'd left them, they'd still be in trouble.

"Somethin' must be wrong with us. We're defective."

"You think so, Andria?" Bella winced at the level of sarcasm in her tone and gentled her approach. "We've been raised by outlaw brothers, and we're used to doing their biddin'. We dress in men's clothes, and we shoot like men."

"Well, it doesn't help that the only things we know about being a woman come from reading the books Ma had lyin' around before she died."

"Ma did a good job of trainin' us before she passed away. She gave us a good start before the boys took over and messed everything up. At least she taught us to read." Bella felt the fabric give as she found the correct opening and her head cleared the neckline. "Yes! I've made it through one openin'. There's hope for us, Andria."

"Can you shoot a rifle in your current position?"

"No." A sigh slipped past Bella's lips. Her arms were still lost in the innards of the fabric mess. "Not without reversing the process and startin' all over. I could slip the rest of the dress back up over my arms and shoot in my undergarments, though that hardly seems proper. And I think that would sort of mess up our plans to eavesdrop and spy in town."

"Well, the good thing about that situation is the poor soul on the receivin' end would be so startled by a half-dressed female pointing a weapon at him, he'd likely not have time to react. You'd have a clear shot." Andria panted. She almost tipped over as she tilted and hopped at an odd angle. She looked more like an Indian warrior dancing around a fire than a fair maiden dressing for a trip to town.

"Right." Bella snorted. "They wouldn't be a bit distracted by your crazy dancin' and antics. And our brothers would thank us for taking the clean shot and ruinin' our scoutin' opportunity in town."

"Hmmm." Andria's head popped through her neck hole, and she sent Bella a pompous grin. "Then we'd best get to it and find our armholes so we can shoot proper-like."

"Well I for one, don't intend to shoot anyone, dressed or not. I want to sashay into town, do our business, and be on our way. We have some plannin' to do."

"Oh, in that case, we're almost there."

Bella laughed out loud. Andria's hair stuck out every which way. Half the collar on her dress was tucked inside the neckline of her garment. The dress was twisted a quarter of the way around. One sleeve hung down her front and the other down her back. Andria looked like she'd just fought a very large bear and had come out on the losing end.

"What?" Andria frowned. "Please tell me I don't have it on inside out?"

"That would be the least of your worries." Bella would help her, but her own arms were still lost in the fabric. She twisted and turned it every which way. "I'm thinkin' someone sewed the armholes shut by accident. I don't think my dress has any."

"That's because they're tucked inside. Your dress *is* wrong side out. The sleeves are, anyway." Andria tugged and shifted her pink fabric. "This bodice is so tight my arms won't fit through the armholes. Bella, what if the dresses don't fit?"

"They'll fit. Ma was bigger than either of us." Bella looked over to see the early morning sun rising a bit too quickly in the sky. "Slip the dress off your shoulders and lower the bodice down a bit. If you do that, your arms should be able to find the sleeves and you can pull it back up with everything in the proper place."

Andria did as told and sent Bella a smug look.

"You wouldn't be so far ahead if I hadn't walked you through the process," Bella muttered.

"If we'd pulled the dresses on feetfirst, we wouldn't have had such problems."

"Now you tell me," Bella muttered. "Why didn't you figure that out fifteen minutes ago?"

Andria sashayed over and pulled Bella's sleeves out properly. Bella slipped her arms through the thin fabric. She exchanged a glance with Andria and smiled. She knew no one watching their latest debacle would ever believe the danger the two women presented to others in their regular, everyday life.

❧

Duncan walked into the stifling heat of the sheriff's office and tossed his hat on the nearby desk. He could hear the sheriff muttering as he clattered around in the small back room. Duncan decided to give his friend some time and talk to Ethan first. He'd speak to the boy's father in a bit.

He turned his attention to the lone prisoner in the cell. "Hey there, son. Looks like you've run into some problems today."

"I ain't your son." The boy's eyes narrowed, but even in the shadowy interior of the building Duncan could see the telltale remainder of tears. Ethan's eyes were red and swollen, but whether the tears were from sorrow or anger remained to be seen.

Duncan raised his arms above his head and braced them on the cool steel bars that separated the prisoners' quarters from the office. He rested his head on his forearms and studied his friend's only son. The boy was small in stature for a ten-year-old. Between that and his father's reputation as a no-nonsense sheriff, Ethan had a hard time of it with the other kids in town.

"Rough day?"

"I've had better." The sullen boy refused to look at Duncan.

"What're you in for this time?"

Ethan's scowl deepened. "Stealin'."

"Again? How many times is that this month? Three? Four? What'd you steal?"

"A lousy piece of candy." The scowl turned to a glare. "It ain't like old man Crawford can't afford it."

"Stealing is stealing, Ethan. It doesn't make it right just because someone has the money to buy more."

Ethan raised and lowered a shoulder.

Duncan walked over and rifled through the stack of odds and ends that lay upon Sheriff Andrew's desk.

"These things yours?" he asked as he picked up a small rock and tossed it up and down on the palm of his hand. Two similar rocks remained on the desk.

"Yes."

"This is a nice one."

"Yep."

"Where'd you find it?"

"Over at Cooper's Creek."

Duncan caught the pebble and turned it on his hand.

"Well, they sure are fine specimens. I think I'll keep this one for myself." He tucked the rock into his pocket and turned to go.

"Hey! Give that back!"

Duncan turned the boy's way and feigned surprise. "But you have two others just like it! What's it matter if I take just this one?"

"It ain't yours to take. You can get your own if you want to walk over there. I spent the better part of a hot afternoon looking for those three rocks."

"But you have three. I'm leaving you two others. You can walk over and get more just as well as I can."

"That don't matter. . . . They're still mine fair and square." By now the boy was standing on the other side of the bars, fists clenched. Duncan was aware that Sheriff Andrew stood just out of Ethan's line of vision in the back room, listening to the exchange with interest.

"Aw, Ethan, it ain't like you can't go over and get more when you get out of here. Isn't that pretty much the same thing as your theory on taking candy from Mr. Crawford?"

Ethan narrowed his eyes before dropping heavily down on the bed. "I get what you're doin'. I ain't dumb."

Duncan walked back over to the cell. "Then you know how Mr. Crawford must have felt when you walked out of there with something that wasn't yours to take."

"I guess so."

"So what do you propose we do about this, son?" Andrew stepped out into the main room. "I'd like to have you on your way home in time for the noon meal. Your ma'll tan your hide if you're late, especially when she finds out why."

"You ain't gonna tell her, are you?" Ethan seemed more worried about his mother's reaction to the theft than he did about his sheriff father locking him up. It was obvious who carried the big stick in the family home.

Duncan cupped a hand over his mouth to hide his grin.

"I dunno. Guess it depends on how you choose to deal with this."

Ethan's eyebrows pulled together in thought as he contemplated his dilemma. "I can tell Mr. Crawford I'm sorry."

"That's a good start," the sheriff said. He didn't seem bent on giving Ethan any breaks in this situation.

"Um." Ethan was silent a few minutes longer. "I can offer to sweep his back room for him." He looked sheepish. "Or maybe he'd rather have me out front where he can see me. I can sweep his porch for a week."

"A month," Sheriff Andrew agreed.

"A *month*? I only took one piece, and I didn't even get to eat it!"

"Keep that in mind next time you have a hankerin' to do wrong." Andrew's eyes narrowed, his expression resembling his son's earlier glare. "One month. I think that'll go a long way in making things right."

"Aw, Pa!"

"And you'll pay for the piece of candy."

"But I didn't get to eat it! That ain't fair! I threw it in those bushes when I heard you comin' and Patch ate it."

"It isn't fair that Mr. Crawford paid for that candy and can't make his profit or recoup his money for it. I guess your dog owes you a thank-you for his treat."

Ethan's shoulders drooped.

Andrew unlocked the cell and motioned his son to clear out. "You head on over to apologize and offer your assistance, then you get on home to your ma. *Straight* home. I'll follow up with Mr. Crawford as soon as I finish talking with Duncan. Don't make me sorry I let you go."

"I won't, Pa." The boy skirted his father and hurried for the door.

Duncan stopped him with a touch to his shoulder. "I want to see you in church on Sunday, Ethan."

"Yessir." Ethan raced out the door.

As soon as it slammed shut, Andrew sank into his chair. "That one's going to do me in, Duncan. How am I supposed to keep the law when I can't even control my own son? I'm feeling the need to hang up my hat."

"You mean, hang up your hat as in turning in your badge? You'd quit as sheriff just because you have a rambunctious son?"

Andrew motioned Duncan into the seat opposite him. "It isn't just that. I'm feeling old and tired. I've lost my edge. I'm hearing new rumblings about the McLeod gang, and people are starting to talk. They want something done about them. I've been after that gang for years and haven't gotten anywhere when it comes to stopping their outlaw ways."

"The McLeod gang is good. Better men than us have tried and failed to capture them."

"I know, but they've become a personal thorn in my side, and I want to put them behind bars. If I can't, I need to find someone who can."

"So you're going to toss that desire to capture them aside and quit?"

Andrew slammed his hand down on his desk. "I didn't say that. I said I *feel like* hanging up my hat, not that I am."

"Just asking some questions based on your comments, Andrew." Duncan raised his arms in mock surrender. His friend was strung tight today. "What do you plan to do?"

"I guess I'll put together a posse and ride up there. See what we can find out."

"A posse?" Duncan didn't like that idea. Several other posses had ridden up into the hills, only to have several come back injured. No one could prove the McLeods were responsible, but speculation leaned in that direction. "I'd rather you not do that. You know what's happened to the others."

"No, we *don't* know; that's part of the problem. We don't know who is behind the attacks. I'd like to find out." Andrew stood and paced the length of the small office.

"You have a wife and son to consider. Let's figure out another way."

"That's just the point. I do have a wife and son to consider. I'm not doing them any favors by sitting down here waiting for the McLeod gang to strike again."

Duncan studied his friend. "You know something." It wasn't a question.

Andrew stared out the window. After a few moments, he turned to look at Duncan. "You had lunch yet?"

"No."

"Let's head over to the diner, and I'll tell you what I know. I trust your intuition and will listen to your thoughts after I've shared."

"I'm ready to head over there now."

Chapter 5

Duncan studied the street that ran through town as they walked to the diner. Other than wisps of road dust hanging in the air from the most recent traveler, the steaming stench of horse manure lingering in the midday heat, and the normal parade of people coming and going from the shops and eating establishments, he saw nothing out of the ordinary. He'd hoped to catch a glimpse of the two sisters when they rode into town, but so far he hadn't seen any sign of them. He supposed they could blend in from afar if they'd decided against the dresses and to instead wear the clothes from the day before.

He and Andrew chose a small table in the far back corner of the diner. The choice gave them privacy to talk while allowing the sheriff a clear view of the room and roadway outside the front windows.

Sheriff Andrew leaned forward, his face close to Duncan's. "Rumor has it that the youngest McLeod family member—Alex—has the missing gold from the big mine heist several years back. Do you remember that one?"

Duncan's blood ran cold as he nodded. He remembered all right. The heist occurred a year before Duncan became pastor of their small town.

"We need to gather another posse to chase the McLeods down and see what they know. We'll bring the youngest member in for questioning. Maybe that'll make the older ones talk, too."

"Don't count on it." Duncan tried to keep his voice steady. He'd turned his life over to Christ years ago and had kept steady in his relationship with Jesus ever since. This news put Duncan in a dilemma. The situation had the potential to collapse his carefully constructed life, but at the same time he couldn't let his tenuous situation cause innocent people pain.

"Don't count on finding them, or don't count on the older ones talking to protect a younger one?"

"Both." Duncan shifted on his chair. "You know their reputation. They're mean as snakes and as sneaky as ever. They won't care if you have one of their younger siblings."

"You're sure?" Andrew rested his chin on his hand, his expression thoughtful. "What do you recommend? Someone needs to go up there."

"Give me some time to think and pray about it." Duncan would do more than think. He'd figure out a plan that didn't involve the sheriff or a posse.

The door to the diner opened, and the room grew silent. Duncan and Andrew turned their attention to the newcomers. Two women stood in the doorway looking around the room with discomfort as every eye in the place stared them down.

Duncan had been wrong when he'd thought Bella and her sister could slip into town unnoticed. Cleaned up, they were two of the most beautiful women Duncan—and apparently almost every man in the diner—had ever seen.

Several men jumped into motion at once. One even tipped his chair over in his hurry to get to the entry before the others. The two women stepped backward in alarm. They obviously hadn't foreseen or planned to create a stampede when they entered the establishment.

Madelyn Steeples, the diner's owner, bolted through the kitchen doorway and bustled toward the newcomers. She waved her heavy arms in the air. "Shoosh now! You men go on back to your seats and sit yourselves down. Imagine getting all caught up in a frenzy just because two pretty ladies walk through our door." She hemmed and hawed as she hustled across the diner.

No one questioned Maddy when she was on a mission. Several men left, and the few remaining men hurried back to their seats and conversations as directed, but their eyes remained focused on the women. Maddy glanced around the room. Her search ended when she noticed Duncan and Andrew in the far corner. She motioned for the two women to follow her and led them to the table across from the men. The dark-haired woman stumbled, and the other steadied her with a hand to her arm.

"Sheriff? Parson? I assume you two can welcome these ladies into your conversation without causing a disturbance?"

"Of course we can." Duncan hurried to stand and pulled out a chair for the nearest woman, Bella, the one with the fiery-colored hair. Both sisters had vivid blue eyes. Andrew stood and pulled out a chair for the younger, dark-haired sister.

"Bella and Andria, right?"

Bella froze in place, gaping at him.

Duncan smiled. "I'm Duncan Bowers. We met on the trail yesterday afternoon. I heard you refer to each other by name. I was one of the men blocking the path when you rode down the trail."

Bella relaxed and settled into her seat. "I remember."

"Allow me to introduce the sheriff, Andrew Walker."

"It's a pleasure to meet you, Sheriff Walker." Duncan noticed her discomfort. She looked anything but happy to meet him.

"Sheriff Andrew is fine."

"Sheriff Andrew, then."

Andrew didn't move. The women's expressions went from uncomfortable to panicked.

Duncan hurried to finish introductions. "I'm sorry. Sheriff, this is Andria and Bella. . . ?"

"Um. . ." Bella hesitated.

"McLeod," Andria supplied.

Bella flinched and stared forward, not meeting Duncan's or the sheriff's eyes.

McLeod? Providence. Yet again.

Duncan smiled. "Andria and Bella McLeod."

"Nice to meet you." To his credit, Andrew didn't bat an eye as the ladies identified themselves as possible relatives of the gang Duncan and Andrew had just been discussing moments earlier.

Maddy walked up and delivered Duncan's and Andrew's food. The savory scent of pot roast and baked vegetables—herb-topped potatoes, carrots, and onions—drifted up and teased Duncan's senses. Maddy placed a basket of yeasty-smelling bread and a small container of butter on the table between them before turning to take Bella's and Andria's order. Andrew tucked a napkin on his lap, and Duncan picked up his fork, ready to enjoy the succulent meal. As soon as the women were distracted with their menus, Andrew sent Duncan a pointed look, and Duncan nodded imperceptibly.

After Maddy moved off to the kitchen with their order, Andrew began his interrogation. His experience as sheriff showed as he mixed bites of food with well-targeted questions.

"So what brings you ladies to town? Do you have business here? Or do you have family in the area?"

This time Bella sent Andria a look and stepped into the position of spokes-woman. "A little bit of both. Our family lives up in the hills, but we came to town to order some supplies."

"I see." Andrew casually leaned back in his seat, folding and unfolding his napkin. "Will you be here for a few days, then?"

"No, we'll see to our business and be on our way in the mornin'."

Duncan watched as the sheriff leaned forward. He frowned. "I have to say I'm surprised and a bit nervous to see two women travelin' such a distance without a chaperone. As sheriff I know the risks of such a thing."

Bella exchanged a glance with Andria and smiled. "I appreciate the concern, Sheriff, but we can handle ourselves just fine."

"I'm sure you can, but it doesn't seem right for me to let y'all ride out in the mornin' without a proper escort."

Duncan had a feeling he wasn't going to like what Andrew was going to say next.

Bella apparently felt the same way. A hint of irritation passed over her features. "I can assure you, Sheriff Andrew, we're completely able to take care of ourselves. We've never had a problem travelin' alone before, and we've traveled the hills quite extensively."

"I'm glad to hear that, but all the same, you're here on my watch. I couldn't in good conscience let y'all leave here without proper protection." He smiled and motioned toward Duncan. "Duncan often acts as my deputy, in addition to his duties as the parson. He's completely trustworthy in both capacities. If Duncan is in agreement, I'd like to have him accompany you home."

Duncan cringed. He didn't feel comfortable with Andrew forcing his company on the women, but he felt even more uncomfortable with the sheriff's words of affirmation. The only thing he'd ever kept from the sheriff was that in his former life—before turning his life over to Christ—he, too, had lived as an outlaw. His past wasn't all that different from the McLeods'.

❦

Bella watched as Duncan's mouth gaped open. Bella felt hers do the same. They exchanged similar horrified glances. The only sound came from Maddy, who worked at the far end of the diner wiping down tables and carrying dirty dishes from the tables to the kitchen. The room grew uncomfortably quiet as the other diners trickled out the door to return to their afternoon obligations. Bella wished she and Andria were ready to do the same. But it wouldn't do to draw further attention by leaving before their meals arrived.

"I appreciate the consideration, but an escort is not necessary." Bella bit out her words through clenched teeth. She kept the smile pasted on her lips, but she knew the smile didn't reach her eyes. Instead she felt pure panic at the thought of this kind and peaceful man escorting them home. "We don't need a chaperone."

Wayne wouldn't be happy to have a man brought into their encampment, let alone a law-abiding one. Bella had no idea how she could warn or protect the parson without giving herself away. The sheriff didn't seem to recognize their family name when Andria blurted it out, but Wayne would be sure to cover their tracks when it came to a stranger approaching their territory. And she had no doubt that Wayne would find out.

"The trip is long and hard. We don't live close by. We couldn't possibly ask the parson to make such an arduous trip."

Duncan seemed to gather himself. He grinned at her statement. "I'm sure I'm up to the trip. I mean, you two seem to have made it here just fine. I'm sure I can make it up the mountain just as well."

Bella studied him. He wasn't the kind of pastor she was familiar with, not that she had a lot of experience in that area. The one who'd buried her father and mother had been a skinny, mean, beady-eyed old man who walked stooped over his cane. His eulogies, as far as she could recollect, at each of her parents' funerals were something to the effect of "good riddance." Her father had deserved such a send-off; her mother did not.

Bella knew that in most of her neighbors' eyes—not that the neighbors were that much better—her mother was guilty by association. It didn't matter that she came from back East and had an educated background. She'd married a scoundrel, which placed her in a similar category. The horrible old man who buried her momma made sure the few people at the funeral knew that, too.

Duncan, on the other hand, was the complete opposite of that other pastor. He was tall, strong, and ruggedly handsome. He wore his long dark hair pulled back at the neck, and he had compassionate brown eyes. Even in the midst of her horror at the thought of him accompanying them home, she could only imagine what it would be like to have someone like him watching out for her and Andria. She could think of far worse company to keep—her brother Wayne's for starters. The thought quickly reminded her of why she didn't want nor need the parson to ride along with them to their homestead.

"Actually, our older brother will be ridin' out to meet us. He won't take too kindly to us appearin' in the presence of a man he doesn't know." She hesitated. "Nothing personal or anythin', but he'd shoot first and ask questions later."

"I wouldn't do anything different if you were my sisters," Duncan observed.

"But you would have arranged for a proper escort for your sisters in the first place," Bella stated, her voice flat. The man didn't back down easily.

"I would have, yes." He nodded, his eyes warm. "And if they'd snuck off on their own, I'd have ridden out to find them."

He must think their brother a complete miscreant. Of course, if Duncan did think that, he'd be right.

"Well, you aren't our brother. And we didn't sneak off on our own. Our brother knew where we were going. He sent us here. He had business to attend to elsewhere. But I'll have you know he's very possessive—I mean, protective—in his own way."

"I can only imagine."

"Then you'll understand why you can't escort us home?"

"No." Duncan shook his head. "I'll still escort you. I'll just be on my best behavior, and I'll be ready when we meet up with your brother."

Bella sighed none too quietly. She started to say something else but decided against it. She'd just have to come up with a plan to dodge him. They would leave at daybreak. She'd make sure they were long gone before Duncan-the-parson ever had a chance to join up with them.

Chapter 6

M cLeod, Andria?" Bella admonished the moment they'd finished their meal and cleared the doorway of the diner. "Why didn't you just hold up a sign that says SISTERS OF THE NOTORIOUS McLEOD GANG?"

"Well, I didn't see that you were comin' up with anything better. You just sat there stutterin'—your eyes all big and startled-like—while you floundered around in your head for a last name that would work. Do you seriously think that looked any better than my just tellin' the truth? And we aren't just 'sisters' of the notorious McLeod gang, we're a *part* of it."

Bella walked in silence for a moment, considering Andria's words. "I, for one, prefer to be known as the McLeod clan."

"Prefer whatever you want, but the hard truth is, we're in this as deep as our brothers, reluctant participants or not."

"I don't want to be a part of it, Andria, and I don't want you to be, either. We've gotta get out."

"How we gonna do that with Deputy Parson on our heels? That'll be a fine mess when we lead him straight to the homestead. Wayne'll be beyond thrilled. Have you forgotten how he knocked you from that horse? He'll do far worse when we show up with the law."

"You don't think I know that, Andi? We've gotta come up with a plan." Bella had been deep in thought throughout their entire meal and still hadn't figured out the best way to handle things. If they slipped out early, they'd draw attention. The wrong kind of attention. But showing up at the homestead with a man wasn't an option either.

"Do you think he's onto us? Neither one of them seemed too familiar or surprised when I shared our last name."

"Can't tell with the likes of them. Sheriffs and preachers can be clever that way. I didn't see either one of them as bein' stupid." Bella ducked into the mercantile to place their order. She pulled out her short list and handed it over to the proprietor.

"Hello, ladies." The man's lecherous eyes surveyed them from top to bottom as he leaned forward with his elbow braced on top of the counter. "Ain't seen neither one of you around these parts before." He smirked. "And I would have remembered if I'd seen your pretty faces before."

"We're just passin' through." Bella's smile felt tight. "We have some other business here in town so we'll be on our way. Would it be possible for you to wrap our order and have it ready when we return?"

"I can do better than that." He glanced around and leaned closer. His yellow-toothed smile looked more predatory than friendly. "Tell me where y'all are stayin' for the night, and I can personally deliver your order right to your door."

"That won't be necessary." Bella slipped her small money pouch over her wrist.

The man eyed them suspiciously. "What's your business in town?"

Bella started to tell him to mind his own business, but Andria stilled her with a touch of her hand. Much to Bella's disgust, Andria batted her eyes at the despicable man and gave him a conspiratorial smile. "You seem like the kind of man who knows what's goin' on around town. Any word on the outlaw gang that's rumored to live up in the hills? Is it true they're robbin' and raidin' and that people are gettin' upset?"

"Why would two women like you care about some ole gang?"

Andria smiled, her eyes dreamy. "I just think it'd be so excitin' to meet up with the likes of someone like that."

Bella almost choked. Contrary to her sister's ruse, they wanted to be far away from the likes of Wayne and his outlawin' ways.

"Well, hon, you want a rebel-type man, you got someone like that right here in front of ya."

Bella's stomach turned. "We need to go—"

"Oh please, sis. I just gotta find out if the rumors are true." Andria returned her attention to the proprietor. "*Are* they?"

"They're true, all right. According to local gossip, the sheriff is forming a posse to go up into the mountains and force the whole mess of 'em out of the hills and into custody. He'll take 'em dead or alive."

Bella shivered. She could fully imagine Sheriff Walker uttering similar words during discussions on how to best capture the gang.

If what the proprietor said was true, it was likely the sheriff knew exactly who she and Andi were and that's why he'd suggested Duncan ride along. Duncan would be able to scout out the situation under the guise of accompanying the sisters on the trip home. And if Duncan found out they were indeed related to the McLeod gang, she and Andi would be arrested—or worse—right along with their brothers.

"We have to be goin' now." Bella pulled Andria by the arm when it appeared her sister wanted to pump the man for more information.

The proprietor slicked back his oily hair with his hand while leering at Andria with a grin. Bella frowned with disgust. He used the same hand to pick up the list of items Bella needed to take home, leaving a greasy oil spot on the previously pristine piece of paper. She scowled. "We'll be back top of the next hour."

"I'll be waitin'." His answer was directed toward Bella, but his gaze and innuendo were focused on Andria.

Bella hurried from the store. "No way does the sheriff not recognize our name, Andria."

"I was thinkin' the same thing." Andi frowned. "Question is, what are we gonna do about it? You still want to give that sheriff the slip? They could arrest us before we report to Wayne if we do."

Bella considered her words. "I don't think so. I think they would have arrested us already if they wanted us in custody. They want Wayne and Charlie."

"Or perhaps they want all of us together."

"That's possible, too."

They headed toward the far end of town. Bella was too riled up to stick around in any one place while they waited for their purchase to be gathered. She moved quickly down the walkway. She had a thought and whirled around, nearly knocking her sister over. "But then again, maybe they don't see us as outlaws. Maybe they assume we're innocent victims of our brothers' wild ways—which we are to a point."

Andria's eyes lit up. "And if they capture Wayne and Charlie, we'll be free to move on and start fresh."

Bella grinned. "That means our little farce is workin' out. The sheriff must see us as the innocent women we've been trying to portray."

They reached the end of the walkway and turned around.

Bella admitted something that was bothering her. "I hate to think of Charlie facin' the same future as Wayne. Charlie still cares. We might have a chance of reachin' him. What do you think?"

"You want to let him in on our plans?" Andria's face scrunched. "I'm not sure I trust him that much."

"No, I don't trust him either. I think his loyalties run toward Wayne. As much as I love him, I think he's closer to becomin' like Wayne than wantin' to be like us."

"He did take up for you when Wayne knocked you from the horse. You have to remember that."

Bella reached back and touched the knot that had formed at the back of her head after Wayne had knocked her down. She knew she had a large bruise on her shoulder, considering the raw tenderness she'd felt when she'd tried to lie on her back the night before. "He did. But then his only counsel was for me to be more careful around Wayne. He didn't say anythin' that would give me the idea that he was tired of the way Wayne treats us."

"You have a point." Andria folded her arms. "What do you think will become of them if the posse locates the other homestead? If anything happens to the boys, we'll be completely on our own."

"We've pretty much been on our own since Momma died, Andi. Losin' our brothers won't change things much."

"True." Andria shrugged. "In that case, I guess things would change for the better. I don't want to wish ill on them—I want them to change and do better things with their lives—but if they weren't around, we could stay on at Momma's place, fix it up, and continue our lives here. I could resume my friendship with Sarah, and it would be like old times."

Andria had a point. The boys had made their lives miserable, so why should she and Andria be the ones to leave? If they could get their brothers to go out West without them, they'd be able to set up a new life of their own. "But what if they leave for a while and then return? We'd always have that concern to worry about."

"Then we need to continue with our plans to leave and hope that the boys make it through whatever they end up facin'."

Bella nodded. She didn't want to think about her brothers' fate. At the moment, their fate was too intertwined with her own. And with Andi's. Whatever happened to Wayne, Charlie, and herself, she had to make sure Andi escaped and had the chance to live a life free of their outlaw ways. She was so young. She didn't have many memories of their life as a family. She deserved a chance to be happy and to find a family to settle down with.

But Bella was concerned that if Andria alone made it through whatever came their way in the future, Andria'd be so angry she'd never settle for a normal life. Instead, Bella figured Andi would gravitate toward the saloons and meet up with someone there and her life wouldn't be any better than it was at the present.

Bella felt there had to be something more out there. Something good. After all this was over and they were free, she'd find a parson and talk things over with him. Duncan came to mind. He intrigued her as much as he annoyed her. She'd love to spend more time in his company if things were different.

Bella stood at the end of the walkway and surveyed the street that ran through the mountain valley. Earlier that morning, when they were on their way in, Bella hadn't taken the time to see the small town's charm. Nestled in the foothills of the mountains, the town had looked smaller than it really was. It boasted a good-sized bank and two mercantiles. If Bella had noticed that fact before, she'd have left the one they'd patronized and would have gone on to do her business with the other one. She continued her perusal. The town also had a milliner, the diner, and a dress shop. A good-sized livery finished out the far end of the strip on the opposite side of the road.

Their side of the street held two saloons, a boardinghouse, the general store where they'd placed their order, and at the far end, the sheriff's office.

People bustled in and out of the various establishments, going about their day. No one paid Bella or Andria any mind as they stood forlornly at the end of the road. Bella tried to imagine living in a place like this, a place where neighbors called each other by name and waved to one another with friendly familiarity, a place where others were there to look out for you when you were ill or were facing hard times.

Bella shook herself out of her musings and glanced back toward the diner. Duncan and Andrew stood just outside the door of the establishment, deep in conversation. Duncan glanced her way and grinned. He sent her a small wave, and the sheriff looked over. Bella felt her face flush with guilt, though in theory—or at least as far as they knew—she'd done nothing wrong. She walked over to the wooden rail that separated the walkway from the road and leaned her elbows against it. If she couldn't even stand in the same town with Duncan without blushing and feeling guilty about her family's outlawin' ways, how would she ever travel all the way home with him by her side?

On the other hand, she had so many questions about life and how things worked out in the normal world, she would enjoy having a few moments alone with the parson. Maybe he could help her know how to live a different life. If she had a chance, she'd ask him about God and what He thought of people like her. She'd ask him how she could help her sister find more to life than the hand they'd been dealt so far. Maybe he could intervene in Andi's life and help her find a better way. Bella longed for a better way, but she didn't feel she deserved it.

It wasn't like she didn't know what her brothers did. They stole from people on the trails—robbed unsuspecting travelers—and left them stranded far from town. And as she and Andi had discussed the previous day, Bella had her suspicions that Wayne's outlaw ways had reached new levels in recent months.

Something deep inside Bella warned that he'd escalated to harsher crimes and that she and Andi needed to get away. The feeling had intensified when she'd been in the presence of Parson Duncan. She felt he held the reins to her future, but unfortunately—for his safety and their own—she and Andi would have to head out long before he had a chance to hand them over.

Chapter 7

Bella looked like a lost lamb. More than likely, based on her family history, she was a lost lamb—at least in the eyes of God. Duncan parted ways with Andrew and wandered over to lean against a nearby wall. He took the opportunity to study her. A few moments earlier when he and Andrew had exited the diner, Andria and Bella had been in deep conversation. Now Bella rested against the rail in front of her, looking as if she carried the weight of the world on her shoulders. Andria paced back and forth behind her, looking bored. After a few more turns, she glanced around and headed down the walkway. She kept her eyes focused downward as she approached.

When she walked by, she tossed her black curls over her shoulder and sent him a saucy grin. She didn't stick around long enough to offer a chance for conversation, which was fine with Duncan. If he spoke with anyone, he wanted it to be Bella. Duncan nodded his head at Andria, looked back at Bella, and decided he'd take advantage of this opportunity and talk with her while she was alone. He knew she wasn't happy about their upcoming trip, and he felt he should try to alleviate any concerns she might have about the travel arrangements. Maybe if they could talk a bit, she'd be more open to his company.

Bella didn't react to his approach. Either she was really good at ignoring people she didn't want to talk to, or she was so caught up in her thoughts that she hadn't heard him walk up behind her. He suspected the latter. And if it was the latter, he had all the more reason to accompany them home. It wasn't a good idea to be unaware of your surroundings when traveling away from home. Like Andrew, Duncan wouldn't rest until he knew Bella and Andria were safely back at their place in the hills.

Duncan cleared his throat to announce his presence. "I guess you've already finished your shopping?"

Bella jerked upright and spun around. Even at full height she was still a good six inches shorter than his six-foot-tall stature. He towered over her. In an instant her expression changed from contemplative and wistful to challenging and hard. She glared up at him.

"I've placed my order, yes, and I'm waitin' for it to be filled." Her tone was defensive. "We'll head out as soon as it's ready."

"Head out, as in going home? Or head out, as in leaving town and staying put until morning?"

She blatantly ignored the question.

He took her place at the rail, hoping the casual action would put her at ease. She held her position, standing rigidly behind him and slightly to his right. He waited to see if she'd answer. Most women hated silence and would fill in any awkward moment with lame conversation. Since the silence didn't seem to bother her, Bella obviously wasn't one of them.

Duncan watched as a horse and wagon came into sight from around the farthest building to the south of town. A young family sat upon the front bench, smiling and talking as they rolled past. Duncan wondered if he'd ever have such an experience. He kind of hoped so. The family seemed so content.

He decided to break the silence. "Thomas Mercantile or Sundry's Dry Goods?"

"Pardon?" Bella stepped closer, her forehead crinkled with confusion.

"We have two stores in town. Which shop did you place your order with?" He looked over at her. She looked like she'd rather be anywhere else but there.

"Oh—" She leaned around him and glanced down the road toward the two shops and read the closest sign. "Thomas Mercantile, I guess."

"Sundry's might be a better choice next time—that is, if you ever plan to come back down this way. Thomas can be a bit much to deal with, especially when pretty women enter his shop alone."

"So I noticed." Bella flushed. "But I didn't know before we went in. I'll keep that in mind for the future. Thank you."

"My pleasure. I'm here to help the townspeople—or those like you in the surrounding areas—in any way I can." He sent her a grin that she didn't respond to. He felt his smile falter. "Anything a person might need or might want to talk about—spiritual guidance, advice on situations that occur in day-to-day living, safety issues that might cause concern. . .all you have to do is ask."

She flinched. He wished he could ask outright about the conversation he'd overheard the previous day, but he couldn't.

"I'm not much for askin'." She stood close beside him but kept her gaze on the building across the street. She hugged herself tight, her arms wrapped defensively around her chest.

"So I've noticed." He chuckled.

Her brilliant blue eyes narrowed as she turned to stare into his. As he watched, a few tendrils of her gold-tinged hair fell forward to frame her face. The slightly curled tresses cupped her cheeks and softened her features. "Are you laughin' at me?"

"No!" He straightened, his arms raised in a gesture of innocence. "Of course not. Never."

"Then why did you laugh?"

"I wouldn't exactly call that a laugh."

"What *would* you call it?"

He thought a moment. "I guess if I had to call it anything, it would be a chuckle."

"Why did you *chuckle* at me?"

He sighed in exasperation. "I didn't laugh or chuckle at you! I found your words to be amusing. You leave no doubt that you're perfectly capable when it comes to your ability to take care of yourself or to find your way on your own. Based on that, I figured you for the type to resist asking for help, even if you needed it."

"Oh. Capable." Her tough facade cracked a bit, and she scowled. "I wouldn't go that far."

Duncan knew enough to proceed with caution now that he'd found a chink in her armor. He remained silent, letting her take the lead.

She didn't elaborate further.

"You have doubts about your capabilities, Bella?"

"I have doubts about pretty much everything. Doesn't everyone?"

"I'm sure they do." He was pleased with himself. This was the longest conversation he'd had with her since they'd met. Their conversation at the diner was forced, with her mostly answering their questions in as few words as possible. A warm breeze blew past and rustled the leaves on a nearby magnolia, distracting him. He figured Bella would look pretty with one of the tree's white blossoms tucked into her hair.

"What are yours?"

Distracted by the direction of his musings, he lost his train of thought. "My what?"

"What are your doubts?"

The question caught Duncan off guard. He was used to being in control of conversations. Bella seemed to have a way of keeping him off balance. He was used to doing the asking and getting answers from everyone else. No one came to see the parson to ask about his life or to see to his needs. They came to him when they needed something from him, which was exactly what he expected.

Of course the women in town took good care of him, dropping by regularly to stock his pantry or to drop off a baked good or two in appreciation of some service he'd rendered. The men in his congregation came around now and then to drop off a stack of firewood for the parsonage or to fix something on the church grounds. The single women kept his dinner table well stocked when he was in town, which was part of the reason he liked to roam around the hills as much as he did during his off days. The townspeople took good care of him, but they never asked questions about his well-being. They never asked about his personal thoughts or feelings.

That is, no one had until now.

Duncan suddenly found himself on the receiving end of questions he wasn't sure he wanted to answer. Questions he didn't want to think about. He figured for a man in his position, he doubted far too much as it was. And he wasn't sure he wanted to admit that. He knew better. He studied the Word. But still he found himself questioning God in various areas. Not all the time, but far too often. Like when someone in his small church passed away unexpectedly and he had to help the family with their grief. Or when a family worked hard to bring in a crop and too much rain or not enough moisture took everything they had. And on the other hand, he found himself surprised when God acted in ways that caught him off guard, but he figured he shouldn't be surprised at God's provision at all. He was still a work in progress. "I'm not sure how to answer that."

Bella's mouth turned up at the corner. The smile radiated through to her eyes. She had a beautiful countenance. "So the preacher doesn't like to admit his shortcomin's? Or does your strong faith allow you to cast aside all your doubts? Perhaps you don't ever have any?"

"I wish I could say that." He smiled. As pastor, Duncan wanted to reach out and use this small connection they'd forged as a way to get to know Bella better. He also wanted to be sure to represent himself in a way that was honest and reflected where he was on his faith journey. But he didn't want to be a stumbling block to someone who was obviously searching. "I'm sure I'm no different than you, Bella, or anyone else in this town. I often struggle with doubt. Faith is an ongoing process; trust isn't something that happens overnight."

"But you're a pastor."

"That doesn't make me perfect."

"Hmm." Her forehead wrinkled, and she nibbled on her lower lip. "That's an interestin' way to put it."

"Why?"

"I just always thought preachers had faith, and that was that. I didn't figure they struggled with the same things us common folks struggle with."

"I have complete faith in my Lord Jesus Christ and His ability to do what's best for me. But like anyone else, I tend to let my doubts about how things are going to work out creep in now and again." He turned to face her. "Everyone struggles, Bella. Pastors, believers, nonbelievers. The difference is that faith helps a believer get beyond the struggle and on to the other side."

"Believers? Nonbelievers? I'm afraid I have no idea what you're talkin' about."

"Believers are those who turn their lives over to Christ. They want to live a life that's pleasing to Him. They're followers of Jesus. They turn to the Bible for advice on how to live their life, and they want to do good."

"So you're sayin' if I'm a nonbeliever, I have no hope of comin' through a struggle on my own?" She frowned, her frustration evident.

"No, I'm not saying that at all. You can come through your struggles just fine, but you're going it alone. We all sin—we all do bad things or have moments where we choose to do wrong in our lives. A relationship with Jesus means you don't have to go it alone. Jesus forgives those sins. All a person has to do is ask. Faith brings peace and gives hope. That doesn't mean the hard times go away; they're just easier to handle when they do come."

"So you're sayin' as a nonbeliever, I have no hope?" Bella looked as lost as she sounded. Her hands rubbed up and down her arms as if she were cold.

Duncan's heart went out to her. He softened his voice. "I'm saying with Jesus there is all hope."

❧

Bella wanted hope. She also wanted peace. Her thoughts were in constant turmoil. The constant unrest in the life she lived exhausted her. She wanted to know and understand the deep faith that shone from Duncan's brown eyes. His eyes were kind and compassionate in a way she'd never seen before, and she had a hard time looking away from them.

In fact, she had a hard time looking away from his face in general. Everything about him was pleasing to the eyes. Gold streaks wound through his wavy brown hair and spoke of a man who spent a lot of time outdoors. His jaw was strong and his lips—well, she had the silliest urge to lean in and see what they would feel like against her own. Never in all her life had she ever given consideration to such a thing! Her emotions were making her crazy.

Duncan was kind in nature, too. His strong physique hid a gentle spirit. No man had ever taken the time to talk with her like he had. He listened to her and spoke to her like she mattered. He acted as if he had all the time in the world to stand there and answer her questions. She wished she had all the time in the world to listen. He made her feel safe. But she knew she had to go.

Bella sighed. No matter how much she wanted to experience the things Duncan had talked about, she still didn't understand how it all worked. And she hated to ask more questions than she already had. She didn't want him to figure her for stupid—if he hadn't already.

Maybe she *was* defective, as Andria had said earlier that morning. Maybe her mind didn't work in a way that would ever allow her to get close to God. She figured with her family background, her sins were bad enough that she'd never have that kind of relationship or closeness with Him. She'd been born a McLeod, and she'd die one. Momma had been a good person, and still, in the end, she'd been judged by her name alone.

Based on that, Bella didn't figure God would ever see past her many sins and give her Duncan's kind of hope and faith.

She consoled herself with the fact that the conversation wasn't a total waste. Now that they'd talked, Bella was pretty sure Duncan and the sheriff hadn't put together the McLeod connection. There was no way a good, upstanding man of God like Duncan would linger around on the public walkway, talking to a sinful member of the McLeod gang about Jesus if he had any idea of her true identity. If that was the case—if Duncan and Andrew had known who she and Andria were—surely they'd have arrested her and Andi on the spot and would have hauled 'em in for questioning. They might even have held them at the jail in the hope that the rest of the family would come into town to find them. Bella knew better than to believe that would ever happen. She and Andi were only of use when it came to helping in the hills. If they ever became a liability, they'd be dropped from the gang on the spot. Her brothers had no loyalty. She and Andria were expendable.

Now that she thought about it, Bella needed to figure out where Andria had wandered off to and round her up before she got herself into trouble. It was time to pick up their supplies. If they were to leave the pastor behind, they'd need to be on their way. She wanted enough daylight to make some serious progress before nightfall. She didn't want to travel the mountain trails in the dark of night.

She glanced over at the handsome man standing next to her. She was everything evil to his everything good. She needed to make her excuses and be on her way before Duncan saw through her guise and looked into the darkness that was her heart.

"I appreciate your time and kind words, Reverend Bowers. I'll take what you said to heart. But for now, I'd best collect my sister and be on my way."

He studied her a moment then nodded. "Where shall I meet you?"

She hesitated. "We're stayin' near Cooper's Creek, just outside of town. We'll leave from there." She felt bad deceiving the nice man. She didn't exactly lie—she just avoided telling the full truth by not disclosing *when* they planned to leave. Instead of leaving at first light, they'd leave long before. Still, she hated the fact that God could add another sin—a sin of omission—to the long list He probably already had on her. He probably didn't take too well to people betraying His pastors. This was just another confirmation for Bella that she'd never be good enough for God.

Chapter 8

Ican't believe you went into that establishment after I told you not to. I specifically told you not to go in there! The saloon isn't a place for someone like you to visit. It isn't a place anyone should visit. You're only seventeen. You don't belong in there. Oh! You exasperate me to no end." Bella hurried Andria along, anxious to broaden their distance from town. The whole town experience had bred nothing in her but dissatisfaction and frustration. "Just when I think we're gettin' somewhere, makin' plans for a new start, you defy me and do somethin' stupid. Saloons aren't safe, Andi. Why do I have to keep tellin' you that?"

"I was safe. You might not have noticed, Belle, but you're not my mother. You're not my father. You're my sister. I have a fine mind—you're always tellin' me that yourself—and based on that, I wish you could see that I can take care of myself. That includes making my own decisions. I wanted to find out if anyone would talk about a posse or talk about what's goin' on with that. I don't mean to be disrespectful, Bella, but you have no authority over me."

"That's quite obvious." Bella stalked ahead, furious at her sister's attitude. "Though in this messed-up clan that we call a family, I do have authority over you."

"Just like Wayne and Charlie have authority over us? That makes me want to *obey*, all right." Andria's words dripped with sarcasm. "And it seems to me, you aren't plannin' to *obey* much longer yourself. What makes it okay for you to refuse what they say or to plan against them?"

Bella lost some of her momentum. "That's not fair and you know it. What I do, I do in your best interest. I want you safe. Charlie and Wayne only use us for their future gain. They don't care about our well-bein' or safety. There's a huge difference."

Bella was at her wit's end. Earlier in the day it seemed she and her sister had gained some solid ground in their relationship, just to have her sister pull this. Now Andi was back to being her normal frustrating self. Bella sighed and slowed to a walk. "I don't want to see you hurt, Andi. I don't tell you things like this to irritate you."

"I'm not gonna get hurt, Bella."

"You don't know that. The men who hang out in those types of places aren't nice. You're far too young to be in there."

"I'm old enough to help our brothers make a livin'. I should be old enough to slip into a saloon and ask some questions."

"No, you aren't old enough to help our brothers. It's their responsibility to provide for us. Our brothers don't care about that, but I do. They shouldn't use you—or me—to do their biddin'. We've talked about this. We're going to make things right. Dallyin' in a saloon won't fix anything. That behavior will just create more problems."

They'd almost reached the clearing where they'd left their horses and supplies. Andria placed a hand on Bella's arm. Bella stopped and turned around to face her.

Andria closed her eyes and took a deep breath. "I'm sorry. I don't want us to fight. I just wanted to talk to someone besides family. I won't do it again."

Bella let out a sigh of relief. "Maybe you can get together with Sarah soon. I know you miss visitin' with her."

Andi smiled.

"I do. I saw her a while back, last time we went to Momma's cabin. But the visit was far too short." A look of guilt crossed her features. "I forgot, Bella. I did mention findin' some gold to her. I didn't tell her how much, but I showed her the three gold nuggets."

"Don't tell anyone else, and don't bring it up to her again."

"Maybe I should tell her next visit not to say anythin' to anyone else."

"Then we'll try to get there soon, after we clear everything up with the boys."

They picked up their pace and soon reached the area down by the water where they'd left their horses and belongings. Everything seemed to be as they'd left it earlier that morning.

"I told you this was a secure place." Bella beamed with relief. They'd found a small path leading away from the water they'd bathed in the night before, which led to another, smaller clearing. The second clearing ran alongside the creek. They'd set up camp and had left their things behind while they'd gone into town.

Andria stepped up beside her. "Are we still leavin' at first light? Or do you intend to sneak off in the night before your reverend comes to find you? If I have any say in this, I personally think we should stay the night and then get up early—that is—*if* you truly want to avoid him." Andria grinned.

"What do you mean 'if'? Of course I want to avoid him! And he's not 'my reverend.'" Bella stopped her tirade. Her voice was rising in pitch. She sounded guilty. She took a few breaths and calmed down. "We'll leave now. I want to get away from here long before he heads out to meet us. If we stayed through the night and overslept, he'd be hot on our heels all the way home."

Andria's face fell. Bella wondered if she had plans to sneak back into town or to do something equally nefarious. Her eyes narrowed. "You don't like that idea?

What exactly did you have in mind that requires you to be near town?"

"Stop being so suspicious." Her sister shrugged. "The idea's all right, I guess. What I do like is that reverend. I think he likes you, too. I kind of hoped you'd relent and let him escort us home. I—for one—would appreciate the company."

Bella just gaped at her younger sister. The two years that separated them might as well have been decades. "He doesn't *like* me, Andria. He's a preacher. They have to be kind to everyone."

"Yes, but he seems to be *extra* kind to you. You never know. . .he might like you enough to stick around."

"Andria, a man like him—a man of God—isn't going to stay around for a woman like me."

"You could change."

"I *plan* to change. That's not the point."

"Then what is?" Andria folded her arms across her chest and waited for Bella's answer.

"I'm afraid if we come home in the company of Duncan, our brothers will try to kill him."

"I've never known them to be violent. Not like that."

"Were you not there yesterday morning when Wayne knocked me from my horse?"

"You know I was." Andria blushed. "But that was a random incident. You know better than to talk to Wayne that way." She appeared to rethink her words and hurried to add, "Not that that makes his actions right or anythin', but still, you know better than to confront him."

"What about the people he robs? You've never seen him react violently when they refuse him?"

"I guess he has." Andria paled. "I've always tried to move forward and not give much thought about what happens after a robbery."

Bella was glad to see her sister still appeared to have a heart. No one should have to live like they did. They lived in constant fear of their brothers. Andria didn't like their life under their brothers' control any more than Bella did. "We're going to fix this. We're going to get out. But we won't use that kind man to make things any easier."

"I think he'd be willin'. I saw the way he looked at you."

"Andria! He's a *pastor*!"

"So?" Her sister laughed. "He's still a man. The whole time we were talkin' he couldn't take his eyes off you. And he looked at you like you were the most beautiful sight he'd ever seen."

"He did not, so just stop it." Bella knew she was blushing from head to toe. Her sister was spouting off crazy talk. Bella stalked over to the bushes and pulled her dry traveling clothes from the branches. She couldn't wait to put them on and leave the town behind. She tossed Andria's set to her. "Hurry up and change out of that dress and ready your horse for the trip."

"I'm more than happy to oblige. I'm ready to be out of these clothes. I've waited all day to get into somethin' more comfortable. I have no idea how women can get anythin' done in those constrictin' dresses."

"Most women don't ride the mountains and abandon angry victims like we do, Andi."

"I've never thought about that." Andria looked contemplative. "What do you suspect other women do all day anyhow?"

"I dunno. According to the books at Momma's place, they do things like bake, clean, and sew."

"How can that fill a whole day? I'd be bored out of my mind."

"I suppose I would be, too. But I'd sure like the chance to try it out and see. I think it would be relaxin' to sit out on the porch and look out over the mountains while darnin' socks and talkin' to my kin. You could while away the time as the sun sets on the horizon." Bella sighed. "Such a life would be peaceful and relaxin' for sure."

Andria stared at Bella as if she'd grown an extra head. "Darn a sock? How can you imagine sittin' there doin' something you hardly ever do?"

Bella smiled. "The darnin' isn't what's important. I'm just sayin'. . .we've never had the opportunity to live a normal life like that. We've never had the chance to do domestic things and enjoy the easy life most other women live. Seems to me it'd be a nice way to fiddle away our time."

"I dunno. I've seen Sarah's mom goin' about her chores, and they look pretty hard to me. She's always doin' somethin' or other and hardly gets a moment to rest. Momma used to work pretty hard, too."

Bella shrugged. "I'd prefer to settle in and take the time to really see what's happenin' around me. It isn't any fun to always be lookin' over our shoulders, wonderin' when the law's gonna catch up with us. Domestic life would set right well with me."

"You have a point. I guess it would be a nice way to live, sittin' around doin' nothin'." Andria looked at the garment in her arm. "Maybe I'd even enjoy wearing the likes of this dress if we had a life like that. You have to admit, the dresses were cooler than these pants once we figured out how to wear 'em."

"Yes, they were." Bella slipped into her pants and finished dressing for the trail. The dress was definitely cooler, but the pants allowed them more freedom of movement while on the trail. The trail they were now ready to follow so they could get themselves far away from town—and Duncan.

❧

Duncan grinned as he watched the McLeod women ride out of the clearing at a fast pace. He'd been sure Bella would try to give him the slip, but Andrew said after watching them talk in town, he thought Bella would wait around for her escort. Duncan had hurried home to pack, just to be on the safe side, and it looked like his precaution paid off.

From all appearances, it seemed Andrew had lost their bet and would owe Duncan a dinner next time they met up. Duncan decided to tail the women at a distance for a while. He'd make his presence known after they'd gained some ground. It'd go better for him if he followed them with discretion. No need to get them all riled up and angry if he could avoid it. He could watch out for them just as well from afar as he could if he rode along with them.

In all honesty, he'd probably keep his focus on protecting them better from way back here. Bella had a way of distracting him, and he couldn't afford that. If she wasn't distracting him with her rare but pretty smile, she'd be arguing with him. He couldn't afford to be caught off guard if and when they met up with her brothers.

The women were skilled on horseback. They moved at a fast clip, making it hard for Duncan to keep up, watch his surroundings, and keep out of sight. He wondered if they'd try to ride all night or if they'd pull off at dusk. He'd have a harder time following them at night.

The sun was low on the horizon when Bella and Andria ducked into a stand of trees and disappeared from sight. Relieved, Duncan slowly made his way in that direction. He didn't want to ride all night. He wanted to catch some sleep so he'd be fresh for whatever Bella's homecoming brought along with it.

He heard their voices as they moved about setting up camp. He debated whether he should quietly settle in nearby or if he should make his presence known. Since they'd so casually stopped off where they had and didn't seem to give a thought to their surroundings or safety, he decided to alert them to his presence and let them know they weren't as observant as they thought.

He left the trail and burst through the thick trees and into their encampment. Both women screamed.

Duncan tipped his hat and gave them his most cocky grin. "Evenin', ladies. Seems y'all left somethin' behind."

The women spun around with weapons raised. Andria had snatched up a nearby log, while Bella had her rifle trained on him.

"Whoa, it's just me!" Duncan raised his arms.

They stood and stared at him for a few moments before recognizing him and lowering the weapons. Bella leaned against hers and glowered while Andria stood with a hand to her heart. Andria looked as if she'd seen a ghost while Bella returned his cocky glance and looked over at their belongings. "I don't see anything of importance missin', Andria, do you? Whatever could we have forgotten, Reverend Bowers?"

"Me."

Bella rolled her eyes. "In order to 'forget' you, I would have had to plan to bring you along in the first place. In case you didn't notice, I didn't plan any such thing."

Duncan feigned shock. "You didn't plan to bring me along? You snuck out of there without me on purpose? I thought it was an oversight."

"My only oversight was leavin' without checkin' things out better. And there was no sneakin' involved. We merely changed our plans and decided to make some progress while we had daylight to burn."

"I've been meaning to talk to you about that."

"About burnin' daylight?"

"About leaving without checking things out better."

"How much time could you possibly have had to 'mean to talk' to me about anythin'? You've only been here a few moments."

"Thought-filled moments. And I've followed you for hours since you ducked away from town while trying to dodge me."

"And yet here you stand."

"Obviously, your efforts were in vain."

"I can see that. Thanks for fillin' me in."

Andria stood a few feet away from them, still holding on to her log, looking from one to the other as they continued their verbal sparring. "Are y'all 'bout done?"

Duncan glanced over at Bella.

Bella shrugged.

"Guess so."

"Yep."

Andria dropped the log. "Well then, now that we have that all figured out, maybe we can finish figurin' out the important things like settin' up camp before night falls?"

"Sounds like a plan." Duncan looked around for something that needed his attention. "What would you like me to do?"

Bella sighed dramatically. "What *I'd* like you to do is—"

"Why don't you start us a nice fire, Reverend Bowers? We'll finish up our other preparations in the meantime."

"I don't need to be referred to as Reverend Bowers, Andria. Duncan will do just fine. I don't go on formalities, especially way out here."

Bella spoke before Andria had a chance. "So we noticed when you pranced in here all arrogant-like on your high horse."

Duncan laughed. "Since when did being a pastor mean you couldn't be comfortable with those around you? It seems I bring more people to my side by making them feel at ease than I do while standing in judgment."

Bella didn't comment; she just stood and stewed. Andria grabbed her sister by the arm and dragged her away from his side. Duncan couldn't hear what they were saying, but he could hear the anger in Bella's voice.

After a few minutes, they'd apparently reached a mutual decision because both walked over to join him. Bella didn't look any less angry, but she went about her business as he prepared the finishing touches for their fire.

"I hope you brought along your own food. I didn't pack enough for an extra person." Bella's words were a mix of irritation and apology.

"I'll be fine. Don't worry about me. I'm here to help, not to hinder."

"Then you should've stayed behind," Bella muttered.

Though she first appeared to be angry, Duncan noticed an undercurrent of panic in her voice. He felt bad that his presence caused her frustration.

Andria glanced up at him to gauge his reaction. He winked at her before turning to Bella. Andria's eyes widened in surprise.

"I couldn't do that, Bella. I know you're upset with me for following you. You have every right to be offended. But Sheriff Andrew and I both felt we needed to make sure you reached your home in a safe manner. We'd never forgive ourselves if we found out something had happened to you on the trail. Something my presence could have prevented."

"Yes, because men of cloth are known to be such good gunfighters in battle. What can you possibly do for us that we can't do for ourselves? If you get hurt because of us, *we'll* be the ones who can't forgive ourselves."

"You owe me nothing, and I take responsibility for my own choices. I had a life out in these hills, Bella, before I decided to live for the Lord. I've dealt with the likes of those who live out this way. I've worked with Andrew in various situations, and I've had to lay down the law for those on the wrong side of the badge more than once. You just say the word once I have you safely home, and I'll leave."

Bella looked at him with indecision. Whether she was debating taking him up on his offer or still trying to figure out how to send him packing, Duncan didn't know. She had a cantankerous look about her that said her mind wouldn't stop when it came to thinking up ways to lose him again as soon as she could. "I don't see that I have any choice in the matter."

Duncan felt bad. Maybe he should have stayed out of sight and just followed them in without their ever knowing.

The irritable spark in Bella's eyes grew larger. "You know what? We could've had you tied up and lyin' flat on the ground if we'd wanted to. We went easy on you because of who you are."

Andria's mouth twitched.

Duncan stared at them, incredulous. "You're tellin' me you knew I was back there all along?" He laughed. "If that were the case, why didn't you let me know? Why did you look so startled when I walked into the clearing? I don't believe it."

Bella shrugged. "We didn't want to make you feel bad."

For a moment, Duncan didn't know whether or not he should believe them. He finally decided it didn't really matter. Not as much as it mattered that he was able to accompany them home. He needed to make peace.

"It seems like you have everything under control. What's the plan for tomorrow?"

"We'll get up early and head out first thing. You'll need to choose a spot far away from us when you go to sleep. I don't wanna have to worry about the snoring keepin' anyone up."

"Aw, your snores can't be all that bad. I'm sure they won't bother me a bit. I'm a heavy sleeper."

"I wasn't talking about *my* snoring botherin' *you*, I was talking about *your* snoring botherin' *us*!" Bella huffed.

"So you do snore?"

"No! I do not."

Andria tried to hide her laughter behind her hand.

Duncan turned to her. "Andria, does Bella snore?"

"Not often, and not real loud or anything. Her snores are more like quiet little snuffles."

"I don't snore!" Bella's horrified screech made Duncan laugh.

He asked, "What makes you think I snore?"

"Don't all men? My father and. . ." Her voice drifted off. "Other family members have snored. I've heard them all the way from the barn to the house."

"That doesn't mean all men snore."

"Well maybe not, then. But all the same, you need to sleep far away from here. I don't want to hear you or know you're nearby."

"I bet if you hear a large bear rustling around in the trees you'll want me nearby soon enough."

"The only sound of a bear rustlin' in the trees will be you tryin' to scare us."

"I'd never do anything of the sort." He softened his voice, wanting her to know the teasing was over and he meant the statement. "I'll stay out of your way, but I'll be close enough to help if you run into trouble."

Chapter 9

A rustling in the nearby trees moments later had Duncan on alert and reaching for his rifle. Andria stepped closer to Bella. Bella held her own rifle at the ready.

"Whoever you are, make your presence known."

Duncan's strong voice at Bella's side made her jump. She had a momentary vision of a large black bear rushing out of the woods with paws raised in fear. Instead, a small boy with unruly red hair and a scowl on his face slowly walked out of the thick stand of trees and moved into the clearing. His green eyes reflected in the firelight as he surveyed the three adults gathered around the blaze.

"Ethan?" Duncan roared. He lowered his rifle. "What on earth do you think you're doing following me around like this and wandering through the woods? You almost got yourself shot."

"I knew you wouldn't shoot me."

"You're right, Ethan. I wouldn't knowingly shoot you. But I didn't *know* it was you, did I? I was expecting a bear or an outlaw to walk out of those trees, not you."

Ethan looked from Duncan to Bella to Andria. "What are you doin' out here all alone with these two women? I thought preachers weren't supposed to do things like that."

"Do things like what?" Duncan looked confused.

"Be alone with strange women in the woods."

"I'm protecting them from bears and outlaws," Duncan muttered. "Your father wanted me to chaperone them and keep them safe until they reached their home."

Bella couldn't help but laugh.

Duncan turned his stormy expression on her. "You find this situation to be amusing?"

"No." Bella tried to corral her emotions. "It's just that you were standin' here not too long ago lecturing us about being more observant and how we needed to be aware of our surroundin's, and yet this small boy apparently followed you all the way from town without your knowledge. Just seems a bit ironic is all."

"I was focused on keeping you safe."

"I ain't small," Ethan sputtered.

"I didn't mean any offense," Bella hurried to say, trying to tamp down her amusement. "To either of you."

She had to admit it was nice of Duncan to watch out for their well-being. Her brothers certainly hadn't ever concerned themselves with such a thing. But Bella couldn't keep her jaded thoughts from wondering what Duncan's ulterior motive was. In Bella's experience, all men had one.

She hoped the preacher proved her wrong, but she wouldn't count on it.

"Come on over to the fire." Bella wrapped an arm around Ethan's shoulder. "I bet you're pretty hungry after all that ridin'. We'll see if we can find you something to eat."

"What?" Duncan widened his arms. "I'm here on your behalf, with the best of intentions, and all I get is yelled at, threatened, and told that I won't be eating. Ethan walks in here unannounced when he shouldn't be here at all, scares us all to death, and you welcome him with open arms?"

"He's just a boy. His parents must be worried sick."

"She has a point." Duncan turned suspicious eyes toward the boy. "What did you tell your parents?"

Ethan dug his toe in the dirt. "I didn't exactly tell them anythin'."

"Ethan! Argh!" Duncan threw his hat on the ground. "Now I have to turn around and take you back to town. I needed to escort these ladies to their homestead, but thanks to you, they're going to be unsafe for the rest of the trip while I tend to you."

Bella's heart trilled. The precious little boy had fixed their dilemma. Thanks to him they'd be able to return home with no worries when it came to their brothers hurting Duncan.

Ethan bristled. "You don't have to take me back. My ma went to visit her sister and won't be back for at least a week. She told me to stay home with my pa."

"And you don't think your pa will be upset to find you missing?" Duncan asked. "Ethan, you've really messed up this time. Didn't we just talk in town this morning about respecting others?"

"I thought we talked about stealin'." Ethan looked confused.

"It's all one and the same. Stealing from someone causes them frustration and makes them upset. Leaving town without telling your pa or ma will cause them frustration. They'll be worried."

"No they won't. Pa thinks I went with Ma. That was the original plan. That is—it was the plan before she went and got all upset with me for killin' her precious flower bushes."

Duncan sat on a nearby rock and rested his forehead on his hand. "Maybe you'd better start at the beginning."

"Ma and I were supposed to go visit her sister, my Aunt Maggie. Aunt Maggie smells like dead weeds, and her cookin' makes me wish I was sick in bed."

Andria unsuccessfully choked back a laugh. Bella nudged her, doing a better job at hiding her own amusement this round.

"Ma told me to dump her cleanin' water. I thought she'd used it to wash dishes, so I threw it on the plants. They all wilted and died. Apparently it wasn't from the dishes after all."

Duncan rubbed his hand across the back of his neck. "Apparently not."

"So, Ma got mad and said I could just stay home with my pa. She was tired of my antics. She muttered something about it being good for the both of us."

"I can only imagine." Duncan studied the young boy for a moment. "So what's your pa gonna think when he comes home to find you gone?"

Ethan's face lit up. "That's the good part! I never did get around to tellin' my pa before I saw you sneakin' out of town. I decided to follow along—since I was in trouble anyway—and see where you was goin'."

"I wasn't 'sneaking,' Ethan. I told you, your pa wanted me to escort these ladies and keep them safe."

"Sure looked like sneakin' to me."

"Well it wasn't."

"Then why did you keep close to the trees and hang back when the ladies slowed their pace?"

Bella laughed out loud this time. Duncan sent her a very unpreacher-like glare.

"I wanted to make sure the ladies were safe without interfering with their trip."

"Like we're doin' now?" Ethan quipped.

"Exactly like you're doing now," Bella agreed.

"How can we be interfering with your trip when you aren't traveling?" Duncan asked.

He had a point.

"You're interferin' with our dinner preparations," Bella responded.

"Would you like me to leave?"

"No." Bella took pity on him. "I'd actually like for you to join us. I know it doesn't seem like it, but we do appreciate your concern for our well-bein'—misguided though it might be."

"So we're stayin'?" Ethan's face lit up.

"For dinner," Duncan answered. "After that, we'll head back so I can return you to your father."

"What if my father isn't there when you return me?"

Duncan closed his eyes. "What aren't you telling me now?"

"Pa got called out of town on business. He'll be gone for several days, too."

"And when did you find this out? After your ma left and before you took off after me?"

Ethan's brows furrowed with deep thought. "After my ma left, but before I took off after you. Yes." He glanced up to see Duncan's glower and hurried on with his story. "I saddled up my horse and was ready to go after you when I saw my dad talkin' to some men and I hid in the alley so he wouldn't see me. I heard them say they were goin' after someone and wouldn't be back for at least a few days. My pa said that was all right and he'd go along because me and my ma were out of town anyway."

"So no one will miss you for at least a week?"

"Right. Not until my ma comes home."

"Where's your horse now?"

"I tied him to a tree outside the clearing so you wouldn't hear me ride up."

Duncan looked thoughtful. "So we have time to escort the ladies back to their homestead and then get home in plenty of time to tell your pa."

Ethan wrinkled his nose at that. "He won't be too happy about that."

"No, I don't imagine he'll be happy at all, but that's the price you have to pay for your deception and disrespect." He grinned at Bella. "And in the meantime, I'll still be able to follow through on my commitment to help these ladies reach their home."

❧

Bella rode her horse into the open area around the homestead midmorning the following day. She exchanged an uneasy glance with Andria.

"I sure hope this plan works, Belle."

"So do I. But it seemed like the best idea at the time."

Bella knew her brothers would show up eventually. She hoped Duncan and Ethan would be long gone before then. She and Andi had stayed up late, trying to figure out the best approach for the trip home. Their final decision was to visit their mother's homestead under the assumption that it was their permanent home.

Duncan rode up behind them. "You have a beautiful place here."

The homestead overlooked the Blue Ridge Mountains. From where they sat upon their horses, the mountains rolled away into the distance. Early morning mist hung in the valleys and swirled around them in the yard. The songbirds were well into their singing, the different varieties melding together from the treetops above their heads. The fresh scent of jasmine blew around them on the breeze. It was a magical place.

"Thank you. We love it here." The statement couldn't be any truer. She'd loved their years growing up here before Momma took sick and died. She loved the times their brothers sent them over to wait out whatever was going on in the hills after a robbery. She dreamed of the day they could settle in at the homestead without the fear of their brothers arriving and wreaking havoc.

"I can see why." He smiled. "I feel closer to God up here. There aren't any distractions like I have in town. Up here it's just God and His creation."

Funny, Bella thought, *I've never felt further away from God.*

Most likely because of all the sad family memories, the bad times, the fear she felt during their brothers' escapades. Though the cabin was a refuge, it also bore scars of past hurts. And if Duncan only knew, all kinds of distractions to his peace were waiting just around the corner.

"I wish I felt the same way. But then, I don't feel close to God no matter where I go."

Duncan studied her. The intensity of his probing eyes caused her discomfort. She shifted in her saddle.

"You could if you'd just let Him into your heart. Give Him control of your life."

Bella laughed, the sound harsh as it drifted away like the mist. "You don't understand. Some people don't have the ability to make such a choice."

"Everyone has that ability."

"Not me."

"Yes you. All you have to do is ask."

"Such a thing would completely turn my life upside down. I can't let that happen."

Duncan's expression grew troubled. "Tell me what the problem is. Maybe I can help."

Bella gentled her words with a smile. "No one can help, but I appreciate your concern."

She ended the conversation by dropping from her horse and following Andi into the cabin. The room was dark and dreary. It smelled musty and unused. She left the door open as Andi rushed over to open the opposite door that looked out over the backyard. Light trickled in and brightened the area.

Duncan appeared in the doorway. "I sent Ethan over to the barn with the horses. He'll take good care of them."

"I can help!" Andria seemed all too eager to steer clear of Duncan's presence.

Bella watched as Duncan circled the untidy room. Layers of dust covered every surface.

"I'm not much for housekeeping. You'll have to excuse the mess."

He raised an eyebrow in reply. She knew it was an understatement. The house hadn't been lived in for several years, and she and Andria didn't see much reason to clean it during their brief visits.

Duncan ran his fingers over the titles of the books on the shelves. "Looks like someone liked to read."

"Our mother did. She loved to read. She taught school back East before her father brought the family out here for the Georgia gold rush."

"Did he find gold?"

"No, and he died before he could be lured farther west after his claim fizzled out. Momma met our pa, and she settled in here at the homestead."

"Where's she now?"

"She passed away a few years ago."

"I'm sorry to hear that. And your father?"

"He passed away, too. After Momma died he started to drink all the time. I think it ruined his health."

"Liquor can do that to a person." Sympathy filled his eyes. "So your brothers took over your care?"

"We were old enough to care for ourselves, but yes, they took on watchin' over us."

Duncan stopped in front of the family Bible. A layer of dust rested upon the sacred cover. He blew it off and looked over at Bella. "I take it no one around here reads the Good Book?"

"Um, not lately."

Their mother had been the last to open the cover of the large book. Her brothers would rather toss the thing into a bonfire than to ever read a word of what lay inside. Though their mother had tried to read the scriptures aloud to her wayward children, her words had fallen upon dry ground. Bella wished she'd been older. She and Andria had been too young to understand back then, and when they were old enough to understand, their mother's breath was too precious to waste with reading.

Duncan opened the book to the page that listed their names and dates of birth. He studied them carefully then frowned. Bella's heart beat loudly in her chest. What would he do when he saw her brothers' names inscribed on the pages of that fine book? Their names didn't even deserve to be located in such a special place. She was sure her own name and Andria's were just as poorly placed.

"You don't have a brother named Alex?"

"No." Confused, Bella shook her head. "Just my sister, Alexandria, but we've always called her Andria or Andi. Why do you ask?"

"I heard the name mentioned in passing. I figured with you being a McLeod, he might be a relative of yours."

Duncan didn't say another word as he closed the book and continued his trek around the room. "The dust around here is mostly untouched. You must not spend much time indoors."

Bella realized her mistake. If they lived at the cabin, it would be clean and tidy. Instead, as he said, the layers of dust coated everything in the room. She and Andria never stayed long when they were sent to the cabin. They gathered whatever items they'd been sent to claim, or they worked around the yard until one of their brothers sent for them.

"With a view like we have outside, would you? It's much better outside with the fresh air and sunshine. But if you must know, the dust gathers fast up here in the mountains."

"It does, does it?" Duncan's mouth turned up at the corners.

Bella couldn't tell if he was laughing at her or if he took her words to heart. She motioned toward the front of the house. "As you can see, we like to keep the doors open for all the light it brings in. The practice comes with a price."

She hurried over to the corner and picked up a worn broom. "I'll tidy up if it'll make you feel better. I don't want you thinkin' poorly of us. We do know how to clean." She placed the broom on the ground and started to sweep with it. The rotted handle promptly broke in half. Bella couldn't do anything but stare at the defective item.

"You've worn that poor broom to a frazzle with all your cleaning up." Duncan laughed. "I'll tell you what. Let me make you a new handle and you can resume your—cleaning—as soon as I get it done."

Bella felt the flush crawl up her neck but refused to back down. "I'd be mighty obliged to you if you did that. Thank you."

He stepped from the room, and Bella sank into her mother's rocking chair with frustration. Dust motes danced in the shafts of sunlight that filtered in through the front door. Now her deception not only had her hiding her brothers' identity, but it also had her pretending to be something she wasn't.

Andria walked into the room. "Duncan said something about making us a new broom?" She looked around. "I didn't even realize we had an old one."

Bella buried her face in her hands. "I know. I didn't realize we had one either. He started talkin' about the condition of the place, and I saw the broom hidin' in that corner over there. I picked it up, and it broke to pieces in my hand. I suppose he knows we're tryin' to trick him into thinkin' we live here. I mean, look at this place!"

Andria looked it over. "It is pretty rough. Momma would be ashamed."

"We'll start today and clean it in a way that would make her proud. From now on when we're sent over to wait things out, we'll make use of the time and keep it up to her standards. No more idle hands for us."

Andi nodded her agreement. "I hate to bring this up, but we have another dilemma."

"Which is. . . ?"

"We have no food to offer them. We have no chickens to lay eggs, no cow to milk, not much grain for all the horses. . . . Don't you think they'll figure out—if they haven't already—that no one has lived here in a long, long time?"

"We have the supplies we brought from town. I know it's not much, but surely they'll realize two women on their own wouldn't have need for a lot of supplies?" She thought a moment. "Perhaps you can run over to Sarah's and buy a couple of chickens from her parents? They used to breed them. I would imagine they still do. Perhaps they'll even loan us a goat for a few days. Tell them we're workin' on fixin' up Momma's place."

Andria's face brightened at the thought. "I'd love to go over there! Sarah will be so excited to know I'm back again."

"Don't get too excited, Andi. You know this is only for a short time. We'll be able to send Duncan off before we know it, and we'll need to head back to the other homestead."

Andria's face fell. "I know. You're right. But for a moment there, I got carried away with the thought of stayin' and fixin' the old place up. It's so much warmer and homier than the other cabin. I hate it there."

"I hate it there, too. We'll be here soon. I promise. And the more we can do now to get it in shape, the better it'll be when we return."

Bella just hoped her promise was one she could keep.

Chapter 10

Duncan watched as Andria hurried off into the trees on foot. The hair raised on the back of his neck. He hoped she wasn't going to warn her brothers about their arrival. He couldn't risk Ethan's safety. He'd need to act fast if the rest of the McLeod gang arrived unexpectedly. He couldn't imagine that Bella or Andria would set them up, but one never knew. They seemed genuine, but he'd seen outlaws turn for all sorts of reasons. Number one reason for the McLeod women to betray him was that they were terrified of their older brothers. Or at least that was the impression Duncan had received when listening in to their conversation the day he'd first met up with them.

He finished up the final touches on the new broom and tested it on the dirt floor of the empty barn. It seemed to sweep just fine. He headed for the house. Bella puttered around, tidying up the kitchen area.

"I just saw Andria head off into the woods. Is everything all right?"

Bella nodded but didn't look him in the eye or stop wiping the table with the old rag she clutched tightly in her hand. "She's going over to retrieve our livestock from a neighbor's house."

"You take your livestock to a friend's when you leave for a couple of days?"

"We don't have anyone who can come over and care for them."

She didn't elaborate further.

"I have your broom ready to go. Care to give it a try?"

"Sure. I'd love to." Bella finally turned his way, her nose wrinkled with disdain, telling him the opposite was true. She was too polite to tell him that, of course, but her actions made it clear. It was obvious housework wasn't her strong suit. Based on her favorite choice of clothes and her independent ways, he figured she didn't have much experience with housework in general. The cabin's condition attested to that. It looked to him like nobody had lived in the house for quite some time.

"As soon as I'm done sweepin', I'll start the fire and get somethin' goin' for the noon meal." She said this with a tone of resignation. She eyed the stove with dislike. "I suppose I'll need some wood."

"I'll get it for you. Just tell me where to find it." Duncan hadn't noticed any wood stacked anywhere around the grounds, but he hadn't exactly been looking.

"Tell you where the wood is? Oh. . ." Bella looked nervous. "I believe we might have used the last of it before we left on the trip."

"You must travel a lot."

"More than I'd like to, yes."

He moved to the door. "I'll see what I can find. Where would I find an ax?"

She frowned. "Perhaps we have one in the barn?"

The comment was more question than statement. Duncan had a distinct feeling Bella and Andria were up to something. He wondered if the place was even theirs. He remembered their names in the family Bible and figured they had some tie to the cabin. But he also knew they could have planted the Bible there at some point. Or maybe the cabin had belonged to their grandparents.

Duncan still had concerns about Andria's disappearance. He kept one eye on the trees while he looked around for an ax. He sent Ethan out to look behind the barn, and Ethan called out that he'd found one. Duncan hurried around the small structure and found the ax buried deep into a tree stump. Judging by the amount of rust on the head, it had been sitting there for a long, long time. He tried to pull it out, but it had become permanently embedded into the wood. Ethan grinned, pleased that he'd been the one to find it.

"Want me to chop the wood for you, Duncan? I can help out that way."

"Thanks, Ethan, but I think you'd do better finding us some wood to cut once I get the ax in working condition. While you're at it, gather up some smaller pieces to use as kindling."

"All right." Ethan's face fell.

"We can't have a fire without wood, Ethan. Finding the wood is every bit as important as cutting it."

"Yes, sir."

"I have to work on this ax for a while before it'll be usable anyway, if it ever will be."

"Yeah. Those ladies should put their equipment away before they leave for town next time."

Duncan nodded his agreement but didn't tell the boy that the ax had obviously been there for years, not days.

Bella walked through the rear barn door and entered the shady clearing that surrounded the back of it. "You found the ax. Good."

"What's left of it anyway. I'll have to see if I can make it usable again. How long has it been since you two had wood anyway? How have you survived here, Bella?"

❧

Duncan's concern made Bella feel even guiltier about their deception. She reminded herself that the deception was necessary for everyone's well-being. "We make do all right. Our neighbors are good people. We all watch out for each other." Which at least was true back before her momma had died.

Duncan looked relieved. "So the neighbors bring you wood for the fire. That would make sense. I'm glad to know you have people watching out for you."

"Right." The only people who had ever watched out for Bella and Andria since their mother passed away were standing right in front of her. Sarah's family had tried to talk Bella's father into letting Bella and Andria move in with them, but their father wouldn't hear of it.

"Are they due to bring more wood soon?"

"Um. I'm not sure." Bella hated this situation. She wished Duncan would leave so they could stop the farce. "We'll be fine though until they do. You and Ethan can be on your way. I don't want his father to worry."

"You heard the boy. His father won't be home for another week at the earliest. I don't have to preach again until Sunday. And I have an arrangement in place so that if I can't get back in time to preach on a given Sunday, a friend in town will cover the service for me. If he doesn't hear from me by Saturday afternoon, he knows he's to step in and preach the next sermon."

"How wonderful." She didn't bother to hide her sarcasm. What were they to do now? Her brothers would show up sooner or later, and they'd turn the place upside down. She couldn't bear it if Ethan or Duncan got hurt. She hadn't known them long, but she related to Ethan more than he knew and she found Duncan's overprotective ways to be endearing. She figured if she told him the truth he'd refuse to leave and would face her oldest brother's wrath. She knew Duncan couldn't stay forever, but she knew she could learn from his presence if she could only spend a little bit more time with him.

"You don't sound very enthusiastic."

"As I've tried to tell you, Andria and I have been on our own for quite a while. We aren't used to anyone else lookin' out for us. I hate for you to miss out on your own obligations while we start gettin' used to dependin' on someone else."

Confusion clouded Duncan's features. "Then you don't have supportive neighbors?"

"We do. . .when we're here. Which isn't often. Which you've probably already figured out."

"Often being—every few years?"

Bella shrugged. "Somethin' like that."

"If you don't mind my asking, where do you live the rest of the time?"

"I can't answer that. I wish I could. We live a solitary life. We're not used to dealing with outsiders." At least that part was the truth. The sad truth.

"Do you want us to leave?"

A heavy feeling settled over Bella at the thought. She did and she didn't want him to leave. She wanted him and Ethan far away from her brothers. But she also wanted to spend more time with him. He'd forced his presence upon them, but he'd been nothing but a gentleman and she longed to know more about him and his relationship with God. She knew she could never tell him about her brothers, but she didn't want to lose the tenuous relationship they were building. Preacher or not, he was the first kind man she had ever known.

She corrected herself. Sarah's father was kind, but he'd been more of a father figure to them back when they were young. He'd tried to step in when her father's manner changed. He'd talked to her brothers when they'd started running wild. That's when they'd moved the girls up to the other homestead.

Duncan, on the other hand, seemed more of a friend, even though she barely knew him. She knew he had to be kind to everyone, his position required it, but it was still nice to know someone cared and was watching out for them.

"I'm sure I should say that I do want you to leave, but in all honesty, I don't. Not yet."

"Ah, you want us to stay and help you put the cabin back in order, is that it?" Duncan teased.

"No. Yes. I mean. . .I'd love to have you help with the cabin. But I also appreciate your concern and the escort and your offer of help. I don't want to take advantage, but it's nice to have someone here watchin' out for us. It's nice to feel safe." She closed her eyes in mortification. She'd said too much. It was one thing to think the words, something entirely different to utter them to his face.

"You aren't taking advantage, Bella. I offered, remember? I wouldn't have offered my help if I hadn't meant it."

"I know."

Duncan leaned against the ax handle. The head was still stuck tight into the stump. "Who or what do you need to feel safe from? Being alone? Because as I said, God is a great companion. Or is there something more that you're afraid of? Because God can help there, too."

"I'm sorry. I shouldn't be talkin' to you about this." Bella turned on her heel and hurried back to the house. She should have told him to go ahead and leave. It would only be harder to see him go, the longer he was there. And he hadn't been there very long as it was. Something deep inside drew her to him. She figured it was her desire to know God, but there was something more, too.

She shook her head. It was probably nothing more than panic over her brothers' possible actions and pure terror at the thought of being alone with them again. She knew she was headed for a confrontation with them, and she didn't relish the thought. She knew she could no longer help them with their outlawin' ways. There'd most definitely be a confrontation.

Having a strong man like Duncan at her side when that day came would do wonders for her confidence when facing them, but was it fair to bring him in? She needed to warn him, but she knew he'd leave.

She and Andria had the little matter of the gold to deal with, too. If her brothers became suspicious about Bella's loyalty, they'd never leave them alone long enough to claim the fortune. The fortune that was their ticket out of their brothers' clutches.

Ethan had carried in the supplies when they'd first arrived home and had laid them just inside the door. Bella went over and dug through the parcels, trying to figure out what to make for dinner. She glanced out the window and saw Andria walk through the trees with Sarah by her side.

"Sarah!" Bella laid the supplies on the table and rushed out to meet her sister's childhood friend. Though Sarah was closer to Andria in age, all three had played together.

Sarah pulled her into a warm hug, turning sideways so as not to knock Bella over with the large bag she carried over her shoulder. "Momma sent over some food for you. I came along to help Andi with the animals." She glanced around. "Not that I see a place for you to put the hens."

"I'll figure something out." Duncan walked up to join them. He looked relieved to see Andria. "Nice cages."

"My dad rigged them up for us." Sarah laughed. "I'm Sarah."

"Pleased to meet you, Sarah. I'm Duncan."

The goat butted Andria in the thigh. She squealed and handed the rope over to Duncan.

Duncan took it with a laugh and led the ornery goat off toward the barn. "Bring the hens to the barn when you get through chatting."

Sarah turned to Andria and said in a loud whisper. "You were right—he is handsome."

"Andria!" Bella looked at Duncan's retreating back for a sign that he'd heard Sarah's declaration.

He didn't miss a step.

"I was just fillin' her in. It's not like it isn't true. You have to admit he's easy on the eye."

"I've never denied it, but he's a pastor. You need to speak of him with respect."

"How is sayin' he's handsome disrespectful? In case you didn't notice, it's a compliment, Belle."

"It is a compliment, but still, you mustn't talk that way about him."

"Pastors marry, too, Bella," Sarah joined in.

"I know. But you need to remember and respect his position."

Sarah went on as if Bella hadn't spoken. "I, for one, wouldn't mind bein' a pastor's wife if I could marry one that looked as fine as he does."

"Absolutely not. Get that thought right out of your head."

"I'm not allowed to marry a pastor?"

"You're not allowed to think about marrying this pastor."

Sarah sighed. "So no hanging on his arm, begging for a walk around the property?"

"Goodness no! Especially not anythin' like that." Bella surprised herself as feelings of jealousy reared to life. She had no hold on Duncan.

Sarah and Andria laughed.

Bella had a feeling she'd been set up. "You two need to get those hens out to Duncan and ask him to come in for the noon meal. Round up Ethan while you're out there. Is there enough food here for everyone?"

"Momma asked how many you had at the cabin. There's plenty of food for everyone, myself included." Her enthusiasm slowed. "That is, if you don't mind my stayin'. I can leave if you'd rather."

"Of course I'd love for you to stay. Andi has missed you so much."

"And you haven't?"

"I certainly have." She gave Sarah an extra hug for good measure.

"Any chance y'all are back for good?"

Bella sent Andria a warning glare. "Not for now. Maybe someday soon, though."

Sarah's face fell. "I miss havin' y'all nearby. It's been too long."

"I know. We want to come home, too. But we have to be with our brothers for now. Speakin' of,"—she glanced over toward the barn—"for the time being, can you not mention them?"

"Why?"

"Duncan doesn't know about them, and I feel it's best to keep it that way. I don't want him asking too many questions."

"He doesn't know about them?"

"He knows we have brothers. He doesn't know what they do."

"So it's true what they say." Sarah looked upset.

"What who says?" Bella had a bad feeling in the pit of her stomach.

"The locals. Word gets around. You know how it is out here." Sarah motioned toward the hills over her shoulder.

"Yes, I know."

"Rumor has it, your brothers are the ones ridin' the hills and robbin' folks. I didn't want to believe it. They said they call themselves the McLeod gang."

"They don't call themselves anything," Bella stated. "And Andria and I are tryin' to figure out exactly what's going on with them. Until we do, please promise you won't say anythin' to anyone about our being here or about Wayne and Charlie while you're around Duncan."

"I promise. I'll keep your secret."

Bella hoped she would.

Chapter 11

Dinner was a noisy occasion with Ethan at the table. The young boy never quieted, even as he ate bites of his food. Duncan was forever correcting him, telling him not to talk with his mouth full; but a moment later, Ethan was asking a question or sharing a story with anyone who'd listen.

Bella picked up the basket of bread and passed it around. Sarah's mother had thought of everything, down to the butter for the bread. The slices of cured ham set Bella's mouth to watering. She hadn't had food like this in years. Not since her mother had been well enough to cook. Their meal in town had smelled wonderful, but she'd been so nervous that day, sitting next to Duncan and the sheriff, that she couldn't enjoy the food. She'd been too worried that they'd figure out her relationship to Wayne and Charlie.

She used a fork to pull two slices of ham onto her plate. She reached for the butter and spread it across the bread. The bread was still warm and melted the butter as soon as she slathered it on. Green beans, fresh from Sarah's family's garden, rounded out the fine meal. Bella decided then and there she'd plant fresh vegetables as soon as she and Andria settled down.

She placed a hand on Sarah's. "Sarah, please tell your mother thank you for the meal. It's wonderful. I haven't had food as good as this in a long, long time."

Duncan grunted his agreement.

"You know how Momma is. She wanted you to come over and eat at our place, but Andria said you'd just arrived and couldn't leave just yet."

"Andi is right. The place is a shambles, and we have a lot to do. I think Duncan has decided to stick around a few days and help us out."

"That's very nice of you." Sarah batted her eyes at him.

Duncan smiled back.

Bella corrected her with a look.

Sarah and Andi exchanged a glance and started laughing.

"What's so funny?" Duncan looked down at his plate and resumed eating.

"Bella."

Duncan looked her way, and Bella wished she could sink into the floor. She shrugged.

"Bella's funny?"

Ethan narrowed his eyes and looked from Andria to Sarah, to Bella, and finally Duncan. "They sound like the girls at school when someone's sweet on someone else."

"They do, huh?" Duncan grinned around his bite of bread. He leaned back and chewed slowly. "So who's sweet on whom?"

"Well it certainly isn't us," Andria hurried to say.

They both looked over at Bella. She could feel her face redden as everyone at the table stared at her.

"Well it certainly isn't me either. I'm not sweet on anyone. Though you *are* rather cute, Ethan." She nudged him with her arm.

Ethan turned bright red and fled the table. "Ain't no girl gonna get a hold on me, I don't care how old she is."

"I think he just called you old, Bella." Sarah laughed.

"Yes, I think he has a bit of work set before him when it comes to dealing with females," Duncan agreed. He wiped his mouth with a cloth. "Ladies, that was one fine meal."

"I wish I could take credit." Bella grinned. "I'm more used to cookin' up the likes of rabbit or fish or venison over an open fire."

"That sounds nice, too," Duncan said. "I hope to get a chance to sample some of your cooking someday soon."

"Really?"

"Why not?"

"You seem so civilized. I didn't figure you for the type to like wild game."

"I haven't always lived in town. I've spent my fair share of time riding around in these hills. I told you that before."

"I guess you did, but it's hard to imagine that." Bella smiled. This was a side of Duncan she hadn't expected to see. She'd love to ride the trails in the hills with Duncan's strong protective presence by her side. Andria's and Sarah's giggles brought her out of the daydream. She'd been twirling a strand of hair around her finger while staring at Duncan like he was her own special Christmas gift. Mortified, she jumped to her feet and started gathering plates.

Duncan, looking flustered, stood and did the same. Their hands connected when they both reached for the same mug and both hurriedly let go. The ceramic mug shattered on the hardwood floor at their feet.

"Don't move. I'll get the broom." Duncan moved across the room with long strides.

Andria's and Sarah's gazes went back and forth from one to the other, their expressions amused.

"You two should go help Ethan in the barn. We need to get the animals settled before nightfall."

"Of course." Andi drew out the words. "You two want to be alone."

"Andria!" Bella gasped. "Go!"

Bella walked over to the front window. Now it sounded like she *did* want to be alone with him! What was her sister thinking? Bella. . .*alone* with Duncan? The last thing Bella wanted was to be alone with him. He had her emotions going in all directions and her thoughts all topsy-turvy. The last thing she wanted was to be alone with the man who had her thinking silly thoughts and making a fool of herself. "I meant you two should go along with Duncan to help Ethan in the barn. You'll need to take some blankets. The men will have to bed down out there. I can get the kitchen in order on my own."

Duncan's touch on her shoulder froze her in place. "They're long gone, Bella."

She spun around. He was right. Her sister and friend were nowhere in sight. "They didn't waste any time gettin' out of here."

He chuckled. "No, they didn't."

"Well as I was sayin', you might as well head on out to help them. I'm sure they have no clue what needs to be done out there, and you seem to have some experience that might help them."

"Bella."

She stopped, halfway to the long board that served as a counter. "Yes?" Her voice shook.

"Am I making you nervous?"

"You are right now."

"I don't want you feeling uncomfortable around me."

"I'll try not to, then."

"You didn't finish your meal. Come over here." He gently took her arm and led her back to her seat at the table. "Sit down and eat. The chores will be waiting when we get to them." He glanced around with twinkling eyes. "Just as they have been for the past few years."

"True."

He sat down across from her, making her feel as nervous as she'd been at the diner.

She pushed the food around on her plate. "I can't eat with you sittin' there starin' at me."

"Why not?"

"I just can't." She took a sip of water. "You unnerve me."

His voice took on a teasing tone. "Is it because you find me handsome?"

The water caught in her throat, and she choked. "I never said that!"

"You kind of did."

"I did not!"

"When your sister was talking earlier?"

"I corrected them. I told them to stop."

"Yet they didn't. They asked what you thought. . . ."

"And I didn't answer."

"You didn't deny it."

"When?"

"When the girls were discussing my finer points just after they brought in the livestock."

"That was their conversation, not mine. If you'll think back, you should have heard me chastisin' them, tellin' them they shouldn't be talkin' about you that way."

"Why? I'm still a man. I appreciate the compliments."

Bella pushed her chair back so fast it tipped over. She'd never felt so uncomfortable around a person in all her life.

"I need to do the dishes."

"Bella." His voice was gentle. "I'm sorry for causing you discomfort. I'll stop."

"It's just that. . .I'm not sure how you make me feel," Bella blustered. "Yes, I do. You—you make me feel flustered. And—and inept. And—and—" She put a hand to her hair, and her shoulders sagged. "And like a complete mess."

"If that's the case, you're the prettiest mess I've ever seen."

She whipped her head up to stare at him. Was the man blind? She wore men's trousers, and her unruly hair was pulled back in a braid. Stray strands tickled her face where they'd fallen out of place. She'd slept on the ground the night before and hadn't had time to freshen up. Yet there he sat, saying such ridiculous things.

She didn't know what to say. No one had ever called her pretty before. Duncan was ruining everything. She'd never be able to be content in her old life now that she'd met him. Though she'd already decided to leave behind their outlawin' ways, she'd been content with the thought of living alone at the homestead with just Andi for company. But now that she'd had a taste of Duncan's sweet compliments, she'd always feel something was missing after he left. She promptly burst into tears at the thought.

Duncan jumped to his feet. "What did I say?" He looked perplexed.

"You just had to get all nice and complimentary, didn't you?" she sobbed. "Now I'm the one who has to live with that."

"But isn't that a good thing? I meant everything I said." He started to reach for her then stopped and let his hands drop to his side. He looked bewildered. "Why is that a bad thing?"

"I can't explain it. I told you, it's hard to put into words. Look, I know it's a part of your profession to say such nice things to the people you meet, and you're supposed to be nice and make people happy, but you really ought to be more careful about who you say them to. Some people might, um, take them to heart and make more of the words than is meant."

"If I said something out of line, I apologize. I never use my words lightly. I always mean what I say. And I'm not in the habit of giving compliments to pretty women. I haven't been a preacher for very long, only a few years, but I know to be careful in my actions toward women. I didn't mean to offend, but something about you catches me unaware. I'm in uncharted waters here, too." He glanced around the room. She figured he was either searching for the fastest way out or for a weapon to use against her if she went batty on him again.

"Really?"

"Really."

"But you seem so confident and always in control."

"Then I do a good job hiding my true feelings, which isn't a good thing. I'll have to work on that some more. I want to be approachable to my parishioners and everyone else around me."

"So you meant the things you said to me?"

"Of course I did." His handsome face tightened with concern. "Why would you think otherwise?"

"I don't know, but you shouldn't say things like that."

He looked hurt, but he nodded. "I think I understand. There's someone else, isn't there?"

"Someone else?"

"Someone else courting you. You have a beau that comes calling, and I've overstepped my position. Is that correct? If so, please forgive me."

"That's not it at all! It's the very opposite of the truth."

"There is no beau?"

"No. I've not even had the chance to ever have one. I wouldn't know what to do with a beau."

His mouth quirked up into a grin. "I'd be more than happy to instruct you on the subject."

"*You're a pastor,*" she whispered.

Duncan glanced around. "There's no one else here. Why are you whispering?"

"I don't want the others to hear. I don't want to be a part of anythin' that could be interpreted as sordid and make you lose your upright standin' in town."

"I promise you my intentions are nothing but honorable. We're well chaperoned here, and I'll make sure to keep my distance so as not to disturb your delicate sensibilities as to what a preacher can and can't do." He leaned close, and she could feel his breath against her cheek. "But I will have you know that something about you calls to my heart, and I intend to find out what it is. I'm not going to abandon you. I might have to leave soon, but if and when I do, you can rest assured that I will be coming back."

With that, he disappeared out the back door and into the afternoon sun.

Bella bustled around the kitchen, cleaning up the dinner dishes, then slamming pots and pans into the wash water so she could clean them for later meals. The man had some nerve.

"I'm still a man."

As if Bella hadn't noticed that fact.

Chapter 12

With Andria and Sarah's help, Bella dug in to finish cleaning the main areas of the cabin. They spent the better part of the day hauling out junk and sorting through their parents' belongings.

Bella stripped the dingy, rotting curtains from the windows and threw them into the fire pit outside. She remembered back to when the fabric was new and her mother had been so excited to put up such bright, cheery fabric. She'd sewn the curtains herself. Bella's father hadn't always had the hard edge to him that he'd had in his later years. He'd bought the fabric as a surprise for Bella's mother on a Christmas long ago.

Sarah gave the windows a good scrubbing, and they sparkled like new. Even now, with the late afternoon sun slanting through the windows, the room was brighter than it had been when they'd arrived earlier in the day.

Andria stayed busy with scrubbing down every surface in the room. Bella washed the pots and pans and dusted the few collectibles their mother had accumulated through the years.

They worked together to remove the linens from the beds and wash them in the tub that Duncan had dragged over near the back door. He filled the tub with water from the hand pump, and Bella added hot water she'd warmed on the stove.

Duncan grinned at their enthusiasm as they dipped the dusty linens in the warm water and scrubbed at them with vigor. Bella watched as Duncan hung a length of rope from the corner of the cabin to a large branch on the nearby magnolia. After he was finished, the clean linens were placed on the line to dry. The fresh-smelling sheets swayed back and forth on the line in the gentle wind that blew through the backyard.

"I'm not sleepin' in those fresh sheets with all this dirt and grime on me." Bella looked down at her dusty pants and shirt with dismay. "I'll need a good scrubbin' myself after we've finished all this cleanin'."

Andria nodded her agreement. Sarah, on the other hand, looked as fresh and pretty as she had when she arrived earlier that morning.

The final items to be cleaned were the beds. It took everything all three women had to drag the feather mattresses outside and thrash them with a stick. They thrashed until the dust stopped puffing up into the air.

306

Duncan exited the barn and shook his head. "Y'all should have hollered for me to come and do the heavy lifting."

Bella studied him as he walked over to survey the fruits of their labor. He stood with hands on hips, his dark hair blowing in the breeze. Bella couldn't help but notice the hard muscles under his white, rolled-up sleeves. He looked like he belonged in the hills, working the land; and at the moment, Bella found it hard to imagine him in town, standing behind a pulpit.

She shook herself out of her musings.

"We managed to get 'em out here just fine," Bella retorted with a grin. "But we'll be more than happy to let you carry the heavy ticks back inside now that we're finished. We don't want to chance draggin' them on the dirty ground after all the hard work we put in gettin' 'em clean, do we, ladies?"

"Certainly not," Sarah agreed.

"I'm sure not startin' over," Andria chimed in.

Duncan heaved the first one on his shoulder and carried it inside like it was nothing. He returned for the others while the women watched with interest. He was right. It would have been much easier to let him carry them out in the first place.

With the bed frames clean and the mattresses in place, they decided to rest for a bit. They sat in a circle around the open chest at the end of Bella's mother's bed. The fresh scent of spring blew through the open doors and windows. Her mother's personal items lay in the trunk before them.

"What are you going to do with all your ma's dresses?" Sarah picked up the pretty pink gingham that lay on top and held it against her chest. The garment flattered her fair appearance. The pink in her work-flushed cheeks accentuated the light blue color of her eyes. The humidity set her hair into blond ringlets. Bella knew she looked a fright when compared to her pretty friend.

"I suppose we should fix them up and wear them." Bella sighed. "We can't exactly run around in men's pants and shirts forever. That is, we can't if we end up stayin' here."

"Oh, I agree." Sarah beamed. "And I do want you to stay."

Bella exchanged a look with Andria. "We want to, but we have to take care of some final business first."

"How long will it take?"

"We aren't sure, but we'll be back as soon as possible."

Sarah's face fell. "Do you have to leave right away?"

"No, I think we'll sit tight for a couple more days at least. We might as well finish puttin' the place to rights before we move back in."

Bella lifted a blue floral dress from the trunk and felt something hard press against her leg.

"What on earth. . ." She reached into the pocket and pulled out a polished stone. "Momma's prayer stone."

Sarah leaned close. "What's a prayer stone?"

"Momma found this pretty polished stone one day over by the stream, and she put it in her pocket. She said she'd carry it always and would remember to pray for each of her children every time she felt it. It was like a reminder for her to pray for us. I have a feelin' she knew the lot of us would require all the extra prayer she could summon up. Even with that, look how things turned out."

"Why would you say that?" Sarah's brows knit together in confusion. "I don't think y'all turned out so bad."

"Thanks." Bella forced a smile. There was so much Sarah didn't know about them. She and her family simply thought the McLeods had moved away.

Bella turned the smooth stone over and over in her hand. The stone felt cool to her touch. She liked the idea that her mother's hands had last touched the stone. "Andi, do you mind if I keep Momma's stone with me? I'd like to use it in a similar fashion. Maybe Duncan will teach me to pray better and I can pick up where Ma left off."

"I'd like that, Bella. It would feel mighty good to know someone was prayin' for us again and askin' God to watch out for us."

Bella slipped the stone into her pocket. "I'm not sure my prayers will account for much, but I'll surely give it a try."

"Why wouldn't you think your prayers would be heard?" Duncan entered the room as Sarah folded the last dress and placed it next to a stack of aprons that had been draped over the bed frame.

Bella sent him an incredulous look. "You have to ask? Surely you've noticed by now that we aren't the most traditional women in these here parts."

"I've noticed, but God loves you anyhow. He loves you no matter where you are and no matter what you're doing."

Bella didn't understand why and told him so.

"Do you remember hearing the Bible story of the prodigal son?"

"Vaguely."

"The woman at the well?"

"No."

"The Bible is full of stories about people who chose the wrong path and how God later led them back to His fold."

"His fold?"

"God is our shepherd, and we're like His sheep. He cares deeply for each and every one of us. If you stray, He'll come after you."

"Oh, I don't think He has a mind to come after me. Or Andi." She placed a hand on top of Andi's. "Sorry, Andi. But I'm sure that's true."

Andria shrugged, not appearing too surprised with her lot in life.

"But it's not true," Duncan interrupted. "Let me show you some examples." He picked up their mother's worn Bible and opened it to a passage. He read it aloud and flipped to another. He read passage after passage that told about bad choices and God's redemption of the sinners.

"So all those folks in the Bible were outlaws and God took 'em back into His family and forgave them?"

Duncan laughed. "Yes, although I'm not sure the term 'outlaw' existed way back then."

"Thank you, Duncan. That gives me some things to think on. I find it interestin' to know that God might still love me, poor dressin' style and all."

"He does love you and don't you ever forget it. He doesn't care about how a person dresses. He only cares about the heart." Duncan headed for the door. "I need to go see what Ethan is up to. I'll be back in a bit."

Bella turned to her sister and her friend. "If y'all don't mind, I think I'll head over to the stream and freshen up. Now that we have the cabin tidy, I feel more like a mess than ever."

"You do look a mess." Andria laughed. "And I'm sure I do, too. Maybe we should try out some more of Momma's dresses."

"I think I'd like that."

Sarah bounced on her chair. "You try them on, and I'll fix 'em up for you tonight when I get home. I can take them in and hem 'em up and make them fit y'all just fine."

Andi's eyes lit up. "You can? No more trippin' on Momma's long skirts?"

"I can do better than that. I'll teach you how to hem, too, so we can get it done faster."

The younger girls waved Bella off and turned to their sewing chores. Bella grabbed up the blue floral print and tossed it over her arm. Even when messy, Sarah looked like a proper lady. Bella suddenly had the urge to look like a lady, too.

❧

Bella stripped out of the ill-fitting, confining pants and shirt and tossed them toward the stream's shore with disgust. The filthy outfit floated on the water in the shallows. Dirt and grime slowly seeped from the fabric and made the water murky.

Only a couple of days earlier Bella had hated the thought of donning a dress. Now she wished she could wear one proper-like. Surely Duncan would appreciate her more if she looked and dressed like Sarah. She shook her head to clear the silly thoughts. Bella had surely lost her mind if she thought Duncan would ever show any interest in her.

She glanced over at the pretty blue dress that lay carefully draped over the branches of a nearby bush. She hoped the dress would make her look more feminine. Stacked up to Sarah, she didn't have a chance. Sarah had a sweet nature about her and she'd grown up in a God-fearing home. Chances were, she was the kind of woman Duncan was looking for—if he was looking for a woman at all.

The bar of lye soap she'd dragged along with her waited for her on the shore. She swam over to it and worked it into a thick lather. She washed the grime from her body, spending extra time on her hair. She felt better already, just by being clean. It was exciting to have a fresh outfit ready. She usually scrubbed her pants and shirt just before bed and hoped they'd be dry before she had to put them back on the next morning.

Bella lay on her back in the water and floated in the stream. Though the stream wasn't very deep—only a few feet in depth at the middle—the pool where she'd bathed was deep enough to allow her to float above the water-polished stones that lined the bottom.

She thought about the stories Duncan had read to her. She'd never felt worthy of being a good person, not with the family she'd been born into. But apparently God didn't discriminate according to such things. And her mother had loved the Lord dearly, that should count for something. Bella had only focused on her father's and brothers' choices and habits in the past couple of years, but maybe she should put more weight on her mother's love of the Lord.

If what Duncan said was true, it was possible for Bella to have a relationship with God. Bella's whole life would be changed for the better. She wouldn't have to watch her back anymore. She wouldn't have to wonder if and when and where they'd be caught and taken into custody for their deeds. Her life would be redeemed, and she could turn her back on her outlawin' ways.

Because she and Andria weren't ever willing outlaws, Bella didn't think God would hold their actions against them. She figured He'd just want them to turn away from their former actions and change their ways, like the men and women Duncan had told them about. Bella would be more than happy to do just that. Of course she'd confess everything to Sheriff Andrew just to be sure. If he had a mind to punish them, she'd face whatever charges their sins brought her way.

Her mother would be so happy to know that Bella was considering such a thing. For once she'd feel her prayers had been recognized. Bella suddenly remembered her mother's prayer stone and sat up. She frantically glanced around for the pants she'd left drifting in the stream. How could she have been so careless? She'd just taken possession of the stone, and now she'd possibly lost it.

For a long moment she didn't see the pants. She worried they'd washed downstream. She finally located them in some heavy overgrowth near the shore. She tugged them out of their resting spot and dug her hand into the pocket. She breathed a sigh of relief as her hand closed around the hard stone. She kissed the wet object and waded over to tuck it securely into the pocket of the dress. She'd be more careful with the treasure in the future. Though her own heart was well on its way to being redeemed, she still had work to do when it came to her sister's and brothers' well-being.

Chapter 13

Two days later, Bella, Andria, and Sarah stood and looked over the transformed homestead.

Pride like Bella had never felt before seeped through her being. The work was much harder than she'd first expected. "Sarah, without you, we'd still be standin' here starin' at a filthy cabin. Thank you for comin' and helpin'."

"That's what friends and neighbors do." Sarah grasped Andi's hand and swung her around in circles. "I so want you both to come home."

Bella watched with mixed feelings. Her outlaw sister looked so normal spinning around and laughing with her childhood friend. But she'd missed out on so many other experiences like this. This should have been Andi's life, not the outlaw one their brothers had forced them into. She was more determined than ever to right the wrongs and get Andria back where she belonged.

Sarah headed over to the clothesline to take down the newly tailored dresses.

Bella took advantage of the moment and pulled Andria aside. "I've been thinkin'. We have to turn in the gold."

"What?" Andria's face fell. "I thought we were going to use it for our fresh start. I don't want to go back to our outlawin' ways. Bella, please reconsider."

"We aren't goin' back to our former ways, Andi. But I want us to have a fresh start. If we take gold that isn't ours to start out with, we're as good as stealin' it from whoever it belongs to."

"I hadn't thought of it that way."

"Neither had I until I started listenin' to Duncan and readin' Momma's Bible these past couple of days." She motioned around them. "Look at what we have here. We have everything we need. We need to trust God to provide anything else we might need."

Andria looked doubtful. "You really think He'll come through for us?"

Bella nodded. "I do. And if you'd start readin' the Good Book, I think you'd agree."

Andi dug into her pocket. "Then I can't keep these gold nuggets I took from the cave. We'll have to return them."

Bella placed them in the pocket of her dress, right next to the prayer stone. "We'll do that as soon as Duncan leaves to take Ethan back to town. We need to talk to Wayne and Charlie, then we need to talk to Sheriff Andrew. We'll tell him about our past, and we'll tell him about the gold."

"What about Duncan?"

"I want to tell him before he leaves. He's been so good to us—he deserves to know the truth."

They headed for the house and met Sarah inside.

The familiar bark of a dog carried through the woods and into the open windows. Bella looked out front, her heart filled with dread. She glanced over at Andi, whose expression mirrored her anxiety. Their worst fears had come true. Wayne had arrived at the cabin.

Sarah glanced from one to the other. "What's wrong?"

"Wayne's here."

"Well, that's a good thing, isn't it? Aren't you excited to see your brother?"

"Not right now."

"Why? Do you think he'll cause a problem?"

"We know he'll cause a problem. Multiple problems."

"Can I do something to help?"

"I don't think so." Bella turned to her. "Or maybe you can. Do me a favor and go out to the barn and try to keep Ethan and Duncan distracted while we talk to Wayne."

"How do I do that?"

"I don't know, think of something! But hurry. Ask about the chickens or the goat."

"I'll be happy to do that." Sarah hurried toward the back door and slipped into the warm afternoon sun.

"I'm sure you are," Bella muttered. She had no doubt her friend had noticed the preacher's good looks. Sarah had admitted as much. What surprised Bella were her feelings of jealousy at the thought.

The barking grew louder.

"Let's go out and meet him. Duncan will be out front before Sarah can stop him if he hears the dog."

They hurried to the path that led to their other homestead. Wayne rode slowly up the trail. He looked harder than ever. His dark hair hadn't been tamed, and his blue eyes were bloodshot.

"Well, lookee at what we have here." His words were slurred, a sure sign that he'd been drinking. "The prodigal sisters have finally come home."

"You're right, Wayne. Now that you mention it, we have come home. Home. Right where we belong." Bella didn't know why she started out with an attack. Wayne wasn't nice at the best of times, but when he'd been drinking he was all but impossible to reason with. Bella and Andria knew to stay clear of him when he was in this condition. Unfortunately, in this case, he couldn't be avoided.

"Home is where I say it is." Wayne leaned forward with his finger jabbing the air and almost fell from his horse. "And I say home for y'all is at the top of the mountain with me and Charlie."

"Speakin' of, where is Charlie?" Bella asked. Charlie wasn't ever very far from Wayne's side.

"He's workin'."

"Workin' where?"

"Well Bella, maybe if you'd come home like you was supposed to, you'd know where Charlie was and what Charlie's been doin'."

Bella didn't respond. She wouldn't let Wayne goad her.

"Care to tell me why you didn't come home, *Bella*?"

She glanced over her shoulder but didn't see any sign of Duncan, Ethan, or Sarah. "Something came up."

Wayne laughed. "What could possibly come up? I told y'all what to do, and you defied me. You know that's not gonna go unnoticed."

Andria stepped forward, her hands clutched at her side. "We had our reasons, Wayne, and if you'd just listen, you'd appreciate our decision not to come home."

Wayne looked surprised to see Andria stand up to him. "You wanna get in the middle of this, baby sister?"

"I want you to leave Bella alone."

"Cain't do that."

"Why can't you?"

"You know why. We need you both to help out. We cain't have y'all actin' disrespectful. We need to count on you."

"What if we don't want to help out anymore?" Bella stood tall and folded her arms across her chest.

Wayne laughed. "You never were what I'd call willin'. But we cain't do it on our own. We depend on you to distract the targets so we have a chance to act."

Bella jumped back in. "It ain't right what you do, Wayne. There are other ways—better ways—to make a livin'. You and Pa used to run moonshine. Why couldn't you stick to doin' that? Or better yet, do somethin' upstandin' that'll make you proud. Robbin' people—it ain't right at all."

"When did you go and grow a conscience anyway? It didn't use to bother you. What's changed?"

"It's always bothered us. We never wanted to be dragged into your law-defyin' ways. But we've grown up. We know that what you do is wrong. We don't want to be a part of it anymore."

"You ain't gettin' out of it, Bella."

Bella hadn't ever been one to pray, and she wasn't sure she even knew how, but she figured it wouldn't hurt to reach out to God and see what happened.

Maybe, just maybe, they'd be able to talk some sense into Wayne and they'd be able to stay on at the homestead right away.

She whispered a prayer for God to help them out.

"Who you talkin' to, Bella? You talkin' to yerself?"

Wayne's interruption caused her to jump.

She wondered if she should explain, but Duncan's welcoming shout from the doorway of the barn made her forget what she wanted to say. Ethan and Sarah were nowhere to be seen.

"Who's the man?" Wayne's whole posture changed. "I *told* you not to show up here with a man."

"No, you told us not to go into town and get ourselves hitched. I've hardly done that." Though the thought of being hitched to Duncan wasn't a totally unpleasant one.

"Then who's the man you dragged home with you?"

"He's the parson in town. He didn't think it right that we were travelin' on our own, and he insisted on escortin' us."

"Did he now. And you couldn't figure out how to say no?"

"We did say no," Andria stated. "He followed us out of town anyway, even though we left the night before we said we'd leave."

Duncan was getting closer.

"You'll get the man away from here, or I'll take care of him for ya. You hear me?"

"We hear you," Bella spat.

"Tell him I'm askin' for directions. Don't let on that I'm your brother. You have two days to send him packin' before I return and take care of him myself."

Duncan walked up and introduced himself. Wayne reached down and shook his hand. "The ladies here were just givin' me directions. I'm afraid I got turned around on a trail somehow."

"That's easy to do up here the way some trails twist and turn," Duncan agreed. "Did they set you straight?"

"I think we came to an understandin', didn't we, darlin'?" He stared down at Bella.

"Sure we did. If you'll just follow the right path, you should be just fine."

Wayne squinted his eyes and looked over at Duncan. "There's a right path for everyone to follow, right, Reverend?"

Duncan studied Bella's brother. "It's true there's only one right path for everyone to follow. It's each person's choice whether he or she follows it or not."

Wayne cackled like the crazy man he was. "Says you."

"Says the Bible." Duncan frowned. "I take it you're not a believer?"

"Not in the least." Wayne spat a stream of tobacco onto the ground near Duncan's boots.

Bella closed her eyes in shame. Duncan didn't know the uncouth man was her brother, but if she didn't hurry up and get him away from there, he'd figure it out soon enough. And then what would he think of her? She needed to explain things in her own way, in her own time.

Duncan stepped forward and used his body as a shield for Bella and Andria. "You'd best be on your way. I hope you make it safely to your destination."

"Sure ya do." Wayne cackled again. "I'll be sure to let you know."

"No need." Duncan's words left no room for argument. "I think it's best if you head out and don't come back."

"What?" Wayne leaned forward and stared with bleary eyes into Duncan's face. "Preacher man, saver of lost souls, is tellin' me to get lost?"

"You're already lost if you don't abide by God's Word. Only you can change that."

"I thought preachers were supposed to be kind to everyone."

"I don't see that I'm being unkind. I'm merely asking you to leave and not come back. These ladies don't need the likes of you harassing them."

"The likes of me? Maybe they don't want the likes of you harassin' them." Wayne glared at his sisters. "What do you say, ladies? You want him or me?"

"Listen. We gave you the directions you asked for. The sun's gettin' low in the sky. You'd best be goin' on, or you'll get lost for sure." Bella wished her brother would just leave. Her stomach was in knots. Once he decided to let go with his cover, he wouldn't bat an eye at hurting Duncan, and at the moment Duncan was unarmed. They all were.

She should have warned him about Wayne. At least then he'd have had his rifle at the ready. If anything happened to him, his fate would rest on her conscience. And if Wayne went on a rampage, how would she keep Wayne from discovering Sarah and Ethan in the barn? She hoped Sarah had cleared the area when Duncan headed their way. Bella knew Sarah would take Ethan back to the safety of Sarah's home if she needed to. They owed her an explanation, too.

Wayne debated for a moment, and much to Bella's relief, he turned his horse to leave. They watched as he rode silently into the woods. Jake, their dog, stood indecisively at the edge of the trees. Wayne called him, and with one last backward glance, the dog ran off to join his master.

Duncan turned to Bella. "You should have summoned me as soon as that man rode up. This is exactly why it isn't safe for you and your sister to remain here alone."

Bella continued to stare into the trees. "I didn't know what to expect. I didn't want to bother you unnecessarily."

"That's why I'm here, Bella! I want to be here for you. I want you to call me if you need me."

Andria backed away a few yards then turned and headed for the barn.

"You've only just met us. You're only here for a short while. I'm not sure why you feel compelled to help us out, Duncan, but you can't watch over us forever. And when you do leave, we'll be on our own again, dealin' with situations just like this every time our brothers are away on business." Bella looked hard into his eyes. "Who are we gonna summon then, Duncan?"

"That's my point, Bella. Why don't you consider coming back to town with Ethan and me? I can find you a place to stay. I can help you find work. I can't explain why I'm drawn to you, but I am. I want to know you're safe. Andrew sent me up here, but my heart is telling me to stay. When I leave, I want you to come with me."

"We can't do that."

"Why not?"

"We have a life up here. We don't belong in town." Bella paced a few feet away. "I'll not make the same mistake again. Does that make you feel better? I'll keep my rifle at arm's reach. Havin' you here has given me a false sense of security. I let down my guard, that's all. It won't happen again."

"That doesn't make me feel any better." Duncan towered over her, hands on hips. His brown eyes glared down at her. "I don't understand this any more than you do, but I know we were brought together for a purpose and I intend to wait and see what that purpose is."

"You don't even know me, Duncan. For all you know, I could be the worst thing to happen to you as far as your position as preacher goes. You need to leave. You need to go back to your people. You need to get Ethan home to his family."

"I'm not leaving. Not yet anyway. I have a few more days before Ethan's parents return. If you won't come with me, I'll stay here and pray I have some answers before I have to leave."

"Nothin' I can say will make you leave sooner?"

"No. I feel God wants me to stay. I don't want to offend you or cause you any concern, Bella, but I need to follow through on what God has placed on my heart."

Bella panicked. Wayne didn't fool around when it came to this sort of threat. She'd prayed for God to intervene, and Duncan had come to help them. Could he really be sent by God to watch out for them? Was it possible that he was the answer to their problems and that somehow God would use him to get them away from Wayne?

She said another prayer and asked God to make it clear if so. A small seed of hope started to bloom in her heart. Maybe, just maybe, God did care, and He'd help them in this time of need.

Chapter 14

Bella woke early the next morning and decided to enjoy the view of the sunrise from the cabin's porch. She dressed quietly and wrapped a blanket around her shoulders to ward off the early morning chill. She slipped outside and settled into her mother's old wooden rocking chair. The side porch had the best view of the mountains. It was Bella's favorite place to sit and think.

As she watched, the early morning sun began to rise up over the trees. The sky turned from dark blue, to light blue, then lavender, pink, and finally orange as it worked its way higher in the sky. The birds welcomed the morning by calling back and forth to each other from the treetops.

The cacophony of birdsong was so loud, it didn't surprise her to see Duncan walk out of the barn. He headed over to the newly primed pump and shaved before splashing fresh water on his face and hair. He spotted Bella on the porch and headed her way.

She greeted him with a smile. "Beautiful mornin' today."

"Aren't all mornings beautiful up here?" He climbed the steps two at a time and walked up beside her to lean against the rail. He watched quietly for a few moments as the sun climbed higher in the sky. "Nothing I've seen beats the beauty in these hills."

His tender glance swept over her, and for a moment Bella had the strangest sensation that his words described more than just the scenery. Duncan was so breathtakingly handsome that Bella had a hard time keeping her mind on their conversation. She had to agree with his observation when it came to the beauty that surrounded them. The comment suited him as well. With his dark hair still damp from the hand pump and the fresh scent of shaving soap wafting her way in the gentle morning breeze, it was all she could do to speak.

She finally found her tongue. "I s'pose you're right. It is mighty pleasant to sit out here and enjoy the view." So much for witty conversation. Bella smiled. At least she was being civil. She hadn't been all that nice when they'd first met. She forced her eyes away from him and concentrated on studying the low-lying, mist-covered valleys. It had been a long time since she'd taken time to appreciate the beauty of their surroundings.

She wasn't used to letting down her guard. Duncan's presence on the porch and his nearness made Bella feel safe and secure. She wasn't used to either sensation. She wondered how empty the porch would feel once he was gone. Bella was afraid the entire homestead—maybe even the whole mountain—would feel the loss of his presence.

She kept her eyes averted as she spoke, afraid her emotions would be written on her face. "You don't sound much like a city boy at the moment. What part of the mountain are you from? You seem familiar with the area."

"I grew up right here in these hills." He turned to her with a smile. He pointed to the next mountain over. "I was born and raised on that mountain. And I'm wondering at the moment what I was thinking when I decided to settle and preach in town." He sighed and shook his head. "Sometimes you don't know something's missing until it's staring you in the face."

Bella knew what he was saying. She felt the same way about the homestead, but even more so, she felt that way about Duncan. "It seems to me you were in town because God told you to settle down there."

"I guess He did, but I think now He might be calling me in a new direction."

"Just like that?" Bella wished she had such clear direction from God.

"Just like that." Duncan rested his elbows on the rail and looked over at her.

Bella shifted in her chair so she could see him better. "And what would that new direction be?"

"I'm not sure, but I think maybe He's calling me back into the hills."

"You'd leave your church?" Bella's heart skipped a beat at the thought of Duncan living nearby. She didn't want her selfish thoughts to interfere with what God had for Duncan, but if what he said was God's will, she sure hoped he took God up on the offer. "What would you be doin' way up here?"

"Same thing I did down there." He grinned. "I'd still preach, I'd just preach to a new group of faces."

Bella frowned. "I'm not so sure you'd have a good reception. Folks up here tend to hold a person at arm's length when it comes to outsiders. My momma learned that the hard way, and she lived here most of her life."

"Good thing I'm not an outsider then, hmm?" He nudged her with his shoulder. Her arm tingled from the contact.

"You'll have to convince them of that first."

"I'm sure we can find middle ground after we start comparing kin. My family goes way back in these hills."

"Mine, too. Or at least they did." But now most of Bella's family was gone, and she had only her wild brothers and Andria as far as family went. "Why would you want to settle way out here anyway? It has to be easier in town."

"Easy isn't always best."

"I s'pose not."

"I want to ask you something. That rider, the one who dropped by yesterday afternoon. . ."

A high-pitched shriek just beyond the trees had Duncan standing upright. He motioned for Bella to stay put, snagged his rifle from its perch on the steps, and hurried over to see what had caused the noise. Bella slipped inside and reached for her own rifle. She reached the porch in time to see Duncan assisting Sarah from the path. He'd slung his rifle over his shoulder, and Sarah leaned against him for support.

"She twisted her ankle."

"Oh, Sarah! I'm so sorry." Bella turned the rocking chair so Sarah would have easy access when she got to the porch. "Bring her up here. I'll get somethin' for her sore ankle to rest on."

Bella hurried inside and woke Andria. Andria got up to dress then headed to the well to fetch some cool water for a compress.

When Bella stepped back outside, Duncan had situated Sarah in the chair.

"I feel so clumsy." Sarah fought back tears. She drew in a breath and exhaled. "One minute I was hurryin' over here so I wouldn't miss a moment of our day together, the next I was trippin' on an arched tree root. My foot stayed stuck as the rest of me went down."

Bella cringed. "That must have hurt somethin' awful."

"It did and still does."

"Andria went for cool water."

"Thank you." Sarah tried to gather herself. "I have no idea how I'll get back home."

"I'll make sure you get there." Duncan looked relieved to have something he could do. "I'll put you on my horse and lead you home that way."

"That would be wonderful." Sarah's face lit up. "Ma's wanted to meet you and Ethan, and she's wanted to see Andria and Belle ever since I told her y'all were here. Why don't you come along and we can make a day of it. Ma would love to make a big dinner and catch up while you're there. Ethan would have fun playing with my brothers."

Bella hesitated then realized this gave her the perfect opportunity to slip up to the caves and check out Andria's golden treasure. "I'd love to, but I have some things I need to do today."

Sarah's enthusiasm waned.

Bella felt bad. "Andria and Ethan can still go along with Duncan. I'll be the only one missin'. I'll finish up what I need to do here, and I'll have a hot supper waitin' when everyone gets home."

Duncan was already shaking his head. "I won't want to leave you on your own here. What if that drifter returns?"

"I can handle the likes of him. I doubt he'll return this soon, but if he does, I'll make sure I have my rifle by my side."

"I don't know. I still don't feel right about leaving you on your own."

"We'll be on our own anyway once you leave to take Ethan home." She stared up at Duncan. "If you're serious about movin' up here and makin' a fresh start, it'll do you good to visit with Sarah's family. They have a lot of standin' and respect in these parts. Their word and encouragement will go a long way in helpin' you start out."

"When you put it that way, it does sound like a good opportunity." Duncan looked impressed. "Thank you, Bella. I'll do just that."

"Glad I could help y'all out," Sarah teased from her perch on the chair.

"I'd rather you not have hurt your ankle, but it does give Duncan a good opportunity to meet some people." Bella laid her hand on Sarah's shoulder. "Tell your ma I'll come to visit soon."

"I'll go round up Ethan and the horse, and we'll be on our way. That ankle is only going to hurt worse as the day goes on. I'd like to get you settled at home before it gets too bad." Duncan leaped from the porch and headed for the barn.

Sarah turned her attention on Bella. "You're sure you can't come along? Can't your chores wait?"

"Not really." Bella didn't elaborate. "But my stayin' here will speed along the process so we can move back here permanently."

"Then get whatever it is that needs doin' done!"

Bella laughed. "I'll get on it as soon as y'all head out."

Andria returned from the well, and Bella slipped inside to get an old rag. They dipped the rag in the cool water and placed the compress on the rapidly swelling ankle. Bella sent Andria inside to gather her things. Duncan and Ethan arrived with Blaze and led him over to the porch.

Duncan left Sarah and Ethan with Andria and motioned for Bella to step around the corner of the cabin. He reached for her hand. "I don't feel right about leaving you here alone. Why don't you join us? I can help with whatever it is that you need to do after we return."

"It's not something you can help me with," Bella hedged. "I need some time alone. I'll be careful, and I promise I'll keep my rifle close at hand."

Duncan was too much of a gentleman to argue, but Bella could tell he wasn't happy about the arrangement.

"I want to talk to you tonight." Bella figured that evening would be as good a time as any to tell him about her family and past. "There are some things about my family and my life that I want to share with you."

"I look forward to my return, then. I want to know you better. We'll stick around Sarah's family's place until after dinner, but we won't stay all day. I'll make our excuses and head back as soon as I can." He leaned forward and kissed Bella on her forehead.

She wondered what it would be like to have him press his lips against her own.

"Until later, then." He moved away and led her toward the others.

Bella knew he'd be later than he thought. When Sarah's family had a visitor head their way, they had a way of making the event a day-long celebration. She nodded, knowing she had to make haste if she wanted to get all the way up to the caves and back before he returned.

꿈

As soon as they were gone, Bella headed for the barn. She readied her horse and swung up onto the saddle. The skirt of her long dress hindered her movements, and she wondered if she should change into her pants and shirt. She decided that would be best. She dropped down and walked to the cabin to change. As she neared, she saw that Wayne leaned against the cabin's back door.

Her airway closed off, and she found it hard to breathe. "Wayne."

This couldn't be good. She glanced back at the trail where she'd last seen Duncan. She willed him to come back. She knew he wouldn't—all his attention would now be focused on Sarah and her painful ankle. And even if he did come back, the resulting battle wouldn't be good.

"Looks like you're in a hurry to get somewhere, little sister."

"Not really. I was just headin' out for a short ride. I haven't taken Steadfast on a trail for a few days and figured he'd be ready to run around a bit."

She wondered if she had time to jump back up on the horse and get away before Wayne could stop her.

He guessed her thoughts and leaped from the porch, landing by her side. He grabbed her by the arm. "Don't lie to me. I always know when you're lyin'. And don't be thinkin' you can get away."

She jerked her arm from his grasp. "What do you want with me, Wayne? You said we had a couple of days. I said I'd get rid of the preacher, but I need more time."

"I have a better idea." He grinned at her, his eyes cold. "What do you think about comin' with me now? The preacher will leave soon enough if you're out of the picture."

"My presence doesn't have anything to do with his visit here. I told you, he wanted to make sure Andi and I made it safely back to the cabin."

"Seems to me you made it back, and he's still lingerin' around."

"He's thinkin' 'bout movin' back to the hills to preach. That's the only thing holdin' him here. He's tryin' to meet some of the locals to see if they'd be receptive of his preachin'."

"Then it won't matter if you come with me."

"It'll matter to Andria. She'll be frantic."

"Go inside and write her a note. And while you're at it, change out of that ridiculous dress. You won't be of any use to me if you're wearing that." Bella's blood ran cold. The only way for her to "be of use" to Wayne was to help him rob innocent travelers. She couldn't do it again. She wouldn't. She had to refuse. "No."

Wayne stared her down, his eyes crazed. "No, what? No you won't change? Or no you won't write Andi a note?"

"No to all of it." Bella stood her ground. "I won't have a part in hurtin' innocent people anymore. I won't be an accomplice to your robberies. If you insist on breakin' the law, find another way to do it that doesn't involve Andria or me. We're stayin' put."

Wayne was in her face and had her arm in his viselike grip before she could take a step backward. "You'll do this last run and then you can take your sorry attitude and go wherever you want. But I promise you that after your part in this, you won't be able to point a finger of blame toward anyone but yourself."

"I won't hurt innocent people."

"You'll do what I tell you to do."

Bella would die first. Tears blurred her vision. And she likely would. She might never see Duncan or Andria again after today. Her last words to Duncan had upset him. He'd blame himself if anything happened to her.

"I'll write that note." She shoved past Wayne and headed for the porch, but he followed her up the stairs. He leaned in the doorway and watched as she wrote. "Tell her what you told me. You wanted to take Steadfast for a ride."

"She'll still be frantic if I don't return in time."

"In time for what?"

"I promised I'd make them supper."

"Aw, isn't that sweet of you? I can't guarantee you'll be back for supper, but we'll see what we can do." His sarcasm made it clear he didn't care if he had her home on time or not. And since he preferred to do the robbing in the early morning hours, she knew she wouldn't be back before dark.

Bella chose her words for the note carefully. She had a feeling Wayne wouldn't bring her back at all. She wanted Andria to get safely away from the area, and she wanted to leave a message so Duncan would gather a posse.

In the end she knew she had no choice but to do as Wayne instructed. He'd tear the note up if she defied him, and Andi wouldn't ever know what happened to her. She finished up and stepped away from the table. "I need privacy if I'm to change my clothes."

"I'll be right outside, but I can see the note through the window. If you tamper with it, I'll be inside before you can finish it off. You hear?"

"Loud and clear."

Bella moved to the far corner of the room and hurried to change into her riding clothes. At least she wouldn't be hindered by long skirts if she had a chance to get away. Dresses certainly had their downside.

Wayne was getting restless. She could hear him pacing the porch. He called for her to hurry up. She pulled the prayer stone and the three gold nuggets from the dress pocket and walked over to the table. Wayne straightened his posture, daring her to defy him. She held the stone and nuggets carefully in the palm of her hand so he couldn't see them and raised her fingers to her lips. She glared at Wayne as she pretended to kiss her fingertips and laid her fingers on the note.

Wayne glared but didn't seem to notice as she laid the small pile of stones on the center of the paper. She walked toward the door, using her body to shield the note from sight. Wayne was none the wiser that she'd left behind a clue. She only hoped Andria and Duncan would figure out what the clue meant.

Chapter 15

Duncan whistled a tune as he led Blaze toward the clearing at the end of the trail. The clearing led him to Bella. The day had been long, and he couldn't wait to get back to her cabin. Though the trip had been a success as far as supporters for a new church went, Duncan couldn't shake the sense of apprehension that had been with him ever since he'd left Bella behind. A few more yards and he'd see the welcoming smoke coiling from Bella's chimney. This late in the evening, she should have supper preparations well under way.

With most of the hard work behind them, he'd enjoy sitting at the table with the group as they told Bella about their day. He wanted to hear what Bella had been up to also. He had a feeling she was on the verge of sharing something important with him. Maybe she finally trusted him enough to share about her brothers. That would sure make things easier for him in the future. He'd be able to open up to her about Andrew's concerns and the need for a posse. He wanted Andria and Bella far away from their brothers when the posse took them in.

Everything was falling in place, and he had a feeling God was getting ready to do some special work in both him and Bella and with the nearby homesteaders. He whistled louder, reflecting his good mood.

Andria laughed from her place on Blaze's back. "Somebody sure is in a cheerful mood this evenin'! If I didn't know better, I'd think you were excited to get back home to my sister."

Home. Duncan would be proud to call the place home. The barn was coming along nicely. He and Ethan had cleaned the stalls and secured the outer doors. They'd fixed a few loose boards in the loft and were ready to fill it with fresh hay. He'd leave that for another time since he didn't know when Bella would be back or when she'd settle there for good.

"If you mean that I'm excited to get back and see that she's okay, then yes, I'm excited to get back to your sister."

"Um-hmm." Andria leaned forward, almost dislodging a worn-out Ethan from his spot behind her. "Are you sure there isn't more to it than that?"

"More to. . ." Duncan choked. "What are you trying to say?"

"It just seems to me that you're sort of protective of my sister. And trust me, Bella doesn't need any protectin'. We've been on our own for a while now, and she's managed to keep us both safe just fine. We've been through a lot."

"I do feel protective—of you both. For whatever reason, God has placed me in a position that allows me to watch over you. Then Ethan showed up, and now he's in my care, too, until I can turn him back over to his father. I think it's all part of God's plan to get me up here in the hills where I can make my time more worthwhile. If I can keep you and your sister safe in the process, I'm happy to oblige."

Andria gave him a skeptical look. Duncan ignored her. He wasn't sure what his feelings were when it came to Bella. She was special to him, but she was possibly an outlaw and he was a preacher. The two didn't mix. She was searching, but until he knew she'd found God, he couldn't move forward with his feelings.

"Seems you'd be happy to oblige in other things, too."

"Andria."

"Sorry, but it's true. I see the way you look at her. My sister doesn't know it, but she needs someone like you."

"I thought she could take care of herself."

"She can, but that doesn't mean she should have to."

"I agree." He frowned as they entered the clearing and he didn't see the expected smoke curling from the chimney. "We'll have to wait and see what happens. In the meantime, why isn't she inside waiting for us?"

Andria's gaze was focused on the dark windows. Worry pinched her features. "Somethin' ain't right."

Duncan handed the reins up to Andria and headed for the house at a run. Andi turned the horse toward the stable.

She called out from the barn doors. "Steadfast is missin'. He ain't in the barn."

Duncan motioned for her to stay put. Andria rode Blaze into the protective frame of the barn. Ethan clung to her back. As soon as they were out of sight, Duncan pushed open the back door of the cabin. The interior was dark and cool.

He found the matches and lit the lantern. The room was empty, just as he'd expected. His boots made a hollow sound on the wood floor as he walked around the room. "Bella?"

There was no reply. He hadn't expected one. He placed the lantern on the table and headed for the front door. He stepped onto the porch. Nothing looked out of place. The rocking chair still sat near the steps where she'd placed it for Sarah. The blanket that had warmed Bella's shoulders at sunrise lay crumpled on the floor where she'd dropped it when they'd heard Sarah's anguished cry. He picked the blanket up and held it close to his chest.

He yelled her name toward the trees as Andria stepped up behind him.

"Duncan, she's gone. I found a note on the table."

Duncan followed her back inside. Ethan huddled in the opposite doorway, watching them with worried eyes.

Andria pointed. The note was on the far side of a vase of flowers. The arrangement hid the note from sight; he hadn't seen it when he placed the lantern there.

A polished stone and three gold nuggets lay on top of the single page of parchment.

"What does it say?"

"It says she's taking Steadfast for a ride. But she wouldn't have stayed out this long, nor would she have parted with the prayer stone if that was the case. Just like our momma, she said she'd never leave it behind. Since she did, she had to have left it as a sign."

"And the gold nuggets? What do they mean?"

"If I'm guessin' right, it means she's headed to the caves where I found a stolen lot of gold. I think the fact that she left the stone behind means that our brother Wayne has her. She wouldn't leave it otherwise. The carrier of the stone has the obligation to pray for the rest of us. She said she'd carry it with her always and it would remind her to pray for our brothers and me. Maybe she figures the stone won't do us any good now that she's with Wayne, but that it'll do her some good if it's with us. She wants us to pray for her. Duncan, I think the fact that she's left it behind means she's in serious trouble."

"This puts us in a real hard place, Andria." Duncan paced back and forth across the hardwood floor. "We have Ethan to watch out for. I need to gather a posse. I don't want to leave the two of you here alone. Wayne might return."

Andria nodded.

He thought for a moment. "I think we need to head back to Sarah's. You and Ethan can stay there."

Sparks shot out from Andria's eyes. "You aren't leavin' me behind! I'm goin' with you."

"I'll do better on my own. If you're with me, I'll be worrying about you every step of the way. Stay at Sarah's and pray for Bella's safe return. Let me concentrate on finding your sister."

"I know what my brothers do, Duncan." Andi stared at him with beseeching eyes. "They lead their victims into the hills and rob them."

Duncan's heart went out to her. She was so young. She looked so guilty at having to tell him about their actions. "Everything's going to be okay, Andria."

"No, it's not. Nothin's gonna be okay." Her voiced choked up with tears. "I know this because Wayne makes Bella and me lead the victims in. We duck out through a small cave that leads to the area while Wayne and Charlie do whatever they do. We hole up here at the cabin, which is why it was in such bad shape. We only get to stay until they come after us."

"So you have no idea what your brothers do after you lead the people in?"

"No." Her voice was choked with tears. "Bella said she thinks they've turned more violent. She felt it deep inside. She said it was like a warnin' and that we had to get out as soon as we could."

She wiped at the tears that coursed down her cheek. "Duncan, she stood up to Wayne. Twice. The first time was the day we left for town. She stood up to him, and he knocked her from her horse. She landed flat on her back. She was bruised all the way up her side and shoulder. She had a huge lump on her head."

Duncan's heart filled with rage. If only he'd pushed them to tell him what he'd overheard that day.

"Then she did it again the other day when he rode up to the cabin."

"The man asking for directions?"

"Yes, it wasn't really a stranger. It was Wayne. Bella said we weren't helpin' him anymore, and he said we were. He looked crazed, Duncan."

"Why didn't y'all tell me?"

"He threatened to hurt you. And he would have. He had weapons; we didn't. Bella wouldn't put you in that position. He gave us two days to send you on your way."

"I had no idea! What kind of protector am I? I've let you both down."

"You don't know Wayne, Duncan. He's dangerous. And I told you Bella's independent. She can handle herself." Her voice drifted off. "Or she used to be able to, before Wayne changed."

"I can be dangerous, too, Andria. Where's your other brother in all this?"

"I don't really know. Charlie has always been at Wayne's side, but he wasn't there the other day. Wayne said somethin' about Charlie workin' when we asked, but he's never sent him off like that before."

"Then we can assume something has happened to Charlie, too."

"He did try to defend Bella when Wayne hurt her." Her eyes widened. "If Charlie's hurt—or worse—that would explain why Wayne needs Bella. When she said that we were done with helpin' them, Wayne said he wasn't goin' to let her go, and instead he'd be initiatin' her into a higher level of service. She's been readin' Ma's Bible faithfully, and she's learned a lot. She said the other day that she wants us to abide by God's Word. We have to get Bella away from Wayne! She'll die before she hurts another person. And Wayne will be happy to oblige that desire if she crosses him."

Duncan stopped pacing and headed for the door. "We'll take Ethan to Sarah's. Ethan can wait there."

"I don't wanna stay there! I wanna help you find Bella." Ethan's angry voice broke into the conversation. "My pa's posse can take care of the bad guys."

"Your pa's posse?"

"Yeah, the one I told you about when I overheard my pa talkin' in town. They said they was goin' after the McLeod gang."

Andria paled. "That's us."

She backed away from Duncan. "Is that why you're here? Did Sheriff Andrew send you to watch over us so's he could go after our brothers? All this time, you were doin' what you did because you were workin' for the sheriff?" She burst into tears. "I thought I could trust you. I really thought you cared about us."

"I do care about you, Andria. I care about both of you." He wrapped his arms around her stiff body and pulled her into a hug. "Everything's going to be okay. I'm here to protect you and Bella, just as I said. We did realize who you were when you arrived in town, but we were after your brothers. We'd heard that a member of the gang found gold, Alex McLeod, but I never heard mention of a family member by that name. I didn't figure it out until I saw the family Bible."

Andria got control of her emotions and stepped back, her gaze wary. "You found what out when you looked at the Bible?"

"You're Alex, right? There are only four listings in there. Wayne, Charles, Isabella, and Alexandria."

"It's true I found the gold. I already told you that. But we were going to turn it in as soon as we had a chance. I think that's why Bella stayed behind today. She told me we couldn't use the gold to start a new life as we'd originally planned when we went into town. She said she'd learned enough from you to know we had to trust God to provide our way. She wanted to turn the gold over to Sheriff Andrew. I think she stayed behind so she could go up there and check things out."

"That makes sense."

Andria glanced over at the table. "I only took those three nuggets as proof of my discovery."

"Who else knew? Somehow word about the gold made its way back to Sheriff Andrew."

Andria dropped her gaze. "I told Sarah. She sometimes calls me Alex. She said she'd keep it a secret. I figured it was safe to tell her about it since she lived way up here in the hills, but she must have told someone else. I didn't tell her where I'd found it, just that I'd found some gold, and I showed her the three nuggets. For all she knew, that was all I'd found. The story must have grown as it made its way to town."

"Stories have a way of doing that." Duncan sighed. "Let's get going. If the story has somehow reached Wayne, Bella won't be safe once she's led him to the treasure."

"I don't think Wayne knows about the gold, Duncan, but I do think he has plans to get rid of her. He was really upset that she defied him. Somethin' inside him is off. He's drinkin' more than usual, too."

"Drinking too much can certainly change a person. We need to find her."

Chapter 16

Andria wound her way around the mountain with Duncan following as close as he dared. They wove through the trees with the full moon lighting their path. Animals scurried out of their way, rustling the brush on either side of the trail. The night noises kept Duncan focused.

Ethan hadn't been happy about being left behind, but Duncan refused to take him along. Sarah's parents quickly gathered the boys together for prayer, and Ethan had settled in with them. Duncan knew the boy was in good hands.

Andria sat tall in her seat. Duncan could tell by her posture that she was upset. "We're going to get to Bella, Andi. You lead me to the back side of the escape cave, and I'll go in after her. The posse should already be in the area. We'll find them. We're going to get her back."

She didn't answer for a moment. Her posture remained tense. "He won't act until mornin'."

"Pardon?"

"Wayne. He never strikes in the dark. He'll wait till mornin' light."

"Then we have time to plan."

"Yes."

They rode for two hours before spotting a small campfire in the trees ahead. Duncan urged Blaze to move up beside Andria's horse. "You sit tight and let me ride up and check things out. I don't want to ride into an ambush."

"All right, but it's probably just some cowboys passin' through and restin' for the night."

Andria had spunk, Duncan had to give her that. She didn't spook easily. "If it's all the same to you, I'd still like to take a closer look before we ride in. It's never a good idea to catch a group like this unawares."

Andria smiled. "We don't usually take the chance to find out. We usually ride away from groups of people out here, not to them."

She and Bella had lived such a different life than him. Even during his own outlaw days he'd made friends along the trail. The McLeod gang was a solitary bunch, which is why they were so hard to catch.

He followed the faint path and cautiously made his way toward the circle of men. He'd acted as deputy enough to recognize Andrew's hat and posture as he neared. He motioned for Andria to join him. Duncan called out to the group before they rode into the encampment.

"Duncan! You're a sight for sore eyes. We're gettin' closer to catchin' the McLeods. As a matter of fact, we might have stumbled upon one of them this afternoon."

His voice drifted off when he registered Andria at Duncan's side.

Duncan motioned to her. "You remember Andria."

Andrew hurried to his feet to help her down from her horse. "Miss McLeod. It's a pleasure to meet you again."

"She knows what's going on." Duncan answered the unspoken question in Andrew's eyes. "Her brother, Wayne, arrived at the homestead yesterday afternoon and threatened Bella. At the time, I didn't know who he was. He told Bella she had two days to get rid of me."

Andria jumped to his defense. "You had no way to know, Duncan. Don't blame yourself."

"This morning Andria and I had to escort an injured neighbor home, and Bella begged off, saying she had things to do." He shook his head. "I should have known she was planning something."

Again, Andria interrupted. "Bella's good, Duncan. If she doesn't want you to know somethin', she makes sure you don't know."

"So I noticed. That doesn't make it any easier to stomach."

He turned back to the posse. "Bella's brother, Wayne, apparently decided to come back a day early. He took Bella with him. Or at least, that's what happened to the best of our knowledge."

Andria explained about the stone and the nuggets of gold. "We think Bella was plannin' to check out the cave with the gold, but Wayne intercepted her before she could get there. He's been actin' mighty funny. And we're worried about our other brother, Charlie. He doesn't usually leave Wayne's side, but he wasn't with him yesterday."

Andrew exchanged an uneasy glance with one of the men. "Maybe you can come over and identify a man we came across yesterday mornin'. He can't talk to us, but we figured him for one of the McLeods."

He led the way over to a small outcropping of rocks. Duncan noticed a still figure lying on top of a bedroll.

Andria hurried over and dropped to her knees. "Charlie!"

The figure didn't move.

"What happened to him?"

"We aren't sure. We found him unconscious at the top of the trail. Looked like he was hit pretty hard on the head and tried to make it to help."

"Is he gonna be all right?" Tears poured down Andria's cheeks.

"We sure hope so. We've tried to keep him comfortable. We don't want to move him too much since we aren't sure about the extent of his injuries. Mason rode for Doc. They should be back anytime. We figured it was Doc ridin' in when you arrived."

He lowered his voice and talked to Duncan as Andria turned her attentions back to Charlie. "We figure we'll keep Doc around until tomorrow afternoon. He can stay with Charlie while we go after Wayne. We might be needin' his services again before the day is out."

Duncan walked over and knelt at Andria's side. "He's resting comfortably. His breathing looks good."

"I've never seen Charlie so quiet."

"He'll be fine. Let me pray for him."

She lowered her head and listened along as he prayed for her older brother. She said a quiet "amen" when he finished up the prayer.

Two men on horseback announced their arrival on the heel of the prayer.

"That's Doc in the black coat," Duncan explained. "He'll take good care of Charlie."

A chill was setting into the night air, and she shivered. Duncan led Andria over to the fire. "We're going to make sure Charlie is okay, and we're going to get Bella safely home. In the meantime, tell us everything you know about Wayne and what he might have planned."

Andria glanced around the circle of tough-looking men. Most women would be too intimidated to speak to such a group, but Andria lifted her chin and began to talk. Duncan felt as proud of her as he would if she were his own sister. He admired her gumption.

"Wayne will wait in a small clearin' in the trees up the hill from the cave trail. The main trail is safer, but lots of folks take the cave trail to save time. Bella and I move out of the trees as soon as we hear travelers approachin'." She took a moment to gather her thoughts. "Every once in a while we run into someone we know. If we do, we have to pretend we're out for a ride. We wait for them to leave, and the process starts all over again."

"So Wayne's attacks are chance, not something he plans in advance?" Andrew leaned forward, focused on every word.

"Right. He sits back and chooses his victims as they pass by."

"So what happens when someone you don't know passes down the trail?"

"Wayne whistles, mimickin' a bird when he wants us to lead someone in. We hesitate near the fork in the path, and when they ride up, we tell them we're tryin' to decide if we want to go along the more populated trail or if we want to take the faster trail through the caves." She shuddered. "Usually they'll encourage us to take the faster trail and will offer to escort us in."

"I take it you've had some bad experiences with that?"

"Many." She closed her eyes. "Most of the men attack us before Wayne and Charlie ever decide to show up. Wayne says he prefers for that to happen. Says it makes it all the sweeter to be able to protect helpless women in need while robbin' the poor fools who fall for our act."

"He put you and Bella at risk for his own gain."

"As often as he could get by with it."

"What did Charlie say?"

"Charlie was our defender. If Wayne waited too long, we could always count on Charlie to come through for us. Even the time one of the men almost had his way with Bella. . ." She let her voice drift off. She cleared her throat. "Charlie got there in time. He was fightin' mad."

"How long ago did this happen?" Duncan felt his face redden with anger. He prayed he'd be the one to take Wayne down. He didn't think it was the most appropriate prayer he'd ever lifted up to God, but he also figured God understood his anger.

" 'Bout three weeks ago, I s'pose. That's the first time Bella asked Wayne to consider changin' his callin'. Wayne laughed in her face and said he'd never change. Charlie got in Wayne's face and told him he'd best not put either of us in that situation ever again."

"What happened after that? Did Wayne change his ways?"

"Not in a good way. He sent Bella to the homestead to gather up a couple of Momma's dresses for our trip to town. Meanwhile, he used me to lead a group in on my own." Her face pinched. "I hadn't ever had to go in alone. Charlie said he'd watch out for me, and he did. Wayne said I'd best not tell Bella or I'd be sorry. He was so different he scared me. I didn't tell Bella until later. I told her when we went to town."

A look of horror rushed across her face.

"Charlie isn't up there to protect Bella. Wayne will take a sick satisfaction in seeing Bella hurt. If he had anythin' to do with Charlie's beatin'—and I think he did—he'll not hesitate to let Bella get hurt, too."

"Not if I have any say in it." Duncan was well aware of Andrew's questioning look. "I'll ride up there tonight if you tell me where to go. Bella won't be hurt at Wayne's hands."

"It's not Wayne's hands I'm worried about in this case," Andria muttered.

"I know."

Andrew intervened. "If you'll excuse me for interruptin', I'd like to say a few words as sheriff."

Duncan motioned for him to go ahead.

"First of all, we aren't goin' to go rushin' into this all willy-nilly." He stared hard at Duncan. Duncan kept his focus on the fire. "Second of all, Duncan,

I have half a mind to keep you back here with Andria, Charlie, Doc, and Doc's assistant when the rest of us ride in."

"You aren't keeping me from rescuing Bella."

"That's what I thought."

Andrew's contemplative expression rubbed Duncan wrong. He knew he needed to get control of his anger and his thoughts, but this was Bella they were talking about. "I'm not sitting out when Bella's in trouble."

"You won't do anyone any good if you ride in there and aren't thinkin' straight. You need to settle down."

"I'll settle down after she's safe. This is *Bella* we're talking about. What if it were your wife or your son?"

"I'd do anything to keep my family safe, Duncan. You know that. But I'd also act within the law as much as possible. I'd think things through so my actions didn't have the wrong result and end up gettin''em killed."

Duncan blanched at the thought. There were so many things he wanted to say to Bella. They'd talked enough during the past couple of days that he felt pretty sure she had a good grasp on God. She'd asked Duncan to pray with her several times. And based on his conversations with Andria, he felt pretty sure Bella had given her heart over to the Lord. But there was so much more he wanted to teach her. He wanted to be by her side as she learned to trust and rely on God. He wanted to be by her side as she started her new life on the homestead.

"You've fallen in love with her, Duncan." Andria's eyes lit up at the thought. "We'll get through this, and then you need to tell her."

Duncan didn't even care that a group of the toughest men in town heard her words. Most of them were hitched anyway and understood what he was going through.

"We'll get them, Duncan," Andrew said. "But you know when we do, Bella will be tried for the crimes right along with her brothers."

Andria gasped.

"I'm sorry, ma'am, but that's the hard truth." Andrew looked Andria in the eye. "I'll do my best to prove that you were both reluctant to participate at the very least. And because you're so willingly workin' with us now, I think we'll be able to keep you and Bella out of trouble."

"Thank you." Her voice was barely a whisper. She looked terrified for a brief moment then quickly pulled herself together and covered up all emotion. "Duncan, maybe you should tell him about Ethan."

"Ethan?" Andrew's eyebrows rose. "What's the boy done now?"

"He followed me up the mountain and didn't show himself until it was too late for me to turn back."

"That can't be right. He's supposed to be with his mother in Atlanta."

"Apparently she got upset with him and left him to stay with you. He rode into town and overheard you mention that you were going with the posse. I was leaving town, and he got the idea to tag along."

"That boy!" Andrew pulled his hat from his head and ran his fingers through his hair in frustration. "Where is he now?"

"He's safely tucked away at Bella's neighbor's house. They'll take good care of him until we can get back up there and retrieve him."

"Good."

Doc entered the circle and settled down next to Andria. "Your brother should be good as new once he rests a bit. He has a concussion, and he'll have quite a headache before he feels better. Someone hit him hard on the head. It's a miracle he's alive."

"Charlie's always had a hard head."

"Well, in this case his hard head saved his life. I'll stay close and watch him through the night." He patted her hand. "We'll talk more in the mornin'. This old man needs to get his tired bones in bed for now. I'll be up and down checkin' on my patient while y'all sleep."

"You'll have company," Andrew stated. "We'll take turns keepin' watch. I don't expect Wayne to show himself down this way based on what Miss McLeod has told us, but it won't hurt to be prepared just in case."

"I'll go first." Duncan stood up and sent Andrew a look that said he wouldn't take no for an answer.

"I'll spell you in a bit. We have enough men here that we can each take an hour and still be fresh in the mornin'."

"I want to leave at first light." Duncan thought a moment. "No, I think we should leave sooner than first light."

"I'm callin' the shots here, Duncan." Andrew glared. "If you can't abide by that, you'll be locked in handcuffs and left with only a tree for company."

"I'll see you bright and early." Duncan figured he wouldn't sleep a wink. He might as well offer to stand watch all night. But he knew Andrew wouldn't allow it and would likely prove his point with the handcuffs.

Duncan wished he'd never joined up with the posse. While it was good that Andria would have company and could sit by Charlie's side, Duncan would prefer to be standing at the right end of the trail instead of sitting at the wrong end. If he found a way, he'd sneak off after his watch and settle himself into place.

Chapter 17

Bella pulled at the ties that bound her wrists and tried to loosen their hold. Instead of loosening, the ropes dug deeper into her skin. Tears of frustration threatened to spill over, but she blinked them back. The last thing she wanted to do was let Wayne know how upset she was.

She glanced over at him. "I haven't had anything to eat."

Wayne glared at her. "What's that matter to me?"

"I won't be much help to you if I pass out from hunger."

She hoped he'd release her from her bonds long enough to eat. If he did, she'd take her chances and try to get away. So far he'd kept his rifle propped against his leg, allowing no opportunity for escape. He'd spent the better part of their time together drinking. If she caught him at the right moment, she could probably escape. Even if he was able to reach his gun and aim before she ducked behind some trees, he wouldn't be too accurate a shot with all the whiskey he'd consumed.

"I'll take my chances. I'm not givin' you any vittles. Stop aggravatin' me."

Bella sank back in despair. She didn't want to help Wayne with his next robbery, even this one last time. He scared her.

"Why won't you tell me where Charlie is?" She tried to find a more comfortable position and winced. The ropes had rubbed her raw in several places, and every time she shifted she reopened a wound. "What have you done with him?"

Wayne spit. "What makes you think I done somethin' to him? Maybe he's just busy."

"He's never been too busy before when it came to helpin' you out. I used to think it was because he was so committed to you and the robberies. But you know what I think now?"

"No, but I'm sure you're gonna tell me." He sounded bored, but his words were beginning to slur. "What do you think, Bella?"

"I think he also told you that he didn't want to be a part of this anymore and you did somethin' to hurt him. That's why you need me so bad. You need money for your next bottle of whiskey, and you don't have any help. Far be it for you to get up and make your own livin' in a legal way." Her voice rose with anger as she stated each word. "You prefer to make us all do your illegal work while you sit all safe and sound hidden up here in the trees."

"I've done my part through the years. And for your information, I can make my own livin' if I want to. But why do that when I can use you?"

"You can't use me. I won't help this time. I already told you that."

"And I already told you that you will help or you'll pay a heavy price."

Bella had already set herself straight with God. She knew the price she'd pay if she refused Wayne. But she'd also pay a price if she went against what God wanted her to do. "I'm willin' to pay that price. I won't help you out, Wayne. Not now. Not ever. You're on your own this time."

"Then you must not know the price I'm askin' of ya, little sister."

"Oh—I think I do. But I won't put my own safety above that of an innocent stranger's."

"Innocent? If I recall properly, some of those *strangers* tried to take liberties with you and Andi. You think that's what upstandin' people do? The men we rob deserve every bit of what they get and then some."

"No, I don't think upstandin' people do things like that, but that still doesn't make what you do right."

"I ain't never said it was right. And I reckon that I don't care."

"Why don't you care? You weren't like this when Momma was alive. Papa wasn't either. Was it her death that set you two off? We lost her, too, you know."

"I haven't ever taken the time to think it out, Bella. We did what we had to do."

"No. You didn't. Papa took care of us just fine. You and Charlie could have looked for honest work. And maybe you should take the time to think about it. You didn't have to become outlaws. You chose to."

"Yep."

"And you dragged the rest of us along with you."

"That we did."

"It wasn't right."

"Agreed."

"Then why'd you do it? I hate when you act like this. I might as well be talkin' to this tall pine tree you tied me to."

"I'm uppin' the ante, Bella. How's that for talk?"

"Uppin' the ante how?" Bella narrowed her eyes.

"I want you to be involved with the entire process. You won't ride off after we corner the victim. You'll stay to help this time."

"I just told you I won't help you anymore. Are you even listenin' to me? I'm not helpin' you lead anyone in. I'm not leavin' anyone alone with you. And I'm not gettin' more involved with the process. I quit. I'm done. And so is Andria."

"See, Bella, that's just the thing. You don't have the privilege of quittin'. You have to do as I say."

338

"No I don't."

"Yes you do." Wayne moved close. The stale odor of whiskey mixed in with his unclean body assaulted her senses. "You will do exactly as I say, or you'll regret it."

"I already regret everything I've done for you in the past, Wayne. I won't add more regrets to the list. You'll have to kill me first. I have my life right with God, and you can't intimidate me anymore."

Wayne's face turned purple with rage.

"How dare you defy me!" He slapped her hard on her cheek.

Bella's head snapped back against the tree, and she saw stars. The tears broke free and poured down her face. "I won't do it."

"You'll not only do it, you'll kill the person we rob. How do you like that? You'll never be able to point your self-righteous finger at me. The whole time you're robbin' the person, I'll have my rifle sight trained on the back of your head."

Bella's head ached, and she wished he'd just finish her off then and there. "You said I'd pay a heavy price. I'll pay it now. End this."

He laughed. "What price do you think you'll pay?"

"I s'pose you'll make me pay with my life. I'm ready to do that."

Her mind cried out that she wasn't ready. She wanted to be there for Andria. She wanted to keep her safe. Bella uttered a desperate prayer for the safety of those she loved. She prayed that God would intervene and keep her safe. She'd never been so afraid in her life. She hoped Duncan and Andria had figured out her clues, but she didn't see how they could gather help and arrive in time even if they did. She said a final prayer in the hopes that God would direct Duncan to watch out for Andria if anything happened to Bella.

"I'm not takin' your life, Bella. That wouldn't be nearly as much fun as watchin' your face when I bring Andria into the fold. It's time she became a bigger part of things, too."

"You leave her alone!" Bella fought the ropes that held her, tearing more skin in the process.

Wayne only laughed.

He knew he'd won. She'd do anything to avoid Andria being hurt. Bella felt peace that Duncan would watch out for Andria, but he couldn't watch her every moment and she knew it was only a matter of time before Duncan let his guard down and Wayne went after their sister.

❧

"Wake up, little sister. It's time for us to go." The early morning sun formed a halo around Wayne's head.

Bella squinted as she pushed herself up from the hard-packed earth and tried to see her brother's face. It was hidden in shadow. He towered over her, his rifle in one hand and the horses' reins in the other. "C'mon. I want to get an early start."

Bella shifted around so he could cut through the ropes that bound her hands together. If he noticed the damage they'd done to her wrists, he didn't let on.

The ground shifted away from Bella as she stood. She leaned on the tree for support. Tired, dizzy, hungry. . .she wasn't feeling real confident when it came to pulling off whatever her brother had in mind.

One thing she was sure of—she wouldn't hurt another person. Andria's face came to mind, but Bella pushed it away and focused on praying instead. *Lord, please keep Andi safe. Please be with me in this time of need and help me stop my brother from whatever it is he plans to do. In Jesus' name. . .amen.*

Bella realized that as woozy as she was, she'd be hard-pressed to make a fast escape. That explained Wayne's reluctance to let her have dinner the night before.

"Can I have a bite to eat before we go?"

Wayne stared down at her. "After we finish our day's work."

He half lifted, half pushed Bella up onto her horse. She continued to pray that God would show her the way out. Wayne motioned for her to follow him, and she did as he requested, though she continuously scoured the countryside for any signs of help.

They were just approaching the split in the trail when a huge explosion rocked the air. The horses reared, and Bella fought to keep her hold on the saddle horn. Wayne continued to battle his much larger horse, and Bella took advantage of the opportunity. She urged her horse to run, guiding him in the direction of their escape route. She knew Wayne would be on her heels in an instant, but she felt her only chance would be to lose him on one of the many winding trails.

She and Andi were much more familiar with the area than Wayne, and Bella used that to her advantage. She took some of the lesser-used paths, knowing that Wayne seldom came this way at all. He and Charlie took the faster route home and rode out the way they came in.

Andi and Bella took pride in finding new paths, cutting new trails, and disappearing as soon as they were spotted by any of their victims who happened to ride after them.

She rode hard, her breathing matching the horse's as they ducked through low-lying branches, jumped over stumps or large rocks, and tore through openings in the brush. She could hear Wayne behind her but didn't dare to look back to see how far behind he was.

The passage twisted and turned, and for a brief moment she panicked, knowing nothing but empty trails waited for her on the other side of the mountain. *Lord, please help me get out. I have so much I want to say to Duncan. I want to tell Andi what I've learned about trust. I want her to know You.*

The crashing neared, and Bella bent low on her horse, riding for all she was worth. He was gaining on her. And she had no doubt that when he caught up with her this time, she wouldn't get away again.

Movement to her right caught her off guard. Her horse slowed as a large figure burst from the brush and headed straight for Wayne.

Duncan!

He yelled for her to keep moving, and she did as he requested.

Wayne screamed—whether in terror at being thwarted or anger that someone had bested him, Bella didn't know. She didn't stay around long enough to find out either. She heard a huge crash in the trees behind her and kept moving forward.

Bella couldn't slow down. She knew she had to make as much progress and get as much distance from Wayne as she could. She began to cry. So many bad things had happened in these hills because of her brothers. Now Charlie was missing and Duncan was alone where she'd left him, fighting a madman. Bella had left Duncan in her dust to fight her battle. And she had no idea where Andria was or how she'd keep her safe.

"Bella!"

Bella was so deep in thought and so filled with terror that at first she didn't register that her name had been called. Her only thought was to get far away.

"Bella, stop, please!"

Andria's voice started to break through the panic. Bella glanced around.

"I'm over here. Slow down."

Andria rode up beside her and took the reins.

Bella leaned into her arms and cried. "You're safe."

"Of course I am," Andria crooned. "Duncan kept me safe. You're the one we were worried about."

Bella wiped her eyes and reached for her reins. Andi saw her wounds and gasped.

"Wayne did that to you? He tied you up?" Tears of anger and sympathy filled Andi's eyes.

"Duncan went after him alone. We need to get help."

"Sheriff Andrew and some others are already on their way. They took the south trail in case Duncan and I missed you. They'll meet up any minute now."

Bella tried to get her emotions under control. "Charlie wasn't with Wayne. I asked about him, and he wouldn't give me a straight answer. I think Charlie's in trouble."

"Charlie is fine." Andi filled her in. "He's injured, but Doc says he'll be just fine after a few days' rest."

"Wayne hurt him, didn't he?"

"I assume so. He's not conscious right now, but someone roughed him up somethin' awful."

"I want to see him."

"He's just outside the passage. Doc is there with him, and we'll have him look at your wrists. Follow me."

Chapter 18

Bella waited by Charlie's side until Duncan and the men rode into the encampment. Sheriff Andrew trailed behind with Wayne draped across his horse.

"Is he—?" Andria paled.

"He'll be fine. He put up quite a fight, but we managed to subdue him." He glanced over at Duncan. "We'll head on into town so we can get him in a cell before he wakes. You finish up here and meet up with me later."

Duncan nodded. "I'll gather up Ethan and see you in a bit."

"I want to go with Wayne." Andria glanced over at Bella, her eyes begging for understanding. Bella nodded her approval.

"I'll stay here with Charlie. We'll join you as soon as he's ready to travel."

Andria gave her a spontaneous hug.

"It's okay." Now that the shock had passed, Bella resumed the role of older sister and fell back into her usual habit of reassuring Andi. "We'll all be fine. I'll be right behind you."

One of the men in the posse was giving Bella a strange look. "What about the rest of 'em, Sheriff?"

"What about the rest of who, Clive?" Sheriff Andrew looked annoyed to have been stopped by the member of the posse.

"The rest of the gang. You aren't goin' to leave 'em behind, are you? What if they scatter?"

Sheriff Andrew looked incredulous. "Don't you think Bella would have left already if she'd had a mind to escape?" He shook his head. "And Charlie there can't do much, what with him bein' unconscious and all."

"For all we know Miss McLeod here could be fixin' to run as soon as your back is turned. She knows her siblings are in custody."

"I'll take responsibility for them, Clive. Don't you worry your pretty little head."

Clive glared, and Ben backed him up.

"I have to agree with Clive. These women have been active in the gang from everythin' I've ever heard. We can't go lettin' them walk just because they're of the fairer persuasion."

"Andria is coming to town with you, Clive, and I'll personally make sure

Charlie and Bella arrive by nightfall." Duncan spoke from behind Bella. He was close enough that his breath warmed her ears.

Bella waited for the posse to move on and saw a flash of guilt pass through Duncan's eyes when he turned to her.

Her heart sank. "You knew who we were all along, didn't you?"

"I did."

"You're no different than any of the others. You said you were here to protect Andi and me. Instead, you used us to lead you to our brothers."

"That's not true." He reached for her, imploring her to listen, but she only wanted to distance herself from his lies.

"I never expected you to use trickery and deceit in such a way. I thought you were honest and upstandin'. I figured you for the preacher you said you were, not this imposter of a man of the cloth."

"I am honest and upstanding, Bella, or at least I strive to be."

Bella turned her back on him. She didn't want him to see her tears.

"My actions were honorable when it came to protecting you and Andria. I heard you talking in the trees that first day, the day you almost ran us down on the trail. You mentioned your brothers and that one of them had hurt you."

Bella remembered but hadn't realized he'd overheard their conversation about their brothers.

"I didn't know who you were at the time. But when you walked in the diner and introduced yourselves—that's when we knew." He paused. "Your brothers are dangerous men. I wanted to help protect you and help you break free of their hold."

"Why didn't you tell me this from the start?"

Duncan looked amused. "Would you have trusted me?"

"No."

"That's why I didn't tell you. I had to gain your trust."

"By deceiving me?"

"I didn't intentionally deceive you. You just weren't privy to the full situation." He touched her arm, encouraging her to look into his eyes.

Bella obliged.

His deep brown eyes searched her own. "I could say the same about you, ya know."

"That I deceived and tricked you? How do you figure?"

"You didn't let on that you were with the McLeod gang. You insinuated that you lived on the homestead. You knew my heart but didn't let me have any inkling that you were involved with an outlaw gang."

"We do live on a homestead, just not that one. Not very often anyway."

"You didn't tell me Wayne was your brother that day when he first rode in."

"I knew he'd kill you if you figured out who he was and approached him."

"And the fact that you've lived as an outlaw?"

"A reluctant one. I've never wanted to be in the family 'business.' I hate the outlawin' lifestyle."

Duncan sighed and looked out over the trees. The hollow was cool. Bella noticed that the birds continued to sing and dart from tree to tree. Life around her went on, even though her own life was falling apart.

"The posse will want to know where the gold is."

"We never touched it." Bella remembered the three gold nuggets and flushed. "I mean, other than Andi taking those three nuggets. I meant to put them back, but Wayne found me before I could return them."

"That's probably a good thing."

"In what way?"

"If Wayne had followed you up there, Andria and I wouldn't have had a chance to follow. Wayne would be in charge of the treasure."

"They're going to blame Andi."

"Maybe. Maybe not."

Bella stared at him with confusion.

"The gold came from a heist committed several years back. I know Andi didn't have anything to do with it."

"How can you be so sure? The townspeople won't agree."

"I know because I used to ride with the gang that stole the gold."

Bella gaped at him. "You're tellin' me that you, an upstandin' Bible preachin' man, had something to do with a gold heist?"

"I haven't always been the *fine upstanding* man that you see today." His words were laced with sarcasm.

"I don't believe it." She stared at the handsome man before her. "What could you possibly have had to do with a gold heist?"

"I rode with a gang, a family gang, for years." Duncan shook his head. "Ever hear of the Marshalls?"

"I have."

"They're my brothers. Well, the gang was made up of me and my brothers." He scowled.

Bella knew the feeling. Once you knew right from wrong, you wondered how you could have possibly made the wrong choice for so long.

"I found out about God from a traveling preacher and decided to change my ways. But even before that, I'd started to question why we did what we did. I was the youngest of my brothers. Our way of life was all I knew. One day I slowed enough to see the pain on a victim's face. We hadn't hurt her, but we'd taken something precious from her. Her security. I couldn't get her pain out of my head. I knew that because of us, she'd have to live with fear for the rest of her life. I didn't want to ever see that look on another person's face."

Bella's heart went out to him. She understood what he was describing all too well. "I've seen that look. That moment when a person realizes that something they're going through is out of their control and that the circumstance will affect them for the rest of their life."

Duncan nodded, his face filled with pain. "That's it. I realized our actions lasted longer for the people involved than the few minutes it took us to do a heist. I told my brothers I wanted out, and they laughed. They couldn't imagine why I'd want to quit. They didn't understand why I'd even question what we'd always done. It was our way of life."

"What happened?"

"They cut me out and went through with the gold heist when I was out of town. When I realized what was going on, I rode as hard as I could to get back to them. They'd all been shot. Two of them were killed while doing the heist. One died at our family home. He made it back there, but I wasn't home to help him. The papers said all four were shot, but I never did find out what happened to my fourth brother, Danny."

"I think I know."

Duncan looked at her in surprise.

"Andria said there was a skeleton in with the gold."

"In the cave?"

"Yes."

Duncan nodded. "That would make sense. Danny made it to the cave but couldn't get any farther." A momentary look of defeat filled his eyes, and he paced a few steps away. "I've always hoped that he made it out of there, that he'd found medical help and would someday reappear. I'd hoped he'd also see the wrong in what they did and would come back a changed man. I guess I have to let that dream go."

"Well, we can't know for sure it's him. Not until you look things over."

"True. But I doubt that anyone else found the gold and left it there. It makes more sense that Danny made it there, a place he'd planned to meet up with the others, and that he died from his wounds."

"I'm so sorry." Bella wondered if she should have kept that part to herself, but figured he'd know soon enough anyway.

She looked up to see him studying her.

"You're hurt."

Bella looked down at her wrists. Doc had cleaned the wounds and bandaged them. "Just a little. The cuts aren't deep. They'll heal quickly."

"I'm sorry I wasn't there."

"You couldn't have known." Bella smiled, not used to the compassion. She figured she could settle down with a man like Duncan after all.

"We'll need to go into town and tell them everything we've shared with each other."

"I know." Bella bit her lip. "What do you think they'll make of us—Andria and me? Will they want justice served in full?"

Duncan reached forward and tucked a strand of Bella's hair behind her ear. "I think, after they hear what we have to say, they'll realize we all were victims of our families and that you and Andria did what you had to, in order to survive."

"We?"

He pointed from his chest to hers. "We. I intend to share my past with the townspeople. I've built myself up to a position of respect with them. I prayed daily that my past would never catch up with me. My whole ministry was about being genuine with my parishioners, yet I kept my past from them. I always felt something was missing from my ministry but couldn't put my finger on what was wrong."

"I don't want you to bring all this up on our account."

He smiled at her. "It's time I came clean with the whole sordid story. I don't think it'll matter to my believers. They'll welcome the idea that I'm no different than they are. And trust me, I know all their secrets and sins."

Bella sighed. "I wish none of this had ever happened."

"Bella." Duncan smiled and pulled her into his arms. "God doesn't make mistakes. He's had a purpose for you from the very beginning. He'll use your past to help others in the future. You'll be able to give hope and compassion to whoever He puts in your path."

"You're sure?"

"I am." He tilted her chin up so she had to look him in the eyes. His brown eyes were filled with love. "We'll go into town, we'll share what we've been through, and I feel sure that you and Andria will be set free. Charlie will face charges for his part in things, but I think he'll come around. Wayne will be in longer, but I pray we can reach him with patience and perseverance."

"I certainly hope so." Bella couldn't take her eyes off Duncan. His warm breath fanned her face. Her heart fluttered at his closeness.

"And you and I . . ." His words drifted off as he smiled. "You and I will marry and live happily ever after."

"We will?" Her voice came out in a squeak. She'd gone from confident outlaw to giddy female in a moment's time.

"We will," he whispered. He leaned forward and claimed her lips, sealing his promise with a kiss.

A Letter to Our Readers

Dear Readers:

In order that we might better contribute to your reading enjoyment, we would appreciate you taking a few minutes to respond to the following questions. When completed, please return to the following: Fiction Editor, Barbour Publishing, Inc., P.O. Box 719, Uhrichsville, OH 44683.

1. Did you enjoy reading *Georgia Brides* by Paige Winship Dooly?
   ❑ Very much. I would like to see more books like this.
   ❑ Moderately—I would have enjoyed it more if _____
   _____
   _____

2. What influenced your decision to purchase this book?
   (Check those that apply.)
   ❑ Cover   ❑ Back cover copy   ❑ Title   ❑ Price
   ❑ Friends   ❑ Publicity   ❑ Other

3. Which story was your favorite?
   ❑ *The Lightkeeper's Daughter*   ❑ *The Displaced Belle*
   ❑ *The Reluctant Outlaw*

4. Please check your age range:
   ❑ Under 18   ❑ 18–24   ❑ 25–34
   ❑ 35–45   ❑ 46–55   ❑ Over 55

5. How many hours per week do you read? _____

Name _____

Occupation _____

Address _____

City_____ State_____ Zip_____

E-mail _____

HEARTSONG
P R E S E N T S

If you love Christian romance…

$12.⁹⁹

You'll love Heartsong Presents' inspiring and faith-filled romances by today's very best Christian authors. . .Wanda E. Brunstetter, Mary Connealy, Susan Page Davis, Cathy Marie Hake, and Joyce Livingston, to mention a few!

When you join Heartsong Presents, you'll enjoy four brand-new, mass-market, 176-page books—two contemporary and two historical—that will build you up in your faith when you discover God's role in every relationship you read about!

Imagine. . .four new romances every four weeks—with men and women like you who long to meet the one God has chosen as the love of their lives—all for the low price of $12.99 postpaid.

To join, simply visit www.heartsongpresents.com or complete the coupon below and mail it to the address provided.

Mass Market, 176 Pages

- -

YES! Sign me up for Heartsong!

NEW MEMBERSHIPS WILL BE SHIPPED IMMEDIATELY!
Send no money now. We'll bill you only $12.99 postpaid with your first shipment of four books. Or for faster action, call 1-740-922-7280.

NAME _____

ADDRESS_____

CITY_____ STATE _____ ZIP _____

MAIL TO: HEARTSONG PRESENTS, P.O. Box 721, Uhrichsville, Ohio 44683
or sign up at WWW.HEARTSONGPRESENTS.COM